Elizabeth Wait  e until she was thirty-four ed as a bus conductress at er husband moved to Dev

Now retired, they live in East Sussex.

Third Time Lucky

ELIZABETH WAITE

sphere

SPHERE

First published in Great Britain in 1995 by Little, Brown and Company
Previously published in 1996 by Warner Books
This paperback edition published in 2010 by Sphere

A CIP catalogue record for this book
is available from the British Library.

ISBN 978-0-7515-4484-8

Printed and bound in Great Britain by
Clays Ltd, St Ives plc

Papers used by Sphere are natural, renewable and
recyclable products sourced from well-managed forests and certified
in accordance with the rules of the Forest Stewardship Council.

Mixed Sources
Product group from well-managed
forests and other controlled sources
www.fsc.org Cert no. SGS-COC-004081
© 1996 Forest Stewardship Council

Sphere
An imprint of
Little, Brown Book Group
100 Victoria Embankment
London EC4Y 0DY

An Hachette UK Company
www.hachette.co.uk

www.littlebrown.co.uk

Writing has brought me many new friends but none that I value more than Beryl Kingston. I have to thank her for all her help, her advice and most of all for her loving friendship.

Chapter One

PASSERS-BY COULD BE FORGIVEN for thinking that the tall thin man, who wore a suit and a tie even though it was a Saturday afternoon, and the pretty blonde-haired lady, who had freckles on her nose and was smiling happily as they walked arm in arm, were husband and wife. Most would also assume that the two attractive young girls who were skipping excitedly alongside of them completed a happy, normal family.

Nothing could be further from the truth.

Evie Smith had met Edward Hopkins in the summer of 1938 when she'd been barely seventeen. In no time she had fallen in love and got herself pregnant. Happy as a lark, she'd wanted nothing more than for Ted to marry her. But it was not as simple as that.

Edward was twenty-five years old. He'd had a wife since he was twenty-two. The childless marriage was not a happy one and he was all for seeking a divorce and marrying Evie, thrilled at the thought that he was to be a father. It wasn't his fault that his wife had suffered a stroke and been an invalid ever since. But his sense of duty prevented him from deserting a sinking ship.

The family turned off the road and made to cross Albert Bridge. Evie and Ted were both quiet, each thinking of Monday morning when Ted would leave London once again and return to that totally different life that he lived in Lytham St Anne's.

Looking across the river, Catherine, Evie's twelve-year-old daughter, cried, 'Look at the lights. Aren't they lovely?' She came running back to her parents, calling, 'Hurry up you two.' Her cheeks were flushed, her fair hair glinting with the sun shining on it.

'We're coming,' her father said, ruffling her hair. 'You're turning into a real beauty,' he told her solemnly.

Catherine loved her father. So much it hurt sometimes. She thought he was handsome with his dark hair and deep-set brown eyes. Absolutely outstanding. Much better than the fathers of most of her school friends. They were a scruffy, ordinary lot. Catherine adored him. He could do no wrong. She had only one wish: that her father could live with them all the time.

Evie sighed. 'Go on with you,' she interrupted. It was all right for Ted to treat Catherine as if she meant the world to him, but come Monday he would be gone again. She took Catherine's hand and pulled her to her side. 'Keep hold of your sister's hand, we don't want her wandering off.'

'Yeah, I want to come with you,' Jenny, her six-year-old sister, agreed. 'And listen, you can hear the music from the fairground. Will we get to 'ave a go on all the rides, Dad? You did say we could.'

'And I meant it, my darling. You won't miss out on a single roundabout, and you can have all the candyfloss an' toffee-apples that you can eat.' Her father was laughing as he swung Jenny high in the air and she spread her legs to sit astride his shoulders.

Evie brightened as she remembered that, taking all in

all, her life and that of her girls wasn't so bad. Many a man would have dumped her long ago, and this evening they were going to give their daughters the time of their lives. She had come through the war, survived two years of living in a Nissen hut and now London had all the fun, fantasy and colour of a festival year to offer.

It was 1951, the Festival of Britain. The postwar gloom was temporarily forgotten as not only North and South Londoners flocked to cross the river in their thousands, but people from all over the country and, indeed, if the papers were to be believed, from all over the world were coming. Twenty-seven acres of derelict, bomb-damaged London, near Waterloo, had been transformed into an exhibition site. Down river, at Battersea Park, there was a display of open-air sculpture, alongside of which were the Festival Pleasure Gardens.

They had hardly got through the gates when Cathy grabbed Jenny's hand and the pair of them surged ahead in leaps and bounds, eager to decide which ride would be their first. They could already see some of their school friends, who laughed and shouted at them. Cathy let go of Jenny and was off like a flash.

'That Cathy, I'll give her such a thump. She ought to know by now she shouldn't race off an' leave her sister like that.' Evie didn't wait for Ted to answer her, she was yards ahead of him. 'You all right, luv?' Evie panted, grabbing Jenny so tight she almost sent them both flying.

Ted caught up with them. Evie regained her balance and they set off to catch up with Cathy.

'Catherine,' Ted's voice held that note of command, 'just you hang on a minute and don't be charging off on your own.'

'Slowcoach!' called Cathy.

Evie belted after her. 'If you don't learn to take notice of what I say to you, Catherine, I'll 'ave to find other

ways of making you, won't I? You mustn't rush off an'
leave your sister like that. Anything could 'appen.'

Catherine went a bit red. She didn't like it when her
mother blew her top.

'Hello, Cathy,' two girls called brightly, saving the
situation.

'Who are they?' Evie asked, returning to her usual
good-humoured self.

'They're in the same class as me at school. One's Linda
Brown, the other one is Vera Clarke. You know her, lives
at the back of us.'

''Ello, Mrs Smith. It's great 'ere at the fair, ain't it?'

The two school friends and Ted and Jenny joined the
group simultaneously. As far as Ted was concerned it was
time to see that the kids started to enjoy themselves.

'How about us all going on the Dodgems,' he suggested.
'Course, your friends can come as well,' he added quickly.

What a scramble! Evie and Ted, with Jenny squashed in
between them, were in a red car – Jenny's choice. The
three other girls, in a blue car, were grinning broadly as
they waited for the off.

'We'll show 'em, won't we?' Vera asked the question.

'Crikey, not 'alf we won't. Don't forget, tug the wheel
hard an' we'll ram them first,' Cathy insisted.

'All right,' agreed Vera.

'Your dad's nice, ain't he?' Linda grinned.

'To tell ye the truth, Cathy, I didn't think you and
Jenny 'ad a dad.' Vera Clarke was smirking at her.

Catherine gave a loud sniff. It was the insolent way she
had said it. She knew that Linda and Vera were laughing at
her, and she wasn't going to stand for it. Ever since she had
started school it had been the same, one or other of the kids
taunting her because her dad wasn't always around.
'Course we got a dad. Everybody 'as, yer daft ha'p'orth. He
works away and don't get 'ome too often, but it's great

when he is 'ere. If you want to make something of it, Vera, you just say the word.'

Linda sneered. It wasn't often anyone managed to ruffle Catherine Smith's feathers.

Vera felt she was squashed too close to Cathy to make an issue of it. She lost her nerve.

'Well?' Cathy demanded an answer. She was fed up with all the harassment. Vera was silent for only a few seconds.

'Course not, Cathy. I didn't mean nothing by it. Honest I didn't.'

To her relief, Catherine was saved from having to pursue this awkward subject. The music was blaring, blue sparks were flying from the electric poles which were attached to the cars, there were loud screams of delight, and they were off.

It was quite dark when they arrived home. The girls were too tired to talk, too tired and full up to want any supper, but not irritably tired. Jenny kissed her father goodnight and willingly allowed her mother to carry her into the bedroom. Catherine lingered.

'Will we go to the zoo next time you come home?' she asked her father.

'Of course we will. And to the pictures and the museums if you like. We'll even have our dinner out. How does that sound?'

Catherine started to speak again, then changed her mind. 'Goodnight, Dad.'

Edward Hopkins lowered his head to his chest and sighed deeply, thinking of the strange hand of fate that had dealt him two illegitimate daughters, the mother of whom he adored, while keeping him trapped in a loveless marriage without a hope in hell of being able to do anything about it except wait.

Evie made cheese omelettes and a pot of coffee. She

would rather have had tea but she bowed to Ted's preference. They ate in silence, then with the table cleared they talked. It had all been said before. One minute they were calm and speaking of alternatives to the way they were living. There were no alternatives. Evie lost her temper, taunted Ted and said he had the best of both worlds. No other man would stay with a bedridden wife when he had a healthy mistress and two lovely daughters who would welcome him with open arms. No other woman, apart from herself, would put up with his comings and goings. She and the girls were lucky if they saw him for three or four weeks, twice a year.

Then it was his turn. He upset her by saying she couldn't really love him if she was going to start a row when she knew he had no option but to go back up north. Did she want him just to send her an allowance and to stay away altogether?

Then came the tears. If he never came to stay with them again, what would there be to look forward to? No father for her children, no marriage – what else mattered? When she argued this point with herself she sounded as if she was on the defensive and she became cross with herself. Her girls didn't lose out, not when it came to food and clothes, nor yet love, especially not love. She and her mum saw to that.

Evie wasn't daft, not by a long chalk. She was painfully aware that Ted shut her out of the main stream of his life. She would readily admit he did his best to make up for it in the time they were together. It was worse after his visits. She missed him so much. Why was she always the loser? She was only human, and if the truth be told she was unreasonably jealous of Ted's wife, even though she recognised that no normal sex life could exist between them. She was sorry his wife was bedridden. She was glad to be a healthy woman, a woman with sexual desires and well able to please a man. Not that the opportunity arose very often.

'Come on, my darling, all this talk is getting us nowhere. Let's go to bed,' Ted pleaded.

Evie was in bed first. She sat up, pulling a shawl tightly around her shoulders, watching Ted get undressed. Then he was beside her. At once his arms were around her, holding her fast.

'Please, Ted –'

He stopped her words with his kisses, urgent, demanding, passionate kisses. She protested for a while then gave in to him. But she wasn't submitting, it was more than that. A whole lot more. She responded willingly now, with a passion equal to his own, her demands as strong as his. It was she who made the running, dragging every ounce of feeling from him.

With all passion spent, they lay back against the pillows, his arms still around her, her bare breasts heaving. Minutes passed. He broke the silence. With a sob in his voice he began to murmur, 'Evie, oh my darling Evie, if only.'

Evie sat up. Her hands shook as she straightened her nightdress and fastened the buttons. She was trembling. Her love for this man never lessened, nor would it ever, probably not until the day she died, much good that it did her!

'Please listen to me, Evie,' Ted whispered.

She didn't want to listen. She had heard it all before, so many times before, over the past twelve years. She opened her mouth to shout at him, but she couldn't say the words.

His head bent, his lips covered hers, softly, gently now. Together they lay back down again and, cradled in his arms, Evie slept.

Sunday was a day taut with emotion. Even the children felt the atmosphere wasn't right.

'You take the girls with you to get the papers,' Evie suggested to Ted, adding quickly, 'and maybe you can go on into the park, give me time to get the dinner ready.'

By the time two o'clock came Evie breathed a sigh of relief. Dinner was over and all washed up. She brushed Jenny's brown hair and tied the ends of her plaits with pale blue ribbon, which matched the colour of the cardigan she had on.

'Are you ready, Catherine?' Evie asked, as she opened her purse to give both girls a couple of coppers for the collection at their Sunday school.

'Yes, I'm ready,' Catherine answered and, looking up, Evie smiled. Her eldest daughter looked as pretty as a picture and so grown-up. A short tweed jacket with a brown velvet collar, which Evie herself had made, fitted nicely over Cathy's summer dress, and white cotton gloves gave the finishing touch.

'Bye Dad, bye Mum.' They were each kissed in turn and then suddenly the living room seemed empty and very quiet.

Evie sighed, a great sigh that came from deep within her. Edward hesitated, hand on the top of the bed-settee. He had been going to suggest that he open it up and that he and Evie spend the afternoon cuddled up together. Now he too sighed. Nothing would be gained by that.

'I wish you were going today,' Evie said, her eyes not meeting his. 'All this hanging about only prolongs the agony.' Her voice sounded calm, even to herself, but inside she was weeping with frustration.

He came to stand beside her, took her hand, raising it to his mouth, gently moving his lips over the tips of her fingers. Evie swayed, felt the blood in her veins start to rush. My God, he was a charmer! She longed for him to hold her, to say that he would stay, but of course that wouldn't happen, any more than it had on all the other occasions over the years. She pulled away.

'Don't sulk, Evie,' he protested. 'I've been here four weeks as it is. I can't possibly leave Mabel any longer.'

For an instant he saw jealousy flash in Evie's eyes. He retaliated quickly. 'You knew the situation from the beginning, Evie.'

'All right, all right, don't start going on, but you might give a thought to me now an' again. It doesn't get easier with time you know. You wanna be here sometimes when Cathy starts asking questions. Perhaps you could give her the right answers because I'm blowed if I can.'

Ted's cheeks flushed red with anger. He didn't want this row. It was no way to end what had been a grand break for him, but he wasn't about to let Evie make him feel guilty by laying all the blame at his door. His smile was cynical.

'As I remember, it was you that wanted to have both babies. You wouldn't even discuss an abortion, even though I offered to pay all expenses.'

'What? All that came later. First off, you played the proud father, proved to yourself that you were capable of fathering a child. Going to buy a big house, weren't you? This district wasn't good enough for your offspring to be brought up in. And what happened?' Evie was shouting now. Tit for tat, he had asked for, and that was what he was getting. 'Poor Mabel became an invalid, an' I'm not taking the mick, I do mean poor Mabel, but that wasn't the only reason you stayed. Your job an' your expense account went a long way to persuading you. I might not have believed that was so when I was seventeen, but this head on my shoulders has got a lot older an' a damn sight wiser since then.'

By now, Evie was having difficulty drawing breath. She did love Ted but, much as she adored her two girls, sometimes this on–off situation was more than she could bear. She made to leave the room. Ted barred her way.

'And that's it?' said Ted wryly.

'It? Oh, you mean have I said all I've got to say? Yes. Well, not much point in going on, is there?' She pushed past him.

'Wait a moment,' said Ted. 'D'you mean you want us to end everything?'

'Don't seem much point in us going on,' she answered, her back to him.

Ted's voice softened. 'Evie, d'you mind turning round and facing me when you say a thing like that?'

Still with her back to him, she said with a catch in her voice, 'I can't bear these partings.'

'Evie, look at me.'

She turned about, and Ted saw that her blue eyes were filled with tears. Amazing. Despite all that he had put her through, she still cared for him.

'Evie, I do love you, probably more than you realise. You shouldn't need me to keep telling you how much you and the girls mean to me. You should know by now. There just isn't any way that I could leave Mabel, not while she needs me. She depends on me totally. That doesn't alter the fact that we do have something worthwhile. Don't we? Not that it is the life I would wish for.'

Nor me! Is that what she nearly said? Instead she sighed.

He gave her a long look. She saw the tenderness come into his eyes, the pleading way he tilted his head, and the soft, sweet smile. She was utterly defeated.

He held his arms out to her and she went forward gladly to be encircled by them. It was impossible for her not to love this man to whom she had given herself when just a slip of a girl but who, over the years, had given her two daughters and gradually moulded her into the woman she was today.

'You're up early,' Ted said with a smile he didn't feel.

'You said you had to make an early start.' Evie gave him a hug before handing him his tea. He took the mug gratefully. 'Shall I make you some toast?'

'No, no thanks. I'll get breakfast on the train.'

They sat at the table, facing each other, sipping their tea. Soon they automatically reached for each other's hand. They gave each other encouraging smiles. They weren't silent out of pique or because they had lost heart. It was just that they had gone through these partings so often there didn't seem anything left to say. Evie was pondering on the fact that twelve years was a long time.

'How long before we see you again?' Evie asked.

Ted didn't answer. His shoulders were shaking. He was crying, but he didn't want Evie to see. He went to the window and looked out at the dismal terraced houses. He stood there a long time and Evie found no words to comfort him.

Would he make Christmas? Evie doubted it. A lot of water would flow under the bridge before then, and Evie was almost ninety per cent sure that she would discover she was pregnant for the third time.

Chapter Two

EDWARD HOPKINS FELT VERY guilty as he closed the front-garden gate of number 32 Brick Lane, Merton. How he wished he could take Evie and his daughters right away from here. His intention in the beginning had been to buy a house in Hampstead. Very close to the heath. He had got as far as arranging the mortgage, and even if he hadn't been able to obtain a quick divorce it wouldn't have bothered Evie. They would still have set up home as man and wife. Man can make all his plans – they're blown away in the wind if fate decides to step in.

Edward's footsteps faltered. Should he turn back? That would only prolong the agony. He looked about him. On each side of the lane was a row of mean little houses, their brickwork blackened by soot and grime, every chimney belching out smoke. Sanitation hadn't come into being when these dwellings were built. Evie had thought she was in clover when she had first been given the chance to rent the upper part of one of these houses for ten shillings and sixpence a week.

In the downstairs passageway, as in the majority of the houses nearby, was a door to the right, close to the front door, which led into what was known as the ground floor flat. A door at the foot of the stairs led to the upstairs flat. The stairs rose steeply. He had paid for these to be carpeted and held in place with brass stairrods. On the first small landing was a toilet, and five steps up again were two rooms with a gas cooker out on the landing, beside which was a sink with a cold water tap.

With his help, Evie had made these quarters into a comfortable home which, despite the luxury he was used to, he would have given his right arm to be able to share with her and the girls on a permanent footing. At least that was what he told himself when he was with Evie!

It hadn't been easy to begin with. The walls of the house had been infested with bugs. Fumigation had been the first job on a long list. A gas geyser installed over the stone sink had been the next item, for there was no running hot water. Ted smiled to himself as he remembered how easily pleased Evie had been when they'd gone in search of suitable furniture. A pleasant chintz-covered three-piece suite, four white wooden chairs and a wooden-topped table, and the front room had become crowded but very pleasant. The one bedroom had an iron-framed double bed, a chest of drawers with a mirror on top, and a black-leaded fender fronted the small fireplace. There was no room for anything else. Clothes were hung on hooks behind the door. Since the arrival of Jenny, the settee had had to go, replaced by a bed-settee which, when folded up, stood along the main wall.

Evie's talents were especially dressmaking and crochet work. Hand-crocheted runners of dazzling white cotton helped to brighten the rooms, and her sewing ensured that her girls were always neat and tidy. The house should have been condemned and pulled down long ago, the battle against dirt, grime and damp being an endless one. But Evie came through with flying colours. Her home and her girls were known to the neighbours and to the members of staff at the school the children attended as spotlessly clean.

The guilt persisted in Edward's mind as he turned into the high street to wait for a bus that would take him to Wimbledon Station. Now, in his mind, he was comparing the dwelling he had just left and the home to which he was returning. Detached house, sweeping lawns rolling down to the sea. Clean, sweet-smelling St Anne's, far away in Lancashire. Eight rooms for two people and a resident nurse. That was how he lived at least nine months of the year. Just him and his wife, Mabel. No children. The way of life bore no comparison. The very air in Brick Lane was sour.

The bus came and he got on, taking a seat downstairs, just inside the door. It was only a short ride to the station. He checked his watch: seven-fifteen. Another half hour and the buses would be packed, everyone rushing to get to work on time this Monday morning. He had some things to be grateful for. He was given a lot of leeway as to his comings and goings. Mabel's family were rich and influential in the North.

Yes, he said to himself, *and you were flattered to think that their only child set her cap at you. You were conned, old son, and it served you right.*

Mabel's parents had known she was ill, even then. What they had hoped for was that Mabel would become pregnant right away, hopefully produce a son. A much needed son to carry on the business. From the off, the marriage hadn't worked. Mabel was too fragile to lead a normal, healthy life. Again he rebuked himself. It was nobody's fault but his own. He'd had a decent job on the shop floor of Walker's Engineering Company. It wasn't enough; he'd wanted more, tempted by greater rewards. Mabel's family still held the purse strings, not that more money could buy happiness – not for Mabel or for himself. A little more would be useful when it came to his second family, but he wasn't in a position to explain that. Besides, when it came to the crunch it hadn't all been bad. *If I'm being honest about things not working out between Mabel and me, maybe I should count up the plus side. The reason I always give to Evie, about not deserting a sinking ship, is partly true. Course it is.* He shook his head, amused at his own thoughts, then he scoffed. He also knew damn well that he owed Mabel's parents a very great deal.

The bus pulled into the station forecourt. Edward bent to retrieve his suitcase from where he had stowed it on the platform beneath the stairs.

'Going on holiday?' the cheerful conductor asked.

Edward grinned. 'No. As a matter of fact, I'm going home.'

Evie closed the front door and leant against it, listening to Ted's footsteps go down the short path to the front gate. The last words he had said were, 'I shall miss you.' *Not nearly as much as I'll miss him,* she thought, feeling thoroughly wretched, while at the same time experiencing a sense of anger. Once again it was left to her to explain to the girls why their father had to go. She wished someone would explain it to her. For all the guarantees she had, Ted might just have walked out of her life forever.

She wouldn't cry. She was past all that. Even so, dry sobs racked her body, and the lump in her throat was almost choking her.

Just turned seven o'clock in the morning, and she was clad only in a thin cotton nightdress. Her feet were bare. Autumn was almost here, and at this time in the morning there was a nip in the air. She shivered and pulled her nightdress tighter across her chest before going towards the stairs. It was no good standing here having regrets, wishing things could be different. Wishing got you nowhere. Quietly, she turned the handle of the bedroom door.

Catherine opened her eyes. 'Mum?' she queried as she struggled to sit up.

Evie came to the side of the bed, put her hand against Cathy's shoulder and forced her back against the pillows. 'Go back to sleep, my lovely, it's early yet.'

It was good to watch her daughter obey her and relax. She heard the toilet flush and she stood in the doorway to watch Jenny climb the five stairs. Jenny looked up, a grin on her face as she saw that her mum was up.

'Has Dad gone again?' she asked, her eyes bleary with sleep.

'Yes dear, he had to. Hurry up back into bed and keep warm.'

'Can't I crawl in with you?' Jenny pleaded, and her voice was so sad it tore at Evie's heart strings. Without giving her mother time to reply, Jenny said, 'There's loads of room in the big bed. Come and get in with Cathy an' me. Go on, Mum, please. We can all 'ave a cuddle.'

'Yeah, course I will.' The look of tenderness on Evie's face as she picked her youngest daughter up into her arms and carried her back into the bedroom was unbelievable. She placed Jenny on the far side of the bed and slid into the centre between her girls.

'H'm, that's nice,' said Cathy softly, as she tucked herself up tight against her mother.

Catherine knew the score. Evie was sure of that. At twelve years old she had to be told the truth; the time for fairy stories with her was long gone. Catherine was known as Cathy Smith. She would probably never be able to call herself by her rightful name of Catherine Hopkins.

Sounds of Jenny crying could be heard, even though her head was buried in the pillow.

'What's up with little 'un?' asked Cathy.

'Nothing,' said Evie. 'She just got a bit cold going to the lavatory.'

'Mum, you know that's not the truth. She don't like Dad going away any more than I do.'

'I know, I know,' said her mother, thinking to herself, *That sod does have the best of two worlds* and, to her embarrassment and disgust, she too began to cry.

'Oh, Mum. I hate it when you're upset like this. Shall I get up an' make you a cup of tea?'

Her mother didn't reply straight away. She put her arm around Cathy and bent over to kiss the top of her head. 'Another ten minutes, then you can, and I'll tell you what. You and Jenny can have the day off school an' we'll all go an' see Nanna. What do you think about that?'

'Smashing, eh Jenny? Did you hear what Mum just said?'

Jenny lifted her tear-stained face. 'Yeah. Can we 'ave our dinner there, stay all day?'

'Course we can, but only if you give us a kiss and tell us you're gonna be happy.'

Jenny sat up and kissed her mum. 'I don't feel happy.' But she was beginning to smile.

Chapter Three

FLOSSIE SMITH, EVIE'S MOTHER, lived in Upper Tooting, which to most working-class people was a posh area. Worlds apart from Tooting Broadway. It didn't make an atom of difference to Flossie. She was a legend in her own lifetime.

Coming out of Tooting Bec Underground Station into Upper Tooting Road, Balham lay to the left and Tooting to the right. Making the crossroads was Trinity Road, where the Police Station lay and, further on, Wandsworth Common. On the opposite side of the high street was Tooting Bec Road, which led to Tooting Bec Common, with its popular boating lake and avenue, lined each side with great noble oak trees. Both roads boasted prestigious houses, worthy of the district.

Not so Chetwode Road, which was the first turning on the right in Trinity Road. Houses here were of a more modest type. However, compared to where Evie and her daughters lived they were palaces: double fronted, with three rooms downstairs and three bedrooms and a bathroom upstairs, and that wasn't all. There were two lavatories! One just outside the back door and a second on the first landing. Hot water in the tap. Well, there was if you could afford the coal to keep the fire in the living room alight. A boiler was situated at the back of this grate.

Catherine and Jenny arrived at their nanna's house yards in front of their mother, having run all the way once they turned the corner into Chetwode Road. The front door was wide open. It was hardly ever closed.

'Nanna!'

Getting no answer, Jenny rushed down the passage calling, 'Nanna, we've come for the day. We're not gonna go to school.'

In the kitchen, Flossie Smith was hanging washing on to five long wooden slats. It was difficult to see her between the wet sheets and underclothes. ''Ello, my darlings, I won't be a minute,' she called, tugging on the rope of the dangerous pulley system, which sent the contraption high up to the ceiling.

'Can I do anything to help?' Evie asked as she came into the room.

'It would be nice if you meant it,' her mum cried.

'Oh don't start the minute we get 'ere, Mum. Tell me what you want and I'll do it. D'you want me to make a pot of tea?'

Flossie stepped down from the chair on which she had been standing, turned around and smiled at her daughter. 'Making the tea would be nice, but there's no milk. I've bin waiting for you to turn up an' go to the corner shop.'

'Nanna, I'll go.' Cathy sounded eager.

'Not before I've 'ad me kiss an' cuddle. Ain't seen you for a week and what do I get? No greetin' from either of you.'

Jenny pushed herself in front of her sister. 'How could I kiss you when you were up on that chair?'

Their nanna laughed. 'Come 'ere, the pair of you. God, but you're a sight for sore eyes.'

They loved their nanna. She was pretty, bubbly and always laughing. Happy-go-lucky is how most people would describe her.

Nanna wrapped her arms around the two of them, hugging them close to her chest. Kisses were flying from one to the other, and that made Evie smile with delight. This house was still her home. A place full of love, a place where you often got shouted at but where there was never a shortage of love. She watched her mother straighten up and felt a twinge of envy. Flossie's figure was still trim, her skin good, her hair nice if it wasn't for the dark roots that were beginning to show. She would need to peroxide it again soon. Flossie wore a pale blue jumper that stretched tightly across her firm breasts and a grey skirt that hugged her hips and emphasised her small waist and flat stomach. Even at this time in the morning her face was expertly made up and earrings and beads had not been forgotten.

Flossie had been just eighteen when she had given birth to Evie, and Evie had been just eighteen when Catherine had been born, the contrast being that Flossie had been married, at Wandsworth Town Hall, just ten weeks before the baby had arrived. Evie had never been married. And much good marriage had done Flossie! Jack Smith had cleared off within six months. Got himself a job down the coal mines, somewhere up north, so the first postcard had informed her. Jack had sent money, at least in the beginning. He'd even showed up on her doorstep periodically over the first two years of Evie's life. With each visit he had caused enough trouble to last a lifetime before disappearing once again. He'd been dead and buried for three months before his sister got round to writing to Flossie with the news that he'd suffered a heart attack.

Flossie got by taking in lodgers. No one permanent.

She liked men in general too much to tie herself to one in particular.

Affectionate, generous and open-hearted, she'd make any man really happy if she took to him. Half the trouble was that she'd picked some wrong 'uns in her time.

As this thought struck Evie, she burst out laughing. After twelve years of putting up with Ted's comings and goings, she'd hardly win a prize herself for good judgement.

The lid of the tin kettle rattled as it came to the boil, reminding Evie that she was supposed to be making the tea.

'Put your coat back on, Cathy, if you're going to fetch the milk. Where's your purse, Mum?'

'I might 'ave known you'd need the money first. Too much to 'ope you'd fork out a few coppers for a change.'

Evie ignored the sarcasm and nodded at the window. 'It's come on to rain.'

Flossie turned to look. 'Just my blooming luck! I've got a great bowl of woollens there on the draining board all ready to 'ang out.' At that moment, the clothes from the pulley line, all of them still dripping wet, fell on top of Flossie's head.

'Damn an' blast!' Flossie let rip.

Then there was a silence, and Evie wished she hadn't come so early. What was the point of visiting her mum if she was going to be so bad-tempered? Before anyone could go to Flossie's aid, the back door was pushed open, thudding into her backside and sending her sprawling forward. She let out a yell of pain and surprise as she slammed against the kitchen table.

Jimmy Tyler, runner for the street bookie, his face red, his flat cap knocked lopsided, had his head poking round the half open door.

'You there, Floss?' he called needlessly.

'Well I was, till you knocked me for six, you daft bleeder.'

'Mum! There's no need to swear. Jim didn't know you were behind the door,' Evie said, trying not to grin as she helped her mother scramble to her feet.

'Well he knows now so he'd best sling 'is 'ook before I land 'im one.'

''Ang on, Floss, don't be so 'asty. 'Ow you come ter pick an outsider like that on Saturday beats me. But I've got a tenner for you. Your bet came up.'

'Did it, by heck! That's a different story. Come on in.'

Catherine and Jenny thought it all great fun. Their giggles and the fact that she had won ten pounds put Nanna into a much happier frame of mind.

''Ello Evie, luv. Quite a stranger, ain't you? What ye bin doing with yourself?' Sure of a welcome now, Jim walked across the floor to give Evie a peck on the cheek. He'd known this girl since the day she was born.

'Evie, you go for the milk and get some custard creams while you're about it. I'll put the kettle on again and you, Jim Tyler, can get me tin bath in from the garden. Come on Cathy, an' you Jenny. 'Elp me pick this lot up an' we'll put it all in to soak again. Later on I'll find some bloke to mend that damn clothes dryer.'

Evie was grinning as she made for the front door. She had no doubts that her mother would do just that. Fellas fell over themselves to do jobs for her mum!

Cathy and Jenny picked up the smaller articles of wet washing and Jenny began telling their nanna that their dad had gone away to work again.

'Mum was ever so upset this morning,' Catherine said, her voice sounding sad.

Flossie's mouth tightened, and she gave Jim a long look. She mustn't let her feelings get the better of her. Not in front of the children. Just looking at them made her heart ache.

Catherine was tall for her age, fair haired, with a pale complexion and a nose that tended to peel when she'd been in the sun. So very much like her mother, Flossie thought as she remembered the times she had rubbed cream into Evie's skin to stop it from peeling.

Jenny took after Ted Hopkins, God help her! Much darker, and her skin tanned easily, though she wasn't as hardy as Catherine. Her frame was tiny and she seemed to catch every cough and cold that was going.

When at seventeen Evie had taken up with Edward Hopkins, Flossie had wanted to murder him. She had screamed at him. 'She's only seventeen, for Christ's sake, and you're a married man!'

All the shouting and murderous meditation had changed nothing. Alone with her thoughts, she had had to chide herself for having had a go at Evie. Talk about the pot calling the kettle black.

'Well I better get back to me pitch. Thanks for the tea,' Jim said to Flossie and immediately got to his feet. ''Ere you are, girls. Buy yourselves a couple of comics. Or whatever it is you like to read now you're so grown-up,' Jim added, looking at Catherine. He thought guiltily of Evie, who'd been like a daughter to him over the years. Long ago he had considered offering to marry Flossie and take care of her and Evie. He'd let things slide. That bloke Hopkins had come on the scene and Evie, barely out of school, had fallen for him hook, line and sinker. God! To this day it made his blood boil to think of it. He'd learnt not to mention the subject in Flossie's hearing. She was all for knifing the fella when it first came to light, and she wasn't past doing it now.

'Go on then, don't just stand there.' Flossie looked at Jim, a smile playing around her lips.

'We'll walk to the corner with you, Uncle Jim.' Catherine slid by her nanna, taking the two-shilling piece held out by Jim. 'We won't be long, Mum. Only going to the paper shop.'

'Make sure you keep hold of Jenny's hand,' their mother called after them.

As the door closed behind the three of them, Flossie's manner became different. 'I've got a bit of news. You'll never guess what, not in a million years.'

'I won't have to guess if you tell me, will I?'

'Old Maisie Brown died. God rest 'er soul.'

'Not exactly unexpected, is it? Happy release if you ask me. Maisie was a dear old soul. She didn't deserve to suffer, and she was coming up to being ninety. So? What's so astounding that's making you so cagey?'

'Slow on the uptake this morning, ain't ye? You don't get the point, do ye?'

Evie's head came forward, her features frowning. 'What are you on about?'

'You an' the girls moving into number forty-two, ye great dope. Get yourself down to the council.'

'An' what chance d'you think I'd stand, no man behind me? They won't accept that I could pay the rent. 'Sides, I don't come under Wandsworth Borough no more.'

'Gawd save us! Ain't you never 'eard it said that God 'elps those what 'elps themselves.'

'Yes, an' many's the time you've drummed into me that it's Christ help those that get caught helping themselves.'

'Don't be so daft. This ain't like that at all. Nobody's asking ye to pinch anything. Just get in there an' fight for yourself for a change instead of letting anyone an' everyone trample all over you.'

'But Mum, even if I got away with letting them think I still lived in the district, it's a regular payer, 'usband in regular employment, that's what the council will be looking for.'

'Listen, luv, I've already 'ad a word. Paved the way like. Be a load off me mind knowing you were only three doors up the street. Go on, 'ave a go. You'll find you've got friends in 'igh places. You'll see if I'm not right.'

'Mum! I've a funny feeling you've been getting at Mr Cole. It is still Mr Cole that collects the rents around here. Isn't it?'

Slowly, a grin came to Flossie's face, then the two of them were laughing fit to bust. The same thought was running through their minds. Tom Cole would do anything for Flossie Smith!

At Wandsworth's town hall, Evie's first port of call the next morning after dropping her two girls off at the school gate, she was waiting for a Mr Simpson, the housing officer, having spoken to him on the telephone the previous afternoon.

'You can go in now.' The smart young lady smiled at her from behind the tall counter. 'First door on the right in the corridor.'

Evie knocked.

'Come in,' a deep voice called.

Evie entered. Her legs were shaking. She felt this was going to be an awkward interview.

Mr Simpson looked up from his desk. His dark hair was flecked with grey. He had bushy eyebrows that gave him a wise look.

'Good morning, Mrs Smith,' he said. And his broad smile made Evie feel a whole lot easier in her mind. 'That's right, come in, take a seat.'

'Thank you,' Evie murmured and sat down in the chair that faced his desk.

'How's your mother?' asked Mr Simpson, his enquiry sounding sincere.

'Fine, thank you,' she said, wondering how the hell a

well-dressed man such as Mr Simpson came to know her mother.

'From what you told me on the telephone yesterday, I gather that you would like to rent number 42 Chetwode Road. A few doors from your mother.'

Evie swallowed hard. 'Yes please,' she said.

'I'll give it to you straight, Mrs Smith. I know something of your circumstances and I have great respect for the way you cope with a young family under what must be very difficult conditions. However, this vacant property needs a lot of repairs, and we are not just talking about odd jobs here and there.' Mr Simpson's phone rang. He listened, then spoke into the mouthpiece. 'I'll get back to you later.'

'Sorry about that,' he said to Evie as he replaced the receiver. 'Now, I'm sure you are aware that Chetwode Road was badly damaged by bombs during the war and that many of the houses on both sides of the road had to be demolished.'

Evie nodded.

'New houses were built on the right-hand side, Alfred Butt Apartments were erected on the left, number 42 being the first of the row of houses to be salvaged, though with hindsight one wonders if it wouldn't have made more sense to demolish a few more houses even further along rather than patch them up. Down to the powers that be that was, I'm afraid.' Mr Simpson paused, rustling through a sheaf of papers that lay on the desk in front of him, fierce, but kindly underneath.

He might be a bigwig but he has a heart, Evie thought, feeling a lot more at ease now than when she had first come into the room.

Alfred Butt Apartments! The very thought made Evie laugh to herself. They were a nice enough small block of flats built soon after the war ended, and people who were allocated one felt very privileged. Grass had been laid both to the front of the building and to the rear, which was in Holdernesse Road. This in itself was something different for the area. The building had been named after Sir Alfred Butt, Unionist Member for the Balham and Tooting Division of Wandsworth from 1922 until 1936. At least that's how her mother told the story. This was the first time Evie had heard them referred to as apartments!

'It's against our rules to allow anyone to jump the queue, but that wouldn't be so in this case. You have been on our housing list for a number of years, and the fact that you were born in the district carries some weight.'

Evie didn't know what to say, so she kept quiet. She could hardly believe that he was taking her request so seriously.

Mr Simpson looked up. 'There is another point in your favour. Not everyone would be willing to take on such a property.' He opened a drawer, took out a folder, glanced at a form on top of the contents, then wrote something on a pad. 'One downstairs room in number 42 is uninhabitable. It would have to be sealed and its window boarded over. Would you have any problem with that?'

Evie looked up at him. Her eyes were misty. 'None at all,' she said a little gruffly.

'So that proposition would be agreeable to you?'

Evie gaped.

'Good,' said Mr Simpson briskly, getting to his feet and coming round the side of his desk to where Evie sat.

Evie stood up. They shook hands.

'I'll be in touch,' he promised, ushering her to the door.

Flossie Smith stood in the doorway of her living room and watched Evie, whose back was to her, ironing. Evie was a good girl and had proved herself a damn good mother.

There was nothing on which anyone could fault her Evie when it came to her girls. Men! Now that was a different story. It was history repeating itself.

'You don't 'ave to do all that lot for me, not in one go,' Flossie said, stepping into the room and holding out the letter she had just picked up from her front mat.

Evie glanced over her shoulder but didn't stop ironing. 'I might as well keep going. I'll soon be finished here and then I'll do the girls' school blouses I brought with me.'

'Right, but don't you want to read your letter? It's from the council.'

'From the council!'

She'd almost given up hope that she was going to hear from them. It had been three weeks since her visit to the town hall.

Flossie knew this was an important letter, one she prayed would bring her daughter the good news she deserved. She couldn't stand and watch. 'Would you like me to go an' make a cup of tea?' She smiled.

Evie thought her mum was being extra nice. 'Yes, please.' She smiled in reply. With the room to herself, Evie turned the letter over and over in her hand. Should she read it now or save it until later? 'You're round the twist,' she told herself, knowing full well she couldn't wait.

She slit open the envelope with her thumb and after reading only a few lines she let out a whoop of sheer delight. 'Mum! Mum, I've got it.'

Evie bashed into her mother, who was coming out of the kitchen as she made to go in. They flung their arms around each other and did a little dance.

News travels fast. Numerous friends and neighbours, male and female, came through Flossie's front door during the rest of the day. Their remarks were all in the same vein.

'Good on ye, Evie.'

'My, but we're glad you're coming 'ome.'

'Yeah, an' your mum will be over the moon 'aving you all just up the street.'

Especially Catherine and Jenny, thought Flossie. Now she would be able to keep both eyes on those two darling grandchildren of hers, and if she had her way the wind wouldn't blow on either of them.

Three council workmen were waiting for Evie on the doorstep of number 42. Evie used her new Yale key to open the door, and together they entered the house.

In need of some repairs was the right description. Upstairs two windows were broken, one bedroom door hung from only a single hinge, giving it a cockeyed look, and the toilet wouldn't flush. Downstairs the boarded up room made the hallway dark. In the kitchen a house brick was the only thing holding the wooden draining board in place, and cardboard had been used to cover the cracked panes of glass that formed the top half of the back door, which led into the garden. The garden itself was a tip. The large living room was damp, Evie thought, sniffing the air and gazing at the peeling wallpaper. Perhaps it just smelt that way because it was cold and had been neglected for so long. Poor old Maisie. She'd been living on her own for as long as Evie could remember.

One of the workmen turned to Evie. 'Do you think you'll be able to cope?'

'I do,' Evie stated emphatically. 'Once I get a fire going we'll soon feel a difference.' Silently she was vowing to herself that she would do her utmost to make this place into a comfortable home for her girls.

'Go down your mum's and get her to make us all a cuppa and then we'll get started. We'll go through this house like a dose of salts. Deal?' asked the workman, extending a hand to Evie.

A grinning Evie, not in the least put out by his grubbiness, shook hands with him. 'Deal!' she agreed.

'You there, Evie?'

The three workmen stood drinking their tea. Evie was upstairs, trying to decide where to start.

'Evie?' The voice was louder this time.

Evie came out of the bedroom and looked down over the bannisters. 'Oh, Joan, it's you. I'll be right down.' Evie's voice was filled with surprise. 'Mum told me you an' Bert had got one of those new 'ouses opposite. Cor, I ain't 'alf glad to see you. We seem to 'ave lost touch since we left school.' All this had been said as she came down the stairs. The two women met halfway down the passage and hugged each other fondly.

'Yeah, but now we're gonna be neighbours. Great, ain't it? I should 'ave come over sooner. I told your mum I would give you a 'and to get straight once you moved in.'

Evie laughed. 'Don't make rash promises you ain't prepared to keep. Wait till I show you over this place. It won't be one hand you'll need to be offering if you really mean to 'elp, it'll be both hands an' a lot of bloody elbow grease. Still offering to 'elp, are you?'

Joanne Watkins, now Joan Killick, and Evie Smith had been inseparable from the day they could crawl until men had come into their lives and they had taken different paths.

Joan took a deep breath, pushed the sleeves of her blouse up beyond her elbows and laughed. 'Lead me to it.'

'Got to go down Mum's first. Borrow her bucket, brushes an' cloths. Come on, she'll be ever so glad I've got some 'elp. All she's offered to do is mind me two girls.'

'That's enough, ain't it? She can mind my two an' all if she likes. Get on my bloody nerves, they do, at times. Bert's never 'ome. He's up the pub every night. Honest, Evie, you don't know just 'ow pleased I am that you're gonna be living 'ere now.'

Evie glanced at Joan. She hadn't altered that much. Her hair was a softer colour now, though still red. The fights the two of them had got into when they were kids because Joan hated to be called ginger! Her green eyes were the same. Maybe they had lost some of their sparkle, but that was to be expected. She certainly hadn't put on any weight. Not an ounce. Two girls she'd given birth to: Shirley, about the same age as Catherine, and Norma, who was six months older than her Jenny, and still Joan was skinny.

'I don't believe it,' cried Flossie, having been given the conducted tour of number 42. 'You've worked wonders here.'

'Yeah, it's smashing, ain't it, Mum? I'm ever so grateful to you and to Joan Killick. Mind you, we've 'ad a helluva lot of laughs while we've scrubbed this place from top to bottom.'

'I can guess! And got through a lot of gossip, if I know you two.'

The house did look nice. Besides Evie's own furniture, there were several pieces that Flossie had kindly offered her and which she had accepted gratefully.

'I've got the kettle on downstairs. You will stay an' 'ave a cup of tea with me? There's stacks of time before I've got to go an' meet the girls from school.'

'Course I will.' Flossie smiled.

Evie didn't have the nerve to tell her mother straight out why she wanted her to stay. Better get her sitting down with a cup and saucer in her hand before she fired the first shot.

Flossie had made herself comfortable in the armchair. Evie poured the tea and passed a cup to her mother. On a side table she had set small plates, and a larger one had a doyley, on which there was a victoria sponge, its top dusted with icing sugar.

'Gonna 'ave a piece of sponge, Mum? I made it this morning. It's raspberry jam in the middle.'

Flossie grinned. She loved Evie. She admitted to herself that she hadn't been able to keep her on the straight and narrow, though God knows she'd tried. The two of them could never live under the same roof, they were too alike for that, but when it came to knowing her daughter she could read her like a book.

'She said softly, 'Yes please, love. I'll try your sponge. And when you've cut it, don't you think it's about time you spit out what ever it is you have to tell me.'

Evie sniffed and gave her mum a funny look. 'Oh, you, Mum.'

'Never mind, "Oh, you, Mum". You've been prancing around for the last 'alf hour. Now sit down and tell me, whatever it is.'

'Mum, I'm pregnant,' Evie said quickly. Now that she had come right out with it, it sounded callous. Her voice was steady, but inside she was trembling. Evie felt even worse when she saw the shock on her mother's face.

'Oh no, Evie! Not again.' Flossie was stunned. She sat on the edge of the chair, staring at her daughter. How many more was that bleeder going to dump on her? When Evie had become pregnant at seventeen Ted Hopkins had boasted loud enough about how thrilled he was to know he was going to be a father. He was going to divorce his wife, marry Evie as quickly as possible and everything was going to be fine. Instead of which Evie's life had been ruined because that posh, selfish git had persuaded her to lie on her back for him. Then he had sodded off back to his wife and his highfaluting way of living, leaving Evie to bring up the baby.

It wouldn't have been so bad if it had all ended there. At least Evie would have been given the chance to find someone else. But no! When that man wanted his oats he made sure he got them, turning up on Evie's doorstep whenever the fancy took him. And she, daft cow that she was, welcomed him with open arms. Did he ever think of staying to take care of her and the two girls? Did he heck as like! Three or four weeks till his craving was satisfied, and he was off on his merry way again. Even war time hadn't put a stop to his capers. He'd still managed to cover the distance from north to south and leave Evie pregnant for the second time. *Good job he's not here this minute. There'd be murder done.*

'I suppose Ted Hopkins is the father?'

'Mother! What a thing to ask.'

'Now don't come the innocent with me. You don't exactly lead the life of a nun, now do you? Not that I'm blaming you, cos I'm not. But I've got eyes in me 'ead an' you've 'ad enough boyfriends to form a bleedin' football team.'

'Well I'll be blowed! Coming from you that's rich. You've given me more uncles than 'ot dinners. Even when I was a toddler one uncle would take me to school and a different one meet me, cos you were too busy.'

'You cheeky bitch!'

It was on the tip of Evie's tongue to say, 'I must take after you,' but she found herself compromising by saying, 'Mum, when Ted's with me I can't help myself. Caution gets thrown to the wind. I love him, Mum. That's all there is to it. But I'm only human, an' I do get lonely.'

Flossie leant forward and kissed Evie's cheek lightly. Suddenly she felt weary, old. 'Get yourself ready. I'll come with you to meet the girls. We'll muddle through, won't we luv? You know what they say: each baby brings its own love with it. And you've got to admit that's more than true when it comes to Cathy an' Jenny. Christ, can you imagine life without the pair of them now, cos I can't?'

Evie went upstairs to fetch her coat.

Downstairs Flossie poured herself a second cup of tea. Closing her eyes, she began to pray. 'God give me the health and strength to stand by my daughter and the wisdom to show my grandchildren how to tread a different path through life to what me and their mother seem to have chosen.

Chapter Four

EVIE COULD WRITE TO Edward, care of his office, and she also had a telephone number where she could leave a message in case of disasters or a crisis. She had never yet used the number. Nor did she write regularly. When she did send a letter she did her best to make it funny and full of entertaining things the girls had said and done. Often she had a job to hide the hurt and humiliation. Not a word must she say about his wife, his other life in such different circumstances.

Ted had adored his first-born, Catherine. Carried her around on his shoulders. Right little daddy's girl she had been when he was about. When he left it was a different story, especially as she had grown older. Jennifer's birth had also pleased him, or so he had said at the time. And he would still pander to her with boisterous play when the mood took him. At least he had never failed to send her an allowance each month, by way of a registered letter. And for that she would be eternally grateful. What he would have to say about her being pregnant again now, she had no idea. She had written to him, very briefly, and told him she was three months' gone.

She took the telegram out of her bag and read it again. When the ratatat-tat had sounded on her door this morning and she had opened up to find a telegraph boy standing there, she had felt the colour drain from her face. Telegrams always spelt bad news. She could not believe it! She read it yet again. CALL THIS NUMBER SEVEN O'CLOCK TONIGHT. LOVE, EDWARD. Underneath was a phone number.

It crossed her mind that maybe he wasn't too pleased. But there again he had put 'love, Edward'.

It was going to be a long day. Her mouth was dry and she felt a bit dizzy. The teapot had gone stone cold. She would clear away the girls' breakfast things, go upstairs and make their beds and then she would make a fresh pot. Should she pop along to her mum's? No. Flossie was acute. She would be able to tell, just by looking at her, that something was up. Of course she could go over to Joan's. They were the best of mates again now, just as they had been in their school days. Often had a night out together at the pictures or up at the Brixton Empire.

Flossie was always good-natured when it came to minding the children, she never complained. In fact Evie got the impression that the more kids her mum had in the house, the happier she was. The girls loved spending the night at their nanna's, as did Joan's two girls. God knows what her mum let them all get up to.

Evie waited outside the telephone box until her watch told her it was five past seven. She didn't want to appear too eager. She put her money in the slots, dialled the number and suddenly she heard Ted's voice.

'Hello? Who is this? Is that you, Evie?' He sounded worried.

She swallowed heavily and pressed button A. 'Ted.'

'It is you.' She heard the relief in his voice.

The line went quiet as each waited for the other to speak.

'I'm coming down to see you, Evie. I'll be there about ten o'clock on Saturday morning. Is that all right?'

'Oh Ted! Since when did you need to ask?'

'Since you got a whole house to yourself.'

She laughed. 'You'd better watch out. Remember my mother only lives three doors away.'

'I shall be in fear of my life, but I'll come just the same.'

She could practically see him grinning, could hear it in his voice. 'See you on Saturday then.' She replaced the receiver and shivered with sheer joy. Ted was coming home. Only now it was to her new house. Would he stay for good this time?

Saturday promised to be a dry, cold day. There was a sharp frost, and Edward Hopkins stamped his feet as he waited on the platform for the train that was due at ten minutes past five. It wasn't yet light, but with this being the first week in December it was only to be expected. A shrill whistle announced the coming of the train. It shuddered to a halt. He leapt into an empty carriage and began his journey to London. To Evie's house. He wasn't looking forward to it one bit.

Since the day he had first set eyes on Evie he had experienced an all-consuming passion for her, which hadn't diminished with the passing of time. With his wife being an invalid, there had been other women over the years but never any who affected him like Evie Smith. Every warning bell in his head was ringing at this moment, but he wasn't sure how he was going to play it. All he was really sure of was that he was going to spend a marvellous weekend with Evie. Sleep with her. Make love to her. Wake up with her beside him.

For most of his life he crept about the house giving in

to his wife's every whim. Now he was being forced to leave England. Because Mabel had developed a chest infection, the doctors had advised that he take her first to a sanatorium in Switzerland and later to a warm climate where she might possibly recuperate more quickly. Trouble was, he wasn't in a position to be able to say no. Mabel's parents, and indeed her two brothers, were all for it and, seeing as how they would be meeting all expenses, he could hardly object. Having received Evie's letter, he had acted on impulse. Last fling of the condemned man, so to speak. He laughed to himself. Once abroad, God alone knew how long he would be away. And another thing God alone knew at this moment was, how the hell was he going to tell Evie?

Evie watched her girls, together with Shirley and Norma, practically run down Chetwode Road. They were off to the Saturday morning pictures at the Mayfair, and then Joan was going to meet them when they came out and take them shopping. She stood at the gate for a few minutes after they had turned the corner. She felt so nervous. What if Ted was going to kick up a stink about this new baby? Probably moan that it would be a drain on his resources. From what she had gathered over the years, Ted lived the life of Old Riley up there in the North, but when it came down to actual cash, he had to answer to his in-laws, who were his employers, for every brass farthing.

It would be another mouth to feed. This house was lovely, but it cost more to heat, and the rent was an extra five shillings to what she had been paying in Merton. It all had to be found. The girls needed more, especially Catherine. She'd soon be a teenager, and you couldn't stop her wanting to go out and about and do all the things that the other youngsters were doing. Their clothes didn't last forever, and shoes were a nightmare. The money had to come from somewhere. And now there was Christmas coming up!

Neither of her two girls would fare half as well as they did if it weren't for their nanna. Her mother came up trumps every time. It wasn't fair though. Not when Edward had everything he could possibly want for himself. Still, it wasn't his fault, and she had missed him so. If only she could get to see him more often. But there it was. That was the way the cards had been dealt to her and she didn't see what she could do to alter things unless she wanted to lose Ted altogether. *No, as long as I know he loves me and our girls I'll manage, even if we do have to scrimp and scrape.* She turned and went into the house.

When she finally heard his footsteps crunch up the small front path she felt herself glow all over. He did love her just as much as she loved him. *Oh thank you, God, for letting him come. Please can he stay a lot longer this time?*

She went into the passage and opened the front door. Oh what bliss! Ted was back.

Then, without a word being spoken, she was in his arms, she was being kissed. This was how it should be. Every day. He was kissing her face, her eyes, her neck. Taking hold of his hand, she led him into her neat front room.

'It does you credit,' Ted told her, his eyes taking in the fact that there were no carpets on the floor, only linoleum.

'Cup of tea?' she offered.

'How about something stronger?' He undid the zip of his bag and brought out a bottle of wine. Evie fetched two glasses from the kitchen. Edward had his coat off by the time she came back.

She ran her hands up and down his back as he opened the bottle. 'I've been dreaming of this from almost the moment you left,' Evie confessed.

Edward was moved. His hand shook as he poured the wine. He spilled some as he passed it to her.

'To us.' She smiled.

'To us,' he repeated and they both drank. She stared into his eyes and saw in them exactly the same feelings of love and desire that she knew were showing in her own. 'Bed?' he asked.

'Bed,' Evie agreed. Taking his hand, she led him slowly up the stairs and into the big room, which held a double bed and which, up to now, she had shared with no one. It developed into a race as to who could get their clothes off first. Evie won, and she shrieked as she dived between the cold sheets.

'I'll soon warm you up,' Ted laughed, getting into bed and reaching for her.

'Oh, Ted! It seems so long,' she murmured.

He kissed her, his passion mounting. His hands began moving over her, touching, caressing.

When it was over they rested in one another's arms. Evie fell asleep, smiling contentedly.

Saturday evening and their dad was home. What's more, he was taking them out to eat. The girls were too excited to remain still. 'Are we going to a café, or is it pie and mash? I wish you two would make up your minds,' Edward snapped at the girls at the same time looking towards where Evie was adjusting her hat. 'That hat really suits you. Makes you look terrific. Why don't you be the one to decide where we are going to eat before I die of starvation?'

'No!' Cathy and Jenny chorused. 'Fish and chips.'

'Fish and chips it is then,' their father enthused, thinking it would be amusing to see Evie sit down in a fish shop wearing her best hat.

'Not any old chip shop, Dad. We'd like to go to that big

one that Nanna takes us to sometimes. It's just past Clapham Common,' Cathy declared.

'We like it there.' Jenny smiled, adding quickly, 'Cos you can get pineapple fritters for afters an' they are lovely.'

Outside the wind was bitter. 'Wouldn't be surprised if we don't have snow during the night,' Edward remarked thoughtfully.

The inside of the fish shop was warm and steamy. The other customers looked up and smiled at Evie.

'They're all envious of your hat, especially that feather which won't lie still.'

'You mean they wouldn't give me a second glance if it weren't for my hat?' she teased.

'I didn't mean that at all, you know darn well I didn't.'

With a grin she whispered, 'I think I'll wear it in bed tonight, nothing else!'

He raised his eyebrows. 'That I can't wait to see!'

It took some time for them all to decide what fish they were going to have but the decision regarding their sweet was unanimous. Pineapple fritters all round.

Evie smiled at Ted when he'd sat down again after having been to the counter to give their order. She reached across and touched his arm. 'You haven't said what you'll be wearing.' She paused and he saw her eyelid drop in a saucy wink. 'Which reminds me, where have you put your suitcase? I don't remember seeing it.'

He stared at her, suddenly grateful that they were in a crowded café. 'I didn't bring one, only my weekend bag.'

'Ted! You aren't only here for a couple of nights, are you?'

He looked sheepish. 'Can't help it, luv. I'll explain later.'

'I know why you came down, because of my letter, but we haven't even mentioned that yet. Surely we have to have a good talk.'

'Yes. Yes of course we do, but leave it now, Evie. We'll sort it all out when the girls have gone to bed tonight.'

'Sort what out?' Jenny had been earwigging.

Thank God! Edward breathed a sigh of relief. Their table number was being called. 'Come on, you two, come and help me carry the plates.'

Evie's imagination was running away with her. All this way for two nights. Ted had never done that before. She placed her hands around her large mug of tea and began to sip it slowly. The meal had been great. The faces of her two girls were a joy to behold, flushed and thrilled to be out at this time of night with both their mum and their dad.

'By the way,' Ted suddenly said, 'why is that room opposite the kitchen boarded up? It makes that small passageway very dark.'

'I thought I explained that when I was showing you around. That was one of the reasons the council let us have the place. The workmen told me the floorboards were rotting and although the outside end wall was plastered when the demolition was finished, the inside was very damp. Black mould, so one of them said, and it's a job to get rid of that.'

Ted was appalled. If the floorboards were rotten, heavens above knew what that room would be like if it was sealed up for any length of time. Breeding ground for rats, most likely. Still, he wasn't about to throw a spanner into the works by voicing such thoughts. Evie was made up with her house, the girls were happy to have a bedroom each, and which ever way you looked at it 42 Chetwode Road had to be a vast improvement on Brick Lane in Merton. Far better for him to keep his opinions to himself.

'What shall we do when we get home, Dad?' Jenny asked, nudging her father with her elbow.

'I don't know. We can't exactly go on anywhere else in this weather. What would you like to do?'

'Play ludo.' She laughed.

'Sounds good to me.'

'Not to me, it doesn't,' Cathy piped up. 'I'd rather play cards.'

'We'll do both, and tomorrow night we'll all go to the pictures.'

Evie remained silent. She wouldn't be able to think straight until she and Ted had had their talk.

'Evie. Evie, lift your head up and look at me. I've been honest, I've set out the facts for you. I don't like it any more than you do, but you tell me what alternative there is, because I can't think of one.'

Evie lifted her head, she was crying openly. 'Oh, Ted! I half expected you to be mad about the baby, but to tell me you are going abroad for God knows how long. I can't take much more of this, not after today. You weren't even man enough to say anything to Jenny, but I know you heard what she said.'

'Jenny? I'm not with you.'

'Oh please, Ted, spare me that much. You heard as plainly as I did, "Cathy, is our dad gonna be home for Christmas?" That's what your youngest daughter asked. Like me, her sister couldn't answer her. Words choked her.'

'Evie, if I could stay with you all forever I would, I swear I would.'

'Yeah, I know, Ted. I'm also beginning to know that talk is dirt cheap.'

'That's a terrible thing to say, Evie,' he scolded gently.

'I know, but in your case it's true.' She smiled ruefully. 'I'm used to coping on my own. I doubt there is anything that will come up that will be worse than what I've had to deal with these past years.'

He caught her hand and tried to squeeze it. Evie did not respond. What had started out as such a wonderful day had degenerated into one of the blackest of her life. She mustn't try to persuade Ted to stay, she told herself, and she mustn't let herself become bitter. She must think of the girls, what their best interests were, and not take into account what effect this would have on her.

'It's going to be difficult, I know,' Ted croaked, finding his voice at last. 'I'll do everything I can to help you. Truly I will.'

Except leave your wife and marry me. Her thoughts were bitter.

She heard the scrape of his chair as he stood up.

'I'll put the kettle on,' he whispered. 'I'm sure you could drink a cup of tea.'

'Thank you,' she murmured. As she looked into his dark brown eyes, she was aware of how much he had changed over the years. Not in looks but in attitude. He was a hard man now. A selfish man. At thirty-eight years old he was still good-looking. His dark hair wasn't even touched by grey. Like most handsome men, his age suited him and she couldn't help but wonder how many glances, and more, he got from the ladies in the North. Edward hadn't enjoyed the last hour one bit, but then neither had she.

As he came back from the kitchen she watched the different expressions flicker over his face and sighed. It wasn't any easier for him than it was for her. Or was it? It had always been the same. Love him she did, as much as ever, but now she had come to realise that she could never rely on him to be of any help in any way, shape or form. He just hadn't got it in him. Self came first with Ted. For the first time in years she needed him and he was going abroad!

She watched him fumble with the teapot. Her tears had been wiped away now and suddenly she felt her body was heavy and she was very tired. Tired of trying to work out how she was going to manage and what she would do next. She straightened up as Ted passed her a cup of tea and she made a decision. All she could do now was look out for her two lovely daughters and for this unborn baby, who after all hadn't asked to be born. What her mother was always telling her was right: self-pity never helped anyone. She must keep reminding herself of that fact and look to the future.

Flossie had been sitting looking out of her front window for the last half hour. When she saw Ted Hopkins stride off down the street she let her net curtain drop and moved her chair near to the fire. She hated that man. He was a selfish sod. Self first, self second and anything left over was still for himself. If Evie ever saw him again, she'd be lucky. Or would she? She'd be a damn sight better off if that git stayed away forever. Oh, she knew that much. Every time he came back on the scene it broke her Evie up. Yesterday, when the girls had come in and told her their dad was going to leave again in the morning, she had felt she could kill him. It was a pity really that she hadn't got the guts to do just that. It would be worth swinging for. Just to free Evie from him and let her get on with her life before she was too old. All her best years were slipping by, ruined by that pompous ass who thought he was God's greatest gift to women.

Evie, coming down the stairs, her arms full of dirty sheets she had just stripped from the beds, faltered for a moment as she saw her mother opening the front door.

'Oh, 'ello,' said Flossie, glancing upwards.

Evie came quickly down to the passage to welcome her mum.

'Thought you'd be doing yer washing, seeing as 'ow it's

Monday morning.' Flossie felt deep relief that at least Evie was acting normally and didn't appear too upset. 'Just thought I'd pop along to tell you I've got plenty of cold meat if you'd like to join me about one o'clock. We can 'ave a bit of bubble-and-squeak with it, and there'll be plenty over for the girls. They'll like that with a load of pickles. Save you cooking today. What d'ye say?'

Evie was well aware that was not the reason her mum had come calling so early in the morning. She'd come to check if she was all right, and Evie loved her for it. Another thing, her mum's bubble-and-squeak was smashing, crisply browned the way the girls loved it and the way Evie could never get it to brown when she fried it.

'Well, are ye gonna come or not?'

Evie laughed. 'You know very well I am. Besides, try keeping Jenny away, let alone Cathy.'

'See ye then.' Flossie turned to go.

'Mum.'

'What is it, love?'

'Don't go. Stay an' 'ave a cup of tea with me, please.'

'Bless ye, course I will. You go ahead and get yer sheets into the copper and I'll put the kettle on.' She's bloody crying inside, thought Flossie, knowing she'd guessed right.

The washing was all sorted out, the small bits already pegged out on the line.

'I'll take the girls' blouses,' offered Flossie. 'I'll put 'em in with my whites and I'll give 'em a nice blue rinse.'

'Mum, will you please stop fussing. Sit down an' pour out the tea, and for Christ's sake ask me all the questions you are dying to have the answers to.'

Flossie shook her head. 'Oh Evie, you're a daft lummox most of the time, but there ain't no flies on ye when it comes down to rock bottom. I see Ted going off real early this morning, dressed to the nines as usual, new overcoat an' all.'

Evie didn't make any comment as she passed a cup of tea to her mother.

'Well? At least tell me what he said about the baby.'

'He didn't say much at all.'

'Didn't he even strut a bit? Y'know, say 'ow much he'd love a son?'

It was too much for Evie. She burst into tears.

Minutes later, with her mother's arms wrapped around her, the whole story came pouring from her lips.

'He isn't even gonna be able to keep sending me my registered letter. His in-laws will be managing all his money affairs. Aw Mum, what am I gonna do?'

A sharp hissing breath came from between Flossie's lips. She wasn't surprised. Not in the least. He hadn't been man enough to come along and see her before he had slunk off to take his invalid wife abroad. Bloody ponce! Living off his wife and her family and still coming down south for years, using Evie as if she were on the game. 'So 'elp me I 'ope he never makes it 'ome. I 'ope he falls from the train an' breaks his bleedin' neck.'

'Aw Mum, you shouldn't say things like that. You've always told me that curses 'ave a way of coming home to roost.'

'Yeah, well!'

'Mum, he 'as left me two hundred pounds.'

''As he now? An' 'ow long does he think that will last? What you better think about doing, Evie, is bringing things out into the open. That sod 'as got away with murder over the years and if you want the truth, my girl, you've encouraged him. It's about time you started thinking of yourself and the girls. Remember there'll be three children that will want feeding an' clothing before long, and that's gonna take some doing.'

'Don't go on, Mum, please,' whispered Evie.

'I'm gonna give you one more piece of advice and then I'll shut me mouth. Give yourself a couple of days to breathe out, an' then take yourself up to Lavender Hill. Get the law courts to 'elp you take out a maintenance order against the sod. That'll shake 'im. Yeah, that's what you ought to do.'

What I ought to do and what I will do are two different things, Evie said to herself. What she said aloud was, 'Come on, let's tidy up an' go back to your house for this lovely dinner you're going to produce, seein' as 'ow you're being extra nice to me today.'

'Saucy bitch,' said Flossie, but there was a wide grin on her lips as she gathered up the teacups and took them out to the scullery.

Evie's third baby was born on a Wednesday morning in the last week of June 1952. It gave a lusty cry the moment it breathed air. Another girl, tiny but perfect, her head tufted with fine blonde hair.

When the midwife put her into her grandmother's arms, Flossie murmured, 'Oh you sweet little mite.'

'Hey, I'd like to hold her, if you don't mind.'

Flossie, still standing at the side of the bed, the baby in her arms, pushed the midwife to one side and gave Evie her daughter. Then, her voice almost breaking on a sob, she said, 'Well done, love, but make it the last, eh?'

'Can't promise that, Mum,' There was a glint of mischief in Evie's eyes as she smiled at her mother.

'Right! Wait till I see that Ted Hopkins again.' *If we ever do,* Flossie muttered to herself. 'If he won't tie a knot in it then I'll do it for him.'

'Ee!' Evie glanced at the midwife, her cheeks flaring up. Luckily Mrs Bennett had her head down, but she wasn't deaf and Evie knew darn well she would take great delight in repeating what her mum had said to all of the neighbours. Still, Evie grinned to herself, what a thing to come out with. Her mum did take the biscuit and no mistake!

'I'm going to take these things downstairs to be washed,' the midwife said over her shoulder as she crossed the room, her arms full of stained sheets and towels.

'Wait a minute,' Flossie cried, 'I'll open the door. Come to that, I'll come down with you. We'll get the copper going and put the kettle on at the same time. You be all right, Evie?'

Evie nodded, settled back against the pillows and stared intensely at her baby's scrunched up little face. She held the tiny bundle to her chest and began rocking her gently to and fro. As she did so she felt the tears sting her eyes and wondered what Edward was doing. She hadn't heard a word from him since he had come down for the weekend before Christmas. Would he be thrilled to know that he had a third daughter? She doubted it. If she was honest with herself, she would have to admit that even if he were here at this very minute he probably wouldn't be feeling over the moon.

Chapter Five

FLOSSIE SMITH LOOKED AT the sweet face of her youngest granddaughter and her heart went out to the child. 'You look lovely, Rosie. I bet you'll be the smartest girl in the class.'

It was 1957. Rosie was five years old and she was starting school on 5 September, which was only three weeks away. She smiled at her nanna, did a twirl and said, 'You're only saying that. Everyone has to wear this uniform so we must all look alike.'

'Yeah, but not all the girls will be as pretty as you are.'

Rose Mary Smith, as she had been christened, had a head of hair just like the picture of 'Bubbles' that often appeared in magazines. Tight fair curls that were shiny and bouncy, and there was no way of combing them any differently. She had big blue eyes and a sweet smile. Her mother called her Baby Doll. Her nanna called her her little princess. This third daughter of Evie's had come to know early in life that you got a lot more given to you by smiling and saying thank you nicely than you did if you sulked and cried.

'You're always saying I'm pretty, Nan,' Rosie said,

putting her arms around her nanna's neck and kissing her cheek.

'Pretty or not,' her mother butted in, 'you'd better get upstairs an' take that lot off before you go out in the street to play.'

Her mother and grandmother listened to Rosie dash up the stairs.

Evie sighed. 'Don't seem possible that she's starting school, does it mum?'

'No,' her mother agreed, while thinking to herself, *Five years and not sight nor sound of her father.* She turned to her daughter and said, 'She's a credit to you Evie, an' the other two are as well. You've nothing to reproach yourself for, the way those girls 'ave turned out. Many a woman on her own would 'ave give up the ghost, but not you. You've done any job that cropped up and one way or another you've managed. That reminds me. I was gonna collar you before you went shopping this morning. I wanted to give you a couple of pounds towards Rosie's uniform, and yer uncle Jim left an envelope on my dresser for you. Said for you to get Rosie a decent pair of shoes.'

Evie's lips trembled, her head moved, and she whispered, 'Thanks. There wasn't any need. I managed. I 'ad a five pound provident cheque off Mrs Norman. You know, five bob a week for twenty-two weeks.'

Flossie let out a deep breath, vowing to herself that she would see Mrs Norman and give her a few of the payments in advance. She yearned for something good to turn up for this only child of hers, who was getting old before her time. 'What you gonna do this afternoon?'

'Well it's too hot to do much, ain't it Mum? I thought I'd 'ave a sewing session. I've only got the hem to finish on that skirt I'm making for Jenny and then I'll get on with that dress that you cut out for Rosie. That's lovely material, Mum, ever so pretty an' it feels like silk.'

'All right then, luv. You'll be down for your tea?'

'Don't we always come down to you for our tea on Saturdays? Course we'll be there. Shellfish, celery, watercress, crumpets and fruit cake – wouldn't know it was Saturday if you altered the menu!'

'Cheeky cow! You never alter, do you?'

'You wouldn't want me to, would you, Mum?'

'No.' She laughed loudly. 'See you later. Hope Catherine will be home.'

'No more than I do,' Evie said aloud to herself as she picked up her work basket and carried it up the stairs. From her big front bedroom she could see the whole street. Keep an eye on what young Rosie was up to. Besides, if she flung the window up as far as it would go she might even be able to feel a breeze. My, but it had been hot this week.

Before she started on her sewing, Evie leaned her head and shoulders out over the windowsill. Down the far end of the street she could see Jenny, sitting astride a wall, her arm linked with that of Norma Killick. They were watching a gang of boys playing cricket, their makeshift wicket chalked out on the end wall of the last house.

Evie had to smile. Best of friends, those two were. Stuck up for each other through thick and thin. Never a moment's trouble. She and Joan agreed: where one of them was to be found, there for certain would be the other. It was the same with their two eldest girls. Well, it was about them being the best of pals, but as to being no trouble, she wished to God that that was true. But it wasn't.

Her Catherine and Joan's eldest daughter, Shirley, were both coming up to being eighteen years old. They had left school three years ago. Evie sighed and pushed her hair back from her face. She had lost count of the number of jobs the pair of them had had. She didn't like the way

Cathy was using heavy make-up. She didn't need it. Her skin was so fair and unblemished. No one would ever call her a blonde, but her hair was fair, straight and sleek, and whatever style she combed it into it seemed to suit her. She had a marvellous figure, tall and slim with a firm bosom, which her clothes set off to perfection.

On the other hand Shirley dyed her hair blonde, which was sad to see in a girl so young. She too had a nice figure, not as tall as Cathy, but just as slim. When they walked down the street the lads whistled and stared. The pair of them loved it. But where was it all leading? She worried more over Catherine than she did over her other two girls put together. Evie settled herself in a chair as close to the open window as she could get it. She pulled a length of cotton from the reel, bit off the end and selected a fine needle to thread. She loved sewing and she found it soothing. Good job she did. She would never be able to buy all the clothes the girls seemed to get through. Against her will, she thought of Ted. She didn't often do this now. Never a word. Didn't he ever spare a thought as to how she was managing?

She had a job as a barmaid up at the Wheatsheaf Arms three nights a week, and the welfare lady who came around quite regularly wasn't at all the old bat that people said she was. She saw to it that Evie got all the allowances to which she was entitled. It still didn't go far.

It was always her mum who bailed them out and saw to it that the three girls didn't go short of much. And Jimmy Tyler, uncle to her for as long as she could remember. Last year when the winter had been bitter, snow had lain for days on end. It was Jim who had seen that her coal bunker was always full to the brim. Jim never seemed to be short of a bob or two. Then again neither did her mum.

Evie giggled, she couldn't help herself. The whole

street had laughed when Flossie had first let her intentions be known. Sick and tired of working for a pittance, Flossie had decided to become a pie lady. Four days a week, Tuesdays, Wednesdays, Thursdays and Fridays, Flossie made and sold pies. Had done for the past four years now. She had got a hard and fast routine. The sideboard was pushed underneath the window, a crisp starched white cloth spread along the top to make a display stand and Flossie was ready to sell her pies.

She set them out attractively. Savoury ones, steak and kidney, minced beef and onion, chicken and ham to one end, a line of fresh parsley to make a division, and then she stacked the fruit tarts and pies.

Many of Flossie's men friends had allotments, and fruits of the season made their way to Flossie's kitchen before the men's wives got a look-in. Raspberries, blackcurrants, plums and apples served to make the delicious sweet pies. Flossie's butcher was also very obliging!

Regular customers didn't mind a bit that they had to queue in the front garden and more often than not along the pavement. Flossie Smith's pies were well worth waiting for. The pastry melted in the mouth. Meat and thick gravy, flavoured with onions and herbs, had the men drooling. The fruit pies were a bonus. Special orders could be had for the asking: a huge deep apple pie, enough for a large family, made in a china dish, as long as a shilling deposit was left on the dish. Not that anyone dared to try keeping one of Flossie's dishes. Two days, three top whack, and Flossie would be hammering on their front door. They knew her too well to cross her.

By and large, though, Flossie Smith was a firm favourite in the whole of the neighbourhood. That didn't stop the bitchy ones from agreeing that she'd had more men in her life than they'd had hot dinners. Once the police had almost put a stop to Flossie's business venture. As it was, Maggie Turner, who lived round the corner in the next street, never put a foot into Chetwode Road these days, and if she did it certainly wasn't to buy one of Flossie's pies. Flossie would kill her first.

What a day that had been. Frightening but at the same time hilarious. Evie would never forget it. Nor anyone else come to that! She had been in the front room, helping her mum, taking the money and putting the pies into greaseproof bags. They were serving through the open window, and the voices of the women in the queue out in the street carried clearly.

'Like mother, like daughter. Bad blood. It's bred in them,' exclaimed Maggie Turner, whose husband was a dustman. 'Morals? They ain't got one between them. Right pair of alley cats if ye want my opinion.'

'Me mum says she don't care what Mrs Smith gets up to, she likes her,' Dottie Carson said, laughing as the queue shuffled forward up Flossie's front-garden path. 'Me dad does an' all. He says Tuesday's dinner is the best of the week, and that suits me mum down to the ground.'

'That's as may be,' Maggie sniffed, 'I still say she's on the game.'

Flossie wiped her hands on her apron and stared at Evie in disbelief. Evie recalled how she had tried to hold her back. It wasn't possible. Maggie Turner got the shock of her life as Flossie came storming out into the road, brandishing a knife.

'What did you bloody well say? Go on, repeat it to me face.'

'You're mad, you know that.' Maggie's voice sounded terrified. 'And I ain't standing 'ere any longer.'

'Just as well, cos you wouldn't sodding well get any of me pies if you stood there till bleedin' doomsday. Now sod off, before I really stick this knife into yer rotten fat belly.'

That had done it. All hell had been let loose. It had been ages before order had been restored that day.

Her mum could say what she liked to Evie, but give her her due: let anyone so much as whisper a bad thing about Evie and Flossie was at them like a scalded cat.

Evie knew full well what it was that got up the noses of some of the older women: the fact that George Higgins paid her a lot of attention! Her mum couldn't stand the sight of him. According to Flossie, George Higgins was a real viper in the nest. All of six feet tall, he was flashily dressed in good suits and silk ties and never without his grey trilby hat. And he seemed to have money to burn. Where he got his money from was anybody's guess.

First off, Evie had resisted all his proposals, but not for long. He was a charmer when it came to women. He paid attention to small things, like a box of chocolates when he took her to the pictures. He was a show-off, never arriving without a bunch of flowers, always making sure he walked on the outside of the pavement, pulling her chair out in restaurants, helping her on and off buses and in and out of his car. Oh yes, that car! A shiny black Humber. The light of his life, but why did he always have to park it right under her mother's front window? To annoy her. Evie knew that and so did Flossie. And why did he disappear for weeks on end? Turning up again without any warning and offering no explanations, but always bringing gifts for her three girls.

Jim Tyler would only laugh when Flossie started on about George being a no-good layabout. He knew he was anything but that. There were times when even Flossie would admit that George showed her Evie a good time. Most important of all he made Evie feel wanted, and Flossie couldn't begrudge her that.

Would George ever come to be an important part of her life? Evie pondered the question as she sewed. No, she didn't think so. She had been flattered when he had first noticed her. She looked back to that day. *I was lonely,* she admitted. *In fact I've been lonely every day since Ted was last here.* True, she had the girls, her mum, and there was always Joan to go out and about with. Joan had a husband and her mum had Jim Tyler. *I've got no one.* She was staring out of the window now as she told herself, *Whatever the outcome, at least George Higgins has brought a bit of excitement into my life, and for the moment that'll do me.*

Evie had finished hemming the bottom of Jenny's skirt. She folded it carefully and stood up to place it to one side and start on Rosie's dress. Her hands felt hot and sweaty. 'I'll have to nip downstairs and wash my hands,' she muttered, thinking of the fine material she was about to start work on. She went to the toilet first, had a quick wash, splashing cold water over her hot cheeks. 'Oh, I can't be bothered to do any more sewing,' she said aloud, 'it's too ruddy hot.'

'You look nice, luv,' her mum said as Evie stepped into her kitchen. 'Bit early, ain't you? Tea's nowhere near ready.'

'That's all right, Mum, I'll give you a hand. I just got bored being on my own an' I didn't feel like doing any more sewing.'

Flossie cursed beneath her breath. 'Fed up with being on her own – a lovely young woman of thirty-six? It wasn't right. You only get one life and Evie was halfway through hers. Her daughter's feeling for Ted Hopkins, Flossie knew, had been something very like her own when she had first met Jack Smith. Each of them had only been in their early teens. God above knew each of them had paid dearly for what at the time had seemed to be the greatest love of all time. She only wanted what was best for her daughter, for her to find some degree of happiness, but how she could help to bring it about was more than she could fathom.

Flossie watched Evie stroke the thick fair hair back from her forehead, and she said, 'I'll just spruce meself up a bit, then I'll make us a cold drink. In the meantime why don't you put a couple of chairs out in the garden. May as well sit out there for a while.' She now beamed at Evie. 'I won't be long.'

The heat of the sun and the comfort of the armchairs had sent both Flossie and Evie off into a light doze. A voice from somewhere behind the garden fence brought them both wide awake with a start.

'Go on, admit it. You're chicken. Afraid of what yer mother will say.'

Evie knew that voice. Reggie Monks.

Flossie confirmed her suspicion by saying, 'Oh no! Not that gormless boy. I wonder what our Catherine sees in 'im. He's got to be one brick short of a load, the daft way he carries on.'

The smile slid from Evie's face as the back gate opened and Cathy and Shirley came into the garden, followed by Reggie Monks and another lad whom she had never set eyes on before.

'"Ello love, where've . . ?' Flossie's voice trailed away as she gazed at the two lads.

'Mum, Nan, you know Reggie, an' this is Bill Osbourne, and as to where we've been, Nan, if you must know we've been up to Wandsworth Common.' Cathy's manner was cheeky as she finished on a high note.

'Well, well!' her nanna exclaimed before Evie had a chance to find her voice. 'You'd better all go through to the kitchen. There's a bottle of cream soda an' one of ginger beer on the side. You all look as if you could use a cold drink.'

One glance at her mother's face and Cathy turned quickly and led the way without further comment.

Evie and her mum stayed silent for a few seconds, surprise showing clearly on their faces. Then, turning sideways, Flossie asked, 'Do you believe it? What do they look like?'

Evie was bursting with laughter. 'Ee! You're right, Mum. Those boys do look a sight, an' no mistake.'

'D'you suppose they think they resemble Edwardian gentlemen?' Flossie asked as she tried to smother her merriment.

'Teddy boys.' Evie giggled.

'What?'

'That's what they like to be known as, teddy boys.'

'On a boiling hot day like this! They must be out of their minds.'

Now they both turned their gaze to where the four youngsters were leaning against the windowsill, glasses in their hands, and still it was all they could do to stop from laughing out loud.

The girls looked pretty enough in their cotton dresses, which reached down to their calves and had full skirts; that was what the new look demanded. The lads had long draped jackets with velvet collars and cuffs, drainpipe trousers and thick crepe-soled shoes. Their hair shone with the amount of grease they had used and was combed well back from each side to meet in a point at the back of their necks.

Evie leaned across to where her mum sat and whispered, 'Note the hairstyle. They have Elvis Presley to thank for that. You know, the American rock singer. Catherine's got a big poster of him on the wall of her bedroom. His hair is styled like that. It's called a DA.'

'What's a DA for Gawd's sake?'

'Duck's arse.'

'Evie!'

'Well you did ask.'

Flossie's face was screwed up with amusement. She shook her head in disbelief. 'Dunno what the world's coming to. I mean it's not as if both those lads aren't big-made, burly types. You wouldn't think they'd wanna dress up like bloody ponces, would you?'

'Oh Mum,' Evie was creased up. 'Don't for God's sake let the girls hear you talking about their escorts like that. Come on, get up. I think we'd better go inside an' see about getting the table laid for tea.'

'Just so long as Catherine doesn't expect me to ask those twits to stay. Just imagine 'aving to sit through a meal looking at that pair!'

Evie did imagine it. And it was with great difficulty that she kept her face straight as she walked down the garden and into the house.

The Saturday ritual of high tea was over and cleared away. The table was now covered with a rich, red chenille cloth, its heavy fringe of tassles almost reaching the floor. Rosie sat one side, a colouring book and pencils keeping her busy. Jenny had a pack of cards, engrossed in a game of patience.

Catherine was standing in front of the mirror, which hung over the mantel shelf, being finical because her hair wouldn't lay just right. Her grandmother was smiling when she said, 'You know, Cathy, there's many as would say you're a brazen young hussy, and Shirley Killick an' all, chasing the boys like you two do.'

Flossie expected her to come back with some quip, but she didn't. Her head went back and she let out a ringing laugh.

'What would you know, Nan? That'll be the day, when I have to do the chasing. Most lads are more eager for my company than I am for theirs. They'll be fighting over who's going to pay for me and Shirl to go in to the dance tonight.'

Evie took a step towards Cathy, and her voice was harsh as she went for her. 'You mind who you're talking to my girl. There was no call for you to speak to your nanna like that.'

'Sorry, Nan—' Flossie cut off her words. 'That's all right my love, you should think before you speak though. Don't be so 'asty.'

Cathy grinned at her.

Flossie, sensing this could turn into a disagreement, said quickly, 'Evie, you 'aven't opened the envelope Jim left for you.'

Knowing full well that her mother was pouring oil on troubled waters, Evie rose and crossed the room. The envelope that was propped up was not the usual size for a letter. It was a long cream-coloured one.

'Very posh.' Evie smiled, and now all heads were turned towards her as she slit open the top. There was a pound note and a ten-shilling note, which she supposed was meant for new shoes for Rosie, as her mother had said. What was intriguing her was a pink booking form. She read the heading aloud: 'Butlins Luxury Holiday Camp, Clacton.'

Catherine swung round. Jenny and Rosie now jumped up from the table and came quickly to where their mum was standing. Evie looked at her mother, and as she did Flossie burst out laughing.

'You knew about this, Mum?'

'Yeah, Jim told me a coupla weeks ago he was gonna try and get booked up, but I didn't know till today that it was all settled.'

They were both laughing now, as Catherine leaned over Evie's shoulder and read aloud. 'One chalet for five, one chalet for two, for seven days from 14 August until 21 August. That's next Saturday!'

Rosie had slid down on to the floor. Jenny was tugging at her nanna's arm. 'Nan, does that mean we're all gonna go on holiday?'

'It certainly does, me darlings,' Flossie cried, sweeping both of her young grandchildren into the circle of her arms.

'I can't believe it!' Evie murmured, still gazing at the booking form. 'Why would Jim go an' do a thing like this? And who is the chalet for two for?'

'Don't knock it, Mum,' Cathy pleaded, 'I think it's smashing of Uncle Jim. I know a girl whose family went to Butlins last Easter an' she ain't never stopped talking about it. She said the entertainment there is out of this world. Never a dull moment, there's so much going on all the time. And we 'aven't got to wait long – only a week an' we'll be off. Oh, it's great, ain't it, Mum?'

Everyone was laughing now as Catherine, well and truly out of breath, felt for a chair, falling over backwards as she did so.

There was a tap on the back door and Jim Tyler's voice called, 'All right to come in?'

Evie was surprised at how different Jim looked today. Quite handsome in fact. He was wearing a navy blue blazer with a white open-necked shirt. The jacket had cost quite a bit – it was so well cut it hid some of his big stomach.

''Ello Floss, how did they take it?' His nod included Evie and her three girls.

For answer, Cathy looked at him as if she would like to eat him. Rosie flung her arms around his legs. Jenny's smiling face showed that she adored him, while Evie cast her eyes over this tall man with dark eyes, several laughter lines and a healthy red face, and her eyes were brimming with tears as she murmured, 'Thank you Uncle Jim. You are far too good to us.'

Flossie and Jim exchanged glances of relief, and he, all smiles, held his arms wide to Evie, drawing her close in a bear-like hug. 'As long as you're pleased, pet.'

'Pleased?' all their voices answered.

'Who's sharing a chalet with you?' Evie asked.

'No one first off, but George is 'oping to get down there for a few days. I've booked 'im in for the whole week. Just in case like.'

'George Higgins?' Flossie hissed the name.

'Do we know any other George?' Jim asked slowly and quietly.

Flossie took the hint and kept her thoughts to herself.

Evie wasn't sure if she was pleased or not. She was so happy now just looking at the faces of her children. She'd take things as they came and be grateful to this big softie of a man. The girls were all talking at once, clamouring for his attention.

'Uncle Jim, how are we gonna get there?'

'Will the camp be near the sea?'

'Mum, I ain't got a swimming costume. It got too small an' you gave it to Jenny.'

'You can 'ave it back an I'll 'ave a new one if you like.'

'I shall need a decent case. Cor, we'll have to start packing tomorrow, won't we?'

This last statement was from Catherine, who seemed to have forgotten that she'd been on her way out when the news of the forthcoming holiday broke.

'Girls, will you stop it?' Evie's laughter was bubbling over. 'No, I mean it. Give your uncle a bit of peace. What, with one an' another of you all asking questions at the same time, he don't know whether he's coming or going, let alone how to answer you.'

'First things first,' Jim told them when the laughter had died down, 'all you ladies,' he paused to let Jenny and Rosie have their little giggle, 'will be travelling on the orange coach, which you will catch from just along the Balham High Road. It will drop you right at the entrance to the camp. I can't say exactly what time I'll get there. Depends on 'ow 'eavy the off-course betting is next Saturday.'

Everyone started talking at once again.

'I'm going up the Wheatsheaf with Jim,' Flossie shouted at them.

'I'm going to go over to Shirley's, Mum,' Cathy called over her shoulder, a wide grin spreading over her face.

With the room now quiet and Jenny and Rosie seated back at the table, Evie let her thoughts wander. A whole week by the sea. George Higgins would be coming down. He'd more than likely take her out in his car, see something of Clacton, outside of the holiday camp. It should be a wonderful week!

Lovely accommodation, three great meals every day and nonstop entertainment. So successful was their Butlins holiday that nobody wanted to go home. It was Friday evening. The four adults were in the bar having a drink. The three girls were off to see the early performers. They had had their last dinner, and in the morning, after breakfast, they would be going back to London.

'You two get off, if you want to.' Flossie drained her glass and set it back down on the counter. 'The girls will be fine with us, won't they, Jim?'

'Course they will. Last night an' all that – might just as well let them stay up till they're ready to drop. 'Sides, we're gonna 'ave a job prising Catherine away from that new boyfriend she's so eaten up with. You've got t'admit it though, they're great all-rounders, these lads an' lasses they call redcoats. They all dance well, an' 'alf of them are better at putting on a show than some of the professionals.'

'Yeah,' Evie sighed. As usual she was worrying over her eldest girl. 'Keep your eye on her, Mum, please.'

'I will love. As soon as it gets dark I'll see she stays where we can see her.'

'Shall we get going then?' George asked Evie, at the same time holding out her white stole that had silver threads running through it.

They had had drinks in two different pubs, and now George had parked the car as near to the edge of the sea as he could get.

'Ain't it marvellous?' Evie breathed. 'So peaceful.'

Coming up for ten o'clock, not quite dark yet and still very warm. The pretty lights reflected from the promenade shimmered on the soft waves as they lapped the shore.

George couldn't believe his luck. He had been here since Monday and never a cross word. Even Flossie had shown a bit of goodwill towards him, and Evie had been delightful. Putting his arms around Evie's shoulders, he gently drew her close.

Instinctively she sat up straighter. He groaned.

'Oh, Evie. You're beautiful . . . You really are! You're so different.' He covered her breast with his hand and she jumped. Already her heart was hammering and her breathing was irregular.

'Evie, I would never do anything that you didn't want me to.'

She believed him. In all the times that he had taken her out he had never yet overstepped the mark. Though she was sure that her mother would take some convincing on that score.

'I love you, Evie. God, I love you.'

He had never said it before, and if he were never to say it again she would remember those words for the rest of her life. They made her feel special. She wished that she could tell him that she felt the same about him. But she knew, deep inside, that she didn't. She had tried hard to convince herself that she would be all right with George for the rest of her life if only she would let herself go. She also knew that, given the right place and the right time, she would probably abandon all her doubts and surprise him with the strength of her lovemaking. She was, after all, as human as the next woman, and George could be very persuasive. She felt his lips on hers and she responded with a passion that she hadn't allowed him to know before. Before long the thrill of their anticipation and their needs was getting the better of them both.

George had never dreamt that Evie could act as she was at this moment. Unfortunately they were in the front two seats of his car, parked on the main parade where people were still taking a stroll.

George kissed her long and hard. 'Can we carry on from where we are leaving off when we get back to London?'

'I think so,' she whispered, at the same time running her tongue over her lower lip and thinking that life wouldn't be so dull from now on. They each straightened their clothing. He kissed her again and then started up the car.

'We'll just have time to get a round in before the main cabaret.' He grinned, taking one hand off the steering wheel and placing it on her knee.

Evie nodded silently, letting her eyes roam over him. He sat tall in his dark suit. Big and broad shouldered with a head of dark brown wavy hair, he was a man whom women gave a second glance. His face was tanned, his eyes blue and twinkling. He was more attractive than she had given him credit for, and she thought it was impossible not to like him. His smile alone would charm the birds from the trees.

Chapter Six

'BUT MUM, WHY 'AVE you all of a sudden decided that you don't want me to leave home?'

Evie looked at her eldest daughter and said gently, 'It isn't all of a sudden. Ever since we've been back from holiday you've talked of nothing else but getting a job in a holiday camp.'

'Well, what's wrong with that? It's got to be better than standing behind the biscuit stall in Woolworth's waiting for old biddies to decide if they want ginger nuts or custard creams.' Cathy wrinkled her nose now. 'If you think I'm gonna do that for the rest of me life, you've got another think coming, Mum.'

'It's about time that you learned not to be so rude, Catherine. You know full well the job you've got in Woolworth's is only to tide you over until after Christmas. We agreed that in the meantime you could write to Butlins for an application form and maybe you'll be lucky an' get taken on for the summer season. Now you're telling me you want to dash off and get a temporary job that will only last about a week over the holiday. The camps will close again then until Easter, and what would you do for a job until then? Don't you want to spend Christmas with me an' your sisters?'

'Oh, Mum, I do, I do, but I just thought it would be great fun to be in a holiday camp over Christmas with all the entertainment that would be going on.'

'All right, all right. We might not be the best of company for a young lady like you, but just you remember this: you wouldn't be there as a paying guest this time, and you would soon be aware of that fact. You'd be there to work, an' it wouldn't be as a redcoat, cheerleader or whatever it is they call themselves. You'd be a chalet maid, expected to do many a job you wouldn't like, or a waitress, run off your feet, at everyone's beck an' call.'

Cathy sighed, then coming round the table to where her mother sat, she put her arms around her shoulders and kissed the side of her cheek. 'All right, Mum. I'll leave it out for now, but you promise I can go for Easter? That's if I get the job.'

'Oh, Cathy, I've told you that until I'm tired of the sound of me own voice. If I could make life more exciting for you, I would. I do me best.'

Cathy stared at her mother in silence, then she said, 'I know you do, Mum.' Her voice was so quiet and held such a depth of sadness that Evie scrambled to her feet and put her arms around her, saying, 'I'm sorry if I get bad-tempered.'

Cathy broke free from her grasp and said in a low voice, 'You don't 'ave much of a life yerself Mum, do you?'

Evie smiled faintly at her. 'Now come on, 'ow d'you work that out?'

'I've got eyes in me head. You work up the pub and at every job there is going just to feed an' clothe Jenny, Rosie an' me. You don't 'ave much for yerself. Don't you get lonely sometimes?'

Evie took a deep breath, and it was some seconds before

she could bring herself to answer. 'Don't be silly. How could I possibly be lonely with yer gran only just up the street and you girls always around to keep me company? Don't start worrying yerself over me, Cathy. You're not a bit of a kid any more, you're a young woman with your own life to lead.' She looked at the clock and cried, 'God, look at the time. If you don't get a move on you'll be late an' they'll sack you an' you won't 'ave a job at all.'

Cathy pulled on her coat, grabbed her handbag, crying, 'Gee, I didn't realise it was that late. I might get 'ome at lunch time. Depends. If not I won't be late tonight. Bye, Mum.'

The door banged behind her, and Evie went through to the front room to look out of the window and watch her lovely Catherine race off up the street. Standing there, she folded her arms across her chest and shook her head. She had been dreading this for years. The time when one of her daughters would realise there was a great big world out there offering a great many more opportunities than they were getting living here in Chetwode Road. Many times she had wished that she had a husband beside her to discuss their future with, a father for them from whom they could seek guidance and advice. Today she didn't wish for it. She longed for it. Hot, bitter tears ran down her cheeks as she realised the futility of such daydreaming.

It was eleven o'clock in the morning. The youngest girls were safely at school and, hopefully, Catherine and Shirley Killick were both at work. You could never be sure with those two. Joan Killick sat one side of Evie's kitchen table drinking a cup of tea. The kitchen was warm and snug. A well banked up fire burned brightly in the grate, and the window was closed tightly against the bitter cold and the strong, blustering wind. The smell coming from the saucepan on the gas stove was mouth-watering, and Evie was still chopping vegetables to add to the simmering broth.

Watching her, Joan decided that, of all the people she knew, Evie had had the worst of all deals. Evie still had a good figure, was still nice-looking, with no sign of her fair hair darkening, and looked younger than her thirty-six years, with her bright blue eyes and long blonde eyelashes.

'Now,' Joan picked up a writing pad and pencil and pulled them towards her, 'let's make a start on this list, or we're never gonna get our Christmas shopping done.'

'Well the weather's been so bad,' Evie observed mildly.

'Oh, come off it. Since when 'as the weather ever stopped us from going out? Least of all from tramping round the shops.'

Evie sighed. 'Yeah, I know. You're right. We should go.'

Joan looked closely at Evie. She looked exhausted, and her face was so serious. What could be wrong? *Good God! I must be a right heartless bitch! That has to be the answer. Evie hasn't got the money to go buying Christmas presents. Poor Evie! She puts on a brave face to the world, but it must be one helluva struggle for her trying to make ends meet and coping with the worry of the girls with no man behind her.* Her own husband, Bert, wasn't exactly wonder man, but he was always there. Someone to cuddle up to in bed, to talk over your problems with, and he never missed with his pay packet. Even when he did a bit of overtime at the post office, like at this time of the year, he always handed over a bit extra for shoes and things for their two girls.

Evie must feel it sometimes, having no man to turn to, but she would never admit it. Disastrous – there was no other word for it. That was the only way to describe the way that Ted Hopkins had mucked up Evie's life. Though

Evie wouldn't thank you for saying so. Proper on–off do that had been, with Evie welcoming him with open arms each time he turned up. Then there had been the last baby – dear, sweet little Rosie. He'd certainly twisted his way out of that! 'Invalid wife, my arse,' is what her Bert had said at the time. Yet, God love her, there had never been a trace of bitterness in Evie.

Joan finished her cup of tea, set the empty cup down on the table and stood up. 'I'll 'ave to go. I promised I'd pick up Mrs Edward's bagwash. You know she still 'as a job to get about since she 'ad that nasty fall.' She glanced at the clock on the mantelpiece. 'I'll be back in about two hours. I'll bring a coupla pies in with me for us to 'ave midday. Think about our list an' we'll sort out a day to go up to Brixton nearer the weekend. What d'ye say?'

'Yeah, that'll be fine. I'll have the kettle on for when you get back. I'll come to the door with you.'

'Tie yer scarf over yer head,' Evie called, raising her voice against the wind.

'Yes, I will. Go in out of the cold,' Joan called back.

Back in the warmth, Evie sat down again and took up her vegetable knife. Just the thing – beef stew for tonight's dinner. She'd put in plenty of dumplings later on. The girls loved dumplings.

Joan means well, Evie thought to herself. Then, taking a down-to-earth view of the facts, she moaned. Joan had Bert. He earned good, regular money with a lot of extras now, with it coming up to Christmas. What hope in hell had she of finding extra cash? The ten-pound provident cheque she had ordered she had earmarked for new coats for Jenny and Rosie. God knows they needed them badly enough. They ought to have shoes and underwear as well really before she started to think about buying presents.

Since Cathy had started work at Balham Woolworth's, she had taken ten shillings a week off her for her keep. What little Catherine had left she was entitled to. Poor Cathy! She had never had much, and it was only natural that she wanted make-up and nylon stockings like other girls had. She also wanted shop-bought clothes. She was no longer satisfied with what her mum and her gran made for her. But Cathy was still grateful for blouses and dresses, and last week she had been over the moon with that little silk bolero made from a remnant picked up from Smith's in Mitcham Lane, that Evie had stitched and presented her with.

In September, when Catherine had first started handing over ten shillings, Evie had been determined to save it each week, her purpose being to buy a television set in time for Christmas, or at least to be able to rent one. You needed quite a lump sum as a deposit and payment in advance even to be able to do that. About a year ago Jim Tyler had bought a set for her mother. All three of her girls loved to get in front of their nanna's set and watch it, and she herself was loath to miss 'Sunday Night at the London Palladium', though there were times when Evie felt she was imposing on her mum, always assuming that she and the girls were welcome. Of course they were. No doubt about that. Still it would be nice if her mum and Jim were able to sit down some Sunday evenings and enjoy a bit of privacy.

Evie groaned out loud. She had long abandoned such big ideas. Despite the fact that she had had three part-time jobs at one time, she had still somehow got behind with her rent. Three weeks, she had had to find, and she had never let on to Flossie about that. She did enough for her and her grandchildren as it was.

Catherine had made no secret of the fact that she would like to have a record player for Christmas. She had also, accidentally on purpose, left lying about a list of records she would like to have. The cost of half a ton of coal had put paid to that idea. Evie half smiled, saying to herself, *Why can't there be a real Father Christmas?*

When Evie had all the potherbs chopped to her satisfaction, she rose from the table. Taking the chopping board with her, she went to the stove, lifted the lid of the saucepan that held the stewing beef and added the extra vegetables. She put the potatoes into a separate pan, covering them with cold water.

Evie could hear the buzzers from the factories sounding. It must be gone twelve. She looked out of the window, down the street, past the women coming back from shopping with their heavy bags, some of them pushing prams in which rode happy babies, the young mothers laughing as they walked. The sound of a car turning into the road caught her attention, and she grinned as she recognised the Humber. A few quick steps and she was at the door as George parked his car at the kerb side, outside her house for a change.

For a moment she stood looking at this dapper young man and the jaunty way he walked towards her.

'Hi ye, Evie. Pleased to see me, are you?'

She had to smile. 'Oh yes indeed. Don't know how I manage when you're not around.'

'I keep telling you, you should let me into your life. How's the girls an' your mum? By the way, you seem to get more desirable every time I see you.' So it went on until he had walked around the car, crossed the pavement and had reached the spot where Evie stood in the open doorway.

'Come on in, George. It's too cold to stand about out here.'

''Tis an' all. Freeze the balls off a brass monkey, this weather would.'

'Well you're wrapped up well enough. Another new over-coat?' she observed, looking at the heavy camel coat which reached almost to his ankles and noticing that the usual grey trilby hat had been exchanged for a brown felt one.

'Ee, my lovely, you noticed. I knew all along that you loved me.'

'Don't kid yourself, George Higgins. You think every girl that sees you is ready to drop at your feet.'

'It's true an' all.' He leered at her. 'But it's only you that I'm willing to pick up an' raise to such heights of happiness that you will think you've died an' gone to heaven.'

Evie laughed outright. 'Oh you bloody bighead!' Then, looking up at him, she asked, 'What are you doing 'ere at this time of the day? And why 'aven't I seen sight nor sound of you for the last ten days?'

'See! I knew you'd missed me. Been counting the hours 'ave you? We'll 'ave to do something about that.'

Still laughing, Evie made to help him off with his coat as they stepped into the front room. 'What do you fancy, coffee or—'

'I can't stay,' he interrupted her, 'and if I could I'd tell you outright what it is I fancy, an' it wouldn't be coffee.'

Evie's face fell and she took a step backwards. 'Gone off me, 'ave you?'

'No, honestly luv, it ain't that. I've got to go. I don't want to, but I've got a bit of business to see to that won't wait. I just popped in to tell you to make arrangements with your mum to 'ave the girls on Saturday cos I'm gonna take you to the East End.'

There was a bright smile on Evie's face now. 'Well, if you say so, George. If you say so.'

'I do say so, Evie, I do. An' I've said it to meself, over an' over again. I'm gonna take my Evie to the East End, to Whitechapel an' a few places round there. Mates of mine 'ave got warehouses in that quarter, an' you'll be amazed at the gear we'll come back with. Rig the girls out good an' proper, we will. Set them up for this cold weather. Is that all right with you?'

When Evie didn't answer him, he stared down at her face and at the tears that were glistening in her eyes.

'Is there some reason that you don't want to come?'

'No, no, of course not, George.' He had to bend his head to hear her answer because her voice was little more than a whisper.

'Good. Well then, what's your answer?'

She stood on her toes, threw her arms around his neck, put her lips to his ear and murmured, 'And I was wishing that there could be a real Father Christmas.'

He hugged her. They exchanged a smile and he said quietly, 'I really do 'ave to go. I'll pick you up ten o'clock Saturday morning. Be ready.'

From the doorway, she watched him get into the car, switch on the engine and with a wave of his hand the car shot forward down the road.

Evie didn't move until the Humber had turned the corner and was out of sight. Her feelings about George were so mixed up. She liked him – oh yes, very much. But did she love him deeply? Her answer was that it was time she found out. She had better concentrate on all his good points before she lost him to someone else.

George pushed open the front gate and glanced up at the bedroom window before stepping into the porchway. He banged the knocker twice before he heard a scurrying behind the door And then it was pulled open, and there was Evie beaming at him.

'Cor, you're early. You said ten o'clock. It's only just gone nine. Still, I won't be long. Come on in.'

George stepped past her in the narrow passageway and waited while she closed the door.

Evie nodded to the front room door that was ajar, 'Go an' park yer bones. I've only got me face an' hair to do.'

George didn't move. Smiling, he let his eyes roam over Evie. 'You look real dishy. Give us a kiss an' then I'll make meself a cuppa while you're putting the finishing touches to your face.'

Evie, standing still in front of him, said simply, 'George! Oh, George, what am I gonna do with you?'

Bending towards her, he said, 'I rather think the boot is on the other foot,' and such was the look in his eyes and the softness of his voice that Evie felt her heart stir as it hadn't done for years. He took her face between his hands and gently kissed her on the lips. 'Get upstairs an' do what you were going to before I change me mind, cos if I do, neither of us will be seeing anything today except the inside of your bedroom!'

'You're hopeless,' she laughed, but her thoughts were in a turmoil as she slowly went upstairs.

Fifteen minutes later George raised his eyes as Evie stood in front of him, looking, she hoped, very smart in her long beige skirt and brown jumper. Around her neck she had loosely draped a yellow scarf that had a brown and tan edging. Her shoes were a plain court shoe, the same colour beige as her skirt.

'Boy, you were well worth waiting for,' George said, as he looked at her with approval. He helped her on with her winter coat, and Evie hoped that he wouldn't think it was too shabby, thinking at the same time that at least the fur collar still looked good.

George took her arm. 'Is it all right with you, madam, if we get going now?'

'Yes, but . . .'

'No buts. The girls are okay, aren't they?' Evie smiled and nodded. 'Then we're off at last.'

Out in the hallway, Evie giggled. 'I've left my gloves on the arm of the chair.'

George threw up his hands in mock desperation. 'God give me strength! Go on out to the car, I'll fetch them.'

Evie opened the door, stared and felt the colour drain from her face. She gasped as her heart started to thump against her ribs. Standing directly in front of her, his arm raised in midair about to rap the door knocker, was Ted Hopkins. He, too, was lost for words as he gazed at this beautiful, sunny young woman who was the mother of his children.

He was the first to recover. 'Hello Evie.' He smiled, holding out both of his hands.

George Higgins was no fool. He had been told the bare bones of Evie's life by Jim Tyler, and he took in the situation at a glance. Taking a firm hold of Evie's elbow, he propelled her forward, slamming the front door shut behind them. Turning to look over his shoulder, he said, 'Don't know who you are, mate, nor what you want, but do us a favour: sling yer 'ook. We're a bit pushed for time.'

Seated in the car, Evie breathed a sigh of relief. Thank God George had been there. Whatever would she have said to Ted if she had been on her own? She knew that wasn't the end of it. Ted wouldn't just clear off without a word having been said, but at least she had time to think now that she knew he was here in London. What a shock, seeing him standing there after all this time! It must have been just as big a shock for Ted. Did he expect that she would open the door and he could walk straight back into her life?

George was whistling, he wasn't annoyed. People like George didn't get annoyed unless they meant to do something about whatever it was that had upset them. Plainly George was going to ignore the whole thing, and that was fine by her.

George turned his head and flashed Evie a smile. *Forget him. We're going to have a great day,* that's what the smile said.

George was a skilful driver, and Evie was enjoying the ride. Now they were in the City of Westminster, passing the great abbey and the Houses of Parliament, turning on to the Embankment, the dear old Thames wide and fast flowing, with a great deal of shipping going in both directions. Evie hadn't been up this way since God knows when. Her memory of this part of London was of a dark, dusty and dirty place. It wasn't like that now. No sign of the bomb damage and rubble there had been at the end of the war. There had certainly been great improvements made.

'Cor! Isn't that the Tower of London?' Evie asked George, her voice high with excitement.

'Yes, and there's Tower Bridge. It's the lowest bridge across the Thames.'

Evie craned her neck round as the car went on along the Embankment, saying to herself, *I really must bring the girls up to see these sights. Those two towers on the bridge are magnificent. We live right on the doorstep and yet never come to see all that London has to offer.*

George parked his car at the side entrance to the Whitechapel factory, went to the main gates and rang the bell. An old woman came out from the lodge. She wore a shapeless cotton frock and her bare feet were thrust into a pair of old carpet slippers. The varicose veins stood out on her legs, and her face was lined with wrinkles. A great grin split her lips as she spied George.

''Ello, Mister George. Cor, I'm right pleased ter see you. It's ages since you honoured us 'ere at the factory with your presence.'

'And I'm right pleased to see you too, Rachel. 'Ow yer bin keeping?'

'Mustn't grumble,' she said as she turned the key in the lock of the iron gates. 'No bugger takes any notice anyway.'

George laughed as he pushed the gates open wide, then getting back into his car, he called, 'They working full strength today?'

Rachel shuffled to stand beside the passenger side of the Humber and gave Evie a wicked grin. 'Jewish he ain't, though a nice boy he is. Are they working full strength? With Christmas only weeks away, Isaac's is singing, "What a Friend We 'ave in Jesus".'

Evie giggled, and George threw his head back and roared with laughter. 'Still a bit of a card and no respecter of your employer, eh Rachel?'

'Well, the silly bugger don't alter.'

'And neither do you! I'll see you on me way out.'

'Yeah, all right Mister George.' She nodded at Evie. 'You wanna watch the gaffer up there. One look at you an' his trousers will fall down.'

As Evie entered the factory, she wrinkled her nose as she looked about her in the dust-laden air. She wondered how on earth these women could work in such an atmosphere, what with the dust and the noise of the sewing machines. Women looked up as she and George walked down between the long tables. Some of the faces brightened as they called, 'Hi ye, Mister George.'

Further on, a young man pushing a trestle full of swinging garments stopped in his tracks and called, 'See they let ye out then, George?' Then, turning his gaze to rest on Evie, he added, 'Cradle snatching, are ye?'

'Ye cheeky beggar. Seems I only come 'ere to get meself insulted,' George said, smiling. 'Oh, by the way, Wally, how's your little girl?'

Wally Goldman's face brightened. 'A whole lot better than when you last saw 'er, George. Me an' Sadie ain't never gonna forget what you did for us. About time ye come along an' saw the little 'un for yerself. Bring the young lady with you, yes?'

'I'll do that,' George promised. 'Just as soon as the rush eases off. Give my love to Sadie.'

'I will George. Take care.'

By now Evie was feeling bewildered, and there were a dozen or so questions that she was dying to ask. One she couldn't resist: 'What we doing 'ere, George?'

George grinned at her confusion. 'Patience, all will be revealed shortly.'

'Why . . . are you . . .?'

'Enough. Wait an' see,' he responded, his eyes twinkling as he steered her forward. 'Well how's things with the mighty Isaac Solomon?' asked George as they entered a cluttered office.

Isaac was perched on a high stool, his big belly overhanging the top of his trousers, a huge cigar dangling from the side of his mouth. 'My Life! George 'Iggins! You're still alive an' breathing, yes?' All this was uttered as he slid from the stool and came to slap George between his shoulder blades. 'You're a sight for sore eyes, me boy. Say what brings ye to the East End an' it's yours.'

Evie couldn't believe what she was seeing, the welcome George was getting from all quarters. She watched now as he threw out his arms and pulled this portly Jewish man close to his chest, holding him there in a great bear hug. When the two men finally drew apart she was amazed to see the emotion that was showing on each of their faces, and if she wasn't mistaken there were tears glistening in their eyes.

'This is Evie Smith. Evie, this is Mr Isaac Solomon.' George took out a white handkerchief and blew his nose. He really was overcome with emotion.

'I'm more than pleased to meet you, young lady,' Isaac said to Evie. Then, turning to George, he grinned. 'Got yerself a real lovely lady there, but tell me, why are Gentile women always so skinny?'

Evie laughed.

'What's brought you?' asked Isaac, waddling back to his stool.

'Three nice winter coats for three lovely little girls.'

'Ye couldn't 'ave picked a better time. Rose is in the factory terday. You'll find her supervising the packing, straight down past the machines. She sets eyes on you, George, an' she'll think she's seen a ghost, my life she will.'

'Get on with ye, Issy, it's not that long since I broke bread with your family.'

'Try telling that to me daughter Rose. And don't bother ter come back an' tell me what she said. I don't 'old with bad language.'

As Evie shook the podgy hand that held the thick gold wedding ring, she thought to herself what a kind man this friend of George's was. George was once again enfolded in those strong arms and was being squeezed so hard she thought his ribs might crack.

Rose Solomon was a tall, beautiful woman. From the top of her blue-black hair to the tip of the high-heeled shoes that she wore, she was a picture of elegance. She also had the refinement that comes with a good education. Evie felt like a fish out of water as she watched Rose's face light up with surprise and pleasure at the sight of George.

'Mornin', Miss Solomon,' said George briskly.

'George!' Rose cried. 'Come here and let me see if you are real.'

George coughed, shrugged his shoulders at Evie and went, leaving Evie smiling broadly.

When George released Rose, having kissed her hard and long, she grinned. 'All is forgiven,' she told George.

*

George, with Evie seated in the passenger seat, drove through the factory gates an hour and a half later. She had watched George fold a ten-pound note and quietly slip it into Rachel's hand as he had kissed her goodbye. The back seat of the car was loaded with boxes, and still Evie couldn't speak for the lump in her throat that was choking her.

Two cherry red coats, of the finest wool, with navy blue velvet collars to set them off. She could see Jenny and Rosie on Christmas morning parading them for their nanna to admire. Catherine had been well catered for too.

'I just don't know,' Evie had spluttered when asked what kind of outfit her eldest daughter would like.

'Leave it to me,' Rose Solomon had said kindly as she had picked up a telephone and spoken a few rapid sentences into the mouthpiece.

While they had waited, she had served her and George the best coffee that Evie had ever tasted. Before long, three girls, all about the same age as Catherine, had come into the storeroom. Each had been dressed differently. They had walked slowly between the packing cases, turning and pausing in front of Evie.

'They're all so lovely,' Evie had exclaimed as George had asked her to decide which outfit she thought Cathy would prefer.

Each girl had worn a costume or, as Rose said it was referred to, a suit. The material had been the same in each case, a pepper and salt mixture: a kind of tweed, yet smooth like a man's suiting would be.

'Which girl most resembles your daughter's colouring?' Rose had asked.

'Oh, the tall young lady with the fair complexion.'

'Then that's the one you should go for.'

It was a darkish grey in colour, a straight skirt with a long boxy jacket.

'Your Catherine will love the new-look length,' Rose had assured Evie, adding, 'and there is another skirt that goes with it, a flared one, pleats flowing from the hips.'

Evie had been unable to find words to show her appreciation as she had watched the three boxes being packed.

'Happy?' George's question burst in on Evie's thoughts.

'Point is,' said Evie, frowning, 'how am I ever going to be able to repay you?'

'You talk like that an' I'll stop the car an' you can walk 'ome.'

'I'm sorry George. I just can't take it in. Everybody was so pleased to see you. And they were so kind to me. Not one of them asked any awkward questions.'

'True friends don't. If there is anything to be told, men like Isaac know we'll speak when the time is right. Give us a kiss.'

'George! You're driving!'

'Not for long, I ain't. We're gonna turn down 'ere an' you're gonna 'ave the best bit of salt beef that you ever tasted in your life. And after that we're going to another factory that is also owned by Jewish friends of mine, an' your eyes will pop out of your 'ead when you see what we are gonna bring away from there.'

Evie burst out laughing. 'You've got me so as I don't know whether I'm coming or going,' she wailed.

Halfway down Whitechapel Road, George turned the car down a side street on the left, bringing it to a halt on the forecourt of a large public house. 'Come on, this is where we are gonna eat.'

The sharp wind was fierce and bitter cold, sending abandoned wrapping papers and other litter scurrying across the pavement. George pulled his trilby firmly down on his head and held on tight to Evie's arm as they pushed through the doors of the saloon bar. Every man in the bar seemed to stop talking and look up as they made their entrance. Suddenly there was a surge towards George.

Evie wondered for a moment what was happening as she found herself standing alone. George's hand was being pumped up and down, his back slapped and all the while near-the-knuckle bantering was being called.

Evie bit her lip, feeling hopelessly inadequate, and wondered if she should creep out and wait in the car. Who were all these people? It seemed as if half the East End knew George. He certainly was welcomed everywhere. George appeared relaxed enough, he radiated considerable self-confidence and a powerful personality that she had not seen before, and now she found herself looking at him in a very different light.

The sound of George's hearty laugh rolled across the bar and, plucking up courage, she walked to the wall where groups of tables and chairs were set out and sidled into an armchair. George had seen her. He immediately pushed through the throng and came over.

'Sorry about that, luv,' he said, grinning all over his face.

He was so totally happy that Evie smiled back, feeling more relaxed, and said, 'That's all right.'

'I'll get you a drink an' order our lunch. D'you want to see a menu or will you risk it an' leave the choice to me?'

'I'll be a devil an' risk it.'

Fifteen minutes later, a fat white-aproned man set a platter of steaming hot salt beef and boiled potatoes down in front of each of them.

'Get yer gnashers round that lot, and Gladys said to tell ye there's spotted dick an' custard for yer afters,' the man said, shoving George so hard that he tipped forward.

Set on the table between them were an assortment of dishes, some open, some with lids. Evie looked inquiringly at George, who was grinning at her like a small boy.

'Dig in. There's pease pudding, carrots, baby onions in a creamy sauce, and peas the like of which you've never tasted in yer life before.'

When their plates were piled high and they both had started to eat, George said, 'I used to come 'ere for a lot of my meals. Still do when I'm in the neighbourhood. If it's early in the day Jack's wife, Gladys, gives me breakfast. That was Jack that served us. It's his boy, Harry, that is the landlord. His mum an' dad were retired but they got bored so now they see to all the food in the pub. Great, ain't it?'

Evie, her mouth full, nodded her agreement. She was thinking to herself how just lately everything was working out right. It had all been going wrong at one time and then suddenly with George around it came right *But it won't last,* she mused. *Not now that Ted has turned up again.*

George sensed that Evie was lost in thought and he didn't blame her. He knew exactly what was troubling her. Very quietly he asked, 'What's wrong, Evie?'

'Wrong?' she spoke almost abruptly. 'Why should anything be wrong?'

'You seem . . . well, preoccupied all of a sudden.' He stopped and Evie knew he was reluctant to go on. He seemed to steel himself. 'Evie,' he said, 'stop blaming yourself for the past. You were very young, far too trusting. You owe that bloke nothing. Are you listening to me?' He leaned across, put a finger beneath her chin and raised her face so that their eyes met. 'You lived on his promises. I know that to be a fact. Promises which came to nothing. In the end, when you were carrying his third baby, he deserted you altogether. It's beyond me how you coped. It must 'ave been a terrifying time for you. Left with three youngsters and no means. I can't even imagine the heartache and misery you must have suffered. But you didn't give in, did you? You faced up to those responsibilities on your own. And a damn good job you've made of it. No thanks t'that sod.'

Evie grinned. 'Didn't 'ave much choice, did I?'

'Perhaps not. But that don't make it right. I can't get over the fact that he's got the gall to turn up again now. I ought t'ave put my fist in his face. That's what most men would 'ave done. It will probably come t'that in the end if he decides to 'ang around.'

Evie was silent for a few minutes. Horrified was how she'd felt to find Ted standing on her doorstep after all these years. Yet at this moment, having listened to George, she felt a certain amount of relief. She and George were at least talking about Ted.

George took a cover off one of the dishes. 'Have some more of these,' he said, spooning tiny onions and plenty of the rich sauce onto her plate before helping himself to more. 'And Evie, stop looking back. Look forward. This is our day. Our time. Come on, give us a smile, please. Forget him. Don't let his turning up make any difference.'

'He could cause trouble,' Evie sighed.

George chuckled. 'Just let him try! What I don't understand is why. Why would he turn up now after so long?'

Evie looked at him steadily. 'He'll 'ave a reason. A purely selfish one, you bet.'

George leant across again and this time he gripped her hand tightly. 'There is no need to worry about anything any more. You 'ave me now. I'll take care of you. All right?'

Evie sat there smiling now, and suddenly she decided she was enjoying this day. It was one of the happiest she'd ever known, and she wasn't going to allow Ted Hopkins to spoil it for her.

They finished their meal in friendly silence, until

George asked, 'Are you going to 'ave some spotty dick?'

Evie laughed out loud. 'I couldn't eat another morsel.'

'Well, you can sit an' watch me.' He grinned as he got to his feet and went towards the bar.

A number of handshakes and promises to return soon, and they were at the door. Big fat Jack barred Evie's way. 'Don't you worry, luv. He'll be back like an 'oming pigeon, an' he'll bring you, or me an' the missus will wanna know the reason why. He needs a decent girl like you.'

Evie swallowed and said doubtfully, 'I don't know about that, but thanks anyway. I really did enjoy the food.'

'Don't buy so much, George,' Evie said frantically in a hoarse whisper. They were in a long low-ceilinged room that George had told her was a demonstration room, whatever that meant. So far all she had seen was a number of gentlemen in black suits. Each man had greeted George as if he were a long lost son.

Evie stared round, her eyes wide with admiration. This warehouse was far superior to that at Isaac Solomon's factory, and she could only suppose that garments weren't actually made on the premises. Every inch of space had been cleverly utilised. The shelves banked from floor to ceiling held glass-fronted drawers, each carefully labelled with the name of the article it held. The floor was covered in a thick pile carpet, and elegant chairs were arranged by the windows. On the wood-panelled counter there were several order books and an imposing brass ink stand with glass ink holders at each end and several long-handled pens resting in the tray.

Evie marvelled as George felt the material of dressing gowns. 'What do you think? Red for each of them?' he turned to Evie and asked.

She couldn't bring herself to answer, so she merely

nodded as she thought wistfully of how snug and warm her girls would be in gowns such as these rather than the faded wrapround cotton ones they had had to make do with for so long.

'Evie, you order their underwear. Sizes an' such like are a bit beyond me. I'm just off to have a word with Mr Harris.'

It took her a moment to realise that George had left the room and the man behind the counter was laying out warm nightdresses and pretty underwear for her approval. She twisted her gloves in embarrassment, but the gentleman smiled.

'You have three daughters? I myself have two, and two sons. Come, you tell me their sizes and we'll do fine. It is not allowed for you to say no.'

Evie, her face red, smiled. This was a nice man!

By the time George came back, two large boxes under his arm, Evie's fears had vanished, and she was sitting down drinking a cup of tea that had been graciously offered to her. All the same, when their goodbyes had been said and they were once more in the car heading for home, Evie's heart was still racing. She hadn't seen any money change hands, and George had quickly silenced her when she had tried to bring up the matter of payment.

Her house was all in darkness when George brought the car to a stop.

'I'll help you to stack these boxes away an' then I'll walk you down to your mum's.'

'But you can't go yet, George. We've got to sort something out about all the things you've bought for the girls,' Evie said frantically.

'I have to go, Evie dear, but I'll be 'ere first thing Monday morning, and as to what you're worrying yourself silly over, stop it. These are gifts from me for Cathy, Jenny an' Rosie. After all it will be Christmas.'

'Oh George!'

He put his arms around her and held her close. 'I'd like to do a helluva lot more for all of you,' he whispered.

She was touched by his feelings for her. 'George, are you going to spend Christmas with us?'

His arms tightened about her. 'Are you offering?'

She laughed. 'Yes, I'm offering.'

'I'm accepting gladly. Wild horses wouldn't keep me away.'

Evie raised a flushed face. 'It's been quite a day, George. A real eye-opener.'

'I'm glad you've enjoyed it. Now let's get this stuff indoors and stowed away. I really do 'ave to go.'

Evie opened up the cupboard that ran beneath the stairs, and she passed the boxes while George placed them in as far as they would go. Evie turned the key in the lock and smiled. 'I don't think that cupboard has ever been locked before, but we won't take any chances. If I know my girls, they'll be turning the house out once their nanna tells them you've taken me shopping.'

'Leave the light on in the hall,' George instructed her. 'We don't want you coming back 'ere in the dark.'

At the gateway of her mother's house, George took her gently in his arms. 'I meant what I said, Evie. I wish you would think about letting me take care of you and the girls.'

For a moment Evie didn't answer. Was he proposing marriage? She didn't think so. Was he already married? Come to think of it, she didn't know an awful lot about George Higgins. Not even where he lived and whether he lived alone or not. 'You're sure you'll be coming on Monday?'

He covered her lips with his own, and Evie felt a sudden

heat surge through her body. He wouldn't release her and she didn't want him to. They clung together. She closed her eyes, thinking that she had been alone for too long. She was still young and in need of someone to love, someone to love her and to share a future with. Ted had used her when she'd been young and starry-eyed, but George was here, holding her, offering to look after her, to show her a life where she didn't have to scrimp and scrape for every penny. Was it too good to be true? She would have to wait and see.

As Evie opened the door of her mum's front room, her two youngest girls jumped up from the floor, where they had been sitting watching television, and came at her with a rush.

'What did ye buy, Mum?' Rosie wanted to know.

'Nan said you'd gone out with George. Didn't he send us anything?' This was from Jenny.

'Yes he did,' Evie laughed, 'but I've a good mind not to give it to you. It's just being greedy to think that George always comes bearing gifts.'

'Well, he does,' Rosie cried and the look of expectation on her little face was enough to melt Evie's heart and turn it over with love.

'Come give me a kiss and you can both have all that is in this bag.'

There were squeals of delight as they almost knocked Evie off her feet with their hugging. She and her mother exchanged glances as the two girls returned to the television content with their bags of peanuts and packets of crisps.

'Where's Catherine?' Evie asked, almost dreading the answer.

'She's gone dancing at Streatham Locarno with Shirley. She promised me she won't be too late,' Flossie told her, and as Evie sniffed she added, 'You'd better come upstairs before you take your coat off.'

Evie didn't need any telling. This had to be about Ted.

Ah well, better said out of the hearing of the youngsters.

Her mother closed the door behind them and got straight to the point. 'You lumbered me good an' proper this morning, didn't you? That bloody Ted Hopkins arriving out of the blue like that. Gave me quite a shock.'

'Me as well,' said Evie. 'George wouldn't let me 'ang about. He almost pushed me into his car an' told Ted ter sling 'is 'ook. I might 'ave guessed he'd come bothering you.'

'Yeah well, a fella like 'im don't bother me none. He got short change outta me, I can tell ye.'

'Blimey, Mum, you're not telling me he cleared off just like that.'

'No. I'm not telling ye any such thing. If ye must know, I asked 'im in an' then I gave 'im a piece of my mind.'

Evie stifled a giggle. 'Cor, I bet 'is ears were burning like 'ell by the time you'd finished with 'im, Mum.'

'No more than he deserved. The bloody cheek of the man! When you think about it, 'ow long's it bin? I think he thought I was gonna feel sorry for 'im when he told me that 'is wife 'ad died.'

Evie swallowed hard. Pity it hadn't happened years ago. What a wicked thing to even think, she chided herself, then decided it was true; it was a pity for her and her girls. She recovered and asked faintly, 'So what 'appened?'

'Well, the long an' the short of it was, I said he could come 'ere to this 'ouse tomorrow afternoon about 'alf past two. I thought that would give us a chance to get our dinners over an' out of the way an' get Jenny an' Rosie off to Sunday school.'

'All right. What about Cathy?'

'The way I sees it, Cathy is old enough to figure things out for 'erself. Besides, as you've been telling me lately, she asks a lot of questions about her father so if she's around it might be as well to let her see 'im face to face. If not, well, we'll 'ave to wait an' see.'

'Thanks Mum. I'm sorry I cleared off an' left you to deal with him.'

Flossie looked at Evie and her heart ached. If she'd had her way she'd have told Ted Hopkins a lot more home truths, but it was Evie's life. All she prayed was that she wouldn't be daft enough to listen to the selfish git and his sob stories.

She put her hand out to Evie. 'Did you 'ave a good day with George?'

'Mum, you won't believe it.'

'I'm glad. Come on, let's go downstairs before the girls start wondering.'

'Lead me to the kettle. I'm dying for a cup of tea.'

Arms linked, they went out of the room together. *It would take a lot to break the link between us,* was what Flossie was thinking. *When it comes to men though, we're both as bloody soft as each other.*

Evie was well aware of the reason her mother had arranged for Ted to call at her house rather than at 42. *She's afraid I might end up in bed with him again.* Evie was getting impatient. The clock on the mantelpiece showed it was a quarter to three and so far no sign of Ted. Flossie was upstairs in her front bedroom. 'I'll be able to 'ear you if you call,' she had said over her shoulder as she climbed the stairs. Evie had almost answered, 'If you have your way you won't miss a word of what passes between him and me.' Her mum was good though. She'd busied herself this morning.

Evie was sitting in one of the two comfortable fireside chairs. She looked around the room with pleasure. Crisp white net curtains at the bay window, heavy red velvet curtains, looped back during the day, the matching velvet cushion covers on the settee, a cut-glass vase that held bronze chrysanthemums on a side table. By her feet the heavy brass companion set, with its swinging poker, brush and shovel, glittered with the reflection of the flames from the open fire.

The loud knocking on the door made Evie jump, and her foot caught the brass poker as she jumped to her feet, sending it into the hearth with a clatter.

Evie was trembling as she opened the door. She felt her face flush at the sight of him. 'Come in.' She held the door wide and Edward Hopkins walked past her into the house.

'I don't know why your mother insisted I came here rather than to your own house.' He had opened the conversation without so much as a hello or how are you.

'Sit down, Ted.' She smoothed her already tidy hair with a gesture that showed she was nervous and bent to pick up the fallen poker, replacing it on the hook of its stand.

'Are you pleased to see me, Evie?' he asked, making himself at home as he took off his overcoat, then his gloves and lastly his hat.

She drew in a deep breath. 'Should I be, Ted?'

'Well, I thought at least you'd be happy after all this time. Tell me about the girls. Where are they? Were you pleased the third baby was another girl?'

'Oh! So you did get my card.' Her voice was harsh enough to jerk Ted to his feet.

'Evie, my love. I think we've got off on the wrong foot. Shall we try again?'

Evie bit her lip, then muttered, 'A bit late.'

'Listen to me, Evie. Things are different now. Surely you don't need me to tell you that my feelings for you haven't changed? Mabel is dead now. We can be a complete family, have something worthwhile.'

She couldn't believe this was the same man. True he had put on some weight. His hair did now show signs of grey and his brow was marked with deep lines. But hearing him pleading in a way she wouldn't have believed him capable of left her unmoved.

'I love you, Evie. I always have, and I will for as long as I live. There is so much I want to do for you and our girls. Tell me you still love me, please, Evie.'

Something inside Evie snapped. The sudden move Ted had made to touch her had her pulling away in terror. 'Stop it!' She was almost hysterical.

He clenched his fists at his sides, unable to believe that Evie was rejecting him. Evie had always been there for him, ever since she was a young girl. He had come to claim her now, and his children: they were his after all. He was getting older. He wanted a family around him. Somehow, he had to convince Evie of that.

'Evie, let's go down to your home. We must talk sensibly. I've come all the way from Blackpool and . . .'

'What did you do, crawl on your 'ands an' knees?' Her voice, now strong and accusing, cut him off and she stared straight into his eyes. 'It took you six bloody years!' Evie was shaking visibly now but she wasn't about to back off. 'Don't just stand there, Ted. Explain it to me. Not a letter, a postcard, not a word for six years. You knew I was carrying another baby when you went off to Switzerland and God knows where else, you knew we already had two daughters. Did you ever give a thought to them? Their birthdays? Christmas? Were they getting enough to eat? Were they kept warm? Did they have good boots on their feet? How about when they were ill? You didn't know, and you didn't care.' Evie sank back down into the armchair, choking and gasping for breath, the temper that had set her off drained away.

'Evie! I will make you understand.' Ted was bending over her now and he had a grip on both her arms, shaking her until her head bobbed.

'Ted Hopkins! Leave her be!' The words came out almost in a scream as Flossie appeared in the doorway. She advanced towards him, the look on her face so full of hatred that Edward cringed and straightened up. 'I think it's about time that you left my house.' Flossie's voice had dropped to a hiss now, and that sounded even worse than her shouting.

Ted knew he was beaten but he tried to brave it out. 'I came to see Evie, and I'll go when she asks me to and not before.'

There was a moment's silence in the room before Flossie went to where his hat and coat lay on the chair, picked them up in her arms, blundered towards the door, went out into the hall, tore open the door, and threw the whole lot out into the street.

'You won't get away with treating me like this.' Ted had followed her down the passageway, and as he passed her he said, 'I'll see my solicitor. I have a right to see my daughters.'

'You bastard!'

He banged the front door. Flossie ran to open it again. She changed her mind and went back to see to Evie.

'He's off down the street like a bat out of hell,' said Flossie as she let her lace curtain drop. 'And damn good riddance if you want my opinion.'

Evie was feeling deep resentment that the man she had worshipped had not only walked out on her years ago but had had the gall to think that he could walk back into her life and expect her to treat him as if he were a god. Suddenly she was crying.

'For goodness' sake, don't tell me you didn't want 'im to go.'

'That's not why I'm cryin', Mum.' Evie mopped at her eyes fiercely. 'It's that the girls 'ave never known their father.'

'Neither 'ave you really. Now you're making me feel guilty.' Flossie was almost in tears.

'Oh Mum, that's not what I meant.' Evie sniffed and gave her mum a weak smile.

Flossie smiled back, shook her head and said, 'Sometimes, Evie, I wonder about you, I really do!'

Evie managed a shaky laugh. 'Mum, I wonder about you all the time.'

'Right pair then, ain't we, luv? Come on now, let's go out to the kitchen an' make ourselves a nice pot of tea.'

That night, in bed, the tears came. Evie cried and cried. She cried for her daughters who had never known what it was like to have a father, and for herself and all the worries and struggles she had had to face on her own, but mostly she cried because she still had no one to comfort her.

What a Monday morning this was turning out to be! Evie sighed heavily as she looked at the mess in her kitchen. She'd overslept. Been late in calling the girls. Cathy had hogged the bathroom. Rosie had cried because she was afraid her teacher would give her a black mark if she wasn't in her seat when she called the register. She'd just started the washing when the skies darkened, opened up and sent the rain down in torrents.

George hadn't arrived. So much for his promises.

All three girls were coming home for their lunch because there hadn't been time to cut them any sandwiches. About to make herself a cuppa, she had dropped the milk bottle. There had only been about an inch of milk in the bottom, yet when the bottle had hit the floor and smashed she couldn't believe the mess it had made. 'Look at it,' she had cried out loud. The milk had splashed half way up the walls as well as spreading over the floor. 'Damn an' blast,' she had sworn, as the blood squirted from her finger as she attempted to pick up the fragments of broken glass.

Two hours later the milkman had delivered fresh milk. She'd had her cup of tea, found a plaster for her finger. The broken glass was safely stowed away in a cardboard box, she had washed the linoleum and order had been restored. That was until a quarter past twelve when Catherine came home. One look at her face and Evie knew she was in a temper.

'We've got to work an extra hour every night next week,' she wailed.

'Well, it is Christmas week, luv. Think of the extra money you'll get in overtime.'

'Huh!' Cathy sniffed. 'Is that tomato soup?'

'Yes dear.'

'You know I hate tomato soup. Any other soup I really like, so what do you do? You make tomato.'

Evie was trying hard to soothe Catherine. 'I'll make you cheese on toast. It won't take a minute.'

'Just make a couple of slices of toast, that'll do. An' have you got a pair of stockings I can have? We're going out straight from work tonight and I've laddered these. Look at them.' Catherine stuck her leg out for her mother to sympathise. 'It's the blooming counters, they're terrible. I got a splinter in me leg the other day. I'll be glad when I can leave this rotten job.'

'What about your dinner tonight?'

'We're gonna get fish an' chips before we go to the pictures.'

'Oh.' Evie wondered who 'we' were but didn't dare to ask. 'Here's your toast, eat it while it's hot. I'll just go up an' get the stockings for you.'

Cathy did have the grace to say thank you as she took the stockings from her mother. 'Rotten colours you buy,' she moaned, as she glared at her mother.

'For God's sake take yourself off back to work before I lose my temper, you ungrateful young madam.' Evie felt she couldn't stand much more.

'I'll be late home tonight,' Cathy called as she flounced out, bashing into Jenny who was just coming in.

'What's up with her?'

'She's upset she's laddered her best stockings, and don't call your sister Catherine 'her'.'

Jenny was already ladling soup into two bowls, one for herself and one for Rosie.

'Cor, lovely. Tomato,' cried Rosie.

'Yeah, my favourite too,' agreed Jenny helping herself to bread.

Evie breathed a sigh of relief. Nice to be able to please someone. At twelve years of age Jenny was already showing signs of maturity, the only one of her girls that showed a resemblance to their father. Still much smaller than her sister Catherine, Jenny had the kind of beauty that came with a dark complexion, and her long dark hair, still wound into plaits on weekdays, had a glossy sheen to it at all times. Jenny also had a very placid attitude to life, easy-going and easy to please. Pity it wasn't as easy to please Catherine.

Not for the first time, Evie wondered where she had gone wrong with her eldest daughter. She was so lovely to look at, her hair the colour of ripe corn. Tall and slim, her figure had filled out in all the right places. Lately though she spent far too much time posing in front of the mirror, and the amount of make-up she plastered on her face, well! She had given up arguing about it. She shrugged her shoulders, utterly at a loss to know how to handle Catherine.

'Bye, my baby.'

Rosie held her face up to be kissed and Jenny, too, pecked her mother's cheek. 'See you tea time, Mum.'

Their mother stood in the doorway, watching her two youngest set off back to school. Jenny had Rosie firmly by the hand and they turned to wave before rounding the corner.

At least the rain had stopped, though the sky overhead was grey and menacing. She wouldn't be able to get the washing dry today, she thought irritably. Back indoors she gathered up the crocks and put the bread and butter back into the larder. It was going to be a long afternoon.

Evie had her sewing spread out all over the table, pins, scissors, tape measure and bias binding all to hand, when at two o'clock there was a knock at the front door.

She gasped in surprise and admiration when she opened the door to find George standing there, darkly handsome in yet another different overcoat. She resisted the temptation to throw her arms around his neck, smiled, stood back and nodded for him to come in.

'All right, luv?' he asked as he took his coat off and hung it on one of the wall pegs.

'I suppose so.'

'What d'ye mean, you suppose so? Come on, tell me what's wrong.'

She was going to give him a smart answer, but the words froze in her throat.

'Ted Hopkins came back yesterday, did he?'

A deep flush spread over Evie's face as she led the way into the front room. 'I forgot you knew about him.'

'Jim Tyler, he told me the bare bones of the situation a long time ago when I first started taking you out. Don't get me wrong, Evie, it makes no difference to the way I feel about you. It's all in the past and nothing to do with me, at least it wasn't until now. If he thinks he can come out of the blue an' start pestering you after all this time . . . Well! That's another matter.'

Evie leaned towards him impulsively and laid her hand

on his. For a moment the contact sent a tremor through her body and she snatched her hand away, blushing even more. 'You said you were going to come this morning. I wanted to see you. I needed someone to talk to.'

For a long moment they gazed at each other and in that moment Evie admitted to herself that this man meant a great deal more to her than she had let herself believe. There had been feeling on George's part but not entirely on hers. She knew by the look on his face and the tightening of his jaws that something had to come to a head. She had kept George dangling for far too long.

'Come here.' The words jerked from George's throat and he held out his hands to her.

She was in his arms. The contact, the feel of him, even through the layers of their clothing, sent the heat surging through her veins.

'Oh God, Evie!' muttered George as he held her tightly in his arms. She didn't resist as he fumbled with the buttons of her blouse. There had been more than enough waiting for the two of them. They staggered, locked together, out into the hallway, up the stairs and into her bedroom.

To Evie it was unbelievable. The perfect union. Even after that, George didn't leave her. He pulled her round gently so that she lay in the crook of his arm, his face touching hers. He kissed her forehead, her eyes, her nose, then raised his head and smiled at her.

'I love you, Evie Smith.'

'I love you, George Higgins,' Evie said, and knew that although it was the first time she had said it, even to herself, it was true.

'You do? Thank God for that.'

There was no point in telling George that she had been humiliated enough over the years by the shame of having three daughters and no husband. She had been able to bear the scorn when Ted had made regular visits, when she had thought that he loved her and she could dream of the day when he would be free to make her his wife. Now tongues could wag again. The brazenness of the man. A payment of two hundred pounds and not another penny in six years, and he had thought that she was ready and waiting to take him back.

'Evie!' George twitched her ear. 'You've gone away from me again. I'll not 'ave that, not now, not after you've just said you love me. Go on, say it again.'

'I love you, George.'

'That'll do for me, Evie,' he said gently. 'I'll look after you and the girls, all of you. We've a lot of talking to do, a lot of sorting out, but . . .' he grinned mischievously, 'all that can wait.'

She laughed as he released the hand she was holding and used it to lift her body so that it was closer to his.

'I don't only love you, Evie, I adore you. You're all I'll ever want.'

That was like balm to her soul. That was what she needed to be told.

Chapter Seven

'WILL WE LOOK FOR another house?' George asked as they sat in Evie's kitchen the next morning drinking coffee.

Evie considered, then shook her head. 'Maybe we should have that talk before we start making plans. I hate to bring it up, George, but you seem to know everything there is to know about me while I know nothing at all about you. Not even if you 'ave a family or where you live.'

He stared at her, and his eyebrows were drawn tightly in a deep frown. 'Evie, I've always kept my family life and my business life to meself. Business is business, and I suppose there aren't many that can say they don't have skeletons in the cupboard when it comes down to relations.' He hesitated, gnawing at his bottom lip, then said, 'You've a right to know if we are going to be married.'

'What?'

'You mean you didn't think my intentions were honourable? Well they are,' he added swiftly as she opened her mouth to protest. 'If I'm late in my proposal it's only because I 'ave so many matters that I 'ave to get sorted.'

'George, I never expected marriage, not with me 'aving the girls an' all.'

'Don't talk so daft, Evie. Of course we're going to get married. You an' me. That's if you'll 'ave me,' then without waiting for a reply he pressed on. 'I'll be a good 'usband to you, truly I will, an' a good father to the girls. I'll take good care of all of you. Evie, I've never proposed marriage to any woman before. Don't turn me down, please. You did say you loved me, didn't you?' He stopped, not knowing how to go on.

Evie laughed.

'Oh dammit!' he said fiercely, his face red with embarrassment. 'There's no need to laugh at me. If you don't want to wed me just say so.'

'I'm not laughing at you, George,' Evie said in a small voice. 'I just couldn't believe that you would want to take me on with three children.'

'But I do!' George moved in close, caught her in his arms and swung her up until her feet left the floor. 'I love you, Evie. I've watched you struggle to make ends meet, sorting out the problems that come one after the other, always coping on yer own, an' I've badly wanted to offer you financial 'elp for ages now, but you're such an independent bugger, an' I didn't want to frighten you off by interfering. Now just say yes, you will marry me, an' let's get it settled, please.'

She looked up into his dark brown eyes, usually laughing and cocksure, but now pleading, afraid of rejection. 'George, I'd love to marry you.'

His head came down. His lips covered hers, preventing her from saying any more. She clung to him, closing her eyes. For the first time a man had asked her to marry him. She was still young enough to make George a good wife, to love him and to be loved in return. George was offering her a way of life that she had never known. No more loneliness.

Evie picked up their coffee cups, took them to the sink

and washed them. She dried her hands and started to put the china away, then changed her mind. 'I'll make another cup of coffee.' As she poured milk into the saucepan she said over her shoulder, 'You don't have to tell me anything you don't want to, George.'

A flush came to George's face, and he fished in his pocket and brought out a cigar case. 'D'ye mind?' he asked gruffly.

'Not at all,' Evie said, trying not to sound surprised.

There was silence as he put a match to the end of the cigar; he didn't take it from his mouth until the end of it was glowing. 'I'd 'ave told you before but I didn't think you'd understand.'

'What you're gonna tell me, 'as it got anything to do with the fact that I don't see you for days on end?' The question was out before she could stop herself.

Taken off guard, he gaped at her for a brief moment before recovering himself. 'Yeah, in a way.' Then very quietly he said, 'My sister committed suicide, and her death turned my mother's brain. She's still in a home today.'

There was a hissing sound as the milk boiled over the top of the pan. Evie jumped to her feet, resting a hand on his shoulder as she passed him. She put two fresh cups of coffee down on the table, added a spoonful of sugar to one, stirred the coffee and pushed it towards George. 'D'you want to start at the beginning? I'm a good listener,' Evie appealed to him, hoping that he hadn't clammed up.

'Yes, that would be best,' George said, then with a change of tone, he began.

'I was born in the East End of London. I own two factories there, though I don't 'ave to worry. They're managed by men that I trust. I have a one-bedroomed flat in Monkton Mansions, which looks out onto the Thames, and I have more than enough money to enable me to live a good life. Until I met you Evie, I wasn't happy. I used people.'

'I don't believe that,' Evie interrupted without thinking.

George scowled and said sharply, 'I'm nothing like you think I am.' Then he dragged hard on his cigar before saying, 'Just listen, Evie.'

'Sorry,' she muttered.

'It was great when I was growing up. There was just my sister, Glenda, three years older than me, an' me mum an' dad. Dad was a docker, which made us a darn sight better off than a good many of the families that lived in that area. Mind you, me dad took too many chances, an' many a time me mum's 'ad to face up to the police knocking on our front door. Not that he ever got caught but, Christ, looking back, there's many a time when he came a damn sight too near it for comfort. Me an' Glenda were still kids at school when a crane that was unloading a ship on the quayside struck me dad. He was dead when they got 'im to the hospital.' He dropped his head, staring at his clenched hands, and stopped talking.

Evie eyed him thoughtfully but decided to remain silent.

Taking a deep breath, he began again. 'We didn't manage too badly. I was fourteen when I left school, an' I started to learn the tailoring trade. It was Issy Solomon that gave me my first chance. When war was declared I was nineteen and I got myself into the merchant navy. Me sister got taken on at Woolwich Arsenal and stayed 'ome with our mum.'

Here, George sighed deeply and stirred his coffee with such vengeance that Evie thought the cup might break. She put her hand out towards him. He smiled weakly, saying, 'I'm all right.' Then, after sipping his coffee he went on.

'Glenda met a Yank. Her letters to me were full of him. Next me mother knows is Glenda's pregnant. Apparently all the neighbours rallied round, like they used to in the East End. Everyone chipped in an', war or no war, there was gonna be one 'ell of a wedding. That is until me mother opened the door to find an American officer standing on 'er doorstep. Glenda wasn't gonna be no GI bride: the bloke 'ad a wife an' two kids back in the States. It was more than our Glenda could take. When she was in the house on her own she put her head in the gas oven. It were me mum that found her.' George gave a short grim laugh. 'When I got 'ome on leave my mother was in an awful place – a mental hospital. That's about it.'

Evie's coffee had gone cold, and the kitchen was filled with the scent of George's cigar. She didn't know what to say.

Suddenly George lunged forward as though he was going to throw himself across the table at her. 'Well, so now will you still 'ave me?'

'George!' The word was torn from Evie's throat and her eyes were brimming with tears. She got up and went to place her arms around his neck. 'George, it makes not a scrap of difference to us. It all happened a long time ago. No sense in brooding over the past and worrying about what you cannot change.'

He jerked around to face her. 'Evie, there is still me mother.' He had his emotions under control again. 'She's in a good private home now, on the Isle of Dogs, among people who care for her, not that she knows where she is or even who she is some days. Another time I'll phone an' they'll tell me she's as right as ninepence. That's when I clear off and stay near to the home for a few days.' His eyes misted over and, in an entirely different voice, he murmured quietly, 'It's great when she knows me. She calls me Georgie.'

Having whispered that, George wavered. Evie watched in horror as this tough, cocky, hard man broke up.

'George dear, don't. Please don't cry,' she whispered, kissing his wet cheeks. In response his arms went about her and he held her as if he would never let her go. Evie clung to him, and only the sound of the clock ticking could be heard in her kitchen.

When they finally broke apart they were both smiling. George leant down and touched her cheek, smoothing away the wetness left by her own tears. His eyes were brighter now as he looked down at her. 'Tell me again you love me, Evie.'

'I love you, George,' she said, her voice sounding shaky, and he laughed.

'I love you too, Evie, and I promise you, my luv, that from now on we'll 'ave no more secrets from each other. Everything will be all right now for the rest of our lives.'

Flossie accepted the news that her Evie and George Higgins were to marry with a lot less fuss than Evie had expected. Jim Tyler already knew about George's mother, and George had insisted that Evie tell Flossie.

'He can't be all bad, not if he's made 'imself responsible for 'is mother. Seems to me that a lad that not only forks out for 'er to be in a private 'ome but spends a good deal of time with 'er as well is a damn good son.' That was Flossie's reaction, much to Evie's delight.

And within a week or two of hearing about their plans for a summer wedding, Joan Killick was telling Evie that they'd go together round all the shops when it came to deciding what she was going to wear.

'Evie,' Jim Tyler said nervously, the first chance he got to speak to Evie on her own, 'wouldn't it be better if you waited till you knew a whole lot more about George, especially 'ow he earns 'is living?'

'It's all right, Uncle Jim. George 'as told me all I need t'know. I trust 'im, an' he trusts me.'

'Ah well, if you say so, luv,' Jim answered, smiling, letting her see just how much he loved her and that he still thought of her as a young girl. 'Being yer mother's daughter, I know 'ow stubborn you can be. Just remember I'm always around if an' when ye need me.'

'Uncle Jim, you've always been there for me an' my kids. I don't know why me mum hasn't roped you in a long time ago.'

He threw up his hands in mock horror and they both laughed, then Evie took hold of his hand and said, 'It'll work out for me in the end, you'll see.'

'Well, nobody deserves a bit of 'appiness an' security more than you do, my luv,' he told her.

Evie turned to look straight into his brown eyes and for the first time she realised just how much her future and that of her three girls mattered to this man whom she had taken for granted throughout her life. Her voice was calm but full of feeling as she kept hold of his hand and said, 'Of course we could make this a double wedding, Uncle Jim.'

Never again would Evie and the man that she called her uncle be as close as they were in that moment. 'Try saying that to yer mother,' he insisted quietly.

And Evie found herself thinking that that wasn't such a bad idea at all.

At Christmas, Ted Hopkins wrote a letter to each of his eldest daughters, completely ignoring young Rosie. Evie held her breath, dreading their reaction. Jenny was pleased, guarding her letter, not showing it to anyone. She did, however, almost drive her mother and her nanna out of their minds chattering on about her father and his big house by the seaside. Her questions were endless. But the novelty soon wore off and after just one more letter her father's writing stopped.

Catherine's reaction was different. She flung the two pages of writing down onto the table, saying, 'Why does he suddenly want to know me? Why now? He's never bothered about me before.'

Evie knew that feeling so well. 'Good question, Catherine, but he is your father. What does he 'ave to say?'

'Wants me to meet him. You read it, Mum.'

Evie read the letter with a feeling of amazement. Ted hadn't altered. Not one scrap. He wanted his eldest daughter to meet him on Balham station. It wasn't as if he had told her he was making a special journey because he so very much would like to see her. Oh no! He was coming down to Twickenham to see a rugby match. Did he have to tell Catherine that? His party were coming by coach, travelling during Friday night. He would be in London early on Saturday morning and would get the tube down to Balham. Would Catherine meet him there?

Couldn't he have at least wrapped it up a bit? Made his eldest daughter feel as if this meeting was of great importance to him, instead of just slotting her in between his arrival and an all-important rugby match.

Evie paused and took a deep breath before turning to face Catherine. 'It's nice he wants to see you, isn't it?'

Catherine picked up her letter, slowly folded it and placed it back into the envelope before she replied truthfully, 'I haven't made up my mind whether or not I'm going to meet him.'

'Aw, Catherine. You don't need me to tell you he's a selfish man. Always concerned with what is best for him, never giving a thought to you or your sisters . . . God knows I could go on, but this much I will say for him, if he loved any one of you girls, it was you Catherine. You were our first-born and, if I'm truthful, I'd 'ave to say that when you were born I do believe that we both thought there was a life for us together. Don't be bitter, luv. I've tried not to be over the years. Go see him. You'll only be sorry for ever more if you don't.'

There was silence between them for a moment, and then, her voice very low, Catherine said, 'All right, Mum, I'll go.'

The day had dragged. Usually Saturday was a busy day for Evie. Having done her shopping in the morning, she had watched her daughter take pains with her appearance and when she had asked, 'Will you be all right on your own?' she had been rewarded with a cheerful smile and wise words.

'Mum, I'm not a baby. I'm grown up now, and it is my father that I'm going to see, not some stranger.'

Might just as well be a stranger for all that you know about him, was what Evie was thinking as she watched her daughter walk away down the street.

The time now was almost five o'clock. *Do something – knit, sew or read a book, but for God's sake stop pacing back and forth to the front door,* Evie chided herself. *Perhaps Ted decided not to go to Twickenham, has taken Catherine out somewhere for the afternoon. Oh I hope so. That girl needed a break. Wouldn't it be nice if her father showed her that she really did matter to him and that it was only unfortunate circumstances that had prevented him from seeing her all these years?*

Rosie had never ever set eyes on her father, and what she'd never had she couldn't miss. Jenny was a whippy, bouncy girl, taking things as they came. She had never been the only one when her father had been around, not as Catherine had been in those early years, and if the truth be told, Catherine had suffered the loss of Ted much more than she had ever let on.

Oh she's back.

Catherine had just opened the front door. Evie came hurrying towards her, making an attempt at lightness by saying, 'Everything go well, did it? I bet yer father was over the moon to see you. Did he think you were a beautiful young lady, all grown up?'

But Catherine made no reply. She went past her mum to the foot of the stairs, and even with the distance of the passageway between them the hurt was evident in her eyes. 'He didn't turn up.'

It seemed ages before Catherine turned and went up the stairs, and as she did so Evie had to smother a sob. She didn't make any reply because she couldn't think of anything to say, and her thoughts would have frightened her daughter had she had the courage to utter them aloud.

It was five days later when a second letter arrived for Catherine bearing the Blackpool postmark.

Evie watched Catherine as she opened the envelope and read the contents. Evie's heart was thumping against her ribs and her temper was rising fast. *Strikes me we were a damn sight better off when his wife was alive. At least he left us alone then and we knew where we were.*

'Aw, well, that's settled.' Catherine crumpled the paper into a tight ball and threw it down onto the table.

'The coach was late. They were only just in time to see the match.' Her voice showed her distress, and Evie's heart ached for Catherine as she stood and watched her have second thoughts. With quick movements Catherine smoothed out the letter, placed it back into the envelope and resealed the envelope by using a smear of condensed milk to make the flap stick. Then, with bold strokes and using capital letters, she wrote on it, NOT WANTED AT THIS ADDRESS.

Evie lowered her head, closed her eyes and sighed as she heard her daughter say, 'I'm just going to pop this in the post, Mum.'

A short while later, sitting opposite Catherine with a steamy cup of coffee in front of each of them, Evie said, 'Aren't you going to give him another chance?'

'What would be the point, Mum?'

'Well he did say he wanted to see you.'

'Didn't make much of an effort, did he?'

'Not if you look at it that way. I don't suppose he did.'

'No. But I made the effort, and he found he had better things to do. Like he always did have when his wife was alive. He only wants us now because he probably has no one else.'

'You're all het up, aren't you? Take yer time. Think about it and then you can write to him. That would be best.'

'Mum, will you leave it out? Please. As I said, I made the effort, he rejected it. For me, that's the end of the matter. I wouldn't go to the corner of the street to see him now. I'm only glad that Jenny didn't come with me. She's forgotten all about him and I'm going to do the same.'

To Evie's great relief, Catherine was offered a job, starting the week before Easter, at Butlins Holiday Camp at Clacton. The day that Catherine went to London for the interview, Evie felt she had never prayed so hard in her life before. If the answer had been no, there would have been no living with that girl. Ever since she'd worked in Balham Woolworth's there had been tension between them. The way Ted had treated her hadn't helped. Fancy letting your daughter know that she came second to a rugby match. Selfish sod!

There was tension in the Killick house across the road all right. Naturally, Shirley, Catherine's constant companion, had also wanted to apply for what must have seemed to young girls a glamorous job. Bert Killick had put his foot down firmly.

'No daughter of mine is going traipsing off to work an''

sleep with a load of youngsters that we know nothing about an' won't be there to keep our eyes on. And I don't wanna 'ear another word on the bleedin' subject.'

Joan had reported it word for word to Evie, saying, 'I wish t'God he would let 'er go. One less t'worry about.'

Easter arrived, nice and sunny but still quite cold. Evie was surprised how much she missed Catherine and how much quieter and tidier the whole house was without her. She prayed every night that God would keep Catherine safe and that she would be happy in her new job. She also prayed that she had seen the last of Ted Hopkins.

It had been agreed that Flossie, with Jim to keep her company, would stay at home on Easter Monday while George took Evie, Jenny and Rosie on a river trip from Richmond to Windsor, Flossie promising to have a hot meal ready for them when they returned in the evening.

Although Evie had lived only a short distance from the Thames all her life, this was her first trip on the river, and she was as excited as her two girls with the sights and smells and all the people dressed in their Sunday best.

George watched with amusement as they ran along the deck, leaning over the rails, gazing back at the foaming white wake the steamer was leaving behind. He also felt very proud as he noticed Evie clutching Rosie's small hand, while holding her hat on her head with her other hand. He marvelled at the way this beautiful girl and her daughters had brightened up his life since they had come into it. They had given him a reason for living. They all looked so well turned out. Jenny was now a teenager, having had her thirteenth birthday, and was as pretty a girl as you would find anywhere, with glossy brown hair and large, expressive eyes. Rosie still had her head of fair baby curls, though she was coming up to being six years old. Each of them wore the coat that he had bought for them at Christmas, but the dresses they wore beneath had been made by their nanna, and the embroidery on the collars had been skilfully worked by their mother. He was so pleased that neither of the girls had been opposed to the fact that he and their mother were to marry. Quite the opposite. They had always been at ease in his company, now they seemed to welcome him. This morning they had twisted and turned, asking if they were dressed to his satisfaction

'They're just fishing for compliments,' Evie had called out as he had murmured his approval.

'You're like a child yourself, Evie,' George told her as she came tearing up to him. 'Your eyes are popping out of your head.'

'Well it's a wonderful day,' she retorted, 'and one of the stewards has just told us that a piano is going to be played soon.'

'Yes, an' we're gonna sing, aren't we, Mummy?' Rosie was beaming, and neither George nor Evie could have denied her anything.

'How about we go and buy an ice cream before the music starts?' George dropped to his knees in front of Rosie as he asked the question, and when she smiled her reply he gathered her up into his arms and led the way.

Evie smiled. Her heart was speaking to her today, not her head. If she hadn't loved George before, she certainly did now. Laughing, teasing George, making love to her. Serious, thoughtful George, telling her to trust him and that he would never let her down. George being a father! Something Rosie had never known. In Rosie's short life there had been her uncle Jim, and Bert Killick had always gone out of his way to treat her as one of his own, bringing her home sweets and little treats, but that wasn't anywhere near enough. No man had ever tucked Rosie into bed, kissed her goodnight and assured her that he would still be there in the morning. Now all that was going to change. She was going to become a married woman. George would be there to talk to, to share her life and that of her girls. She wouldn't have to deal with any problem on her own in future. She and George were going to face life together from now on.

The girls were sitting on the grass, drinking a bottle of lemonade through a straw. Evie and George were watching them from inside the car.

'Have you enjoyed today?' George asked.

'More than I can tell you.' Then Evie giggled. 'The company makes a difference, doesn't it?'

'All the difference in the world,' George agreed, taking a small box from his pocket. 'This is for you, my darling, to make it official.'

Inside the box, a gold ring with a band of diamonds was clasped in blue velvet.

'Oh George, it's beautiful!' Then she cried nervously as she lifted the ring from its box, 'It must 'ave cost you a fortune! I won't be able to wear it! What will people say?'

George threw back his head and roared with laughter. 'Evie! Can't wear it? I've never 'eard such nonsense. You're worth a thousand times over what I paid for that ring, and the day I see it missing from your finger is the day that I'll wanna know the reason why. This ring is to show the world that you belong to me and that very soon everyone will know that you are Mrs George Higgins.' Strong though his fingers were, they were also nimble enough to slip the ring onto her finger. 'There. I chose diamonds because they are forever, and so will we be.' His lips came down on hers, softly and gently, but his arms were strong about her. 'I can't wait for us to be married,' he whispered before releasing her. 'Better get the girls in the car and be setting off for home, but one thing I want made clear is that we finalise things this week, set the date. This waiting will drive me mad.'

Everything was settled. They were to be married at Wandsworth Town Hall on Whitsun Saturday. The only thing troubling Evie was the fact that she had received only one postcard from Catherine since she had left home.

'At least you know that she arrived safely and 'as settled in,' George said, doing his best to reassure Evie.

'But I've written to her twice an' she hasn't answered. I bet she won't be bothered to come 'ome for our wedding.'

'Leave it out,' Flossie cried as she cut into the large fruit cake she had made that morning. 'I miss that girl as much as you do, especially like today, when we're all gathered for our Sunday tea. What we've all got to remember is that Catherine 'as her own life to lead now. She's working, not on 'oliday. Don't suppose she gets a lot of time.'

When Evie made no reply, Jim got in quickly. 'Tell ye what luv, 'ow about we all think of booking ourselves in to the camp, later on in the year like, when the season there quietens down a bit. You'd like that, wouldn't you, Rosie?'

Rosie yelled her delight.

Evie kept her thoughts to herself, although she did smile at Jim. She wasn't at all sure that Cathy would think it wonderful if the whole family turned up *en masse*. For all they knew it might queer Catherine's pitch with the young men. And that was one thing she'd lay her bottom dollar on: Cathy was playing the field where the boys were concerned. She had a sudden thought. Later on, after the wedding, she'd get George to run her down to Clacton. Just the two of them. Just a quick look around to satisfy herself that Catherine really was all right.

★

Ten o'clock one morning saw Flossie, Evie and Joan Killick climb the stairs of an 88 bus which would take them up to Oxford Street. With George's diamond ring glistening on her finger, Evie clutched her handbag firmly, her mind already buzzing at the thought of all they were going to buy today.

They got off the bus at Oxford Circus and barged into the first large department store they came to.

Three hours later they had worked their way through Bourne & Hollingsworth, Selfridges and several shoe shops. They had stared long and hard at the wonderful window displays of Marshall & Snellgrove but decided that store was too upper class for them. They were now standing outside C & A at Marble Arch.

'Oh no,' Flossie pleaded. 'For goodness' sake let's go an' find somewhere to sit down an' 'ave a cup of tea.'

Joan and Evie, both laden with bags, giggled. They had had a whale of a time.

'All right, Mum. I'll treat ye to lunch. We've only got the hats to get anyway.'

The restaurant was quite busy when they trooped in, but a kindly waitress added a third chair to a table set for two, and they all sat down gratefully.

'I'll get you a menu to be looking at, madam, while I lay another place.'

Evie thought she was too excited to be hungry, but the smells were most appetising and soon they were all enjoying a full meal. They didn't talk while they were eating; each was busy with her own thoughts.

For her marriage, Evie had chosen a cream dress with a fashionably long loose-fitting coat to match. The material was a very fine wool. She had bought a plain bronze-coloured scarf to drape around her neck and had been lucky enough to find a pair of high-heeled court shoes that were almost the same colour as the scarf. She hoped she would be lucky when it came to choosing a hat. Couldn't have a wedding without the ladies wearing hats.

Finding her mother's outfit had proved a difficult task, with Flossie gasping at the prices even though Evie kept assuring her that George had given her plenty of money to spend. In the end, Flossie had settled for a pale blue georgette dress with a high neck and long sleeves, gently draped across the bodice and falling in a flared skirt to mid-calf length. The colour suited her mother, and the new length gave her a bit of height as did the soft cream-coloured kid shoes that she had chosen mainly because the assistant had selected gloves and a handbag that matched perfectly and completed the outfit.

Joan had been the thrifty one, although she had insisted that Bert had given her ample funds and told her to treat herself for once.

'You have lovely hair, madam,' the assistant had said, gazing at Joan's ginger locks. 'An emerald green blouse would set that suit off marvellously.'

So Joan had decided. A navy blue classic tailored suit with a straight skirt and boxy jacket and the silk blouse, items that she would be able to wear for a long time to come. Teamed with a navy handbag and plain navy court shoes, Evie thought how smart her friend would look.

They spent almost another hour in C & A's trying on hats, pulling faces at each other and bursting out laughing at their reflections in the mirror. Wonderful! They each had a hat! Joan's was an emerald green wide-brimmed straw hat that picked up the colour of her new blouse – marvellous for a wedding but impractical for almost anything else. Flossie's was perfect – a soft cream cloche that could have been made for her. Evie's was a bride's dream come true – a bronze silk hat with a mass of veiling which George would raise when the registrar declared them to be man and wife and announced that George was allowed to kiss the bride.

They didn't bother to climb the stairs of the bus going home. They sat quietly on the lower deck, staring out of the window, happy but dog-tired.

They said their goodbyes to Joan at her gate and made their way across the road to Flossie's house.

Jim was buttering bread, Jenny was laying cups and saucers out on a tray, while Rosie was fetching things from the larder.

'Oh you are good girls,' their nanna cried. 'Just what the doctor ordered – a really good cup of tea.'

'Were you here when they got 'ome from school, Uncle Jim?' Evie asked as she took off her coat.

'Yeah, course I was. I said I would be, didn't I?'

'Thanks. You're an old darling, you know that, don't you?'

'Yeah, an' you're full of flannel. Sit yerself down. I thought we'd 'ave toast an' jam, cake an' suchlike, just for now. I'll get us all fish an' chips later on. Bet neither of you two feels like cooking tonight, d'you?'

'You're a life-saver, me darling,' Flossie told Jenny as she placed a cup of tea down in front of her.

'I'll put the news on,' Jim said getting to his feet and going to the television. 'No good going to the fish shop yet. They sell all the stale stuff left from lunch time first.'

They were only half listening when the announcer said, 'Firemen are this evening still at the scene of the tragic fire that started at lunch time in a nursing home on the Isle of Dogs.'

The words 'nursing home' and the mention of the Isle of Dogs had stabbed into their minds. They looked at each other, the colour already draining from Evie's face.

The voice droned on. 'There have been three deaths

recorded so far, including that of a man who was visiting his mother in the home when the fire broke out. It is understood that the man, who has not so far been named, carried his mother and one other patient to safety before going back into the burning building. The staircase is said to have collapsed, trapping the man. He was dead when the firemen got to him.'

The face of the announcer started to slide from one side of the television screen to the other. His voice grew quieter as the buzzing in Evie's head grew louder and she slid from her chair to the floor.

Truth is stranger than fiction, so they say, but this was too much! Flossie was wiping Evie's face with a wet flannel as she tried to tell herself to stay calm, if only for the sake of the girls, who were clamouring to know what was wrong.

'It's just a coincidence, tell me it is, Jim,' Flossie pleaded as she wrung the flannel out so tight the cloth ripped.

'Who knows?' Jim whispered, trying to convince himself that such a thing just couldn't have happened in so short a time.

Evie struggled to sit up.

'Mummy, what's the matter?' Tears were streaming down Rosie's face, and Jenny was as white as a sheet.

Much later Jim went out to fetch an evening paper. 'Man Dies Saving His Mother' was the headline.

Somehow Evie got back to her own house, leaving the girls with their nanna and Uncle Jim. Her bedroom was cold. It would never feel warm again. She and George were going to be together for the rest of their lives, only he hadn't got any life left now, had he? She'd thought she was never going to be lonely again, but she was already lonely – more lonely than she had ever been in her life before. And it wasn't going to get any better. It would always be like this from now on. She twisted her engagement ring that George had placed on her finger and her whole body shook with the shock that she would never see him again. He was gone. All she had was the memory. Only the memory of his kindness, his generosity, his kisses and caresses, his urgent lovemaking and that wonderful day trip on the river when he had said that diamonds were forever and so were they. Only now they weren't. It was only her, on her own as always.

She stood staring out of the window for hours, seeing nothing. The paper said he was a hero. Much good that would do him. 'He's dead,' she cried out loud. Then she got mad. She couldn't pretend that she was glad that he had saved his mother's life. Nor the other woman's life. Two for the price of George. It was a heavy payment. They were old women. They had had their lives. If the truth be told, it would have been a happy release if Mrs Higgins had died in that fire.

Evie stormed across the room and back again. 'George was going to marry me. The first man who had ever considered me good enough to make his wife. I've had no life. I'm still young, but I won't be for much longer. Oh why did George have to make all those promises?' She heard herself going on, ranting and raving. 'Why did it have to be him? Why not his sick old mother?'

Evie's face was red, her eyes swollen and her hair a complete mess by the time she finally flung herself down onto the bed. At last she fell into a deep sleep and woke again as the light came creeping through the window in the early hours of the morning to find that she was still fully dressed and her pillow was soaked with tears that she hadn't realised she had shed.

Chapter Eight

FLOSSIE BROUGHT THE PILE of shopping bags down to Evie's house soon after ten o'clock the following morning.

'Leave them all at the bottom of the stairs. I'll see to them later,' Evie said quietly. She had washed her face, brushed her hair and dragged it into a bun at the back of her head.

She would hang the dress and coat at the back of her wardrobe and cover them with a clean sheet. There might come a time when she'd be able to bring herself to wear them, and perhaps the shoes. The hat, never! She never wanted to see the hat again. There would be nobody to lift the veil and kiss her lips.

Joan arrived, bringing a bag of hot bread rolls with her. 'I didn't think you'd have had any breakfast yet.'

It was Flossie who murmured, 'Thanks.' Her face was sombre.

Evie's face was colourless, and Joan had to sniff hard to stop the tears from falling. 'It doesn't make sense. It's just not fair.'

'No, Joan, it's not fair,' Evie said very quietly. In the long hours since she had woken up she had decided that there was no point in going on about it. She had the girls to see to. Though how she was going to show a brave face to them and to the rest of the world, she had no idea. One day at a time was the only way she might just survive, and God knows she'd need a lot more strength, even for that, than she had at the moment.

If it hadn't been for Jim, Evie wouldn't have known where the funeral was to be held. She wasn't a relative and despite the plans they had made nobody had contacted her.

In the church, which was in the borough of Stepney, she watched dry eyed as George was carried past her in his coffin. What was it they said? 'It's better to have loved and lost than never to have loved at all.' Well that wasn't at all the way she was feeling right now. *I miss him,* she said to herself, *and if I live another fifty years I shall still miss him*. The pews were overflowing and she looked around among the crowd of mourners for a friendly face, but she didn't see one.

The greatest ordeal came when she had to leave the church and shake hands with two elegantly attired gentlemen whom she had never set eyes on before. George wouldn't have had this. He would have shouted from the rooftops: 'This is my Evie. She is going to be my wife.' As she stepped out from the church porch onto the gravel driveway outside, she would have fallen had it not been for Jim.

'Steady,' he whispered, 'it's all over now.'

Jim had been a tower of strength. He wouldn't hear of her coming up to the East End on her own for the funeral, and at this moment she was grateful that he had been so insistent. Evie gripped his arm, let her breath out in a long shaky sigh of relief and said, 'Take me home please, Jim.'

*

Evie was glad when dawn broke. She had tossed and turned all night. She laid the table, prepared the breakfast and set out clean clothes for Jenny and Rosie to wear to school. Then she made a pot of tea and took the whole tray upstairs.

'Wakey, wakey,' she called, kicking open the door to the twin-bedded room that the girls shared. 'Who wants a cuppa?'

They propped themselves up, Jenny still quiet, Rosie bright as a button. She kept telling herself that they were young, that they would soon forget George, but the anxiety was still there for these two youngsters, especially so for Jenny. With her it was more than a niggling unease that bothered Evie.

There was still no word from Catherine, though to be honest Evie hadn't written to tell her of George's death. It probably wouldn't have made much difference if she had done.

Rosie had drunk her tea, slipped out of bed and was already washing herself in the bathroom. Evie sat down on the edge of the bed and said in a rush of words, 'Jenny, how would you like to 'ave your own room? We can redecorate what was Cathy's room. You can pick the colour scheme. You might as well as leave it standing there not being used.'

In a quick, graceful movement, Jenny was up on her knees. 'Oh Mum, d'you mean it? I was going to ask you but then . . .' Her voice broke and Evie held her tightly as she cried her eyes out.

For the next two weeks Evie worked every hour of the day. Jenny and Rosie were rarely out of her thoughts. She felt so sorry for the pair of them. They too had been promised so much that would not now materialise. She wouldn't make fish of one and fowl of the other, so she set to work and scraped the old wallpaper off both bedrooms. Come Saturday, she had taken them both to Brixton. They had made a great game of choosing wallpaper and paint, not to mention pretty little shades for their bedside lamps. It had made a change for her. 'I feel so lonely in that house now,' she told her mother. 'I can't 'elp thinking that George would 'ave moved in with me by now.'

Flossie was at her wits' end to know what to do about Evie. She looked older, more withdrawn, and frown lines seemed to have settled between her brows.

'Let me see, let me see!' Rosie shrieked impatiently.

'Yeah, come on, Mum. Get out of the way an' let us open the doors.'

Not in from school five minutes, they were demanding that Evie revealed the surprise that she had promised them that morning.

'Close your eyes. No peeping, Rosie, and come right up onto the landing – I don't want you falling backwards down the stairs.'

Quietly she opened the door to first one room and then the second room, stood back, flung her arms wide and said, 'Young ladies, you may enter.'

'Cor, it's so pretty.' Rosie was darting from side to side fingering her very first tiny teddy bear, one arm of which Evie had sewn back on. Beside it on a new wall shelf sat two more brown teddy bears. They each had new patchwork trousers and blue cotton shirts. Her grey furry stuffed cat, with its long tail well brushed, lay on the hearth. The second bed, now no longer needed, she had pushed against the wall, removing the headboard and turning it into a divan. The cover had been difficult. Flossie had given her the material, but it had been too thick for Evie's sewing machine and she had had to sew it all by hand. It did look good though, she admitted to herself. Box pleats fell to the floor, covering the ugly legs of the bedstead. Along the back, leaning against the wall, were five brightly coloured cushions that she had made from remnants. Never mind that not one of the fronts of the cushion covers matched the reverse. Rosie could turn them round when she tired of the colours.

'My own desk!' Rosie screamed, straightening the piles of storybooks that lay on the top. The base of an old mangle had been put to good use, thanks to their uncle Jim and all his efforts. A kitchen chair, painted pale pink to match the woodwork of the room, slotted between the iron legs of the mangle.

'I'll be able to do my drawings up here.' Rosie sounded really chuffed.

'I'm just going to see what Jenny thinks of her room,' Evie called to Rosie. Her voice shook, and she put her hand to her mouth for a moment, letting the diamonds on the engagement ring George had given her push hard against her lips. *I've got to go on, be the best mother I can. I've got to, for their sakes.*

Without saying a word, Evie stood in the doorway and watched Jenny. She was obviously thrilled with the lovely bedroom that she now had all to herself. On the top of the tall chest of drawers Evie had arranged bottles of scented bath salts, an oval mirror on a stand, a jar of Pond's face cream and a box of tinted face powder.

Across the bed she had spread a new nightdress that Flossie had made for Jenny, peach-coloured cotton with white ribbons and lace at the neck and at the edge of the long sleeves. Fluffy mules peeped from beneath the bed. These were a present from Uncle Jim.

Jenny's eyes were wide with astonishment, and that was enough thanks for Evie. She crept quietly to the head of the stairs and made her way down. It was as well that she had the girls to keep her occupied, otherwise there was no telling what might have become of her.

The days lengthened and summer came, and Jim Tyler did two things that would endear him to Evie for the rest of her life.

Chetwode Road was never silent, especially not on a Saturday morning. Evie stood at her gate, a frown of bewilderment on her face. Norma Killick had come over quite early to see if Jenny and Rosie were ready to go to the morning pictures. She had seen them off, put on her coat and gone down to her mother's house, ready to go shopping as usual. Most Saturdays they caught the 49 bus to Clapham Junction, getting off at Northcote Road where the street was lined with stalls and barrows, making an open-air market. This morning she couldn't get into her mother's house. There was no answer to her knocking, and the biggest mystery of all was that the front door was locked. Evie was beginning to feel afraid. This wasn't like Flossie at all. She never went anywhere without telling her first. The traffic at the corner of the road was noisy, the buses frequent, and the pavement was thronged with people. But not a sign of her mother. She was just about to turn and go back indoors when the sound of a car horn made her look back. A taxi was coming down the street, slowing down, pulling into the kerb.

The taxi driver grinned at Evie. 'Got a surprise for you, me luv.' He jumped out, came round and stood on the pavement, and with a flourish he opened the door to his cab.

Evie couldn't believe her eyes. Her mouth gaped open. She looked, and looked again. Her mum looked so breathtakingly beautiful that for a moment she couldn't speak. She was wearing an apricot-coloured dress that was embroidered with tiny seed pearls and around her shoulders a creamy lace stole was draped. Her hair had been professionally tinted and set. It looked much softer, no longer the harsh blonde it had been.

Jim Tyler stepped out first, and his appearance was enough to make Evie gape even more. He looked handsome in a dark blue suit, with a crisp white shirt and striped blue tie, and a white carnation in his buttonhole. His eyes were bright and full of laughter. This kind man always seemed full of energy, full of strength that belied his fifty-eight years.

Jim smiled at Evie, made a showy gesture with his outstretched arm and said, 'Allow me to present to you Mrs Tyler, my wife.'

'Oh Mum.' Evie covered the distance between them, almost knocking Flossie off her feet. The two of them stood there, locked in each other's arms. It was an emotional moment.

'Hey, hey, what about me?'

Evie turned and, with tears streaming down her face, she said, 'Oh Jim. I'm so happy for you both. You sly old bugger. Not a word! Why couldn't I be there?'

'Let's get indoors,' Flossie insisted.

'Coming in for a drink, mate?' Jim called to the taxi driver.

'Not now, Jim. But you stay sober. Me an' a few of the boys will be along later on tonight. Can't let a day like this pass without tapping a barrel. See ye,' he yelled as he turned the black cab full circle and drove off back up Chetwode Road.

Evie didn't need to ask why. She knew full well. Her mother had planned it this way rather than have Evie standing in Wandsworth Town Hall wondering why this hadn't happened to her and George. She guessed that her mother hadn't worn the blue dress that they had chosen for Evie's wedding day for the same reason.

'You're happy about this, aren't you, luv?' Flossie asked

as soon as the front door closed behind them.

'Oh Mum! As if you 'ave t'ask. It's been my dearest wish for ages.'

'You're sure? I need your approval but I hadn't got the guts to ask.'

'Oh, Mum.' Evie put her hands on her shoulders and stooped to kiss her on both cheeks. 'I couldn't be more pleased. Honestly, I've always loved Jim, ever since I can remember. The only thing that puzzles me is why the pair of you didn't get married years ago.'

'Wasn't Jim's fault. It were mine. He were what I always thought of as a kind man. To be honest, when I was younger I found him boring. He had both feet planted safely on the ground. Never wanted to do anything exciting. Pity you can't put old heads on young shoulders, cos if you could, I'd 'ave grabbed Jim the minute I set eyes on him.' Flossie paused to push a loose hair out of her face and to take hold of Evie's hand. 'I'm sorry, luv.'

'Mum, whatever 'ave you got to be sorry for? It's a great day.'

'I don't mean that. It's the past. Things that I let 'appen years ago that I regret now.'

'As you're always telling me, Mum, we all make mistakes.'

'Yeah. Me more than most. Jim was always there, even when yer father was around. Helped him out many a time even though he knew darn well that he was a rotten husband and a rotten father to you. And Jim was there to pick me up and dust me off more times than I care to tell you about. I didn't appreciate his worth then. Too busy out dancing, drinking, 'aving what then seemed to me like a good time. All those uncles, as you used to call them. I flaunted them and meself in front of the neighbours, more for devilment than anything else, but I can say, with me 'and on me 'eart, I was never on the game, Evie. Never that. I wasn't a floozie. Picked a few wrong 'uns but that's as far as it went.'

'Will you stop it, Mum? You have nothing whatsoever to reproach yourself for. You've been marvellous to me, the best mum possible. And as for my girls, well, you don't need any telling they think there is no one else in the world like you.'

'Well, it's been some time now since I came to me senses and began to realise Jim's true worth. Then I thought it was too late. I'd missed me chance. I wasn't going to make the first move.'

Despite herself, despite everything, Evie started to laugh. 'Oh you complete pair of idiots! Didn't you know that Jim would have laid down his life for you? At least now I can be happy for the both of you. I think it's great.'

'Thanks, Evie. With things being the way they are, we both figured it doesn't do to keep putting things off.' Her words were casual, but the look in her eyes was gentle and loving.

'I won't be a minute, Mum. I 'ave to go to the toilet.' Evie turned and almost flew up the stairs. She locked the door and stuffed her fist into her mouth, trying hard to stop the tears that were stinging her eyelids from falling. *Please God, don't let me spoil their day. Don't let me be hateful. Don't let me show how jealous I am.* George no longer existed in her life. George was dead. But seeing her mum and Jim as bride and groom had only reminded her of what she had lost. She fell to her knees, wiping hard at her eyes with a length of toilet paper torn from the roll. She would be happy for them.

From the toilet, she went into the bathroom and washed her hands, splashing cold water up over her face. As she walked down the stairs to spend a day with people that she loved dearly she felt very much alone.

*

'Why Mum, that's marvellous,' Evie cried in amazement

as she stood with her two girls and surveyed the wedding breakfast that was set out in the front room of Flossie's house, a two-tier wedding cake on a huge silver stand being the centrepiece.

'That's why me 'ouse was locked this morning, cos Jim an' 'is mates 'ad set the trestle tables up last night, and the reason I told you t'put yer glad rags on and not come down till Jenny an' Rosie were back was because the caterers were setting out all the food.'

Just a dozen of them sat down to eat, their own family of five, Joan and Bert Killick with Shirley and Norma, Flossie's friend Pat, who lived in Brighton but who used to live in Balham, and Fred and Jack, two men who worked for Jim. Since it was no longer illegal to place a bet off the racecourse, Jim, with Flossie's blessing, had opened his own betting shop in Trinity Road.

The meal was finished, speeches all made and now a bar was being set up in the garden. Coloured lights, draped around the fence, were switched on. Four musicians made their appearance via the back gate and soon the party was in full swing. Neighbours, friends and workmates were all welcomed and were sincere in their congratulations. Rosie thought it a huge joke when her nanna explained to her that her uncle Jim was now her granddad.

Everything was going well, and Jim Tyler was more than relieved, although to anyone who knew her well, Evie had a constant look of pain and anguish around her eyes, which frightened Jim, and he could only guess at the agony and despair she must be feeling. He told himself it was only to be expected. She had had a real rough deal.

Jim came to stand by Evie. She smiled up at him. 'Any minute now, Evie, my mate that owns his own taxi is gonna draw up in Holdernesse Road, and I want you to walk out of that back gate with me and collect what I hope is gonna be a very pleasant surprise.'

'Oh Uncle Jim, you've already given me one of the best surprises of me life. Married to my mum! Surely you can't top that.'

'Maybe, maybe not, an' not so much of the Uncle Jim! I'll 'ave you know, I 'ave gone to great lengths to make me life orderly an' legal, an' you, my girl, will pay me the proper respect what is due to me. D'ye get me drift?'

Evie gave him exactly the answer he was hoping and praying for: 'Yes Dad!'

He hugged her to him, his cheeks red, his eyes misty, and at that moment the sound of a hooter blasted loudly over the music, telling them the taxi was back.

'Hi ye, Bob. You got her?' Jim called.

''Course I 'ave, mate. She's in the back. Let the young lady 'elp herself.'

'Good idea, son.' Jim opened the passenger door of the cab and indicated with a nod of his head that Evie should look inside.

Evie gasped. 'Oh! She's really beautiful!'

From the floor of the motor, two deep, expressive, soft brown eyes stared up at Evie. She stooped low, putting her head and shoulders inside the cab. Her hand reached out to touch the softest honey-coloured fur she had ever felt. It was an Alsatian puppy.

'You are perfectly gorgeous,' Evie crooned as she scooped the puppy up into her arms. 'Is she really for me, for keeps?' she asked, nuzzling her chin into the neck of the dog.

Jim's eyes filled with hope. He had done the right thing. 'Yes, Evie. I bought her just for you. Her name is Heidi. She's three months old, house trained and she's fine with kiddies.'

'Oh thank you, thank you . . . Dad.'

Jim laughed and wagged a stern finger. 'Remember,

she'll need a helluva lot of exercise.'

'I can't wait to get her up on the common.'

'Hey, steady on, she's only a baby yet. She still has to go back to the vet's a couple more times. Jenny's got 'er card.'

Evie looked up in astonishment. 'You mean to tell me Jenny knew about this?'

'Sure she did. She chose her, an' she's been with me every time we've 'ad to take 'er for injections. It were Jenny that named 'er Heidi. We didn't let on t'Rosie. We didn't think she'd be able to keep the secret.'

'Oh Dad.' The name already came naturally to Evie. With the puppy still in her arms, she made to go back into the garden, but she paused, turned her head and again said, 'Thank you.'

'Evie, this day is so special to me and yer mum, and I guess I knew it would be kinda sad for you. This was the only thing I could think of to do for you.' His voice trailed off.

Evie went to him. His arms went around her. The puppy squashed between them wriggled, put out her tongue and gently licked Evie's cheek.

'I'm not gonna cry, I'm not,' she muttered, but she was smiling up at her stepfather with tears in her eyes.

'Come on, I can see you're dopey over that dog already. Let's go an' find out what Rosie thinks of her, shall we?' Jim asked, breathing a sigh of relief because everything was going so well.

Rosie swooped on them with a squeal of delight. It seemed everyone was going to love the new member of the family at number 42, even if it was one more female.

Chapter Nine

EVEN THOUGH CATHERINE HADN'T been easy to get along with for months before she had left home, Evie still found that she missed her dreadfully and never ceased to worry about her. While most of Catherine's friends had gone through all the miseries that teenagers had to cope with – spots, greasy hair, agonising over figures that were either too fat or too skinny – Catherine herself had thrived and finally developed into a real beauty, tall and slender, with long fair hair and that lovely creamy complexion that Evie herself had inherited from Flossie.

Throughout the years she had watched Cathy grow with a mixture of pride and concern. Although the girl always made out that she could take care of herself, there was a vulnerability about her that had caused Evie many a sleepless night. There was also that rebellious streak that had been so apparent while she had been working in Woolworth's. She'd been so determined to get that job at Butlins, going off on her own, and scarcely a word from her since. Evie hoped to God that Catherine hadn't lived to regret leaving home.

It was an advertisement in the previous evening's paper that had set Evie thinking so much about Catherine today. An estate agency at Jaywick Sands was offering holiday chalets for rent at very reasonable prices. The advert stated that Jaywick was just outside Clacton-on-Sea. She longed to go down and see for herself just how Catherine was coping in her new surroundings. Maybe she didn't like the job, wasn't happy, but was too pig-headed to come home and say so.

Evie felt she couldn't ask Jim to take her down to Clacton for the day, even though he was doing very well and had bought himself a brand new Vauxhall. If he were to offer, well that would be a different thing, but he was very busy most of the time.

'I know what I'll do,' Evie said aloud, getting to her feet and making a determined effort to find her purse.

Fifteen minutes later she was in the phone box that stood just inside Tooting Bec Underground Station, making a call to Jaywick Sands.

'When is it you break up from school?' Evie asked Jenny, as she fumbled with the straps of her school satchel.

'Wednesday week. I think it's the twenty-ninth, but I'm not sure,' Jenny answered, without looking up.

'What would you say to a week's holiday at a place near Clacton. We'd be able to go and see Catherine.' There was laughter in Evie's voice and it was repeated in Rosie's tone as she raised her head from where she lay stretched out on the rug, her arm across Heidi's back and Heidi's paw resting across Rosie's bare knee.

'Can Heidi come as well?'

'No, sorry darling, but it would only be for a week, an' you know your nan an' granddad would take great care of her.'

'I suppose so,' Rosie murmured, but she didn't sound too sure.

'I don't wanna come,' Jenny told her bluntly. 'Mr an' Mrs Parker said I could work in their surgery during me six weeks' summer holiday. I was going to talk to you about it after we'd had our tea. You know, see if you thought it would be all right.'

'Well! You'll be telling me next that's what you wanna do when you leave school.'

'It is! I'm hoping eventually to become a veterinary surgeon.'

Evie looked at Jenny in utter amazement. All of a sudden she sounded so grown up. 'You don't believe in mincing your words, do you young lady?'

Jenny laughed. 'No point. I made up my mind that's what I would like to become the very first time Granddad took me to the surgery with Heidi.'

'Well I couldn't go and leave you 'ere on your own, now could I?'

'Don't be so daft, Mum.' Jenny put her pile of school books down on the floor and came to where her mother was standing. She giggled. 'Can you see me nan letting me stay here in this house on me own while you and Rosie clear off on holiday? Come off it, Mum! Me nan will be in her heart's delight with you out of the way and me to fuss over.'

Evie had to laugh as she sliced up cucumber and added it to the bowl of salad she was preparing for their tea. She knew full well how right Jenny was.

It was boiling hot on the coach and, though both she and Rosie had enjoyed the ride from London, it was with a sigh of relief that Evie climbed down from the coach and turned to lift Rosie down.

'It's the blue case with the grey strap round it, please,'

Evie said to the driver as he pulled passengers' luggage
out from the side of the coach. 'Thanks.' She smiled as
she gave him a shilling.

'Make the most of this weather,' he grinned at her, 'Ta-
tar, little 'un, 'ave a good 'oliday.'

'We will,' Evie assured him, thinking that it hadn't been
any bother at all really to arrange this break for her and
Rosie. As Jenny had said, Flossie had been only too
pleased to have her and Heidi all to herself for a week.

'Come on then, luv, let's go and pay the balance of the
money an' find out where our chalet is.' Evie picked up
the case, turned to see where Rosie was and was thrilled
to see that she had crossed the grass verge and was staring
wide-eyed at the shimmering sea. 'Won't be long, Rosie.
We'll get these clothes off an' we'll get ourselves down on
that beach. What d'ye say to that?'

'Yeah Mum, let's hurry up.'

With the key held tightly in one hand, Evie trudged
down the rough sandy road. She'd never seen bungalows
like these before, street after street of what were little
more than gaily painted wooden huts, each one detached,
all built up on high stilts, making it necessary to climb a
flight of wooden steps before one could open the front
door.

'Here we are, Rosie, Acacia Avenue. The lady said
number six was the third on the right.' It was just three in
from the seafront.

She put the case down in the road and looked up in
pleasant surprise.

'Cor, ain't it a pretty one.' Rosie squealed in delight.

It was. Painted yellow, the bungalow had a white fence
running down each side, separating it from its neighbours
and continuing on to enclose a small garden at the rear.
Evie could see a clothes line, complete with dolly pegs,
stretching from one side to the other.

'See, Rosie, the people before 'ave been kind enough to leave us some pegs so's we can 'ang our swimming costumes an' things out to dry.'

'Open, the door, Mum,' Rosie called impatiently from the top of the steps.

Evie climbed up, turned the key in the lock, and Rosie pushed past her.

'Aw, it's nice,' they both said at the same time.

The living room was bright and airy. A round table stood in the centre of the floor. Four chairs were set around it and four canvas deckchairs were propped up against the wall. The kitchen was well equipped, and there was a bathroom and a toilet. The lady in the office had said that the toilet was an Elsan chemical toilet, which meant that it was not on main drainage and that a lorry would call each day to change the canister. Also, the cooker used Calor Gas and if the drum ran out she would need to buy a new one from the corner store; a man would be available to deliver and fix it for her.

The two bedrooms took up half of the bungalow. One large room really, with a hardboard division down the middle. In fact, if a child were to stand on one of the beds they would, quite easily, be able to see over the top of the partition.

'As there's only you and me, Rosie, we'll use this room with the double bed, shall we?'

Evie got no reply. Rosie already had the back door open and had gone down the steps to the patch of garden, where she was quite happily chatting away, nineteen to the dozen, to two boys and one little girl who were in the garden next door.

'Rosie,' her mother called from the top of the back steps, 'how about coming in an' changing your frock?'

'Wait a minute, Mum. This is Terry an' Bobby, an' their sister's name is Pat. They've already been 'ere one week an' they're gonna stay another week. They come 'ere every year.'

As Evie stepped down onto the grass, a plump red-faced woman came down the back steps next door, carrying a pail of water.

'Cor, me back is killing me,' she moaned when she reached the bottom step. She swilled the water round vigorously in the bucket then, with a flourish, flung it all out over a flowerbed before making her way to the low fence that separated the two gardens.

''Ello, luv, I'm Joyce Parker and that's me 'usband, Joe,' the woman said, nodding her head to where a well-built man wearing khaki shorts and an open-necked blue shirt stood at the top of the steps.

'Hi ye, luv,' Joe Parker called. 'Just arrived 'ave you? 'Ow many of ye are there?. What d'we call you?'

Evie stared at him; she felt flustered. 'I'm Evie Smith. Yes, we just got 'ere. It's our first time, an' there's only me an' me daughter Rosie.'

Joyce Parker shrieked with laughter. 'Nosy sod, my ol' man. Always was, always will be. But don't let it worry ye, being on yer own. Me sister Annie's in a chalet right opposite with her two kids. She's a widow an' all, so you'll be company for each other. You'll like our Annie, she's nice an' 'er 'eart is in the right place.'

Evie turned to the children, their cheerful grins making her feel welcome. Even so she didn't know quite what to make of the Parkers. They seemed to have assumed that she was a widow, and she wasn't about to enlighten them. How about the sister, Annie? Evie found herself hoping that they would mate up. Be nice to have a bit of company, and already Rosie seemed well set up for mates. Heart in the right place! Evie was grinning to herself. Typical Londoner's daft saying. Be in a right old pickle if Annie's heart was in the wrong place.

'Fancy coming down the club tonight?' Joyce Parker called. 'They 'ave a great room for the kids. There's a bar and a band, an' being Saturday there'll be entertainment as well.'

Before Evie got a chance to answer, Joe Parker, who was by now standing only a few feet from Evie, called over the fence, 'Course you'll come, won't you Evie? It's only along the seafront. You'll come with us an' we'll see ye get back safe. Cost ye half-a-crown for the week's membership, an' well worth it, you'll see. Your Rosie will 'ave a great time.'

'Yes, thank you. I'd like to come with you, if you're sure you don't mind, but I'd better go an' find a shop now, get a few things in for the weekend an' for our tea tonight.'

'Gawd luv ye, Evie, you don't wanna spend yer time cookin'. A van will be round about a quarter to six, sells everything: pies, fish, sausages an' as many chips as ye want. Course, you'll want tea an' sugar an' milk, an' some lemonade powder to make a bottle for on the beach ter-morrow – ain't paying no fancy prices to the kiosks. Bad enough when the kids want an ice cream. 'Ere, our Bobby, put some plimsoles on those dirty feet of yours an' go with Mrs Smith, show 'er where the shop is.'

'Oh, there's no need,' Evie protested, 'I can find it.'

'Move!' Joe barked at his son, which set all the kids giggling as Bobby scrambled over the dividing fence to go with the new lady and show her the way to the shop.

Throughout Sunday and Monday, Evie watched Rosie and thanked God time and time again that she had brought her on this holiday. Rosie had always had a happy nature, now she was in her element – plenty of children to play with, the beautiful soft sand of Jaywick on which to build sandcastles, running back and forth to the edge of the sea, fetching endless buckets of water to fill the moat, and moaning aloud because the water drained away so quickly. Rosie's face was shielded from the hot sun by a white poke sun bonnet. Frequently Evie called her, pleading with her to stand still while she once again rubbed suntan cream into the skin of her bare back. Already Rosie's sturdy little legs were evenly tanned, but Evie was taking no chances.

The weather was glorious, not a cloud in the sky. The sun beat down, making its reflection dance on the waves as the tide turned and, much to the delight of all the kiddies, began to roll in towards the shore. If it had been Jenny, Evie wouldn't have worried half so much about her getting sunburnt. She was dark like her father and tanned easily. Not so Catherine or Rosie. The very thought of Catherine made her shudder. What was that girl up to? Last evening she had found a telephone box and had spoken to a young lady at the camp. 'Catherine Smith is no longer employed here,' was what she had been told.

She had come out of that box in a daze! Where the hell was Catherine? Oh no! Just that statement wasn't good enough. A much more determined Evie had got back on the phone and after a lot of insisting had been told that the staff manager would see her the next afternoon at three o'clock.

Evie glanced at her watch; it was just coming up to twelve.

'Set a couple of towels out, will you, luv?' Joyce's voice carried clearly across the crowded beach.

Evie sat up, turned and watched as both Joyce and Joe came towards her carrying between them a huge wicker basket. Evie knew what was in it. It had been the same yesterday and on Sunday. Evie had boiled eggs and made salmon and cucumber sandwiches today, adding little fresh tomatoes and lots of fruit for her and Rosie. She didn't need to bring a drink with her. Joyce had made that quite clear from the beginning. At eleven o'clock each morning, Joyce and Joe, having settled the children happily on the beach, went back to their chalet and together they prepared drinks for the day and food for their family's midday meal.

Joyce was unloading the hamper, setting out plates, cups and mugs. Joe was in charge of three enormous Thermos flasks, which held pints of hot tea. He also had two bottles of milk and two bottles of bright yellow lemonade.

'Come an' get it,' Joe's voice boomed out.

Annie waved from where she was paddling her feet at the edge of the sea, keeping a close eye on her own two girls, Mary and Lily, and Rosie, and not forgetting her sister's brood of three. She shepherded the whole tribe up the beach and somehow settled them down in a semi-circle. Food and drink were dispensed to everyone.

Rosie, a sandwich in one hand and a hardboiled egg in the other, grinned up at her mother. 'Are we going to the club tonight? Lily said it's bingo tonight an' her mum won nearly twenty pounds last week.'

Evie laughed. 'We were going to go again last night but you fell asleep as soon as we'd had our tea. But we'll see, as long as you behave yourself for Mrs Parker while I'm gone this afternoon.'

'Course I will, Mum, but I can't see why I can't come if you're gonna see our Cathy.'

'Don't start again, Rosie. I've told you Catherine is at work and I shall only be able to 'ave a quick word with her. Far better that you stay 'ere and play with the others on the beach. It'll be ever so hot on the bus.'

'Oh all right,' Rosie agreed, her face lighting up as Joe Parker filled a mug with lemonade for her.

Evie had stuck to her story that she had a daughter of

thirteen who was at home with her nanna and a daughter of nineteen who had a summer job at Butlins Holiday Camp. 'Only natural, like, that ye wanna go an' see 'er,' Annie, Evie's new-found friend, told her. 'But ye don't want to drag little Rosie on the bus an' all, do ye? Not on a boiling 'ot day like today. Christ! I know Balham, where you come from, is maybe a bit better than round the Elephant an' Castle where we all live, but let the kid make the most of the beach an' the sun while she's got the chance.'

'Are you sure Rosie won't be no trouble?' Evie asked once again as she gratefully accepted a steaming mug of tea from Joe Parker. Even on a hot day nothing seemed to quench her thirst like a cup of tea.

'Don't you ever let up, gal?' Joe asked with a wide grin. 'What difference is one more kid gonna make amongst our lot? Or are you afraid we'll lose 'er or something?'

'No, course not.' Evie smiled, feeling a little guilty. There was so much about this family that was nice. They had taken to her just like that. Made her feel she was more than welcome to share in anything they had. They laughed a lot too. Not only the adults, but the children as well. Even down at the club, where he seemed to know all the men, Joe's attitude hadn't changed after quite a few pints of beer – not one cross word as he had told the boys to walk on the outside of the road and not to leave go of the girls' hands as they walked back to their chalets, the time being well past eleven.

Evie left the beach soon after lunch and went back to the chalet for a wash and brush-up. She took a last look in the mirror that was fixed to the back of the bedroom door. 'You'll do,' she told her reflection. She wore a plain yellow linen dress and white sandals. She had piled her hair, brushed until it shone, high on her head in an elegant knot. She wore no jewellery other than the ring that

George had placed on her finger the day he had taken them to Windsor.

Two buses had come along full, and she had almost decided to walk into Clacton when a single-decker bus drew up at the stop.

Evie stated her business at the gate of the camp and was told to follow the path to her left and she would come to the administration block.

'Mr Collier will see you straightaway,' a serious young lady said, and ushered Evie through a door marked 'Private'.

The young man sitting behind a desk got to his feet as she entered. He was a nice-looking blond man in a navy blue blazer and grey trousers. He wore a Butlins badge on his lapel.

'Mrs Smith?' He came around the desk, and shook Evie's hand. 'Please sit down.' He indicated a chair, smiled warmly at her and went back to take his own chair behind his desk.

'I'm very grateful to you for seeing me like this . . . I was so worried when I heard my daughter wasn't here any longer.'

'I can quite understand that, only there is not a lot I can tell you.'

'When did Catherine leave? Why did she leave? Where did she go?' The questions, once begun, came tumbling out.

'I'll take your questions one at a time in the order you asked them.' He was quiet and businesslike and spoke in that precise way that only the upper classes seem able to perfect, and yet he was friendly. He picked up a note pad and read through his notes. 'Catherine was employed here for six weeks only. Two young waiters proved to be unsatisfactory, were dismissed, and your daughter and another young lady took the decision to leave with them.

As to where your daughter went, I can only speculate. However I have been told that another of our present employees has received a postcard from your daughter. It was posted from the island of Jersey.'

Evie waited to see if he was going to say any more. There was a lump in her throat that felt as if it was choking her. How could Catherine do this? It wasn't as if she had been sacked herself. Boy trouble again! Catherine fell for every lad that so much as looked at her. It would be her downfall. Mr Collier was watching her carefully, curious now.

'Thank you again.' It was a barely audible whisper. 'Will you let me know if you or any of your staff hear from my daughter?'

Mr Collier nodded. 'We have your home address in the files.' His voice was now low and understanding.

Evie did her best to smile at him as he walked her quietly to the outer door, shook her hand, and said, 'I'm sorry I couldn't be of more help.'

Evie was very thoughtful as she walked along the lane back to the bus stop. Was Catherine in a load of trouble? That was the first thing she had to consider. Should she warn the police that her daughter had gone missing? The first thing that the police would tell her would be that Cathy was not underage. Should she pack up and go home, discuss this with her mother and Jim? It was a difficult decision to make.

No! she finally said to herself. The whole world couldn't come to a stop just because Catherine was thoughtless and very selfish. A few more days wasn't going to make any difference. She frowned as she remembered that Catherine had only been here in Clacton for six weeks. She hadn't bothered to think how worried she and her grandmother would be. A line or two just to tell them where she was working wouldn't have gone amiss. Christ, the girl must have the price of a stamp.

That did it! *For the rest of this week at least, I'm not going to bother about her. So she's never known what it was to have a father. She still had had a loving family, a grandmother who worshipped her.* Evie looked down at her hands. How many times had she sat up half the night sewing, making her fingers sore as she made blouses and underwear to suit Catherine's faddy taste? Well now she and Rosie were going to enjoy what was left of this week. It hadn't been a wasted journey, nor a waste of money. She had only to look at Rosie with her sundress tucked into her knickers, sunhat on her head, bucket and spade never out of her hand, to know that this holiday was doing her the world of good.

They were all still on the beach when Evie got back.

'Ten choc ices, please,' she said as she delved into her purse. She giggled as the man repeated, 'Ten?'

'That's right, it's a shipping order.'

'Just so long as you ain't been entertaining the British navy.' He smiled back as he put the ten ice creams into a paper bag.

'Saucy,' Evie grinned as she handed over the money.

'Rosie,' she called when she was a few feet away. Rosie looked up, flung her spade down and ran, calling back over her shoulder to the other children, 'Me mum's back.'

'Did you see our Catherine?' Rosie asked as she tucked her little hand that was gritty with sand into that of her mother's.

'Yes, I did,' Evie lied. 'She's ever so well, likes her job an' told me to give you a kiss an' a great big hug from her, so come 'ere.' She took Rosie into her arms and squeezed her tight. 'You're lovely, Rosie. 'Ave ye been a good girl?'

'Course I 'ave.'

Evie smiled to hear that. 'Good, cos I've got ice creams in this bag.' She was thinking about the lies she'd told

Rosie as she suddenly found herself surrounded by children. The lies had been uttered in a good cause. No point in trying to explain to a child that her mother had no idea where her eldest sister was.

Everyone was sucking away at their choc ices when Joe Collier leaned across Joyce and asked, 'Was your daughter all right, Evie?'

'Probably 'aving the time of 'er life, Joe. Thanks for asking.'

'That's all right then.' Annie licked quickly at a dripple of ice cream that was running down her chin. 'You'll be able to enjoy the rest of yer 'oliday now, won't ye?'

Joyce answered for her. 'Too true she will. We'll get 'er down the club tonight. 'Alf the single blokes down there last night were well put out when us lot turned up without you, Evie. So let Rosie 'ave a bit of a snooze when you've 'ad yer tea, and we'll yell when we're ready. It won't be before about 'alf past eight.'

'Suppose ye think I'm gonna knock 'em for six.' Evie giggled, just as a young girl would.

Everyone laughed as Joe put the finishing touches to the conversation. 'One gin an' orange, an' Evie will be out on that dance floor with the rest of us, you'll see.'

Evie said nothing, but inwardly she was vowing to take her time over her make-up tonight. She was glad she had brought Rosie away on holiday and she was going to see that they continued to have a good time. She'd worry about Catherine when she got back to London.

The remainder of the week passed all too quickly. The last evening at the club had been rowdy. Evie had scarcely been off the dance floor, never short of a partner, and come eleven o'clock when the club was supposed to close nobody had wanted to leave. Balloons of all shapes and sizes had floated down from the ceiling as the children surged onto the floor to grab them.

'Mum, I've got two.' Rosie had screamed her delight. 'I'm gonna take them home to show Nanna.'

'Come on, both of you,' Joe Parker had ordered. 'We're gonna sing "Auld Lang Syne".'

Evie had laughed so much she almost lost her footing when Joyce had yelled in her ear, 'Must be New Year's Eve every bloody Saturday night 'ere.'

Now they were packed and ready to go. The chalet had been swept out, and Evie had folded up the blankets neatly, placing the two dirty sheets on top of the case, ready for washing when she got home. Everyone had to supply their own sheets and towels.

'Mum, have you put the rocks in the bag?' Rosie called from the garden next door where she had gone to say her goodbyes.

'Course I 'ave, luv.'

'Well don't forget you're not to give them out, I am. The two peppermint ones are for Nanna an' Granddad, the pineapple one is for Jenny and the sweet shells – you know, those in the jar – are for Norma.'

Evie grinned. 'All right, luv. I'll leave it to you.'

'Now ye promise to write, don't you?' Joyce was holding one of Evie's hand's between both of hers.

'Cross me 'eart an' 'ope to die,' Evie declared.

Despite the fact that they weren't going home until later that evening, having travelled down from London by train, and they could have been down on the beach ages ago, they crowded round the doorway as Evie climbed into the coach and Joe Parker lifted Rosie up the steps. All eight of them were still waving enthusiastically as the coach turned the corner.

Catherine! Just as well we didn't cut our holiday short and come home, Evie thought as she reread the short letter. It had been lying on the table when she came in so Flossie must have picked it up and, judging by the postmark, it had been there for three or four days.

So, Catherine was with another girl called Dorothy and they were both working as chambermaids in Le Coie Hotel, St Helier, Jersey. At least she now had an address for her. What a relief! No mention of any boys, or any reason as to why she had left Butlins. Well there wouldn't be, would there? She had to laugh at the postscript. 'I promise to write as often as I can. Sorry I haven't written before.'

'Children!' was all Flossie said as, having read Catherine's letter, she handed it back to Evie.

'An' what d'ye mean by that?' Evie laughed. 'I was never that much trouble to you, was I?'

Flossie's eyebrows shot up. 'Gawd above, listen to 'er, Jim.'

'So, I take it that neither of you missed me while I was away then.'

'Course we did,' Jim assured her with a great beam of a smile spreading across his face.

'But only at times,' her mother shot back and was prevented from saying more because Evie's arms were tight around her mother's neck and Flossie felt that she was in danger of being strangled.

'Aw Mum, I'm glad we went. It was a great 'oliday, but gee, it's great to be 'ome.'

Chapter Ten

THROUGHOUT THE FIFTIES, EVIE had found it a struggle to make ends meet. With the coming of 1960 Evie looked back and knew that her lifestyle had improved. Most of the improvements she had to thank her stepfather for. Jim Tyler was now a very successful bookmaker. It wouldn't be true to say that he was in the same league as William Hill, but Jim would be the first to admit that he was doing very nicely, thank you.

He now employed Evie in his Trinity Road shop Mondays to Fridays with the posh title of turf accountant! The training had been an eye-opener. Rather than lay Evie open to ridicule, he had first sent her to his other shop, which was in Balham High Road. Wally Harris, an old-timer who had spent most of his life on a racecourse, had been thorough. By the time Wally was through with Evie, she not only knew the betting system from A to Z, she had a firm friend for life in Wally.

Christmas had also opened up another way of life for Evie, and indeed for her mother also. Their eyes had stuck out like organ stops when, on Christmas Eve, Jim had told them both to close their eyes and not to open them until he had led them out onto the pavement.

'A Mini!' Flossie had cried. 'Oh you old darling, you've been giving me driving lessons for ages but I thought it was just a safeguard so that I'd be able to drive you about when you got too old and decrepit.'

'Not just one Mini,' Jim told her quietly, 'the other one is for our Evie.'

'But I can't drive!'

'So we'll get you some lessons. You can take yer time. It does forty miles to the gallon.'

Evie looked at him, stupefied with horror at the thought.

She had, however, soon lost her fear as she sat in the driver's seat. Flossie's Mini was a black one and Evie's was bright blue.

Evie passed her test at the third attempt. Her mother gloated: she had passed first time! Evie hadn't known what to say when she had come across the garage receipt in the office. Their Minis had cost Jim four hundred and ninety seven pounds each!

Having a car made all the difference in the world to Evie. She could get out and about without having to wait for buses or go on the underground. She could ferry the girls about – well, Rosie she still could but, coming up to sixteen, Jenny didn't want her mother around when she went out. Pop music was all that Jenny seemed to live for these days. As for Catherine, there were more times than not when Evie despaired of her ever settling down.

'Oh dear!' she exclaimed softly. 'Why do I always come back to Catherine? It's Saturday, me day off. It's ten o'clock already an' I'm not even dressed yet.'

She put the breakfast plates and cups and saucers into the sink, folded up the newspaper and with a heavy sigh went upstairs to get herself ready to face the day.

*

'Didn't you get a letter this morning?' Flossie asked, as Evie appeared unexpectedly, pleading with her mother to come out with her for lunch.

'You mean from Catherine? No. Why, did you?'

'Yes, it's over there on the dresser. Go on, read it. She says there's a surprise coming to me. Only 'ope it's not an unpleasant one.'

'At least she keeps in touch quite regularly now,' Evie sighed as she folded the one sheet of paper and replaced it in the envelope.

'There you are then. That's something to be grateful for, ain't it?' Flossie looked closely at her daughter. She didn't look happy, in fact she looked downright miserable. Thank to Jim, most of Evie's financial problems had been eased but she spent far too much time on her own. That was half the trouble. She was a damn good mother but, as she herself knew only too well, you couldn't live your life through your kids. She had only had Evie, so it was easy for her to talk. Evie had three of them and that's a handful for any married couple, never mind a woman on her own with no man to turn to. A rotten deal, that's what her Evie had had. First off, when she was little more than a kid she'd got herself tied up with that selfish bugger Ted Hopkins, and then there had been George Higgins. *I'll admit I didn't think much of George when he first appeared on the scene, and I'm sorry to say I still think there was a lot more to George than met the eye. Still, he was good to Evie and her girls. Her one chance to be married and settled down and he has to go and be a bloody hero!* He had got his mother out safely. Why, she raged inwardly, had George gone back into that burning building? He had saved the old at the expense of his own life. What had been the point of it all? How could life be so cruel? She had no answers, only heartache whenever she looked at Evie.

"Mum, when you've finished daydreaming will you please answer my question?"

'What's that, luv?' Flossie tried to make her voice sound light; it didn't do to let Evie know that you worried over her.

'I asked you where ye'd like to go an' 'ave lunch.'

'Well the Wheatsheaf 'ave started doing lunches, an' Jim said they ain't bad at all.'

Evie didn't show much enthusiasm, so Flossie stood up, went to stand in front of the mirror which hung over the fireplace and refreshed her lipstick. 'I'll tell ye what, we'll give it a try, shall we? How d'ye feel about that?'

'Delighted!'

Evie's sarcasm was ignored by her mother, as she said, 'Come on, let's go.'

'What ye gonna 'ave?' Flossie asked as they entered the pub.

'No, you sit down, Mum. I'll get the drinks an' bring a menu over for you to see.'

'Alright, luv. I'll 'ave a Guinness,' Flossie replied.

They were fortunate to find a free table where Flossie sat while Evie went to the bar. Flossie gazed about her, nodding to various people whom she knew. *Say what you like,* she said to herself, *my Evie stands out in a crowd, don't matter where she is.* She was wearing a black pencil-slim skirt and a white silk blouse that was topped by an emerald green jacket. She had on high-heeled black patent court shoes and sheer nylon stockings, the fancy heel of which rose to a point, and the seam ran straight and true up the back of Evie's legs. Many a man in the bar was turning his head for a second look. Evie still had a year to go before she would be forty. Despite her worries she was certainly wearing well.

Evie returned with the drinks and a menu. 'Cheers,

Mum,' she toasted, raising her own drink of whisky and dry ginger.

'Cheers. quite a choice they've got on for lunch. I think I'll 'ave the halibut.'

'I'm gonna 'ave a prawn salad. I didn't know it got so busy in 'ere.'

'Don't suppose you did. You 'ardly ever put yer nose outside the door except to go to work.'

Evie flushed slightly, knowing that her mum meant well, but decided to change the subject. 'Mum, what did you think of Catherine's letter? She seems to be doing all right, I thought. But y'know I can't believe it's almost two years now since we set eyes on 'er. She'll be twenty-one this July.'

'Yeah, I know, luv, but there's two ways of looking at it. She had the guts to go for that job at Butlins an' she got it. Gawd knows why it didn't work out. There again, she didn't come 'ome with 'er tail between 'er legs, whining an' carrying on, did she?'

Evie didn't answer.

'Well? She didn't, did she?' Flossie persisted.

Evie shook her head.

'No! She somehow or another landed up in Jersey. Fantastic, if you ask me. Just think if you or even me 'ad been given the chance at her age to clear off an' land a job in Jersey. Don't know about you, Evie, but I'd 'ave been over the bloody moon. Christ, until the war I didn't even know where Jersey was except that it was near France.'

Despite herself, Evie couldn't help laughing. 'Mum, you always did 'ave a soft spot for Catherine, but honestly, don't you think she ought to tell us a bit more about what she gets up to?'

Now it was Flossie's turn to laugh, and she did, loud and long. 'Honestly! You amaze me, Evie. You've just said yerself that she's nearly twenty-one, for Christ's sake.

You were nowhere near 'er age when you took up with
Ted Hopkins. If you'd told me what you were getting up
to with 'im in the first place I wouldn't 'ave three lovely
granddaughters today, an' you might just 'ave ended up
being an' old married woman.'

Evie's cheeks were really red by now, but she still
couldn't smother her grin. 'Damn you, Mum. Why d'ye
always 'ave to be so right?'

The arrival of their lunches saved Flossie from having
to give an answer.

They'd been in the pub for just under an hour when the
door opened and Jim Tyler walked in. 'There you are.' He
smiled his greeting. 'Joan Killick told me she thought she
had seen the pair of you coming in 'ere.'

'Good! You're just in time to buy us another drink.'
Flossie laughed up into the face of the man that she had
come to think the world of. 'We've been so busy stuffing
our faces and wondering about our Catherine that we've
only 'ad the one.'

'That's funny,' Jim remarked, pulling a letter from his
coat pocket, 'I met Jack Gibbs doing his second round of
post an' he gave me a letter for you, Evie. It's from
Catherine.'

'Well I'll be blowed,' Flossie muttered, 'I 'ad one this
morning from 'er an' all.'

'Right, well while you two are comparing notes I'll get
a round in,' Jim said, picking up their empty glasses and
making for the bar.

'Our Cathy's got engaged,' Evie whispered as she read
the letter Jim had just handed to her.

Flossie's hand stopped in midair. 'She's what?' she
queried.

'Got engaged.'

'Well I'll be . . .' Flossie broke off, momentarily lost for
words.

'It's a surprise to me an' all, I can tell you.'

'Do we know the fellow?'

''Ow could we? I'm beginning to think we don't know our Catherine.'

'Ow's that, then?' Jim came back with a tray of drinks and had caught the tail end of the conversation.

'Cos she's gone an' got 'erself engaged to some bloke we don't even know,' Flossie informed him.

''As she now?' Jim grinned as he settled himself in a chair and pushed a fresh drink in front of his wife and stepdaughter. 'D'we know 'is name?' He got no answer. Evie was continuing to read her letter while her mother was watching her closely, never taking her eyes off Evie.

'It's more than flesh an' blood can stand,' Flossie grunted impatiently.

'Hurry up an' tell us what else she 'as to say,' Flossie instructed. 'Does she tell ye the name of the lad?'

'She's telling us a darn sight more than that Mum. Give me a minute. Let me get to the end an' then ye can read it for yourself.'

A couple of minutes later, Evie breathed out. 'Well,' she said as she handed the letter across the table, 'see what you're able to make of it.'

Flossie was intrigued. She looked up, first at Evie and then at Jim, then began to read again from the beginning.

'So! She's gonna marry this Stanley Caldwell. She don't say whether he's the bloke she left Clacton with,' Flossie commented dryly, and then she gave a hearty laugh. 'At least she's got 'im to put a ring on 'er finger, that's something I suppose.'

'But Mum! Listen to this, Dad. She reckons they'll make all their own wedding arrangements. They'll be married in Weymouth, if you please. From his folks' 'otel. 'Ere's the best bit. Will we make 'er wedding dress?'

''Ang on,' Flossie cut in, 'read that second page again out loud, go on.'

Evie shuffled the pages and found the place, looked across at Jim, who smiled his encouragement, and began to read. '"Stan's parents own the Osbourne Hotel in Weymouth. It's opposite the pier bandstand. Stan used to work for them but he fell out with his dad."'

Evie paused, and Flossie commented, 'Kids!'

'"We're going to stay here in Jersey until the end of the year, see this season out, then we're going to Weymouth because Stan's folks open for Christmas and we are both going to work for them. We hope to have an Easter wedding. Mr and Mrs Caldwell are letting us have their flat in the hotel and they are going to move out into a bungalow. They will still come to work, only Stan and I will be sort of managers."' Evie laid the letter down.

'Got it all worked out, 'aven't they?' muttered Jim, who had been listening intently.

'Not 'alf, they ain't,' added Flossie.

Evie sat silently facing her stepfather, twisting the ring that George had given her round and round on her finger.

Jim knew exactly what was going through her mind and he said to himself, *I only hope Catherine has more luck than her mother did.*

Seconds passed before Evie spoke. 'We must write an' tell Catherine 'ow pleased we are at her news. Tell 'er we 'ope to meet this young man of 'ers before they get married. It would be stupid to do otherwise, don't you agree, Mum?'

Flossie scanned Jim's face. He nodded.

'Yes, luv. You're right. I'll do as Cathy asked. I'll 'elp you make 'er dress.'

Evie ran a hand despairingly through her hair. 'It's so long since we've seen her. It won't be easy.'

'Nothing ever is, but we'll get it sorted, won't we Jim?'

'I've no doubt the pair of you will manage fine,' he

said, getting to his feet. 'Come on, let's 'ave yer glasses.
We've just time for one more drink.'

As Jim came to the side of the table where Evie sat, he
gazed at her, a gaze full of affection, lowered his head
and whispered, 'It's traditional for the bride's father to
pay for the wedding. Do you think a grandfather will
qualify? If she doesn't want 'elp with the actual wedding
you just tell her I'm paying for the material for the gown
an' for the bridesmaids.' He paused, looked across at
Flossie, knowing full well she was listening. 'And that will
include outfits for the bride's mother and grandmother.'

Evie gave him a warm smile. 'Oh, Dad! You're talking
a fortune.'

'So what? It will make you happy, won't it?'

'Of course it will.'

'Then don't forget when you write to her to let 'er
know that I mean it. She only 'as to ask.'

Flossie was the one who got to her feet, came to Jim
and put her arms round his shoulders. 'You're a great big
softie, ye know that? But I love you.'

He laughed. 'Pack it in, woman, or else I'll be too late
to get served at the bar.' All the same, he bent and kissed
her cheek, while Evie nodded her approval. Jim walked
towards the counter. He was feeling very emotional.
'What the hell,' he said aloud. It was smashing to have a
family, and loving someone as he did Flossie was wanting
to make that person happy, and if that included seeing
Flossie's eldest granddaughter well set up, so be it. All
three of Evie's girls were smashing and he vowed he'd do
his best for them all. *I only wish Evie would find someone. It
isn't right, not right at all that one so young and lovely as Evie
should lead such a lonely life. Christ! There isn't much that I
wouldn't do to see Evie happy. But I'm damned if I know just
what I could do.*

Evie was wishing much the same thing. If only she had

someone else with whom she could discuss this turn of events. Her mother was marvellous and so was Jim, but it wasn't the same as lying in bed and talking things through with your partner. She wished with all her heart that George could be here now. She needed him so badly. She shuddered. His death had been so cruel.

'Are you all right, Evie?' Flossie asked anxiously.

'I'm fine, Mum. Memories, that's all.'

'George?' Evie nodded.

'Yes, well, those will always be with you. The good and the bad. Nobody can take your memories away from you. And you wouldn't want them to, not really, would you?'

'No. But I can't 'elp thinking that life for me with George might have been good,' Evie said softly, thinking how good those last few months with George had actually been. It was cold comfort.

Flossie sighed heavily. 'Yeah, life hasn't been too kind to you, luv. Just make sure you don't become bitter, that's all. You know I'm always 'ere for you whenever you need me.'

Evie smiled, stretched across the table and took hold of her mother's hand. 'Mum, I hope I'm as good a mother to my three as you've been to me, and that's not all, you're a smashing grandmother an' all.'

Flossie's eyes were shining with tears as she told Evie, 'That's one of the nicest things you've ever said to me.'

By the time that Jim got back with their drinks, they were deep in discussion about patterns and materials for bridal gowns.

Now they did hear from Catherine regularly, once a week.

'Her letters are not so much full of news as instructions.' Evie laughed as she took the letter out of her bag and gave it to her mother to read. 'I'll put the kettle on,' Evie declared, making for the gas stove.

'I think this is a good idea of Cathy's, to let her buy a

pattern and send it to us. At least we'll know what kind of a wedding dress she's hoping for.'

'Yes, I agree,' Evie replied.

The pair of them had just returned from their Saturday morning shopping spree.

'No matter what design we made up it wouldn't suit Cathy if it weren't of her choosing,' said Flossie.

Evie pulled a face. 'You're like me, you don't think she's changed that much.'

'No, I don't. Not by the tone of her letters. She's hardly become docile,' Flossie answered, smiling nevertheless.

'An' I'll tell ye another thing, Mum. Our Jenny is getting more like her every blooming day. Since she broke up from school she's been down at that vet's surgery morning, noon an' night. Know what she told me this morning? She's not going to be bridesmaid to Catherine, and when I told 'er the wedding won't be till next Easter she turned round an' told me she won't be 'ere by then. Reckons she's gonna get a live-in job working with animals.'

'I wouldn't worry too much about Jenny. At least Mr and Mrs Parker speak well of her. I met them the other day an' 'ad quite a long chat about Jenny. They both said she was a little wonder in the surgery, 'andles animals like she was born to it.'

'Ah, well, it keeps 'er off the streets. I suppose that's something to be grateful for.' Evie opened a cupboard. 'Mum, 'ave you moved the tea caddy? I can't see it.'

Flossie made to get up.

'Sit down, Mum. Just tell me where the caddy is. I'll make the tea.'

Flossie did as she was told. 'Wonder what Mr and Mrs Caldwell are like. I'd feel a whole lot better if we'd met this Stan. So would you, I guess.'

'Of course I would, Mum, but we've been over this dozens of times. Cathy's made 'er choice. She's got definite ideas about what she wants and 'ow she wants it, and nothing you or I can say will alter that. All I care about really is whether Catherine's gonna be 'appy. I've done as she asked: I've written to Stanley's parents. We might be able to judge better as to whether or not she's making a good match if an' when I get an answer from them.'

Evie placed the now filled teapot on the table beside the cups and saucers she'd set out and sat down opposite her mother. 'I'm glad I've got you to 'elp me with the sewing. A wedding dress! We've never tackled anything like this before.'

Flossie considered this. 'Well there's a first time for everything.' They both laughed.

'It's all very well, Mum, but I can't 'elp worrying about getting the size right. It isn't as if she was 'ere to 'ave a fitting. Joan did suggest that her Shirley model it for us, which I thought was very kind. They did used to be about the same size, but who knows now whether our Cathy's put on any weight or even lost some.'

'She 'as sent her measurements,' Flossie said thoughtfully, then a smile broke out on her face and she cried, ''Ang on a minute, I've just 'ad a brainwave! Why don't we make the dress up out of two sheets? We needn't be too fussy about the stitching, and then we could post it to 'er. Cathy could try it on and get one of her friends to make any alterations that are needed with tacking stitches.'

Evie almost choked on a mouthful of tea. 'Mum! You're a genius!'

'I know I am, I've been telling ye that for years,' said her mother and put her hand over Evie's and squeezed it. 'Between you an' me, luv, we'll turn out a dress even Cathy won't be able to find fault with.'

Evie's laughter was a joy for her mother to hear. And Evie was thinking that the prospect of making a wedding dress wasn't as alarming to her as she had previously thought.

A fortnight later, Evie had received a most encouraging letter from Mr and Mrs Caldwell. They had poured their hearts out to Evie. Stanley had been a pest before he'd left home to work at Butlins in Clacton. They too had been worried out of their minds when they'd learnt that he had upped stakes and gone to be a waiter in Jersey. They had been to Jersey for a long weekend, met Catherine, liked her very much and were thrilled that she and their son had decided to get married and settle down.

Catherine's latest letter had contained a page torn from a magazine. It was a picture of a bridal group. 'Mum, I simply adore this style. Can you copy it?' is what she had written.

The dress was gorgeous, the detail intricate. *Be a bloody miracle if I can,* is what Evie was thinking as she studied the picture. In the background of the photograph there were four bridesmaids and two pageboys. 'Wonder she don't want that lot made as well,' she muttered to herself.

Endless hours of pinning and tucking, often using Shirley Killick as a model, and the trial dress was finished.

Flossie patted Evie's hand reassuringly. 'It'll be all right, you've nothing to worry about. Cathy will love it. She can make any alterations she wants and when we get it back we'll start on the dress proper.'

'An' what about mine?' Rosie had just come into the room and decided she wasn't going to be left out of all these exciting plans. 'Nanna said I could come with you when you go to London to buy the proper material an' that I could pick what I liked best for my dress. And the colour. Didn't you, Nan?'

'Yes, I did my darling an' so you shall, but we've got to wait till Catherine says she likes the way we've made the pretend dress before we can start on the real one. You won't get left out. I promise.'

'All right then.' Her response was half-hearted. 'Will Heidi be able to come to the wedding? I think we should tie a big white bow round her neck on that day.'

Mother and daughter looked at each other and hid their smiles. To Rosie this was a very serious matter. Evie formed an answer.

'She won't be able to come to the church, but we shall take her to Weymouth with us on the train and I'm sure she'll be given a place to sit right near you when we 'ave the reception.'

'What's a reception?'

'Another word for it is the wedding breakfast. All the families an' their friends sit down an' 'ave a meal and then the bride an' groom cut their wedding cake.'

'If it's a breakfast, do we have to go to church ever so early, before we've had anything to eat?'

'God give me strength,' breathed her mother. 'No darling. No matter what time of the day people sit down to eat, it is still called a breakfast. And please, Rosie, don't ask me why, because I don't know.'

'Oh,' was all that Rosie murmured, then turning on her heel she said, 'I'll just go an' tell Heidi that she's gonna come on a train ride with us.'

Just in time Evie stopped herself from saying that it would be months before they went to Weymouth. She didn't want to have another string of questions to cope with.

The dress was folded, placed in a cardboard box, wrapped and posted to Jersey. Now all they had to do was wait.

It was Friday evening and Evie was dividing the fillets of plaice that she had bought from Cole's, the fishmonger's.

'They're lovely large ones, Mum, but I still got three for you because I thought one wouldn't be enough for Dad.'

'Thanks, luv. I won't stop for a cuppa. I want to get the potatoes done and sliced up for chips before Jim gets in. We're gonna eat early tonight cos we're going over to the Wheatsheaf. Jim's playing in the final round of darts.'

Evie didn't get a chance to reply. Jim's face was one great smile as he burst in through the back door. 'I'm glad to find you both together. You'll never guess, I've just 'ad Catherine on the phone over in the office. Boy is that girl riding 'igh!'

'Never mind all the remarks,' Flossie protested impatiently, 'just tell us what Cathy telephoned for.'

'To tell you she adores the dress. Fits 'er a treat, she said. Only the length and the sleeves are a bit long. She said 'er mate is putting pins in and she'll be sending it back.'

'Thank God for that!' Evie and her mother breathed in unison.

'Oh, there was one other thing,' Jim added quickly.

'Yes?' Evie asked in a tense voice.

'Cathy said could you send her some samples before you buy the material and something about the trimming, which I didn't understand.'

'Oh my God,' Flossie exploded.

'Don't go up the wall! I told 'er I didn't 'ave a clue what she was talking about and she said not to worry, she'd put it all in a letter.'

'More instructions,' Evie muttered.

Flossie glanced at her. 'At least she likes it and there's no major alterations, at least not according to 'im.'

'You don't think I can take a phone message?' Jim queried, raising his eyebrows at his wife.

'Oh luv, I didn't mean it that way,' Flossie said quickly.

'That's all right then, because I've just told Rosie and

Jenny that I've got five tickets for the Chelsea Palace for tomorrow night. But if you, my lady wife, are daring to insinuate that my grey matter is not up to the mark, we'll leave you at 'ome.'

'Don't say that Jim.' She pretended to plead. 'Come 'ere and let me show you 'ow sorry I am.' She smiled endearingly at him as he crossed the room. It was a smile that meant an awful lot to Jim Tyler, a man who had loved Flossie many a long year before he had had the courage to tell her so.

Another day over, Evie sighed, climbing the stairs slowly. She peeped in first at Rosie, then at Jenny; both were fast asleep. She frowned as she went into the bathroom. *I'll just clean my teeth, I'm too dog-tired to wash tonight.* Betting had been heavy that day but it was that dratted television set, blaring out nonstop, that had driven her clean up the wall. Men! Where did they get the money from that they laid out on horse and dog races? You'd think half of them had no homes to go to, the way they stayed in the betting shop, their eyes glued to the TV. The whole day had been a bugger!

'Don't move, Heidi,' Evie whispered as she stepped over the dog. As if Heidi would! Every night when Rosie went to bed, Heidi went up the stairs with her, staying in her bedroom until she sensed that Rosie had fallen asleep. Then she came out of Rosie's room and stretched herself across the doorway of the main bedroom, and there she remained until she felt the call of nature. Usually about six-thirty in the morning she came to the side of the bed to paw Evie's arm. If that didn't bring a quick enough response, she'd begin to lick Evie's face until she swung her legs out of the bed, stretched her arms and padded downstairs to let Heidi out into the back garden.

*

Evie woke up thinking she'd heard Heidi snoring. 'Oh please, Heidi, stop it,' she murmured, then, uttering a soft sigh, she turned on her side, closed her eyes and snuggled down again. Suddenly she sensed that Heidi was moving. Not only that, the snoring had changed to a growl. Something was wrong! Hardly had she got out of bed than Heidi was up and away, bounding down the stairs, barking her head off.

'What's the matter?' Jenny was in the doorway of her room, clad only in her nightie, slurring her words sleepily.

Evie hesitated. The dog was going mad downstairs. The noise would surely wake up the whole street. 'Wait up here,' she insisted. 'Heidi 'as probably 'eard a cat.' She took a deep breath, then headed down the stairs. 'Heidi!' Evie yelled at the top of her voice, but it was doubtful whether the dog heard her above the racket she was making.

To Evie's surprise, Heidi wasn't at the front door. She was down the short passageway that led to the kitchen, jumping high in the air, scratching away at the boarded up room that was opposite the kitchen. Strange! That room had never bothered her before. In fact it never bothered anyone. It was completely sealed off, and Evie had got so used to it that she had come to consider it part of the wall.

'Down, Heidi!' she commanded, but for once Heidi wasn't obeying. She continued to bark nonstop, sometimes changing the tone to a yelp. Evie grabbed her collar and pulled. This restrained her for a few seconds, then she broke away and dashed up the passageway to the front door.

Heidi wouldn't budge from her position on the mat. Evie recoiled as Heidi bared her teeth and snarled at the wooden framework. *I daren't open the door and let her out,* she thought. *She'd have the whole street up in arms.*

She put her hand on Heidi's back. Her fur was standing

on end. The beginnings of panic were fluttering inside Evie, and prickles of alarm were making her breathe heavily. This was ridiculous; she'd never been frightened of being on her own before. She was now. She caught hold of Heidi's collar and pulled her towards her. 'Come on, pet, calm down,' she whispered as Heidi wriggled in her grasp.

Then Evie's head jerked up. She had heard the sound of a motorbike being started. Heidi had heard it too. The dog became still. Her ears pricked up. There came a roar from outside. It lessened; the motorbike had gone.

Evie sighed. Her head ached. Should she go and wake her mother and stepfather and tell them what had happened, or wait till morning? Wait till morning, she decided. Heidi was quiet now, and she really ought to get back upstairs to Jenny. *Poor little soul! She must be frightened out of her life. What about Rosie? Oh my God.* She hitched up her nightdress and took the stairs two at a time. Jenny was still leaning against the landing wall, barefooted and shivering in her flimsy nightie. She flew into her mother's arms.

'There, there, luv, it's all over. It was only Heidi wanting to get out to chase a cat. D'ye want to go an' get into my bed? Take Heidi with you. She can lie down on the floor beside you. I won't be a minute. I'm just gonna look in on Rosie.'

Evie gently turned the door handle. Amazing! The tight fair curls lay in the middle of the pillow, the tiny cheeks flushed with sleep and one hand was clenched up into a tight ball. Rosie hadn't moved an inch since she had looked in on her earlier. Evie crossed the room to stand beside the bed. 'You are a little love,' she whispered. As the door clicked shut behind her, Evie thanked God that Rosie had slept through it all.

'Good girl, Heidi,' Evie muttered as she bent and fondled

her, before getting back into bed and pulling Jenny into the crook of her arm.

'All right now, Jenny?' Evie asked.

'Mmm,' Jenny murmured, thinking it was nice to be able to cuddle up to her mum.

Sleep was impossible for Evie. One thing she was sure about: that was no cat that had disturbed Heidi. She was in no two minds about that at all.

The first thing Evie did next morning was to go and stand outside on the pavement and stare at the boarded up bay window. Only the top half was visible for the simple reason that Evie had allowed the privet hedge to grow high on that side of the house. The small garden outside her front room she kept neat and tidy. She cut the hedge regularly with a pair of shears, keeping it short so as not to block out the light. She had let quite the reverse happen to the unused room. The less she could see of the boards that were by now dirty and weatherworn, the better she liked it. Everything appeared to be in order. There had been no disturbance that she could see. Anyway, why would anyone want to break into that room after all these years? It wasn't as if they could gain access to the house. The room was completely blocked up from the inside as well as from the outside. It was a puzzle and no mistake, she told herself as she went back indoors to prepare the breakfast.

Evie looked at the clock. A quarter past ten. This was going to be a long morning. She couldn't settle; she was upset, distressed. Her imagination was running away with her. She could see an unknown figure, most probably a man, trying to gain entry to her house. But what the hell for? Should she phone the police? What would she tell them? Perhaps she had better go outside and take a closer look.

Evie shivered uneasily as she opened the front door; this damn boarded up room was suddenly causing her a lot of grief.

Stepping off the pathway Evie stood with her back against the overgrown privet hedge.

'Good God!' she exclaimed. She didn't need to look closer to see that someone had tried to chip away a corner of the dirty old board that had sealed the window up for so long. 'Why?' She asked herself the same question that had been in her mind all morning. Why the hell would anyone want to do such a thing? She was outraged. Through pursed lips she muttered, 'Damn! Why does something like this have to happen to me?'

Heidi came out of the house, ran across the garden and stood panting beside Evie. 'Hello my lovely, you knew someone had been here, didn't you?'

Heidi looked up at Evie and wagged her tail. Evie took a deep breath, still trying to weigh up the situation. What if she phoned the police and they laughed at her? She would look right daft wouldn't she?

'All right,' she declared finally, 'I'm gonna phone the council.' After all it was ages since anyone had been down to look at the house. *Be honest, though,* she said to herself, *the council do inspect the outside wall regularly.* Well they would, wouldn't they? That great big end wall faced the Sir Alfred Butt apartments, and it wouldn't do to have the chosen few who lived in that block looking out over a blank wall that might be the worse for wear, now would it?

'Blimey, that was quick!' Evie couldn't hide her surprise as she opened the door to find two council workers standing on her doorstep less than an hour after she'd come back from the telephone box.

The workmen appeared immensely gratified at being

given such a smiling welcome. 'Speedy, that's us. Now just tell us what's wrong. Kids round here smashed one of your windows, have they?'

'No, you're gonna think I'm crazy. Come 'an see.' Evie pushed past the two men, walked halfway down her path and pointed to the boarded up window.

'Well, what's the matter with it? Been like that ever since I've been at Wandsworth.' The eldest of the two men turned to his mate. 'How about it, Bert? You were one of the men that rendered that outside wall not so long ago, weren't you?'

'I ain't asking you to do no repairs,' Evie said rudely. 'I know full well that room's been like it ever since the houses at that end of the road were demolished.

'D'you use the room above it?' asked the young man.

'Yes, always have. It's my daughter's bedroom. There's still three bedrooms upstairs. I think that's why the coun-cil 'ave never opened that room up for me. Think I don't need the extra room. Which of course I don't.'

'All this is very well,' grinned the young man Evie now knew to be named Bert, 'but could we come in off your step? Then you can tell us exactly why you phoned the council yard.'

Evie knew he was teasing her and she repaid his grin with a smile. 'Yes, of course, an' I suppose neither of you would say no to a cup of tea.'

'Oh you marvellous lady! You must have known how dry we both are.'

Twenty minutes later, and the two men were back out-side.

'Well I don't know, Arthur.' Bert shook his head. 'You ever come across anything like this before?'

'Can't say as I have. Perhaps it was someone just trying to be nosy. They didn't get very far. Ain't even broke a panel. No repairs for us t'do. Even so, missus, you did right to call us. We'll report it to the foreman, see what he has to say. Not much though, I don't suppose.'

Evie broke in. 'Don't seem very serious now, not in the light of day it doesn't, but I can tell you, last night I had visions of being murdered in me bed and my girls were frightened out of their lives. Heidi, my dog, scared them off and I don't think I've ever been so grateful for anything in all my life.'

'Well, we must get on. Thanks for the tea.'

'Yeah, it were great,' Bert added. 'I'd call the police if anyone else tries anything, if I were you. A break-in, or even an attempted break-in, is more a matter for the police than the council.'

'I 'ope there won't be no next time,' Evie cried, and the men laughed.

'See ye luv,' they called as they swung their canvas workbags onto their shoulders and walked towards the van, which was parked by the kerb.

Well, that was a waste of time, Evie mused as she watched them drive off.

Evie entered the Balham betting office by the back door to find Wally Harris staring out of the window.

'Are you all right?' she queried when she saw the expression on Wally's face.

'Yes, I am. It's you that I'm worried about. I've been talking to Jim. You've only just missed 'im. Couldn't 'ave been very nice for you, luv.'

'That was three weeks ago, Wally. I've tried not to think about it since, though me mum does still keep on at me to tell the police. I did get on to the council. They sent two workmen round straightaway but, as they said, wasn't nothing for them t'do. Whoever it was never even broke through the first board. Heidi frightened them off. Was only kids playing about, I expect, don't you think so?'

That wasn't what Wally was thinking at all, but he wasn't about to air his misgivings. To his way of thinking, young Evie had enough on her plate, being on her own an' all, without him putting the fear of God into her. But as he'd said to Jim just now, it was a matter for the police, not the council. No two ways about it. Young woman in the house on her own, two young daughters, and someone tries to break in. Phone the police straightaway. Better to be safe than sorry. Even if it was only kids, seeing the police come round might stop them having another go. Though you never knew with the youngsters nowadays. They were a law unto themselves, half of them.

'My Ada's got the flu. She's been right queer,' Wally said, turning round to face Evie.

'Yeah, so Jim said when he asked me to do the rest of the week up 'ere with you.'

'Aye, well it's an ill wind that blows no one any good, an' it means I get to see my favourite girl, doesn't it?'

'Flatterer.' She laughed as she took her raincoat off and shook the water from it. 'Damn rain! It's been bucketing down for two days now.'

'And there's more to come, according to the weather reports. Probably be some meetings cancelled if the ground gets waterlogged.'

'Well, suppose we can't grumble. We ain't 'ad a bad summer. Weather's been the best that I can remember for a long time.'

'Well remember that, my girl . . . another couple of weeks an' we'll be into November with the dark nights and thick fogs.'

'Oh for God's sake!' Evie made a face at Wally. 'Let's change the subject. D'ye fancy tea or coffee? I've brought some doughnuts in with me.'

'Told you yer me favourite lady. Go on, put the kettle on before the punters start streaming in, an' none of yer fancy coffee – can't stand the muck. I'll 'ave me great big mug filled with Rosie Lee if ye don't mind.'

The blackboard was all chalked up and set up on the wall. There was many a betting man who preferred the old-fashioned way of noting the odds. From then on, to the off of the last race, it was eyes down and hard at it for both Evie and Wally.

It was a quarter past five when Evie said, 'At least it's stopped raining.'

'Not for long by the look of that sky,' Wally replied. 'Just you 'ang on till I go an' fetch me car round to the front an' I'll run you 'ome.'

'No need,' a deep voice called from the back.

'It's you, Dad!' Evie exclaimed, tying her scarf over her hair, which she thought must be in a bit of a mess by now.

'She coming the old soldier with ye, is she Wally?' Jim asked, poking his head into the shop and grinning at the pair of them. 'She's got 'er own car, an' what does she do? She waits till the weather is this bad to decide she's got a flat tyre.'

'Nobody asked you to come an' pick me up.'

'You saucy bitch! For that sweet remark, miss, I've a good mind to make you get the bus 'ome an' also make you wait to 'ear me news.'

Evie grinned. 'Good news?' she queried hopefully.

'I'd take a bet that you'll think so,' her stepfather replied, at the same time winking at Wally.

'Tell me, tell me,' she implored.

He strode over to her, picked her up and whirled her round and round.

'Hey! You old fool,' she protested, laughing at the same time.

He put her down again and placed his hands on her shoulders. 'What if I told you Catherine is coming home an' bringing 'er young man with her?'

Her face lit up. ''Ow do you know? When is she coming? You're not 'aving me on, are you?'

'Nope, it's the God's honest truth.'

'But I 'ad a letter from 'er yesterday and –'

'She phoned. The season's finished. She's coming next Friday, just for the weekend, before they go to her young man's parents.'

'Oh Dad, isn't that wonderful? 'Ave you told Mum yet?' she demanded eagerly. 'I bet she'll be just as excited as I am. Oh dear, I've just thought, where the 'ell are we gonna sleep him?'

Jim looked across at Wally and they both raised their eyebrows in mock desperation. 'Women!' Jim said. 'We've two empty bedrooms in our 'ouse for a start. It's only a hop, skip an' a jump away from 42. I don't expect Catherine will kick up a fuss about that.'

'You're in for a great time, Jim,' Wally commented dryly.

'Aye, I know,' Jim grumbled. 'I'll tell you what, Evie. Instead of us standing around 'ere arguing the toss, why don't you do your mac up an' let's go 'ome so that you can cook your kids' tea.'

'I'm ready. But I'll 'ave to come to your place an' tell Mum before I start cooking.' Evie sighed with contentment. Her Catherine was coming home at last.

Chapter Eleven

EVIE WAS WEARY. SHE had gone hammer and tongs at the house, making sure that every room was extra clean and tidy and that all the woodwork shone. *I'll make meself a cup of tea and have a snooze in front of the fire, she promised herself.* The time was two-thirty. Catherine and Stanley weren't due to arrive until six o'clock that evening.

Her mother had been a saint. Just as thrilled as she was that Cathy was coming home, she had put her back into the preparations. She had had Jim and one of his mates lug a single bed down to number 42 to be put up alongside Jenny's bed. It wouldn't do to upset Jenny by telling her she had to give up what had been Catherine's room and move back in with Rosie. That would have caused ructions.

Flossie had made sure that one of her spare rooms was set up nicely for Cathy's young man. After all, they wanted to make a good impression. His folk owned a hotel! Not that Flossie was ashamed of her home, quite the opposite. Since she had become Jim's wife she had wanted for nothing. Fate had been kind to Jim. He had prospered, and he saw to it that Flossie went short of nothing. 'No more lodgers, and certainly you can knock the pie-making on the head,' he had stated forcibly within weeks of opening his first bookmaker's shop. The only people who used Flossie's two spare bedrooms now were her granddaughters when they stayed over with her for a change.

Evie woke with a start. A cinder falling through into the ash pan had made her jump, and she was surprised to see that it was already dark and that the fire had burnt very low. She'd have to move herself if she was going to have a wash and change her dress before Cathy arrived.

'Oh Mum! That was a journey well worthwhile, just to see you.' Catherine flung herself into her mother's arms and they stood there, hugging tightly for several seconds.

'What about us?' Rosie tugged at her sister's coat. 'Ain't you gonna say 'ello to me an' Jenny?'

'Course I am, baby, come and give us a kiss.' Rosie went to her, and her sister put her arms around her. 'My goodness you've grown, 'an you're so pretty.'

Evie looked at the pair of them. Each had the fairness she and their grandmother had, but young Rosie had that beautiful curly hair and startling blue eyes.

'I'm not a baby. I'm eight now, nearly nine.'

'Shall I tell you something? In Jersey there's a wonderful shop that sells Swiss chocolate an' I've bought you the biggest, thickest bar you've ever seen. Still, if you're too big for chocolate now . . .'

'I'm not, I'm not,' Rosie was quick to protest.

Still with her arm round Rosie, Cathy turned to Jenny and smiled. 'Hello sis. You ain't exactly stayed still either. Quite the young lady now, aren't you?'

'It's good to see you, Cathy. I was beginning to think

you'd left 'ome for good an' that you couldn't be bothered about us anymore.'

Cathy let go of Rosie and pulled her sister to her. 'Don't be like that,' she implored. 'I have been working, but I'm home now an' you an' me will catch up on the news later on, eh? By the way, I didn't bring you chocolate, I bought you the most marvellous bottle of perfume and when you make a purchase like that in Jersey they give you several items of make-up free. You'll love them.'

Jenny felt heaps better. Her sister was treating her as a grown-up. Make-up and perfume. *Wait till I tell Norma.* 'Cor, thanks Cathy. I've never had a bottle of real perfume before. Will you tell me all about Jersey when we're in bed tonight? We've got two beds in your old room.'

'Yeah, course I will,' Catherine told her, only too pleased that her sister wasn't going to be stroppy, and to seal the matter she pulled Jenny closer and planted a kiss on her cheek, which Jenny then returned with vigour.

The sound of a man clearing his throat had them all turning round. 'Oh Stan! I'm so sorry,' Cathy cried, 'I didn't mean to leave you just standing there.'

'Aw, my goodness.' Evie was appalled at her own bad manners. 'I'm sorry, too. Please, don't stand there in the doorway, come on in.'

Catherine took the young man by the hand and brought him forward. 'Mum, this is Stanley,' and then she added, 'an' Stan, these are my two sisters, Jenny and Rosie.'

'Hello,' the two girls said in unison.

Evie held out her hand. 'I'm so pleased to meet you. Welcome to our house.'

Stanley Caldwell was tall and blond. His straight hair hung around his neck. Evie's first thought was that she'd like to tell him to get it cut. *Watch it!* she chided herself, *Mind your own business or else you'll be off on the wrong foot.*

His skin was tanned and his eyes were a light grey. Those eyes had never left her face since he had taken hold of her hand. They were laughing at her. Evie straightaway, in her mind, nicknamed him Laughing Eyes. 'I'm very pleased to meet you, Mrs Smith, and now I can see where Catherine gets her beauty from,' he said, then added quickly, 'and you girls as well. It's great to meet you.'

'Oh he's a charmer, isn't he, Cathy? You better keep your eye on him,' Evie said with a grin.

'I like him. He's nice,' Rosie piped up.

They all laughed. More so when Stan answered, 'I like you too, Rosie.'

'Don't visitors get offered a cup of tea in this house any more?' queried Cathy.

'You're not a visitor,' her mother said sharply, then relented. 'All right, we'll all have a cuppa but then we 'ave to get down to your grandma's. She must 'ave seen the taxi arrive an' she's doing a roast dinner for all of us.'

Everything had gone well. Flossie and Jim seemed to like Stan Caldwell, and Evie breathed a sigh of relief as she at last persuaded Jenny to go upstairs and get into bed.

'I wanted to wait until Catherine comes in,' a tired but happy Jenny pleaded.

'I know dear. She an' Stanley are probably having a good old chinwag with yer nan. You'll have plenty of time to talk to 'er tomorrow, an' she will be 'ere till Monday morning, so go on, be a good girl. I'm coming up meself if Cathy is much longer.'

Evie had just put a saucepan of milk on to boil when the kitchen door opened and a bright-eyed Catherine came in. It was a quarter to twelve. ''Ello, luv. I'm just making some cocoa. D'ye want some?'

'Yes please.' Cathy took her coat off and ran her hands

through her long hair, pushing it back off her face and tucking it behind her ears. 'Gran an' Granddad are wonderful, aren't they? I didn't think they would be that nice to Stan.'

'Why ever not?'

'I dunno. I just didn't. I did hope you would all like him. His parents are real nice. They made me feel they were really pleased to hear that their son an' I had got engaged. After all, they had never met me before, not till they came to Jersey that time for a few days.'

'And you got on straightaway?' Evie asked as she set two steaming mugs of cocoa down on the table.

Cathy smiled. 'Better than I would have believed. Especially as Stanley is an only child.'

'What difference does that make?'

'A helluva lot, according to my mates. Parents of only one kid can be damned awkward. You know, possessive like.'

'And Mr and Mrs Caldwell aren't?'

'No,' Catherine replied. 'I never had any trouble talking to them, and they chatted away to me as if they'd known me all me life.'

Thoughtfully, Evie stirred sugar into her mug, then she raised her eyes and stared straight into those lovely blue eyes of her eldest daughter. 'How old are Stanley's parents?' she asked.

'I've no idea,' Cathy replied truthfully.

'Well I'm so glad you've met someone you obviously love very much, and I wish you all the luck in the world. Though from what you've told me already you'll 'ardly need it.'

A silence fell between them, during which they both slowly sipped their cocoa.

'Mum, there was one thing . . .' Catherine said slowly. 'Meeting Mr and Mrs Caldwell, seeing them together like, made me realise what a hard life you've had. I'll tell you something now, Mum, I hate my father.'

Evie's heart gave a lurch. Was Catherine going to be eaten up with hatred? Please, please God, she wasn't. 'Catherine, hatred is a terrible thing. It can eat away at you, ruin yer life.'

'Oh no, Mum. I won't let it do that. I hate him more for what he did to you. It's your life that he ruined.'

Not trusting herself to speak, Evie nodded instead, and Cathy went on. 'I've never told anyone about this before. I've carried my father's photograph about with me since I was at school.'

Evie's heart ached as she thought of Cathy as a small child and the hurt she must have felt. She hadn't felt any anger towards Ted Hopkins for years. At this moment she was afraid she might betray just how angry she was, and that would never do. It would only upset Catherine more.

'Don't suppose you even remember, Mum. You took the photo of him in the back garden where we used to live. He's got no coat on and his shirt sleeves are rolled up.'

Evie did remember. It had been one of those glorious weekends when she had still believed that Ted would leave his wife and marry her. More importantly, that he would give his name to his daughters.

'You know why I kept it, Mum?'

Again Evie merely shook her head.

'I felt while I had that picture I had a root, a dad somewhere in the background who would come if I really needed him. I wanted to believe we were like other families. Not having had a father when I was little, you'd think I'd have got used to not having one by the time I went to school. But I never did get used to it. I wanted a dad.'

Evie felt she wasn't going to be able to hold back her

tears for much longer. She glanced at the clock. They were talking far into the night but she wouldn't stop Catherine for the world. How little she had known her own child!

'Cathy, why didn't you write back that time that he wrote to you apologising for not coming to Balham to meet you?'

'He'd stayed away too long by then. Broken too many promises.'

'Is that why you like Stanley's parents so much?'

'I suppose so, in a way. They are nice people. They only came to Jersey to check on Stan, but right from the off they seemed to include me, kinda let me know that they had taken to me. It was a nice feeling. Now it's all settled. Stan and I are getting married, we're going to work in his parents' hotel and I feel as if at last I'm gonna have a father.'

'Oh Catherine!' Tears were trickling down Evie's face.

'Please, Mum, don't.' Cathy's voice was little more than a sob. 'I didn't mean to upset you. It hasn't been your fault. There was a time I blamed you, resented the fact that there was only a mum and no dad in our house. Not any more. Leaving home made me realise how smashing you and Nanna have always been to me, and to Jenny and young Rosie.'

'Oh Cathy, why didn't you . . . when you were . . . at school . . .' Evie was incapable of framing a complete sentence. She felt so guilty.

'Mum, did you really fall in love with him when you were so young?'

'Hopelessly,' sighed Evie, 'and I felt that way about him for years. You have to believe that, Catherine. I was pregnant by him three times and it wasn't until I found that I was carrying Rosie that I finally faced the truth that Ted Hopkins had been using me. Stringing me along all those years with promises that he hadn't the slightest intention of keeping.'

Catherine looked at her mother in shocked silence.

'Don't be so upset, please,' Evie begged her. 'It's like yer nanna always says, it's a pity God didn't put old 'eads on young shoulders.'

Evie got to her feet and came around the table. She put her arms about Cathy and rocked her as if she were a baby. Things between her and Catherine would never go back to being what they were. There was a closeness now, a bond of steel, that nothing and no one would be able to break.

'Come on, luv,' Evie said after a long time. 'Let's both wash our faces an' go up to bed.'

Catherine sighed heavily. 'It isn't fair. Even George was taken from you, and he was so nice.'

Oh no! No more probing of the past tonight. She had had all that she could take. She didn't need to be reminded of George. It brought back too many memories of just how lonely she was.

'There's nothing written anywhere that I've come across, Cathy luv, that promises life will be fair. I suppose we all get our just deserts in the end, though like you I sometimes wonder if it isn't the ones that deserve it least that prosper the most.'

For the first time Cathy smiled. 'Oh don't say that, Mum. I'm doing all right at the moment.'

'And long may it continue, though if we stay up for much longer your Stanley will think you've turned into an old hag since you came back 'ome.'

'In that case, I'm away to me bed. Goodnight, Mum. God bless you.'

'You too, my darling. See you in the morning.'

With Catherine gone, Evie sat down, folded her arms on the table, dropped her head and cried as she had not for years. Not since George had died in that fire.

When finally she had cried herself out, she went upstairs and crept quietly into the room where two of her daughters were fast asleep. She bent and kissed Jenny's forehead. Did she feel the same about her father? She looked babyish, younger than her fifteen years, as she lay asleep there. Jenny was the only one of her three daughters that looked like her father. Dark hair, dark complexion and those huge brown eyes. What did life have in store for her?

She turned her gaze to Catherine. She had looked so lovely when she had arrived. So lively, eyes dancing with joy. So excited and enthusiastic about showing Stanley off. Was she glad Cathy had opened her heart to her? Yes! Even though it had evoked memories she would far rather have forgotten. Edward Hopkins had far more to answer for than she had ever imagined.

'I must have been blind,' she murmured as she quietly closed the door.

Chapter Twelve

With Christmas over, the weeks up to Easter had flown by.

'Wasn't it nice of Madge and Alan to let us all come down a day early?' Flossie whispered to Evie as they made their way up the stairs to bed, leaving Jim and Bert Killick downstairs, having a last drink with Stanley and his father.

'Yes it certainly was. Mr and Mrs Caldwell have fell over backwards to make us feel welcome.'

'Now Evie, you know they asked for us all to be on Christian-name terms. You like them, don't you?'

'Very much so,' Evie answered quickly. 'And to ask the Killicks to stay 'ere as well I think was a marvellous gesture. It would 'ave cost Bert a packet if they'd had to go to another hotel.'

'Yeah, four rooms they've given over to our party. Still, they 'ave got a lot more coming from their side than we 'ave. There's only me an' Jim, you, Jenny and Rosie, and the four Killicks.'

'Funny, wasn't it, our Catherine asking Shirley and

Norma if they wanted to be bridesmaids at the last minute?'

'It was an' all.' Flossie agreed. 'And it really pleased Joan.'

'I was only grateful that their dad bought Shirley an' Norma's dresses. And as it turned out their two pale blue ones go ever so well with our two's pale pink dresses that we slogged over. One bride's dress and two bridesmaids' dresses was enough to last me a lifetime, Mum, don't know about you.'

Flossie laughed out loud. 'There were times when I thought we'd never get it right. All those damn little seed pearls. Still, we'll see in the morning if it was all worthwhile. Goodnight luv.'

'Goodnight, Mum.'

'Your dress is magnificent, Catherine,' Madge Caldwell said as she walked round and round the bride.

'Yes, my mum and my nanna have made a tremendous job of it. I'm thrilled to bits with it.'

'We're going to be fortunate with the weather, I think,' said Mrs Caldwell. 'Look at that sun. It's bursting through a real treat, though I don't suppose it will be all that warm. Anyway, I'm going to leave you all to it and I'll see you in church.'

'Mrs Caldwell,' Catherine called.

'Yes, my dear?' Madge was adjusting a fur stole around the shoulders of her navy blue jacket.

Catherine moved towards her, leant forward and gently kissed her cheek. 'Thank you for everything, especially Stanley.'

'Bless you, Catherine.' The older woman was obviously thrilled.

Joan Killick appeared in the doorway. 'That's the four girls gone off in the second car. They did look a picture.'

She came further into the room and gasped in admiration at the bride-to-be. 'God! I never expected that dress to turn out like that. Royalty has never had better.'

Evie and her mother flushed with pride.

The material was pure white silk. The bodice was perfectly plain under a delicate collar made up from dozens of tiny pearls. The long sleeves had cuffs made from the same pearls. It was the skirt that had take so many hours of work. The petticoat beneath was of the same silk but in the very palest shade of pink. Using hoops it had become a crinoline. The hem had been gathered up every twelve inches to form scallop-shaped curves, allowing the hint of pink silk to show beneath it. Dozens more seed pearls had been attached to the edge of every curve. At the top of each gathering, a pink bow had been stitched, the centre of which had again been covered with pearls. The white satin shoes that peeped out from beneath Catherine's dress when she moved were adorned with pearl-covered buckles.

A coronet of apple blossom and a long floating veil completed the picture. Jim Tyler appeared carrying a tray of glasses. He stopped dead, amazement showing on his face. 'Good Lord! he uttered.

'Isn't she gorgeous?' Flossie said quietly.

'Oh, she's more than that. She's bloody beautiful.' Jim smiled in reply. 'I came to boost you all with a drop of champagne before we set off for the church. Don't seem like ye need it.'

'We'd better get going,' Flossie said, taking in Joan and Evie with a look.

'We'll leave the bride and her grandfather to have a drink, seeing as they are allowed to be the last to arrive.'

*

'Are you all right, Catherine?' Jim asked when they were alone in the bedroom.

'I'm fine,' Cathy assured him quietly.

Passing her a full glass, Jim said, 'A toast, if I may. A long and happy life to you an' Stan.'

Catherine studied Jim over the rim of her glass as she drank. She, like the rest of her family, had come to love this kind man. Smiling, she slipped her free hand into the crook of his arm and drew him closer. 'Granddad, I've never really thanked you for paying for all our lovely dresses.'

'Sh, luv, there's no need.'

'But there is need,' she interrupted him, 'you and Nanna 'ave been so generous.'

'Catherine, I've 'ad all the thanks I want just seeing yer mum an' you girls so 'appy.'

Catherine leant forward and softly put her lips to his cheek. 'Most of all, Granddad, I'm thrilled that it's you that's giving me away today.'

He was so choked with emotion by now that he had to make a joke of it or else he was in danger of bawling like a kid. 'Well, let's get it over an' done with. If that young man is daft enough to say he'll take ye, I'll give you to 'im gladly.'

He led her from the room, thinking how lucky he was to have such a lovely wife, daughter and three grand-daughters.

'Perfect, wasn't it?' Flossie asked Evie as they stood outside the church and watched the photographer do his job.

'Oh, Mum, it was lovely. I couldn't 'elp crying. Don't they make a lovely couple.'

'Perfect,' Flossie agreed.

Evie sighed with contentment as she glanced at her

daughter and newly acquired son-in-law with their four bridesmaids grouped round them. Another lovely picture for her to treasure.

'Come on,' Jim called as he came towards the pair of them. 'They want you in the next set of photographs.' Before they moved, he bent towards Evie and kissed her lightly on the cheek. 'Well done, luv,' he whispered. Then turning to his wife he kissed her twice, both times on the lips.

'What d'ye wanna go and do that for?'

'For no reason, except you're the two most beautiful ladies 'ere today and you both belong to me.'

Flossie could have hugged him to death. As far as she could see, her Evie was the only lady there without a partner, and Jim was doing his best to make it up to her. Bless the man. He was a gem. She hoped, as she had on so many other occasions, that she might live to see the day when such a man would come along and make Evie as happy as Jim had made her.

The lovely day was drawing to an end. Everyone was clapping like mad as Stanley and Catherine headed towards the hired car into which their luggage had been stowed.

'Good luck!'

'All the best!'

'Stay sober!'

Many more good wishes were being shouted. Catherine hesitated, looked around until she was able to lock eyes with her mother, then she blew her a kiss.

Evie, who was crying unashamedly now, waved back.

Jim, one arm wrapped around Flossie, drew Evie into the circle of his other arm as they watched the car bearing their Catherine and her new husband away into the distance.

Flossie was thinking to herself, *One down and two to go.* She hoped that Jenny and Rosie might be as lucky as Cathy had been. There again, when they were gone, where would that leave Evie? Lonely was the only word that sprang to her mind.

Chapter Thirteen

EVIE WOKE UP SUDDENLY, fear clutching her insides. She raised herself up on her elbows.

Heidi was growling.

She half got out of bed, then hesitated. This had happened before!

Her forehead was covered in sweat, but she froze as Heidi gave a ferocious bark, got to her feet and bolted off down the stairs. There was no moonlight, and she didn't want to put the landing light on for fear of waking the girls, but Jenny was already sitting up in bed.

'Who's there?' she heard Jenny whisper and, before she could answer, she called again, this time more loudly, 'Who's there?'

'Sh! It's only me.'

'What's the matter with Heidi?'

'I don't know. I'm just going downstairs to see. You stay in bed, but if you hear Rosie wake up, go an' fetch 'er in with you.'

'Don't you want me to come with you?'

'No! I've just told you, stay in bed. I won't be long.'

It sounded like floorboards creaking. Hard to tell with

Heidi barking so loudly. *Funny,* she thought, *I've never heard the boards creak before.* She could feel her heart hammering against her ribs as she gingerly made her way downstairs.

Heidi had dropped down onto her belly outside the boarded up room, her front paws spread flat each side of her head, her eyes focused on the sealed door. For what seemed an eternity, Evie stood still, not knowing what to do, feeling really frightened and with all her limbs trembling. She had to fight to get herself under control.

'What is it Heidi?' She managed to get the question out and then immediately said to herself, 'Ye bloody fool, I suppose ye think Heidi is gonna stop barking an' turn round an' answer you.'

There it was again! Wood cracking! It wasn't floorboards creaking! It was coming from outside the house. Oh my God! Someone was trying to tear down the boards from her empty room.

By now Heidi was out of control, leaping up in the air, snarling and panting.

'What the 'ell can I do?' she raved out loud. She could hear a neighbour's baby crying, then she heard men shouting. She felt her whole body sag with relief. Someone was coming to help her. She flew back up the stairs and into her bedroom. She grabbed her dressing gown and pulled it on. Shoving her feet into her slippers, she went to the window and, as she raised it open, Bert Killick's deep voice echoed down the street.

'Oi! What the 'ell is going on out 'ere?'

The light from his open doorway shone out onto an enormous motorbike, which was parked against the wall of the Alfred Butt flats. Evie shivered, but she wasn't so afraid now.

'Rosie's in 'ere with me, Mum,' Jenny yelled.

Evie ran, popped her head into Jenny's room, and

called, 'I'm going to open the front door an' let Heidi out, I'll come back up to you as soon as I can.'

Heidi couldn't wait as she drew back the bolts. She clawed the wooden framework, still panting, her ears pricked up high.

At last she had the top bolt free. Heidi's paw pulled the door wide and she was out. With just two bounds and a great leap she'd cleared the gate and was flying up the road.

The roar of the motorbike starting up was deafening. Evie strained her eyes but all she could make out was a black helmet and what looked like a dark leather jacket, then the bike was away up the middle of the road with Heidi flying in hot pursuit.

'What's 'appened, Evie?' Bert shouted, coming towards her.

'Don't know yet, Bert. By the looks of this mess he must 'ave been trying to break down these boards. Christ knows why.'

Heidi came limping back. Lights were going on all over the flats.

'Oh, you poor old thing.' Evie's voice was full of pity as she petted Heidi.

'Bloody good job she was around. I reckon she scared the bugger off, don't you Bert?' Alf Martin, a large man with a bald head, owned the corner paper shop and he had always had a great regard for Evie. 'God 'elp the sod if I'd got 'old of 'im. Enough to frighten Evie 'alf to death, and 'er on 'er own an' all.'

'You could well be right, Alf,' Bert agreed. 'Made enough noise to wake the dead, didn't you Heidi, gal? Though what the bloody 'ell the bloke could 'ave been thinking of beats me. You ain't 'ad that room open since you moved in 'ere, 'ave you Evie?'

'No, course I ain't.' Evie shuddered. 'Wish I knew what he was after.'

Joan Killick was crossing the road, pulling the cord of her dressing gown tight as she came. 'You all right, Evie? Blooming fine how d'ye do, ain't it? Mr Simmonds 'as phoned the police. Shall I come in an' make ye a nice cup of tea?'

Before Evie got a chance to agree, a police car sped round the corner and screeched to a halt at the kerb. Evie and Joan came out onto the pavement to meet it.

'You all right, ladies?' The young policeman was concerned for the two women clad only in dressing gowns.

They both nodded.

A little crowd of men had gathered now, and everyone started talking at once.

Sergeant Alan Richardson eased his large frame out of the car and said loudly, 'All right, all right. Calm down, and just one of you tell me what has happened.'

Bert Killick stepped forward. 'Some daft sod 'as tried to break in there.' He pointed to the high privet hedge that grew up in front of the bay window.

'Which one of you lives here?' The sergeant's voice was stern and Evie felt a bit afraid of him.

'I do,' Evie told him.

The sergeant looked at her, then a smile broke out on his face. 'It's Mrs Smith, Mrs Evie Smith, isn't it?'

Evie stared at him, bewildered. There was something familiar about the man but she couldn't place him.

Without waiting for Evie to reply, the sergeant asked, 'Are you all right, luv? Suppose you tell me what happened.'

Evie stepped back off the pavement and onto her garden path and pointed at the damaged boards and the broken pieces of wood and splinters that were lying on the windowsill and on the ground.

Turning to his constable, Sergeant Richardson instructed, 'Go inside the house and switch the lights on.'

Evie was quicker. 'Won't do no good for that room,' she said, reaching inside the house and flicking the switch to light up the hall. 'It's been boarded up for years. You can't get into it even from inside the house.'

The sergeant looked baffled.

'Who ever done that was in a hurry,' declared the constable as he examined the wood panel. 'Seems he was disturbed.'

'What do you keep in that room?' the sergeant asked, his voice now sounding more kindly.

'Nothing. I've told you, it's been boarded up ever since I came to live 'ere. I've never been inside there. The council said at the time the end wall wasn't safe.' Evie was amazed at how crossed she sounded.

'Well, no need to ask you to come to the station. We can't do much tonight. We'll get the council to come and have a look in the morning. That's if you're sure . . .' He left the sentence unfinished.

'We'll see to 'er,' Bert hastened to assure the sergeant. 'Me wife's gone indoors to see to 'er girls an' put the kettle on.'

'Oi, oi, oi, what's 'appened?' Jim Tyler's voice boomed out as he came tearing down the road. 'Evie, are you all right, luv? Christ, what's the police doing 'ere?' Are the kids all right?'

'Calm yerself, Jim boy,' Alf Martin urged, grabbing hold of Jim's arm. 'They're all all right. Bit late, ain't ye?'

'Gawd above, I'm sorry. We sleep at the back. It was only all the lights going on an' the racket that woke me up. Yer mum's just coming, Evie. Now is someone gonna tell me what's going on?'

Evie pointed to the splintered boards that still hung at the dirty window.

'Oh my Gawd!' He grabbed Evie and put his arms

around her shoulders drawing her close. 'Must 'ave frightened the living daylights out of you. Don't make no bloody sense though. Can't be sod all in there, not after all these years, an' there's no way they'd get into the 'ouse from the front, not unless they'd wanna knock a bloody wall down.'

'Well apparently somebody was after having a try.' The sergeant nodded at his PC, indicating that there was nothing they could do at the moment and they might as well be on their way. Then, as an afterthought, he said to Jim, 'You're Mr Tyler, right? You own the bookmaker's shop in Trinity Road?'

'Right on both counts,' Jim agreed.

'And are you a relation of this lady then, sir?'

'Yes, I am, she's my stepdaughter.'

The small crowd had dispersed by this time and Bert Killick had followed his wife into Evie's house.

Sergeant Richardson held his hand out to Jim. 'I think congratulations are in order. Bit late, but still. I heard our Flossie had remarried. Tell her from me there's a lot of us that miss her pies.'

Having shaken hands with Jim, he nodded at his PC and they got back into their police car.

Jim was still shaking his head, taken aback that a copper was on such familiar terms with his wife. He managed to call, 'Goodnight. Thanks, Officer,' as the car moved off.

'Well I never!' Flossie exclaimed as she cuddled Rosie and watched Joan hand mugs of tea around. 'Ain't safe anywhere these days. You all right Jenny? You were a brave girl to stay indoors and take care of Rosie. I'll treat you both to something nice tomorrow. I expect it was only some silly old man who'd 'ad too much to drink. Heidi would 'ave given 'im what for if she'd got 'er teeth into 'is backside.'

Rosie looked up at her nanna and giggled. 'Wish Heidi had got him.'

Don't you worry, pet,' Evie was quick to say, 'Heidi frightened the life out of him. He won't be back.'

Several seconds ticked by while Flossie looked at Jim, and Joan stared at Bert. Each knew what the other was thinking. Even Evie couldn't be that naive.

'So, come on then, let's 'ear all about yer murky past. I wanna know 'ow come it's only now that I find out I've married a woman who is well-known to the police.'

'You're asking for a clump round your 'ead, Jim Tyler,' Flossie answered, grinning widely.

The two girls had been taken back up to bed. Joan and Bert had gone back over to their own house and Evie had been about to say goodnight to her parents. Or rather good morning, for it was now a quarter to three and it would soon be daylight.

'Yeah, Mum. Before you go I wouldn't mind knowing a bit more about Sergeant Richardson. He seemed to know a helluva lot about me an' all.'

'Well 'e should, ye great big dope. You both went to the same school as each other. Though there again 'e must be four or five years older than you. 'Is little girl used to play with Catherine when you brought 'er to see me, before you moved back to Tooting. Shame she died.'

'What? 'Is daughter died? 'Ow old was she?' Evie's voice was full of concern.

Flossie gave a deep, sad sigh. 'Don't suppose you remember it, Evie, though you should, Jim. It were about nine years ago, coming up to Christmas. Shocking 'ow there always seems to be a great tragedy about Christmas time.'

'Mum, are you gonna tell us what 'appened or are we gonna stay 'ere for the rest of the night?'

'Sorry, luv, I was just thinking 'ow unfair it was. His wife – nice young woman: they lived in Tooting Bec Road at the time an' I used to see a lot of 'er – she'd been shopping with Angie. That's it, the little girl's name was Angie. Pretty as a picture, she was.'

Flossie stopped talking, rummaged in her bag for a handkerchief, found one, took it out and blew her nose.

Neither Jim nor Evie had the heart to tell her to get to the point. She was so obviously upset at the memory of whatever it was that had happened.

'They were in a queue, waiting for a bus outside Morden Tube Station. The bus came all right. Straight up onto the pavement – ploughed right into the line of people. Killed about six, I think it was. I know two kids were amongst the dead. The bus driver 'ad 'ad an 'eart attack, so they said at the inquest. It were in all the papers. Rotten for Alan Richardson. He lost his wife an' child.'

'Christ Almighty!' Jim muttered.

There were tears in Evie's eyes as she said, 'There's no justice in this world, is there, Mum.'

'Don't seem like it 'alf the time, luv.'

'Well, this won't get the baby a new bonnet and it won't mend the tear in the old one, so I'd better take you 'ome, woman, an' let our Evie get a couple of hours' shuteye before the council turn up on her doorstep.' Jim was doing his best to be jovial, but neither Flossie nor Evie had it in them to laugh.

'See you later, luv,' Flossie said, giving Evie a gentle hug. 'Send Jenny down to tell me when the council man arrives or if the police come back. I'll come up 'ere with you, see what they 'ave to say. Though for the life of me I still can't fathom out what's going on that suddenly makes that room so important.'

Evie was having exactly the same thoughts as she lay

wide awake in her bed. Sleep was impossible until someone came up with some answers.

The dust that was flying about was awful and the musty smell wasn't much better. Evie stood with her mother and Joan Killick, along with half the street, watching two men in overalls take down the remaining boards from the side windows of the bay.

'Cor, it's gonna be another scorcher,' Flossie complained.

'Don't knock it, Mum. Another fortnight an' we'll be into September an' the nights will start drawing in again.'

'Mrs Smith, would you mind coming into the front garden, please?' Constable Blake, the young policeman who had been here last night, was calling Evie. This morning Sergeant Richardson wasn't with him. A woman police constable by the name of Jane Glover was.

As Evie stepped round the hedge, the WPC was grinning all over her face. PC Blake was covered from head to foot in powdery dirt, and he didn't look at all pleased.

'You must have been barmy, Constable, climbing over the sill before the workmen told you it was safe.' The WPC was still laughing.

Constable Blake ignored her and motioned with his hand for Evie to come closer. The two workmen and the woman sent by the council, Miss Powell, stopped talking as Evie peered into the dusty room. *Must be Women's Lib Day today.* Evie smiled to herself as she now watched the WPC clamber over the sill and join Miss Powell in the far corner of the empty room. Evie was frantically trying to see what they were looking at.

'D'you know anything about this?' the PC asked Evie.

Evie coughed and cleared her throat. The dust was choking her. 'I can't make out what it is,' she complained.

'It's a wooden tea chest.'

'Well 'ow the 'ell did it get there?'

'We're wondering the same thing, Mrs Smith.'

Evie stared hard at Miss Powell. She was a skinny woman, dressed in a severe suit, and Evie didn't like the tone of her voice. But for all that, the woman had her wits about her.

'I'm sorry I can't 'elp you,' Evie said. 'It's the first I've known of anything at all being in this room.' Joined now by Flossie, Evie asked, 'Did you know that chest was in there, Mum?'

Flossie poked her head and shoulders in as far as they would go, and with a smirk on her well made-up face she muttered, 'No, I didn't, but let's 'ope the crown jewels are hid in there, eh?'

Miss Powell had had enough of this. She wasn't at all happy to be messing about in a stinking empty room, getting her suit mucky and ten to one having laddered her nylons. Her voice rose a few octaves as she answered Flossie's quip. 'Well, let's find out, shall we? All right with you, Constable?'

The PC licked his lips. He was well aware that this woman was passing the buck to him and that everyone outside had gone quiet and was listening for his answer. How he wished that Sergeant Richardson hadn't gone off duty. 'What are you proposing, Miss?'

She shrugged her shoulders, her impatience showing. 'To see if the darn thing is empty of course.' Then, facing the two workmen, she ordered, 'Just upend the chest, please. Gently now. Let the contents fall out onto the floor. Careful, careful,' she rebuked them as they bent to lift the chest.

Suddenly it was all too much for Evie. The weirdness of what was going on, coupled with the fact that she'd been frightened out of her life last night and had ended up not being able to get to sleep, took its toll. She lost her temper. Putting her hands on the window ledge in front of her, palms flat, she shouted in through the open window. 'Why the bloody 'ell don't you just let them get on with it? It's probably only a load of old rubbish that got left behind when the room was sealed up anyway.'

Miss Powell was shocked that a council tenant would have the audacity to speak to her like that. She stepped back rather too quickly. There was a distinct crack. The floorboard, rotten with age, had given way and Miss Powell's heel was stuck hard and fast between two boards. The more she struggled to free her heel the deeper it went in.

'Wriggle your foot out of your shoe,' suggested PC Blake, 'then maybe I'll be able to pull it out for you.'

Seeing the straight-laced Miss Powell trying to balance herself on one foot was too much for Evie. She had to cover her mouth with her hands to stop herself from laughing.

The constable got the shoe, order was restored and the two men upended the chest. There was nothing but shavings, and they were wedged in so tightly that very few tumbled out.

Miss Powell, her shoe now back on, shouted, 'You're so slow. Put your hands in and drag the stuff out.'

The onlookers heard the men slam the chest against the wall. The shavings, which must have been in the chest for a long time, came out and with a dull thump a metal box hit the floor.

Evie couldn't believe it. And she wasn't the only one. It was the WPC who picked it up. The box was shiny and clean but not very big. 'About eight inches square and six inches deep,' the constable wrote in his notebook.

'All right with you then, Miss, if we get off back to the station? We'll have to take that with us.' He nodded at the metal box which his colleague was still holding.

Evie's voice was trembling as she asked, 'Who's going to clear this mess up? And what about the floor and the window? Ye can't all just go an' leave it like this.'

The workmen were being gallant. They both stood in the front garden, arms outstretched offering assistance to Miss Powell as she endeavoured to climb out into the fresh air. Once clear of the sill, she stepped away from them as if they had some contagious disease, brushed herself down and with as much dignity as she could muster she moved out onto the pavement to stand beside her car. 'You can rest assured, Mrs Smith, the council will have this property attended to before nightfall.'

'Oh, thank you so much,' Evie murmured, and even Flossie wasn't sure whether Evie was being sarcastic or not.

Miss Powell raised her eyebrows at the policeman and said, 'I presume your station will be in touch with the Town Hall?'

'Oh, undoubtedly,' he answered, using the same high-pitched tone of voice as she had.

Miss Powell sniffed, unlocked the door of her car, got in and, to the relief of everyone, drove off.

'Oh, Mum, I've been worried out of my mind! Look, suppose Dad is right an' there was stolen goods in that box? I ain't got the foggiest idea 'ow they got there or where the 'ell they came from, but who's gonna believe me?' It was just one o'clock and Evie had been asked to come to Trinity Road Police Station at two-thirty.

'Well calm down, luv. I've made us both a bit of lunch an' a drink. Don't know about you, but I'm parched.'

'Mum, will you come with me?'

''Course I will, if ye want me to, though I doubt that I'll be allowed to sit in while they're interviewing you.'

Evie sat still, staring at her mother. Her eyes showed

panic. 'Interview me? What the 'ell can I tell them?' She burst into high-pitched laughter. 'Which prison d'you think they'll send me to if they decide to lock me up?'

'Evie!' Flossie came back with two bowls of soup and a plate of fresh crusty bread and placed the tray down on the table. Then she went to where Evie sat and put her arms around her. 'Come on, luv. Stop talking so daft. Come an' 'ave this soup while it's 'ot. It's not out of a tin. I made it meself – grated all the vegetables and put them on to simmer early this morning.'

'Thanks, Mum.' Evie smiled as she got up and went to sit at the table.

Poor Evie was scared, Flossie knew that much. Perhaps she had a right to be. You heard of such terrible goings-on these days, what with drugs an all. Something had to have been in that box. Something of great value. *I'd stake my life on that,* she thought. *Nobody puts rubbish in an expensive metal container and then hides it in a chest full of shavings. Never in a million years.* There had to be more to it than that. But what? You'd have to be a bloody clairvoyant to know that.

'You'll get through it somehow. They'll probably be very nice to you at the station.'

Evie smiled at her mother sadly. She didn't want the police to be nice to her. She wanted them to leave her alone.

My head's hammering away nineteen to the dozen, Evie moaned to herself as she sat one side of the huge desk and watched the duty sergeant write in his leather-bound book. *If he asks me one more time if I had any knowledge of that ruddy tea chest and its contents, or how it came to be in my house, so help me God, I'll kill him.*

It was only a week since the constable had taken the box away. Christ! It felt like a lifetime.

'Well, Mrs Smith. It's certainly a nice kettle of fish you've got yourself mixed up in.' This was Sergeant Walker, very different from Sergeant Richardson. He was still a big man but gone to seed, Evie was thinking, as she watched a smile come to his chubby red face. His voice was kind and Evie was grateful for that. She cleared her throat.

'I keep telling you, it's got nothing to do with me.'

'Well, young lady, I can tell you this much. The contents of that tin box were very valuable, and we are almost sure we have discovered where they originated from. That's as far as I can go.' He stopped talking very abruptly, almost as if he felt he had said too much already. He linked his fingers together and leant forward on his desk. 'We'll keep you informed.'

The thoughts that were flying round in her head! Valuables? So whatever they were, they had to be stolen, or else what were they doing hidden away in her empty room? Well, it wasn't anything to do with her! It wasn't fair. All this bloody hassle. And for what?

'D'ye mean I can go now?' All the fight had left Evie, and she just wanted to get out of this station.

The sergeant felt sorry for her. Maybe she was telling the truth. 'Yes of course you can, lass. We know where to find you if we need to talk to you again.'

'All right, luv?' Flossie got quickly to her feet as Evie came into the outer office.

'Yeah.' Evie's voice was tired. 'I need some air. Come on, Mum, let's get away from this place.'

She needed time to think.

Evie was listening to the wireless. A story was being read by a man with a wonderful, expressive voice. Jenny wasn't home yet and Rosie had gone to bed at half past eight, an hour earlier. Evie had had a nice hot bath and was now wearing her candlewick dressing gown, making the most of the time to catch up on her pile of ironing. She heard a rap on her back door and knew by the way it sounded that it was one of her parents. Tipping the iron up on end, she draped the blouse she'd finished ironing over the clotheshorse and went out to the kitchen. Through the top half of the back door, which was glass, she saw the outline of her stepfather. Nevertheless she didn't undo the bolts until Jim had called out, 'It's only me, Evie luv.'

She opened the door. Jim bent and gently kissed her cheek, then without saying a word walked past her and into the living room.

'What are you doing 'ere, Dad? There's nothing wrong is there?' She kept her voice quiet. She didn't want to wake Rosie.

Jim squared his shoulders, and Evie saw his face was set in a deep frown. Not more trouble! He faced her and took a deep breath. 'I wanted to 'ave a word with you on yer own, so don't let on t'yer mother that I've been 'ere, there's a good girl.'

Evie was worried. Normally these two never had secrets from each other. 'All right, Dad, but for goodness' sake get on an' tell me what you're on about.'

'Well, luv, there's no way I can think of t'wrap this up, so I'm gonna come straight out with it. At least that way you'll get my version of it and not some daft git's who thinks he's cottoned on t'something big just because he rubs shoulders with a few villains.'

Evie was stunned. 'Dad, it's not like you to talk about villains. Why don't we both sit down an' you tell me from the beginning what it is that's bothering you.' She knelt, unplugged her iron and moved the clotheshorse into the corner of the room, then went to the sideboard and poured her stepfather a stiff whisky.

Jim was seated on the settee, and she sat down beside

him. He took a deep drink of the scotch, cleared his throat and said, 'I was in Whitechapel last night, went to see a boxing match, an' ye wouldn't believe the rumours that were flying about. Talk around the Elephant, in fact all over the East End from what I can make out, is that the police 'ave recovered a load of diamonds which 'ave been missing a helluva long time.'

Evie suppressed a scream. 'I don't think I wanna 'ear this, Dad.'

'Well I think you'd better. Word is that the diamonds were in a safety deposit box, brought into the country by a South African.'

'You mean illegally?'

'Now I never said that, so don't go jumping the gun.' He took another swig from his glass. Evie was amazed to see he was trembling. His face was full of concern, but he kept his voice quiet. 'Seems the South African did a deal with a fellow that suited a whole lot of people. Only trouble was, before the deal could be clinched, the bloke died in a fire.'

The colour drained from Evie's face. Jim put his glass down on the floor and took hold of her hands, rubbing the backs in a circular movement with his thumbs.

'George?'

'Seems likely.'

Evie sat up, stunned, pulling her hands free from Jim's grasp. 'I don't believe what I'm 'earing. What would George 'ave been going to do with them?'

'Oh come off it, Evie. George was no saint. If anyone knew when he was on to a good thing George did. My life, he did!'

'But how? When? Was he such a bastard? He surely wouldn't 'ave planted them in my 'ouse. Oh the conniving bloody sod!'

The words were said in temper, but the hurt look on

Evie's face told Jim the effect this news had had on her. George had been her knight in shining armour. He had been going to take care of her and her girls, see they never wanted for anything. Well if he'd lived to have pulled this job off, they probably would have lived the life of Old Riley.

Evie looked into Jim's lovely deep brown eyes and saw the pity in them. 'You believe it, don't you?'

'Well, he'd 'ave 'ad plenty of opportunity. Can't see much behind that hedge at the best of times, and no one would have given a second glance to see George and a mate or two fiddling at those boards. If anyone 'ad spotted them they more than likely would have surmised that they were doing a repair job for you. I don't somehow see George getting that chest into that room on 'is own. Easy enough for two, though. Remove one panel, chest over the windowsill and in. Box deep inside that. Panel back in place. Bingo! Done an' forgotten.'

'But when?'

'God knows. Could 'ave been months before he died. Had to be when you weren't around, that's for sure. When ye come to think about it, Evie, what better place? Better than a bank vault. You've got to 'and it to him.' Jim laughed for the first time since he had come into the house. 'Wait till yer mother gets wind of this.' He laughed again. 'She's a canny one, your mum. Always said George was as deep as a bottomless pit. Seems she was right an' all.'

'How come someone suddenly turns up to try to get the box back? Who found out it was there after such a long time?'

'Dunno, my luv. Though secrets have a way of being let out. Nothing's a secret for ever if more than one person knows about it.'

It took a few seconds for Jim's words to sink in.

'I suppose so. What should we do?'

'Nothing. Say nothing to anyone. Not a dicky-bird. You've told the police you know nothing an' they can't argue with the truth, can they, gal?'

Evie stood up. 'Suppose we wait for the balloon to go up, eh?'

'We might never 'ear another word about it.'

'Dad, you're a terrible liar.' She smiled as she took his arm and helped him to get up from the settee. 'We'll go out to the kitchen and I'll make us a pot of tea.'

'Not for me, Evie.' He glanced at the clock. 'I've just got time for a pint. Your mother will smell a rat if I go 'ome without so much as a whiff of beer on me breath. Come to the back door with me an' make sure you shoot those bolts.'

Evie heard him whistling as he went down the garden path. It seemed as if all his tension had gone now that he had told her what he'd heard. Not so for Evie. She felt it would be a very long time before she would be able to relax again.

Chapter Fourteen

EVIE ARRIVED HOME FROM work to find her mother waiting on her doorstep for her.

'God, it's suddenly so cold an' the wind is bitter. Why 'aven't you let yourself in? 'Aven't lost yer key, 'ave you?' Evie greeted her mother, banging her gloved hands together.

'I was just about to when I saw your car turn the corner.' Flossie winced as a blast of wind swept her hair into her eyes. 'Damn wind. It's bitter, right enough,' she agreed.

Evie opened the door with her key and Heidi came bounding down the passage.

''Ello, my beauty. Who's missed their mum then?' Evie bent her knees and tickled Heidi beneath her chin.

'Get out of the way, you daft pair,' Flossie urged, pushing her way past. 'I came to tell you there's a big do on over at the Wheatsheaf tomorrow night. Darts final. Jim's playing, so is Bert. Joan doesn't want t'go. She said she'll 'ave Rosie if you want to come with us.'

'No thanks.' Evie spat the words out and was immediately guilt-ridden. 'Sorry Mum, I didn't mean that as it sounded. It's just that I don't like being the gooseberry.'

'Oh luv, you shouldn't feel like that. Not with us. Anyway, there'll be such a crowd there maybe you'll find yourself a nice-looking bloke.'

'Oh yeah! And maybe instead of 'aving a wife an' kids indoors he'll be filthy rich and under sixty years old,' she answered sarcastically.

'Stranger things 'ave 'appened,' her mother replied quietly.

'Not to me. Not with my luck.'

Poor Evie, Flossie thought. First there'd been that business with the police. Thank God, they'd not heard any more on that score so far. Mind you, it had been a nine-day wonder with the neighbours. Folk from Holdernesse Road and even from streets further afield had come to gawp at Evie's boarded up front room. The stories that spread would make your head spin. Drugs, jewels, counterfeit money and even phoney plates that were capable of printing thousands of pounds worth of forged notes had been found and carried away by the police, according to the gossipmongers. All that had been bad enough, yet it hadn't seemed to worry Evie too much. But ever since Jennifer had decided to abandon college and had gone with Norma to work in the West End, Evie had been down in the dumps. Flossie had been about to offer to make a cup of tea, then decided not to.

'Well, I'll go an' see about Jim's dinner. If ye change your mind, Evie, you know we love your company.'

'Yeah, thanks Mum.' Evie tried to smile.

'I mean it, Evie. Why won't you come? I know for a fact you 'aven't been out for weeks.' She stared Evie full in the face. 'Well, you 'aven't, 'ave you?'

'Mum, I appreciate your concern but I'm all right, really I am.' Her voice was husky as she said these words and her sad smile made Flossie want to hug her.

'Well I'll see you in the morning. Send Rosie down to see me when she comes 'ome from school. I got 'er a couple of pairs of new socks and that propelling pencil she was on about when I was down in Tooting this morning.'

Evie shook her head and managed a grin. 'You, Mum! You spoil my kids rotten.'

'That's what grannies are for.' Flossie grinned. 'Bye for now.'

Left alone, Evie shook her head again. This time in irritation. Honestly! What with one thing and another, it was enough to drive her up the wall. She couldn't bring herself to tell her mother the trouble she was having with Jenny. Why had she given up going to college? Because of Norma's tales of the bright lights of the West End and the money there was to be earned there? She guessed that Jenny hadn't needed much persuasion. She never came home until the early hours of the morning. How could any mother sleep? Evie lay awake, night after night, imagining the worst, thinking of the things she read about in the papers. But what was the good of going on at Jenny? She never answered any of the questions Evie put to her, and she had an awful way of making her feel so old.

'What do you know about life?' Jenny had taunted her.

'Enough to stop you making the same mistakes that I have, if only you would listen,' Evie had pleaded.

'Mum, you have to allow me to grow up some time,' Jenny had retorted.

Catherine had been a heavy cross to bear when she'd been in her teens. For more than two years now she had been fine. Happily married. Flat in her in-laws' hotel. Holidays abroad. And she wrote or telephoned regularly now, bless her.

It had been Stanley, her son-in-law, who had insisted she had the phone installed. He'd contacted the post office and paid the full cost of the installation. Catherine had got herself a good 'un there.

With Catherine married and settled down so well, you'd think I was due for a bit of peace, Evie told herself. But no! Jenny was the problem now. And who would have thought it?

Taken under the wing of Mr and Mrs Parker, Jenny had been as happy as a lark working in their surgery, dealing with folks' pets. She'd done well with her exams – well enough to get herself accepted at a college. Whatever it was that had gone wrong at college, Jenny wasn't saying. All the pleading and threatening had fallen on deaf ears. She had chucked the lot. Stayed in bed most days, only getting up to go out at night. As to where she went and with whom, Evie felt she might just as well have been talking to a brick wall for all the information she'd got out of her daughter. It was all so totally out of character. It seemed to Evie that Jenny had become a different person since she'd left school, and she was at her wits' end to know how to handle her, more so since she'd got this job in London.

Evie kicked her shoes off and rubbed at her aching feet. God knows she'd tried hard enough to be a good mother, and didn't life get easier as your children grew up? Did it hell! It got a damn sight harder.

Joan Killick sat in Lyons' tearooms at Tooting Broadway and stirred her tea thoughtfully. She had just come from the hairdresser's. The girl who had done her hair had been chatty. She'd known both her and Evie when they were youngsters in the Girl Guides. *Cheeky bitch said she remembered me as being skinny with ginger hair and green eyes. Well,* Joan laughed to herself, *at least I've still got red hair and green eyes.* It was her asking about Evie that had worried Joan. Seems the whole of Tooting knew that the police had taken stuff away from Evie's house. Poor Evie! She couldn't get her out of her mind. It wasn't right the way she lived, all work and no play. No wonder she got depressed. She'd be ill if she didn't watch out. She pushed the thought of mental illness from her mind. Maybe she should try harder to get Evie to come to the club, or even for a drink in the Wheatsheaf now and then.

''Ello Joan, sorry I'm late. I 'ad a job parking.' Evie sat down at the table and sighed.' My Jenny will be the death of me yet.'

Joan laughed at her friend. 'You know your trouble, you worry too much. You were just the same with your Catherine. D'ye want tea or coffee?'

'Oh, tea please, and a sandwich. I don't mind what it is.'

Joan came back with a fresh pot of tea and two ham and tomato sandwiches, and they sat together discussing their daughters. 'So when is Shirley's baby due?'

Joan grinned. 'Almost any day now.'

''As Bert come round to it yet?'

'Yeah, I think so. Mind you, he won't admit it. Bit of a shock for 'im, but then again, nobody was more surprised than me when our Shirley came in that Saturday afternoon with Bill Osbourne and said they'd got married.'

'Best thing really, wasn't it Joan? Seeing as she was three months' gone.'

'It was an' all. An' as I kept telling Bert, she is twenty-three, coming up twenty-four. It's 'er life. Besides, it saved us a lot of expense and bother.'

'Gonna be a grandma!' Evie teased.

'I don't mind. Especially as they've got a council flat. Out from under my feet.'

'Joan . . .' Evie paused.

'I know what yer gonna say,' Joan butted in. 'What's my Norma and your Jenny up to?'

Evie's cheeks flushed. 'Well, yes, I was.'

'Oh come off it, Evie. Neither of them is kids any more. Your Jenny's turned eighteen and my Norma's almost nineteen. Let's face it, luv, you an' me were married an' well in the family way by the time we were their age.'

'Don't I know it. You'd think they'd learn from our mistakes. Jenny turns 'er back on me if I so much as ask her why she gets home so late. I could break her bloody neck at times.'

'Oh, and you don't think I 'ave all of that an' more to put up with from Norma? Well, don't you?'

'Yeah, I know you do, but you've got Bert to stand up for you an' to sort Norma out if it comes to the crunch.'

'Hmm,' Joan sniffed. 'Fat lot of bloody good he is. If I told 'im 'alf of what goes on he'd go berserk, an' where would that leave me, or Norma come to that? So, what it boils down to is my Norma's chucked 'er apprenticeship in, got fed up with 'airdressing, and your Jenny's packed in college. So what?'

'It's what they're up to now that bothers me. I'd like to know where Jenny suddenly gets all this money she's spending. Satin camiknickers, lacy nightdress, two or three new pairs of shoes, not to mention the nylons.'

Joan grinned. 'They've got jobs in the West End. The pay's much better up there.'

'Oh yeah. And what are they getting paid for?'

'For Gawd's sake, Evie!' Joan put her hand on Evie's arm and squeezed it gently. 'Come on. Give them some credit. What you've convinced yourself is that they're on the game. Right, ain't I?'

Evie bit her lip and nodded.

'Well stop being so bloody daft. I'd stake my life they're not. Mind you, as I said to my Norma, " if I do find out you're more than a hat-check girl in that club I'll beat the living daylights out of you." I promised 'er that, and I meant it.'

Evie bit her lip again, this time drawing blood. Then she burst into tears.

Joan stared at her, long and hard. 'There's something you're not telling me, Evie! Dry your eyes, crying won't solve anything. Come on now, let's 'ave it.'

'Jenny hasn't been 'ome since Wednesday.' The words came out as little more than a whisper.

'Well it's only Friday now, so what's that, two nights or three she's stayed out?'

'Three if she don't show up today. Lately she's been going off about nine in the evening when your Norma calls for 'er and getting in any time after three the next morning. Only Thursday morning she didn't come 'ome. I never slept all night. Then all day yesterday I expected to 'ear from 'er, an' nothing. Not a word. Three o'clock this morning I did expect her to come crawling in, an' I made up my mind that I wouldn't 'ave a go at 'er. I'm worried sick, Joan.'

'Course you are, my luv. The minute we get 'ome I'll 'ave it out of our Norma, you wait. They go to work together an' come 'ome together as a rule, so she must know what's 'appened, an' if I 'ave t'take me slipper to 'er bare backside, big as she is, I'll get the truth from 'er. She'll be all right. You'll see.'

Evie wished she could be as sure as Joan was.

They finally got back to Tooting at a quarter past five. Evie dropped Joan off at her gate and found there wasn't a space outside her own house, so she drove further down and parked close to the kerb outside her mother's house. She felt whacked out. Getting out of the Mini, she locked it and decided she might as well pick Rosie up from her mother's now. The front door opened as she walked up the path and her mum almost pulled her into the hallway.

'There's a policeman an' a policewoman in there.' Flossie nodded her head towards the door of her front room. 'There's been an accident. Jenny . . .'

Evie didn't wait to hear more. She clenched her teeth and burst into the room. 'What's 'appened? Come on, tell me, please. Don't beat about the bush.'

The policeman was big with steely blue eyes and a worried look about him. Evie had never set eyes on him before. The WPC, she had. It was the same one who had come when the room had been broken into.

'Hello, Mrs Smith,' she greeted Evie, looking and sounding somehow much kinder than Evie remembered. 'I'm so sorry to have to tell you . . .'

Evie felt sick. She hoped to God she wasn't hearing right. She thought she was going to faint.

Flossie grabbed a chair and pushed it against the back of Evie's knees, forcing her to sit down.

'What did you say?' Evie asked, her expression showing how frightened she was.

The WPC hated this part of her job. She could feel for this mother. Nowadays it was what all mothers dreaded when the police turned up on their doorsteps. 'It's your daughter, Mrs Smith. Jenny has been attacked.'

Evie stared in horror at the policewoman, fright and pain showing in her eyes. 'Attacked? My Jenny? Who by?' She turned to where her mother stood. 'Oh Mum!' It was like a cry from a wounded animal. 'What are we gonna do? I've been dreading something like this. Our Jenny . . . she's so tiny.'

Her voice broke and she lowered her head and covered her face with her hands. Tears were streaming through her fingers.

'Don't cry, Evie. Come on, pull yourself together. Crying won't 'elp.'

Evie wanted to strangle her mother at that moment. It was the second time today she'd been told to pull herself together, that crying didn't help. What did they want her to do? Laugh!

The policeman cleared his throat. He'd been here long enough, and it wasn't helping matters to stand around and tell the family how sorry they were.

Flossie caught his eye. She pulled her daughter to her feet and into her arms. 'I'll get Jim an' we'll see about getting to the 'ospital.'

The WPC nodded. 'Jenny's been taken to Guy's hospital.'

Evie shuddered. She had to swallow hard before she could thank the two constables as her mother showed them to the door.

Evie sat beside her mother in the back of Jim's car. She felt desperate. Her clenched fists were showing her white knuckles. Was it her fault? Should she have tried harder to put her foot down and stopped Jenny from going to work in the West End? She'd have had a hard job!

Flossie's heart was all of a flutter. When Evie looked at her with those big blue eyes she could see how hurt and confused her daughter was. One had to be fair. Evie had done her best to bring those girls up with no man behind her. She'd always done all she could to help. Between them they'd always seen to it that the girls were nicely clothed, fed and warm. What more could they have done?

Jim Tyler was unusually quiet as he steered the car in the flow of traffic. He was swearing to himself and at the same time praying that young Jenny wasn't too badly hurt. What man got his pleasures from hurting lovely young girls? They weren't men! And you couldn't call them animals because animals would never treat their young so cruelly. Jennifer meant a lot to him. He could see her now, pretty as a picture when she'd been bridesmaid to her sister Catherine. Bloody hell, that was nearly three years ago. *Time flies by when you get to my age,* he reminded himself. It wasn't so long ago that he'd been a lonely man. And a jealous one. Dead jealous of Flossie and her stream of men friends. All that had altered when Flossie had agreed to marry him. Evie and her girls, as they'd come along, had always been part of his life. Now he was proud. Proud of the fact that to all intents and purposes he was father to Evie and grandfather to her children. God, if Jenny was hurt he'd give a lot to get his hands on the man who had done it.

The three of them walked into Guy's casualty department and Jim explained at the admission desk who they were.

'She's been taken up to a ward.' The receptionist smiled kindly. 'I'll get a porter to show you the way.'

'Mrs Smith?' A sister asked, coming out of her office.

'Yes, my daughter's been admitted here. Please, may we see her?'

'I'm sorry, Mrs Smith, you'll have to wait a while. A doctor is with her now.'

Flossie sighed. Waiting would seem endless.

Evie began pacing the waiting room floor and Flossie had to hold herself back from screaming, 'For Christ's sake sit down and keep still.'

Suddenly Evie crumpled.

Jim steered her to a chair and put his arms around her. 'There, there, it won't be long,' he crooned.

'The not knowing is the worst part,' Evie moaned.

'I know, I know. Shouldn't be long now.'

They were sitting like three zombies when a white-coated doctor came into the waiting room. 'Mrs Smith?'

The three of them stood up. 'We're Jenny's grand-parents,' Jim explained.

The doctor placed a hand on Evie's arm, his gaze was sympathetic. 'Your daughter is going to be all right. She has two broken ribs and a good few bruises, and naturally she is suffering from shock. I've given her an injection which will send her off to sleep. Best thing for her.'

'Are you really telling me that Jenny is not 'urt too badly?' Evie queried in a tight voice.

The doctor paused, then said, 'I'm afraid she took quite a beating but as I said she will be all right. Take time though . . .' He broke off, obviously embarrassed to say more.

Jim stepped forward, arm outstretched. 'Thank you, Doctor. Thank you very much,' he said, the relief apparent in his voice.

The two men shook hands and the doctor turned to go.

Evie clutched at the sleeve of his white coat. 'Please, may we see her?' she pleaded, her face looking drawn and white.

'Yes of course, but she will be very drowsy, if not already asleep, so try not to disturb her.'

'Thank you,' both Evie and her mother called after the doctor as he left the room.

Evie had prepared herself, but she still got a shock. Jenny's face was a mass of bruises. One eye was badly swollen. The pillows behind her head were piled high to prop her into a sitting position. Her hair, matted with blood, was spread out over the top pillow. One arm, which lay outside the bedclothes, was strapped to a wooden splint and had a needle attached to a drip inserted in it.

Jim felt rage surge through his body as he had to stand helpless and watch not only Evie's grief but her fear. Jenny wasn't going to die, but all the same, no young girl should be made to suffer as Jenny had.

'She'll be awake when we come back in the morning,' Flossie whispered as she led Evie away from the bedside.

During the journey home, Evie came to a decision. She didn't care what rows or tantrums she had to put up with, there was one thing of which she was certain: Jenny was not going back to work in the West End.

Chapter Fifteen

EVIE WAS ALONE IN the house, and she felt like a caged lion. Rosie had pleaded with her to let her go home with her nanna and sleep in her house. And who could blame her? Even a child could work out that Evie wasn't in the mood for cuddles and story reading tonight. She was much better off with Flossie and Jim. What had happened to Jenny was churning round and round in Evie's mind. All these years she'd struggled on her own to bring up her girls, and the minute Jenny was off out working this had to happen.

She sighed, a deep sigh, dragged up from the very bottom of her heart. Jenny, who'd never given her a moment's worry until recently. Jenny – small and wiry, lively, carefree, full of life, wanting only to work with animals. Damn it! How did she ever come to be working in the West End?

There was a knock on her front door. Evie looked at the clock: it was a quarter to ten. Who the hell was it?

'Come, Heidi,' she whispered, and the dog, sensing her fear, was at her side in one bound. 'Stay. Lay down Heidi,' she commanded as she slowly inched the door open.

Sudden tightness gripped Evie's chest at the sight of the police sergeant but soon turned to relief as she saw it was Sergeant Richardson, though she still felt wary. Was he here to tell her that Jenny had taken a turn for the worse?

He smiled. 'I wouldn't have disturbed you, but I saw your light on. Do you remember me? Don't worry, I'm not here in an official capacity.'

'Oh,' she managed to mutter, feeling utterly bewildered, 'do you want to come in?'

'If I may.'

She stepped further back into the hallway. 'Please, come in,' she said, bending to take hold of Heidi's collar. When he was seated on the settee she let go of Heidi and the dog made straight for the sergeant, sniffing at his shoes. He held out a hand.

'Give a paw, Heidi,' Evie ordered.

The dog sat down on her haunches and lifted her right paw, which the sergeant took between both his hands and shook.

Evie watched, smiling. 'You've made a friend. Now, can I get you anything? Tea, coffee? I don't 'ave much in the way of drinks.'

'No, thank you. I'm fine for the moment, but I wish you would sit down.'

Evie pulled a chair round to face him and did as he asked.

'I didn't know whether to knock at your door or not. I wanted to see if there was anything I could do to help you. I've seen Jenny. It were me that took her statement while she was in casualty.'

Evie's heart instantly went out to this man. How kind of him to bother. He wasn't all that old. What had her mother said? Four or five years older than her? Well, his dark hair was beginning to grey at the temples, his face was weather-beaten and his whole appearance was rugged, but at the moment his dark brown eyes were full of sympathy.

'Jenny is going to be all right, you do believe that, Mrs Smith, don't you?'

Evie didn't know what she believed. Her head was aching like mad. She still couldn't get the picture of Jenny lying in a hospital bed, battered and bruised, out of her mind.

'I feel so guilty, Sergeant,' she murmured. 'I should have put me foot down, stopped her taking that job. She told me it was in a book shop. I've never known Jenny lie to me before.'

Alan Richardson was watching the expression on Evie's face and guessed the torture she was putting herself through. 'Jenny wasn't lying. Not in the strictest sense, she wasn't.'

Evie's head jerked upwards. 'I'm not with you. I was told she'd been attacked by a drunk in the club where she worked.'

'Please, Mrs Smith, don't get so upset. Calm down and let me try and explain. That's really why I came round as soon as I was off duty. I knew you wouldn't have been told the full facts.'

Evie took a handkerchief from the sleeve of her cardigan and wiped angrily at her eyes. She mustn't cry. Not in front of this big policeman. It was his kindness that had brought the tears that were stinging the backs of her eyelids. She tried to drag up the details of what it was her mother had told her about him losing his family. The details wouldn't come. She hadn't her wits about her, not at the moment.

The sergeant coughed, breaking into her confused thoughts. 'Jenny did work in a book shop. Trouble was what went on above the shop. Perhaps she didn't tell you the shop was in Soho.' He heard Evie gasp but went on talking. 'Her friend Norma was taken on as a hat-check girl in the so-called club upstairs.'

Evie chewed her lip as she pondered on this information. 'So what was Jenny doing in the club?'

'Good question. Apparently the agreement was that Jenny would help out if they were short-staffed. It seems she was changing her uniform in what served as a staff room, turned round and found this man staring at her. Jenny hadn't heard him come up the stairs. She grabbed a towel and did her best to cover herself but wasn't quick enough. Whether the man was drugged, drunk or both we don't know yet.'

'Do you know what really happened?' The question burning into Evie's mind was, how far had the man gone? Had he raped Jenny? But she couldn't bring herself to ask, not outright.

'This much I can tell you. Jenny put up one heck of a struggle. The man didn't get off scot free himself. His face is well and truly scratched, and the answer to your unasked question is no. We don't think he got that far. Jenny used her feet, kicked him good and hard, that's probably why he beat up on her so badly.'

'Have you got the man?'

'Oh yes, we've got him. One of the barmen in the club heard Jenny's screams. I took his statement. Alan Richardson paused, and a slight smile came to his lips. 'Would you like me to tell you what the young man said to me? Off the record of course.'

Evie gave a slight nod.

'"I hope the girl crippled him for life, the dirty bastard." That's what he said.'

Why my Jenny? Evie wondered bitterly. *Why her?* She looked across at the sergeant. He had laid his head back against the top of the chair and closed his eyes. He looked as if he too had had a long tiring day. She got up and went to put the kettle on. She took two mugs out of the cupboard and placed them on a tray.

This man had lost his wife and daughter in one fell swoop, that much her mother had told her. He'd had to get on with his life. Apparently he had a good career in the police force. Coming here tonight wasn't in his line of duty. He'd come out of kindness. He must be a caring man.

Evie caught sight of herself in the mirror that was fixed above the sink. Her face was as pale and as strained as the sergeant's. She smiled at her reflection. He was also an attractive man, she admitted to herself. He must have looked after himself well over the years.

'It was good of you to come,' Evie said as she handed him a mug of coffee.

'On these kind of cases we try to be as informal as possible.'

'Oh now don't give me that, Sergeant. This visit is more than that.' Now why had she said that? She was a bundle of nerves. She grabbed her mug, spilling the hot coffee over her fingers.

He was on his feet in a second, pulling a snowy white handkerchief from his pocket. He took her mug and set it back down on the tray, then taking her hand he wiped each finger one at a time. He'd worked it out that by now Evie must be over forty, but this was hard to believe. She was tall and nice looking, her fair hair still thick and shiny, her eyes blue, her skin fresh and lightly covered with freckles, which helped to create this youthful image. He felt so dreadfully sorry for her and couldn't help wondering why there was no man in evidence in this little family.

'It wasn't your fault, you know.' His voice was husky.

'I keep trying to tell myself that, but I still feel responsible.'

'I know,' he said quietly.

A quarter of an hour later Alan Richardson got to his feet and picked up his cap. 'I'd best be off. Let you get some rest. If there's anything I can do, pop in the station. You can always leave a message for me.'

Evie took a deep breath. 'I appreciate that, Sergeant. I'll come to the door with you.'

They both laughed as Heidi got to her feet.

'I'll have to be careful. That dog understands every word you say, don't she?'

'More or less.' Evie smiled.

'Let me know how Jenny is doing.'

'I will,' she promised.

'See you soon then.'

She watched him walk down the path and open and close the front gate, before she bent down to Heidi and whispered, 'I hope that's true. I'd like to see him again, wouldn't you Heidi?'

Heidi put her head to one side as if she were considering the question. Then her tail, a fluffy silken mass of honey-coloured fur, began to wag, as if in approval.

It was hard for Evie to get to sleep that night. She tossed and turned, and went downstairs and had a drink of water. Back in her bedroom she paced the floor, looked out of the window, climbed back into bed and tried once more to close her eyes and go to sleep. She began to wish she hadn't agreed that Rosie could go home with Flossie. At least she could have had Rosie in her bed, a warm being to hold and to cuddle. As always she had no one. Loneliness was terrible.

How would Jenny react to all of this? *It was all my fault, telling her she was stupid to give up college and take a job in London just because Norma had. If I'd kept my mouth shut it might have all blown over.* It wasn't fair, a young girl getting beaten up when she'd done nothing wrong. Especially Jenny. She had such a tiny frame. She'd never been what you could call robust. Even as a child, if there had been any sickness flying around it was always little Jenny who caught it first.

Evie turned in her bed, thumped at the pillow and waited for the daylight.

It rained in the night and as she lay listening to it beat against the window panes her spirits rose a little. The rain would wash the streets and the gardens clean, leaving the shrubs glistening and fresh. The dawn was breaking. Yesterday was over. Please God, today would be better.

She was glad to get up. She'd lain there thinking for too long. She bathed and dressed and went downstairs. Heidi plodded behind her, making straight for the back door. Evie picked up the morning paper from the mat, unlocked the door for Heidi and smelt the dampness of the garden. It didn't feel too warm out there.

Filling the kettle from the cold tap, she decided she'd make do with a pot of tea and just a slice of toast for her breakfast, then she'd go down and see if Rosie was all right before heading straight for the hospital.

Jenny lay in her bed and stared at the ceiling.

Evie bent low and kissed her cheek, smoothing her long hair back from her forehead. 'How's my girl this morning?' she asked, making an attempt to be bright and cheerful.

She got no response.

Evie pulled a chair up close to the side of the bed and sighed.

It was a long ward, made bright by yellow curtains and pretty screens. On the locker that stood next to Jenny's bed was a vase filled with long-stemmed roses. Evie rose to read the card and was struck by the heavy scent.

'"To Jenny, with lots of love from all the staff",' she read aloud. 'That's nice, isn't it, luv? Shows they're thinking of you.'

Still no response from Jennifer.

What the hell was she supposed to say to her daughter now? Yesterday she had felt nothing but anger, anger at the man who had dared to do this to Jenny, anger at herself for ever having allowed Jenny to leave college. But how could she have prevented it? She had no answer for herself. Today in place of her anger there was sorrow. She had done her very best for her girls, yet she had deprived them of the very thing that might have made such a difference to their lives. They had never had a father.

Jenny lay so still, almost lifeless. The bruises on her face seemed worse this morning, stark against her washed-out cheeks.

Evie's thoughts turned back to the years when Edward Hopkins had been the mainstay of her life, to how Catherine and Jenny had always been overjoyed when their father turned up to spend a few weeks with them. It had been marvellous. While it lasted. But all Ted had ever been was a part-time father. *It was me, always me on my own, who had to weave the lies into an acceptable story to tell the girls.*

'Your father travels for a very big firm. Yes, he has to stay in big hotels. He does his best to get home and to be with us as often as he can.'

Had it all been worthwhile? Had she ever managed to convince either Catherine or Jennifer? She doubted it. What about young Rosie? God above knew how she'd turn out. Ted Hopkins really had been a first-class bastard. He'd never once acknowledged Rosie's existence. Safe in his big house up north, he'd lived the life of the rich, only paying Evie and his daughters a visit when it suited him. He wasn't going to shoulder them and all the responsibilities that would have meant, not while his wife was alive and she held the purse strings.

When I think about it, he had a damn cheek turning up after his wife had died. After all those years with never so much as a word! Suddenly Evie smiled to herself. That had been quite a morning! George had given Ted short shrift! And the rest of that day hadn't been so bad. In fact it had been bloody fantastic! Why the hell had George had to die?

'Mum.'

Jenny's small voice made Evie jump. She shook her head to clear it of the loathing she was feeling for Edward Hopkins, and the longing for George Higgins that never seemed to lessen. 'Yes, sweetheart, I'm here.'

Jenny eyes were wide open and she stared into those of her mother. 'Mum,' with an obvious effort she made to sit up, 'I'm sorry.'

'Oh my love, you have nothing in the world to feel sorry about.'

'Aren't you angry with me?'

'Angry with you? Whatever gave you that idea? I'm just so happy that you are awake an' able to talk to me.'

'If you're so happy, Mum, then why are you crying?'

Evie forced a laugh, reached forward to touch Jenny's cheek gently. 'How I wish I could pick you up and take you home with me right now.'

'Oh, Mum. When will I be able to leave here?'

'I shall ask the sister if I can speak to the doctor. He'll tell me.'

'Mum, does Nanna know?'

'Of course she does. She and Granddad are coming in to see you this afternoon. Nanna's minding Rosie now. They all send you their love. And Heidi said to give you a great big lick.'

They looked at each other, really smiling for the first time.

'I think if you come with me, Mrs Smith, we'll be able to find you a cup of tea,' a plump, pretty nurse said kindly.

Evie bent to kiss Jenny's face, a face that was all puffy and swollen. 'You have a nice sleep. I'll still be 'ere when you wake up,' she promised. Out in the corridor, Evie's tears spilled down her cheeks.

The nurse stood silently and let her cry.

It was two weeks before Jenny was allowed home from hospital. Evie was baffled as to what she could try next. Every day was terrible. Jenny stayed indoors doing nothing, staring into space half the time. About the only one she spoke to was Heidi. But when Evie suggested she came with her and Rosie up to Tooting Bec Common to give Heidi a run, all she got was a blank stare and a shake of Jenny's head. Treats and outings, offered with love by her nanna and granddad, were all refused.

Evie was at her wits' end. She'd come very near to losing her temper this morning. All her pleas for Jenny to get out of bed or even to tell her what she would like for her breakfast had gone unanswered. Not a word. The cup of tea she had brought up an hour ago stood cold and untouched on Jenny's bedside table. Evie stood looking down at her daughter, huddled beneath the bedclothes. It was a glorious autumn day, cold but with bright sunshine and soft clouds scurrying across a blue sky, the kind of brisk day when Jenny should be out of the house, living life to the full.

'You there, Evie? Come an' see who I've brought along with me.' Flossie's voice carried up from below, and was Evie glad to hear it!

She hurried out onto the landing. 'Mr and Mrs Parker!

Oh how nice,' Evie exclaimed, running down the stairs.

Evie held out her hand to each in turn. 'It's nice to see you both. It's ever so kind of you to come.'

Mr Parker smiled. 'We were passing and we thought we'd just pop in an' see how Jennifer is doing.'

Evie let out a long-drawn-out sigh. 'Let's go into the front room, it's draughty standing 'ere in the passage.'

'I'll put the kettle on, make a pot of tea, shall I?' Flossie asked. Evie nodded her thanks to her mum.

Mr and Mrs Parker followed Evie. A fire roared in the grate and the room was lovely and warm. The Parkers sat on the settee. Evie took an armchair and smiled sadly.

'I don't know what to tell you. I just can't get through to Jenny. Her face is healing up nicely, though her ribs are still very painful and her arm too, at times. It's as if she were miles away, not in a world of her own, more a nightmare. It frightens the life out of me to 'ave to lie an' listen to her in the middle of the night.'

Mr Parker looked at Evie's pinched face, and his heart went out to her. She shouldn't have to be coping with all of this, not on her own. He got to his feet, put his hand beneath Evie's chin and lifted her head until her eyes were on a level with his own.

'Listen to what I'm going to say to you. This awful thing has happened to Jenny and there is nothing you or anyone else can do to alter that fact. Do you understand that?'

Evie nodded.

'Jennifer will snap out of it. It would be a chilly prospect if we didn't believe that. So here's what my wife and I would like to suggest.' His voice was very gentle as he continued. 'Let Jenny come back and work with us. She has a way with animals, and I'm not just saying that.'

His wife, smartly dressed but a homely woman, interrupted, 'No, really, that is true. It's amazing to watch her at times.'

Evie could have cried with relief at their kind offer. She just hoped to God that Jenny would show the same amount of enthusiasm, but she wasn't at all sure that she would even listen to the suggestion. She fiddled self-consciously with the buttons on her cardigan and was saved from having to answer as her mother brought in the tea and smiled at everyone in general. Evie guessed rightly that her mother had been listening at the door.

'Shall I pour out for us all?'

Evie nodded her head. 'Please, Mum.'

Over the cups of tea and shortbread biscuits it was all arranged.

'Seeing as how it's Friday today we'll let things ride for the weekend.' Mr Parker looked at his watch. 'We'll have to be going shortly but why don't you, my dear, pop upstairs and see Jenny, tell her we miss her and that I'll pick her up in my car eight-thirty sharp on Monday morning.'

Mrs Parker looked across at Evie, straightened the skirt of her suit as she got to her feet and nervously asked, 'Will that be all right? I wouldn't want you to think we were interfering.'

Evie could have kissed the woman.

It was Flossie that settled the matter. 'I'll come to the foot of the stairs, show ye which room is Jenny's, then you go up on yer own. She can 'ardly turn 'er face to the wall when she sees it's you.'

Evie kept looking at the clock. She couldn't relax. She hoped Jenny wouldn't be rude to Mrs Parker.

Flossie had taken the tray of tea things out to the kitchen to wash them.

Mr Parker broke the silence. 'Would it help if you told me a little more about what happened to Jenny?'

He was a short man with hair the colour of straw and a healthy red face. As with his wife, there was no standing on ceremony with him; he called a spade a spade, and Evie liked him for it. She was only too glad to talk. It all came pouring out. She finished her tale with a sob in her voice.

'He didn't rape her, thank God. I don't know what we would 'ave done if it 'ad come to that.'

When Evie had finished, Mr Parker let out a long, low whistle. He was very angry. 'Poor Jenny. No wonder she's so unhappy. We must all do our best to help her through the next few weeks.'

Evie raised her eyes to his and tried, not very successfully, to smile. 'I don't know how to thank you.'

He nodded sharply. 'No need. Everything will turn out fine. You'll see.'

Evie tried to smile again. But it was no good. The kindness of this nice couple had got to her. Then suddenly Mr Parker's arm was around her shoulders and she was sobbing bitterly.

Chapter Sixteen

'STANLEY'S PARENTS DON'T MIND in the least, Mum. They say it's only fair that we come to London and spend Christmas with you this year. I'm writing to Nan to ask her if she and Granddad will let us stay with them over the holiday. I'll phone you Sunday evening, when you've had time to think about it, and you can tell me then if it is all right with you. With lots and lots of love, Cathy and Stan.'

Evie looked up from her letter and gazed out of the window into the street. It was going to be one of those cold, dark, damp days when it never really got light. She could hardly believe that Christmas was almost on them once again. This would be the first Christmas that they'd all been together since Catherine had left home. There'd be quite a crowd. She had no doubts that her mum would insist that they all spent Christmas day at her house. Flossie would love it. She could cope.

The whole tribe of them were grouped in Evie's front room on the Sunday evening when the phone rang.

'Hello Catherine, how are you darling?' Evie asked.

'Give me that phone,' Flossie demanded. Immediately she issued a firm invitation for her granddaughter and her husband to stay for as long as they liked. 'Three days at the very least,' she ordered.

'My turn, my turn,' squealed Rosie. 'I wanted you to have a bed in my room, Cathy,' she yelled down the line. 'Will you tell me what Stanley would like for his Christmas present from me, 'cos I don't know what to get him.'

'Your turn Jenny,' Evie called, holding out the phone.

Something Catherine must have said had made Jenny giggle. That giggle made Evie relax a little. Jennifer was much better. She still didn't smile as often as Evie would have liked, but at least she went to work regularly and was full of stories about the different animals that Mr Parker treated in his surgery. Then again, this was the last year of her teens and nobody would describe Jenny as a starry-eyed teenager. Thank God she had been spared having to give evidence in court. The police had informed them that the man had walked out of a psychiatric hospital where he was being given treatment. In the opinion of the doctors who had examined the man, he was mentally unbalanced and therefore unfit to answer any charges. An assurance had been given to Jenny, in Evie's presence, that the man had been safely locked away this time.

'Catherine wants to say goodnight to Granddad and then she says she has something more she wants to say to you, Mum.' Jenny was smiling as she passed the receiver to Jim.

'For goodness' sake, Jim! You'll wake the whole tele-phone exchange up, laughing like that,' Flossie chided him, her eyes showing deep affection.

'Did ye hear that, Catherine? Your nan is still nagging me t' death. I'd better go. See ye soon.' He passed the phone to Evie.

'Well, I think everyone's 'ad their say now, Cathy. Remember me to Stan's parents. Tell them they're welcome any time they fancy a visit to London.'

'Wait a minute, Mum,' said Cathy, 'I just want to tell you that we've got a lovely surprise for you for Christmas.'

'What is it, luv? I don't want you to go spending yer money on me.' She heard Catherine roar with laughter on the other end of the line.

'Oh no Mum, you don't get it out of me like that! I've told you it's a surprise. It's not long to Christmas, so wait an' see.'

'All right, luv. Take care. Love to Stanley.'

'Bye, Mum.'

The phone went dead and everyone started talking at the same time. It was going to be a great Christmas.

There were only seven shopping days left till Christmas. Jim had given Evie the day off and she had come up to town to buy all those last-minute presents and more decorations for the huge great tree that was already standing dead centre in the bay of Flossie's front room. She knew she'd never find a parking space anywhere near Oxford Street so she had travelled on the 88 bus.

When she had set out, the day had been grey and depressing but at least it had been dry. Much later, coming out of Selfridges, loaded down with shopping bags, she sighed heavily, for the sky had darkened, the wind had got up and it was pouring with rain. She still had to get to Regent Street. No matter what, she couldn't go home without going into Hamley's, that was the only place that you could buy the miniature furniture for Rosie's doll's house. Jim had made the house himself, and she had bought several tiny items for the doll's kitchen weeks ago. It had only been yesterday that she had thought to show them to Flossie.

'Have they miniatures for all of the rooms?' Flossie had asked.

'Mum, you 'ave to see them to believe them,' Evie had replied eagerly.

Straight off, Flossie had dug in her bag and come up with two five-pound notes, ordering Evie, 'Spend one of these on Rosie and the other one on Jenny. I knew I hadn't got as much for them as I 'ave for Cathy, so be a love an' pick something nice for me to wrap up.'

After three attempts, Evie managed to get a taxi to stop.

'Regent Street, please,' she told the driver as she sank thankfully back in the seat.

Inside the great toy store it was like a different world. A fairyland of toys and gifts. The choice! If she had had a hundred pounds to spend it would have been no problem. She made her selections, added the parcels to her already heavy bags and made for the door.

The sudden impact of the cold air made her gasp, and she looked at the torrential rain in utter dismay. She was never going to be able to get a taxi, not on a night like this. There was nothing else for it, she had to walk to the bus stop. The queue was so long. It trailed way out from the shelter. Still, she thought, at least the 88 to Clapham Common ran quite frequently, even if those going all the way to Mitcham didn't. She made up her mind to get on the first one that came along. She could always ring home from Clapham. Jim would be only too pleased to come out and pick her up.

Some hope!

'Two only on top,' the conductor of the first bus called, ringing the bell before the two passengers were scarcely on. The queue had hardly moved.

The next two buses didn't stop at all. 'Full up!' the conductors called as they sailed past.

Evie was so mad with herself. *I should have gone down the underground,* she chided. *Too far to walk now. I can't even put the bags down to give my arms a rest. They're sodden now without getting the bottoms of them soaked.* The rain was dripping off her head, and her feet were squelching in her shoes as she moved about trying to keep warm.

A car slowed down and flashed its lights as it drew to a halt a few yards further on from where she was standing. Then she heard the driver sound the horn. She stood there, feeling daft. The man couldn't be trying to attract her attention, she didn't know anyone up here.

She turned her head to look again. Some lucky soul was about to get a lift. The driver was half out of the car, waving, then she heard him loud and clear shouting, 'Come on, Mrs Smith, be quick.'

She stared, frowning. Then she laughed. Oh thank God. She must have a guardian angel somewhere. She ducked her head and ran.

Alan Richardson leant across and opened the passenger door. 'Get in quickly before I get done for obstruction.'

She didn't need a second bidding. She settled herself in the passenger seat with her wet bags jammed between her legs. Alan leant over her, pulling the door shut with a mighty slam, dipped the clutch, put the car in gear, released the handbrake then put his foot on the accelerator and slowly moved out into the heavy stream of traffic.

Evie breathed out. 'Oh, Sergeant, if ever I was in need of a friend it was at this moment.'

His smile widened. 'What a lucky break that I spotted you. If you'd been standing on the inside of the queue I never would have. Been last-minute Christmas shopping, have you?'

She looked down at all the bags, they both laughed. 'How about you? Are you in uniform under that macintosh?'

'No, day off today. I came up to see an old mate at the Yard. And seeing as how I was up in town I thought I might just as well make a day of it. I've had a look at Oxford Street an' done a bit of Christmas shopping.'

'Like me, you picked a great day for it.'

He turned his head and gave her a quick glance. 'My God, you're drenched through. There's a cloth in the glove compartment. At least wipe yer face.'

They drove in silence for a while, Alan concentrating on the road. He said, 'You know, I've been racking my brains trying to remember your Christian name.'

'It's Evie, short for Evelyn. I do know you're Alan. My mother told me.'

'Well, at least we've got that settled. First names now, eh Evie?'

'Deal, Alan, and thanks again for rescuing me.'

They had passed Balham Station and were well on the way to Tooting Bec.

'Shall I drop you at your house?'

'Yes. No.'

'What does that mean?'

She hesitated. 'Would it be asking too much for you to drop me at my mother's house? She'll have a meal ready, and both my girls are there. Save me running down the street in all this rain.'

He roared out laughing. 'You are funny. Asking too much! What is it, four or five houses further along?'

He turned the car into Chetwode Road, slowed down and stopped outside number 50.

'We're here.' He switched off the engine, and they could both hear the rain beating on the roof of his car. 'Stay here, I'll go and ring the bell, get the door opened for you.'

He sprinted up the front garden and in no time at all the door opened and he was illuminated in a shaft of warm light which streamed from inside Flossie's house.

'Sergeant Richardson!'

'Hello, Mr Tyler, I've got Evie in the car. I gave her a lift back from town.'

'Christ, she was lucky. Bloody awful night, ain't it?'

Alan ran back to the car and opened the passenger door. 'Make a dash for it,' he ordered, 'I'll bring your packages.'

Somehow the whole family seemed to have gathered in the passage to see what was going on, and there was scarcely room for Alan to put the bags down.

'Come along in by the fire, the pair of you. It's nice an' warm. I'm sure you could both do with a cup of tea.' Flossie was in her element when she was in command.

Everyone trouped into her front room. It looked really cosy and inviting. Jim knelt to poke the fire and add more coal.

'What have you bought, Mum?' Did you get that special shaving cream for Stanley?' Rosie wanted to be noticed and she turned to smile at Alan. 'My teacher at school was helping us with our lists of Christmas presents and she said shaving soap is old-fashioned and that cream was what men liked now.'

'Your teacher was right, Rosie. Cream is by far the best,' Alan went along with her, returning her smile.

Jim stood up from beside the fireplace. 'Rosie, why don't you open that packet of chocolate biscuits and spread them nicely on a plate.' Then he looked at Evie doubtfully. 'You'd better get upstairs and get those wet things off. Put yer mother's dressing gown on for now, we won't mind. And as for you, mate, don't just stand there, take that mac off and settle yerself down.'

Flossie came back into the room, her face beaming. 'Well, the kettle's on and the hotpot is ready to dish up, so when you've all sorted yerselves out ye can come an' sit up round the table. You too Alan Richardson, there's plenty to feed you an' all.'

He started to protest, but he was soon persuaded, more so when Jenny quietly said to him, 'You can sit next to me if you like, Sergeant.'

'Thank you, Jenny.' He took her hand and squeezed it. She looked delighted.

The meal was smashing. The meat was tender, plenty of dumplings and lashings of gravy with enough vegetables in separate tureens to feed an army. The talk was all of Christmas.

'Suppose you still spend the holiday with your mother, or are you on duty?' Flossie asked Alan.

'No, I'm not on duty, but my mother died at Easter this year.'

'Oh, sorry to 'ear that. Was she ill for long?'

'Yes, she was actually. I wouldn't wish her back. She suffered too much. Not that she ever complained. I still miss her.'

'Didn't you 'ave a brother?'

'Oh, you remember Bert, then? Him and his wife emigrated to Australia, went about six weeks after my mother died. It was on the cards, but I was glad he didn't go before mum passed away. It made the funeral easier, him being here.'

'So does that mean you'll be on yer own over Christmas?' Jim leant forward, waiting for Alan's answer.

'I don't mind. I'm used to living on my own. I never lived with my mother.'

Jim's voice was firm as he immediately issued an invitation, more an order really, that Alan should come to them for the holiday. 'There's plenty of room 'ere. Cathy an' Stan only need one room.' He said this with a laugh. 'So you can 'ave a good drink. No need to go 'ome, there'll be a bed 'ere. Besides, you'll be doing me a favour, all these females an' only me an' Stan to keep them in order. What d' ye say, mate?'

'He says yes, ye great lummox, if ye'd only give 'im time to get a word in edgeways.' Flossie rounded on Jim.

Alan accepted.

There was a chorus of goodos and Jim was allowed the last word.

'That's settled then.' Bending across the table, he smiled at Rosie and Jenny. 'Gonna 'ave the law on our side this Christmas. 'Ave to watch our step though.'

Rosie giggled, while Jenny said, 'I'm glad you're coming, Sergeant.' And that was Evie's sentiment exactly.

Evie didn't have to wait for Christmas day to get her surprise.

The wheels of Stanley's car had hardly stopped turning when half the street knew that Catherine Smith had come home.

Flossie came running up from her house, taking off her apron as she went, arms spread wide to embrace this beloved granddaughter. Joan Killick came flying across the road, her ginger hair covered in rollers because she had not long since washed it. But of all the noise, Evie's cry of delight was the loudest as Catherine clambered out of the car and practically waddled towards her mother.

Evie gasped in surprise and yelled, 'Catherine! You're pregnant!'

All the neighbours stood laughing as Evie and her eldest daughter stood on the pavement hugging each other, only breaking away as Flossie elbowed Evie aside.

''Ere, let someone else make 'er feel welcome. She's my flesh an' blood too, ye know.'

'Stan! Great to see you,' Jim's loud voice came from the

doorway of the house. 'Come on in, son, leave 'em to it. They're never 'appier than when they're 'aving a good cry.'

'Mum!' Evie shouted, 'I'm gonna be a grandmother.'

Flossie took her arms away from Cathy's neck and linked her hand through the crook of her elbow, the smile slipping from her face. 'Gawd above child, you're gonna make me a great-grandmother!'

Everyone roared with laughter.

'If you stop out here putting on this side show much longer, nobody will be anything, cos we'll all freeze to bloody death.' Stan Caldwell was really feeling chuffed at the reception they were getting, and he grinned as he heaved their cases out of the boot of his car.

'Don't you dare take them in there, you know darn well I've got yer room all ready in my 'ouse,' ordered Flossie. 'Come on down with me now an' we'll get you settled in an' unpacked. Leave Cathy alone with 'er mother for a while. I've got the kettle on.' Then as an afterthought she raised her voice and called, 'An' you, Jim Tyler, can get yerself out from there an' come an' give Stan a hand.'

Stan shook his head in disbelief. 'You're a caution, you know that don't you, Flossie?' He put an arm around her and kissed her. 'You're an angel, too, and I love you. You'll make a damn fine great-grandmother.'

'Get on with ye,' Flossie cried, giving him a push, but there was a cheerful grin on her face as she went back up the road.

There's nothing like a family Christmas when there's a child in the house and all the adults are prepared to act like kids themselves.

Every meal was to be taken in Flossie's house. The great Christmas tree, smelling of pine, glittering with baubles and fairy lights and topped with a silver-dressed fairy waving her magic wand, dominated the bay window.

Breakfast over, Alan Richardson had arrived and there was now noise, gaily wrapped presents and exclamations of delight coming from everywhere. The morning slipped away.

Catherine helped her nanna to baste the turkey and to cut up the cooked giblets ready to make the rich gravy. Jenny and her mother sat at the kitchen table preparing the vegetables. Jim and Stanley, armed with paper sacks, were picking up all the torn paper and ribbons from the floor. Alan lay on his stomach on the floor, with Rosie crouched down beside him, helping to decide where to put each tiny piece of furniture in the beautiful double-fronted doll's house her grandfather had made for her. Evie had thought perhaps Rosie, at eleven years of age, was too old for a doll's house. But this present from her grandfather was no toy! Beautifully made, it was a work of art and a credit to Jim after all the hours he had worked on it. This miniature house and its contents would be a treasure in years to come.

The dinner table looked a picture and the meal was splendid. The girls watched the circus on television, while the adults dozed, too full up to do much else.

Come the evening, and the fun began, although all they seemed to do was play childish games.

'Let's have a go at charades,' Jenny suggested, and Evie found herself sitting side by side with Alan on the settee, trying to guess from Stanley's comical gestures that he was Charlie Chaplin.

Catherine yelled, 'Mum, it's your turn now. You and Alan go out and decide to do one together.' The 'Sergeant' had long been dropped.

'Shall we try "Jingle Bells"?' Alan asked, leaning up against the wall of the narrow passage. 'The very sound of it makes one think of the cold and the snow and everything else that is Christmas, and . . .' he paused, searching for the right words, 'Evie, I haven't had such a happy Christmas for years. I'm having a wonderful time.'

Her heart warmed to him. 'I'm so glad,' she whispered.

On Boxing Night, with Jenny having volunteered to stay in with Rosie, the six adults made for the Wheatsheaf. The saloon bar was full of laughing, cheerful people and for once in her life Evie didn't feel the odd one out.

Alan had to go home, he was on duty the next day, but it was still well past midnight when Evie walked to the front door with him to see him off.

'I can't thank you and your family enough. I'd forgotten what a family get-together was like.' Alan's voice was choked with emotion.

Evie didn't answer.

Alan put up a hand and removed one of the side combs that held Evie's long fair hair in place, and then, using his fingers, he loosened the curls, unravelling them, so that her hair hung loose on one side.

'I've wanted to do that all day,' he said. 'You've worn it in a different style over the holiday to what you did when I last saw you.'

'Fancy you remembering how I did my hair.' For a big tough policeman, his touch was very gentle, Evie was thinking to herself.

'I'll pop in sometime next week, see how you're getting on, and thank your mother and father properly. Goodnight Evie.'

Evie was bewildered by this sudden leave-taking. She watched as he passed beneath the light of a lamppost. His shoulders were very broad.

Somewhere a clock struck one and as the chime died Evie gave a little sigh. Christmas was all over. Had she been hoping that Alan would kiss her before he left? No, of course not, she told herself.

In her heart she knew she wasn't being truthful.

Chapter Seventeen

THE DAY HAD BEEN lovely, long, hot and with the sun high in the sky. Evie hadn't wanted to come on this day excursion to Margate with her mother and stepfather but Flossie had been adamant that if she didn't go then neither would they. It was a once a year charabanc outing organised by the Tooting branch of the Conservative Club.

Jenny was working, and Rosie was going with friends from school to see The Beatles' new film.

The tide was coming in, and Evie was glad that she hadn't allowed herself to be persuaded to go to the pub with most of the party. *I'll go for a swim soon*, she promised herself, sitting up and gazing at the crowded beach. Now, at the end of July, the holiday season was well under way and the sand was covered with gaily coloured beach towels and striped windbreaks. Little girls were running about, some with their frocks tucked into the legs of their knickers, others in bright swimsuits, inflatable rubber rings around their waists. Boys were chasing rubber balls. Their shouting and screaming could be heard above the sound of the swooping seagulls.

A couple of youths ran by, kicking up the sand, which showered Evie. She shook her head and watched with laughter as more lads gathered around a teenaged girl. Her screams seemed to be happy ones as the youths appeared to be dragging her into the sea.

Evie brushed the sand from her towel and lay on her back, looking up at the cloudless sky. *I'm forty-three years old,* she reminded herself. Seven weeks ago her first grandchild had been born. She and Flossie had travelled down to Weymouth and gone to the hospital to see Catherine and to be introduced to James Stanley Caldwell, already being referred to as Jamie. Never would she forget the moment her son-in-law had placed the baby in her arms. Life was supposed to begin at forty. *Well I'm still waiting.* She found herself grinning regretfully, thinking of Alan Richardson.

Did she imagine more than there was to that relationship? Sometimes that man drove her close to exasperation. His visits were never regular, never when she expected him. Soon after Christmas he had kept his promise and come to see her. Since then he had taken her out to dinner, once to the theatre, often to a country pub for a drink, but always seeming to keep her at arm's length. He was away now, in Scotland on a salmon-fishing holiday. She missed him.

It was too hot to lie still for long. She stretched, stood up and ran down the beach.

The sea at first seemed icy. Having swum a good few yards, her circulation had got going and now she was aware only of a marvellous, invigorating feeling of freedom. She lay on her back and floated, doing her best to empty her mind of anything other than this glorious, peaceful day. Lulled by the movement of the waves, she found herself being gently washed ashore with the tide.

That's your lot, she sighed. There was no time for more.

She got to her feet and walked through the shallow water up onto the hot sand towards where she had left her clothes wrapped in her beach towel. The towel felt warm against the wetness of her skin. She pulled her cotton dress over her head and pushed her feet into her sandals.

Most people were starting to pack up, the children all yelling their protest at having to leave the beach, probably tired out and suffering from too much sun. Many of the women were as red as lobsters, shoulders and noses already peeling. *Why do we Londoners always go mad at the first sight of the sun? Most likely it's because we see so little of the sea and beach that we never learn.* Funny though, how much more easily the men seemed to tan. Another thing about life that wasn't fair.

She gathered up her belongings and started up the beach to the ladies' toilets. She needed a wash and brush-up before getting back on the coach. It was just turned five. The driver had said to be back at the coach by six o'clock. She'd have time for a pot of tea before starting to look for her mother and stepfather.

A young family sat at the next table to Evie in the tea-room, the father holding a toddler on his knee, the mother feeding a little girl from a dish of ice cream. Evie remembered Catherine and Jennifer being that age, taking them out on day excursions. There hadn't been many occasions when their father had been with them. She caught the young mother's eye. They smiled at each other.

You're lucky to be a whole family, Evie wanted to say. *Make the most of it. Before you know where you are, they'll be grown up and leading their own lives.*

'I don't want to go 'ome,' the eldest child moaned. The mother made a resigned face in Evie's direction and said, 'Who the 'ell does want to go back to London after a lovely day like this?'

Evie smiled back wryly. 'Yeah, I know 'ow you feel, gonna be a long hot journey back.'

'It sure is. I'm hoping to God the kids will sleep all the way.'

Evie felt sorry for the mother. *But there again,* she said to herself, *at least she's got a man to give her a hand with them.*

Slowly she made her way to the coach park, sniffing at the strong, salty smell of seaweed and fish, listening to the gulls still swooping and screaming overhead. It occurred to Evie that she ought to try to find enough money to take Rosie and Jenny on holiday before the winter came round again. The idea wasn't all that appealing. Jenny probably wouldn't want to come and if there was only to be herself and Rosie, well, as always there would be something missing. They'd never been away as a family. She laughed out loud, a gentle mocking laugh. A man, she admitted the truth to herself. Wherever she went, that was what was always missing in her life.

It was half past eight before they finally got back to Tooting. The coach driver had wisely decided to keep going, not stopping at a pub halfway as he had that morning on the way down. Most of the men had had more than enough to drink already. During the journey Evie had sat beside her mother, giving Jim a double seat to himself. Just as well. He had drowsed sleepily the whole way home.

For once Chetwode Road was almost deserted. More than likely folk were sitting in their back gardens. Best place. It was so close. The very air felt heavy, stale and dusty. The sinking sun, like a great orange ball very low in the sky, promised nothing but another scorcher for the next day.

'What's that van doing parked outside your house, Evie?' Jim asked.

Evie looked blank.

"Ow should I know?'

'It belongs to that fellow that sells different stuff round the markets. A right laugh he is.' Flossie's eyes narrowed as she finished imparting this information. 'That's our Jenny standing there talking to 'im,' she cried.

The three of them quickened their pace.

Jenny looked up, saw them coming and quickly stepped back, putting space between her and the young man, before asking, 'How was Margate, Mum?'

'Very hot,' Evie answered, her eyes on the tall young man.

'It's been like an oven here. Did you have a good time, Nanna?'

Before Flossie got a chance to reply, Jim pushed her aside and looked at Jenny. She was looking very tanned, very hot and rather tired. She had tied back her long dark hair with a white ribbon and was wearing a pretty pale blue sleeveless sundress that exposed her bare shoulders and arms which were already a lovely honey brown. He moved his glance to the young man, taking in the fact that he and Jenny seemed on intimate terms.

"Ello Bernie, an' 'ow long 'ave you known my grand-daughter?'

'Hi, Jim. I've known Jenny long enough to know she's a real nice young lady.'

'Oh yeah? Well we can do without so much of yer flannel.'

'Oi!' Flossie dug her elbow into her husband's side. 'I'm whacked out, dead parched, dying for a cup of tea, so what the 'ell are we all doing standing about out 'ere on the pavement?'

'Mum, Nanna,' Jenny gazed at them both and smiled, 'this is Bernie, Bernie Bryant.'

'Glad t' meet you, Mrs Smith,' he said holding out his hand.

Evie smiled and took it. She winced, it was like putting her hand into a vice.

Flossie had walked by. 'Come on in, the lot of ye. We'll get to the whys an' wherefores when the kettle's on.'

Bernie looked questioningly to Jim, who said, 'Yes, you too young man. You'd better come inside.'

Evie set her bag down and went into the front room. Her face lit up. On the settee lay Rosie, fast asleep. She had on only the skimpiest of cotton skirts and a sleeveless top. Her legs and feet were bare.

'What time did she get home? Who brought her?' Evie's anxious whisper was directed at Jenny.

'Mrs Bailey brought her, about an hour ago. She didn't want anything to eat, only a glass of milk. Dead on her feet she was, but she wouldn't let me take her up to bed, she wanted to wait up for you. Bernie climbed up and opened the top of that window so's she'd get a bit of air.'

'Thank you.' Evie gave Bernie a smile and for the first time took a good look at this young man.

He certainly was a tall lad. Lean and very tanned, with light blue eyes and hair so fair it was almost silver, growing back from his forehead in deep waves. He was also very smart. He wore a navy blue blazer, a white open-necked shirt and a pair of pale grey trousers. His grey shoes were of the softest leather.

'My pleasure.' Bernie smiled back at Evie. 'She was one very tired little girl.'

Jim came into the room carrying a loaded tea tray, closely followed by Flossie with Evie's big brown teapot, normally only used on high days and holidays, which she set down on the hearth.

'Now, sit yerselves down, and you, Jim, tell Evie what you've just told me.'

'About Bernie you mean?'

'Who else d' you think I'm talking about, the archangel Gabriel? Course I mean Bernie, you daft thing.'

Jim grinned across at Evie. 'Bernie's all right. 'Ard working lad really. I meet 'im at racecourses now an' again, like a few weeks back at Epsom. Derby day it was. They always 'ave a fair an' an open market at big meets. He gets 'old of some good gear – china, glass, cookware. And his spiel! Well! It 'as t' be 'eard t' be believed. It's so plausible he could sell fridges to the Eskimos.'

Bernie Bryant was grinning broadly as he watched Flossie fill the cups with the scalding tea. Evie passed one to him and as he took it he said, 'Yes, Mrs Smith, and I 'ave all me own teeth, me 'air's not dyed, I don't 'ave a wooden leg and me intentions towards Jenny are completely honourable.'

You could have heard a pin drop!

Then Flossie exploded. 'You cheeky sod!'

But Evie looked at Jenny and they both burst out laughing.

Rosie sat up, rubbed her sleepy eyes, saw everyone and asked, 'Are we having a party?'

'You'll do, Bernie Bryant,' Jim told him when the laughter died down. 'Just watch yer step, that's all. Just watch yer step.'

Jenny leant over her granddad and whispered in his ear, 'Thanks, you're an old darling an' I love you.'

He patted her bottom and winked at her. 'Any time, but not so much of the old.'

Evie felt a bit apprehensive as she replaced the telephone receiver. Two officers, one from Scotland Yard, would like to come and see her at three o'clock this afternoon. Was that all right? She wondered what the caller would have said if she had told him that it wasn't.

She was angry. Were they still going to go on about that

bloody tin box? *Christ, I've only been home from work ten minutes. Talk about no peace for the wicked.* There had to be somebody who could tell her what to do, some person who would sit down and listen to how worried she was. How the hell could she get the police to leave her alone? She'd told them all she knew about the damn box, which was, whichever way you looked at it, NOTHING! She really didn't know how it had got into her house, let alone where it had come from, so what exactly did they want from her?

Evie was sitting in an armchair, shaking like a leaf. Sergeant Walker and Superintendent Thompson were sitting on the settee opposite her.

'I honestly don't know what more I can tell you.'

Sergeant Walker crossed his legs. 'Remember, Mrs Smith, when I took your first statement, you described to me how Miss Powell from Wandsworth Borough Council found that deposit box tucked away in a tea chest that stood in a room in your house?'

Evie was biting her lip and pressing her fingers tightly together to stop her hands from trembling.

The local sergeant looked at her kindly. 'Surely, Mrs Smith, you're not still asking us to believe that that was the first time you had ever seen that box, or even knew of its existence?'

Evie felt her temper rising. 'I've got to the stage where I don't care whether you believe me or not. I know nothing about the box, I never did. I don't know an' I don't wanna know what was in it, and as to it being in the sealed up room of this house, I'll tell ye this much, if I knew who had put it there an' how they came to get in, not only would I tell you, I'd go after the bugger meself.'

Even the superintendent had a job to smother a smile. Then out of the blue he asked, 'Would you mind telling me what your relationship was with George Higgins?'

Evie felt the colour drain from her face and tears sting the back of her eyes. 'What the hell 'as that got to do with this?'

She couldn't help herself; she was fiddling with the ring that George had bought for her, twisting it round and round on her finger. If either of the policemen noticed they pretended not to.

'Is there any reason that we shouldn't know?' The Sergeant's voice sounded stern this time.

'None at all,' Evie almost shouted. Holding out her left hand for them both to see her ring, she cried, 'This is my engagement ring. George Higgins put it on my finger. If it hadn't been for the fact that he was killed in a fire we would have been married.'

The sergeant had the grace to look sorry, the superintendent looked down at his hands.

Evie cleared her throat. 'I'm not daft ye know. I'd bet my last shilling that what I've just told you is only what you already knew. In fact I expect that by now you also know what I and my kids 'ave for breakfast every bloody morning.'

The policeman from Scotland Yard chuckled. 'I can tell you this much, Mrs Smith, we're ninety per cent sure that George Higgins was involved in this matter, and it says a lot for his integrity that he didn't implicate you.'

'Oh! Suddenly you're telling me that you believe what I've been saying to you all along.'

'Mrs Smith, in that box were some very valuable diamonds. They were brought into this country, from South Africa, legally and above board. They never reached the diamond merchants they were destined for.'

Evie stopped fiddling with her ring. George could never have carried out a big job such as this. Not on his own. That idea was ridiculous. So who the hell had he got involved with? The thoughts that were flying around in her head were making her feel sick. She buried her face in her hands and took a deep breath. It was minutes before she looked up and saw the two policemen staring at her.

'So you think George got hold of them and that it was him that sealed them up in my house?'

'Not on his own, no. But I'm afraid that part of it will always remain supposition. Don't worry, Mrs Smith. You've convinced me that you've been telling the truth all along. I don't think we shall have to bother you further.'

Evie brushed angrily at her tears. *Thanks for nothing,* she almost said.

At the front door, the superintendent hesitated.

'What now?' Evie cried.

He smiled. 'The diamond merchants were offering a substantial reward. Whether you would be in line for it is another thing. Good afternoon to you.'

Evie quietly closed the door and wearily leant her head against the cool wood.

Oh George! You took a chance and you had a bloody cheek using my house. A reward! Would she have claimed it if she'd known the box was lying there all that time. Of course she would have. She'd have been mad not to. Scrimping and saving, watching all the pennies, trying to make ten bob do the work of a pound when it came to dressing her girls. Of course she'd have been the first in line for the reward money. Still, she'd got by. If only that was the end of the matter she'd be grateful. Funny, Alan Richardson hadn't been by for days now, did he know that even Scotland Yard had been investigating her? Perhaps he had been warned to stay away from her. With his job you never could tell.

Chapter Eighteen

JENNY FELT VERY FLUSTERED as she approached her grandfather's betting shop. Should she go in? She didn't have much choice. She had to tell someone what was going on or she'd go round the bend.

She pushed the beaded curtain out of the way and coughed as the smoke-laden air hit her. What a mess. Screwed up betting slips littered the floor; tin ashtrays, perched on the ledges that were fixed to the walls, were filled and overflowing; cigarette butts had been ground out on the faded linoleum. The television set was showing the racing from Goodwood, the volume turned up so high the noise was deafening.

Men's heads turned as she stepped inside. Wolf whistles were cut short as Wally Harris looked up from behind his glass partition and called out loudly, 'Jenny, my dear, what are you doing in 'ere? Come through. Come on.'

Total surprise came through in his voice as he lifted the flap of the counter. 'Yer granddad's in the back room. Why didn't ye come in through that way?' Wally was right het up as he half pulled Jenny through. 'Go on, down the passage. Gawd knows what Jim'll say when he sees you.'

Jenny rapped timidly on the door and had only one foot inside the office when her granddad looked up. He threw down the pen with which he had been writing, jumped to his feet and almost yelled. 'Sweetheart! What's brought you 'ere? Come an' sit yerself down.' He swung his swivel chair round and almost pushed Jenny down into it. Bending down, he kissed her cheek.

'So come on, tell yer granddad what's bothering you, cos you wouldn't be shaking like you are if there wasn't something wrong.'

Jenny smiled, albeit nervously, and decided to come straight out with it. Her granddad was too wily an old bird for her to beat about the bush. 'Granddad . . . would you . . . lend me sixty pounds? I'd pay you back, I promise I would.' The last part of the sentence had come out in a rush.

'Pet, pet, don't get so upset,' he bent his knees and came down until his face was almost on a level with hers. 'Jenny, look at me,' he ordered as he put a finger beneath her chin and lifted her face. 'Silly girl, you know darn well I'll give you the money. Now just tell me what you need it for and I'll see to it.'

That was the last thing Jenny wanted. Things weren't going the way she'd hoped they might.

Jim could see tears glistening in Jenny's eyes, threatening to spill over. God! He wished Flossie was here. There was something fishy about all of this. Young Jenny never asked him or her nan for a penny. Sixty pounds! It frightened the living daylights out of him to think what she might be needing it for. No way could he give it to her. Not just like that. What if it turned out she'd got herself pregnant, needed the money to visit some old woman to get a backstreet abortion? He almost choked on the thought. Flossie would kill him. And if she didn't, Evie would. He had to shake his head to clear it.

'I'll wind things up 'ere for now, pet. We'll go see yer nan, shall we? She'll feed us, make us one of her endless pots of tea. She'll sort out whatever it is that is troubling you.'

He walked to the door, intending to tell Wally that he was going out for a while.

'Granddad, wait, please,' Jenny clutched at his sleeve. 'I'll tell you . . . if you promise not to be mad at me and not to tell me mum.'

'Luvvie, don't you know me better than that?' He stroked her hair, at a loss, really, as to what he should do. 'When 'ave I ever been mad at you? Come on, out with it. Nothing's so bad that we can't get it sorted.'

'Granddad, do you know Joe Jenkins?'

'Offhand, can't say that I do.'

'He's a milkman, works for the Co-op at the Royal Arsenal. I went out with him a few times.'

Jim's heart was hammering against his ribs. 'Did he . . .? Are you trying to tell me he . . . you know . . . that he hurt you.'

'Oh no, Granddad, nothing like that, honest. He took me to the pictures twice, once we went for a drive and the last time it was a Saturday night and we went to Wimbledon dog track.'

Jim's sigh of relief came from him like a rush of wind. 'I'm listening, Jenny, go on,' he urged her gently.

'We had a good time really, until Joe met up with a couple of his mates and then he had to start showing off. Joe's a bit like that. Instead of staying with small bets on the tote he put pounds on with the bookies. He won the first time then after that he lost on every race. He said it was my fault. I owe him sixty pounds.'

Jim fought hard to hold his temper in check. *I'll screw the bastard's neck,* he vowed to himself. 'Daft beggar, I'll give him you owe him sixty quid!'

'Wait, Granddad, he's got to get that money from somewhere. It wasn't his in the first place. He's got to pay it back. I'd rather just give it to him, stop him pestering me.'

Pestering her! His granddaughter! *When I've finished with him he'll be sorry he ever set eyes on her.*

'He's got to have it by this Saturday or he'll get found out. I'll pay you back, really I will Granddad, only don't go telling Mum or Nanna, will you?'

Light dawned in Jim's head. The conniving sod. A milkman. He had to have the money by Saturday to pay in to his firm. He was probably weeks in arrears. He'd collected dues from his customers and stuck to the cash. No wonder he was like a cat on hot bricks.

'All right, Jenny, luv, I get the picture. He stole that money, didn't he?'

'Granddad, he says he borrowed it for me. To show me a good time.'

'Does he now?' Jim Tyler's voice was suddenly very quiet.

'I'll see to it, pet. I'll get it sorted. Have you seen this Joe Jenkins today?'

'Yes, he was waiting outside the surgery when I came out to go for me lunch. I was a bit frightened of him. I couldn't think of who to go to, only you.'

'You did right. By heck you did. I promise you, luv, he'll 'ave the money. That's the end of it as far as you're concerned. Just tell me where you're supposed to meet 'im and when.'

'In Tooting Bec Tube Station by Walton's, the fruit shop, half past five tomorrow evening.'

'Well you won't be going anywhere near there, Jenny, but I will. I'll see he gets the money. Now shall we go an' 'ave that bit of lunch with yer nan? Don't want you being late getting back to work, do we?'

He tucked Jenny's slim hand into the crook of his arm as they walked the short distance to Chetwode Road and held her close to his side. He was fuming. Inside, his anger was almost at boiling point.

'Granddad?'

'Yes my luv.'

'Bernie doesn't have to know about this, does he?'

'My darling, no one will ever know, only you an' me. And you can forget all about it. Men like Joe Jenkins are scum. Certainly not good enough to be allowed near nice young ladies like you. By the way, tell me one thing. Are you getting along with Bernie all right?'

Jenny felt the colour flood to her cheeks. 'Yeah. Do you like Bernie, Granddad?'

'Yes, I do, Jenny. More to the point, do you?'

'You know I do.'

They both laughed.

'That's all right then.'

Jim Tyler parked his car on the opposite side of the road, a vantage point from which to view the young man who was walking up and down outside Walton's. *A right sleaze bag,* Jim declared to himself. If he had his way he'd give the bugger a right good smacking, frighten the life out of him. Better not. There were other ways.

He got out of his car, closed the door, not bothering to lock it, and crossed Tooting Bec Road in just a few quick strides. Always a big man, age had not diminished Jim Tyler. He was fit, healthy and obviously strong. Tonight he had changed his flat cap for a trilby. It added even more to his height. He had dressed carefully: fawn trousers, linen jacket, cream shirt and a brown silk tie. His shoes were the finest brogues. There was a thick gold watch on his wrist and a heavy gold signet ring on his left hand. His turnout indicated what he had intended: money and power.

Jim's first impression was of a man much younger than he had expected, a slim man with dark eyes and close-cropped dark hair. He wore a faded pair of cotton trousers and a loose denim shirt. On his feet were elastic-sided boots. *What the hell did Jenny ever see in this creep?*

''Ello there.' Jim smiled. 'You must be Joe Jenkins. My granddaughter, Jenny, was supposed to be meeting you.' He held out his hand in greeting and the young man had no option other than to put his own into it. Joe Jenkins suddenly knew fear.

'If Jenny couldn't come, I'll be on my way. You shouldn't 'ave bothered. It's not important,' Joe said, doing his best to sound apologetic.

'Oh! Jenny told me it was. A matter of life or death.'

Joe couldn't fathom this man out. Smiling he might be, but somehow his very smile was giving Joe the creeps. 'Really, it doesn't matter, Mr Smith.' Joe took a step backwards, moving away, getting ready to run.

'That's where you're wrong, son. This meeting you wanted matters a great deal. And I'm not Mr Smith, I'm Jim Tyler.'

He waited a few minutes for this information to sink in before saying, 'You've 'eard of me?'

'The bookmaker?'

'Got it in one, son.'

From where they stood, just inside the tube station, they could see the traffic drawing to a halt at the traffic lights, the 49 buses stopping on either side of the road, one taking passengers through Streatham and up towards Crystal Palace, the other one going in the opposite direction, its final destination being Shepherd's Bush.

Joe was left in no doubt now; he was in dead trouble. He knew Jim Tyler's friendly attitude was an act. He felt himself break out in a cold sweat. Could he get past this big man, make a dash for it, jump on a bus? Any bus. Somebody ought to have told him that Jenny Smith was the bookmaker's granddaughter. What a way to find out.

'Would you like to come for a ride in my car?' Jim lowered his voice, his tone now very different. 'You're going to, whether you like it or not.'

Joe wondered whether pleading would help. What was this Jim Tyler up to? His lips were still smiling but his dark brown eyes were like round stones. Joe found it impossible to guess what he was thinking, never mind what he was going to do.

Suddenly Jim had had enough. He grabbed Joe Jenkins by the elbow. 'Right, let's go,' he instructed as he steered him out onto the pavement and across the road.

With Joe settled in the passenger seat, Jim gave him a long hard look and before moving off he muttered, almost to himself, 'You're a nutter, Joe Jenkins. A bloody nutter.'

Jim drove in silence, following the main road through Tooting, Colliers Wood, South Wimbledon and Merton, until Joe asked in a croaky voice, 'Where are we going? Where are ye taking me?'

Jim kept his eyes on the road, not bothering to reply. Up over Carter's Bridge, the enormous Carter's seed factory on their right, until at Shannon's Corner Jim drove onto the Kingston bypass, moving now at great speed.

Joe considered jumping from the car, decided against it. He was too scared. What could he do? He racked his brains. Not much. Except sit quiet and wait and see what Jim Tyler had in store for him. However it turned out, he knew damn well he wasn't going to like it. He heaved a sigh of relief as Jim slowed down and drew into the forecourt of a large roadhouse. By the wall hung a sign: The Ace of Spades, Hinchley Wood.

Immediately the car stopped, Joe made to get out of the car. Jim Tyler laughed, a most unpleasant sound, and sprung into action. He grabbed Joe's wrists tightly.

'So, now you're gonna tell me how come you think my granddaughter owes you sixty quid.'

Joe swallowed with difficulty, his Adam's apple bobbing in his throat. Never in his wildest dreams had he imagined it would come to this.

'Well come on, tell me. 'Urry up about it an' all, before I really lose me bleedin' temper with ye an' give ye the sodding 'iding I should 'ave done in the first place.' Jim was leaning across the seats, his face only inches from Joe's. Joe was petrified.

'I never said that . . . I didn't, honest.'

'Oh, now you're calling my Jenny a liar.' Jim's voice was like steel: it sent shivers of fear through Joe.

'No . . . course I ain't . . . I don't want no money . . . I wanna go 'ome.'

This sod was getting on Jim's nerves; he couldn't stand a bloke who whined. 'You'll go 'ome when I say ye can, 'an you'll be damn lucky if you're still in one piece, time I'm finished with ye.' He could see that he was frightening the life out of Joe and he grinned. It was no more than the bloody creep deserved. 'Now you listen to me. You're a thief, a bloody dishonest, rotten thief. Stealing off women who've got kids. They trust you, pay their milk bills on the dot, an' you pocket the money, running them into debt, playing the big "I am", splashing out on girls with cash that don't belong to you.'

Joe drew his head back until his cheek was touching the car window. Christ, this bloke knew everything about him. He tried to smile. He was about to deny everything, when Jim put a hand over his mouth.

'Tell me one more lie, an' I'll smash yer teeth down your throat, so 'elp me God I will.'

Jim felt his temper getting the better of him. The quicker he brought this to an end the better, before he did something he might be sorry for. 'You made a wrong move, sunshine, when you put the screws on my Jenny – a very wrong move.' Then he grabbed Joe's hair and held his fist within an inch of his nose.

'Don't 'urt me, please. Wh . . . wh . . . what d' ye want me to do?'

'I want you to do exactly as I tell you, so listen good. On Saturday afternoon, one of my men will be outside your yard. He'll give you sixty pounds. He'll still be there when you come out of the office, he'll wanna see your rounds book, check that all your customers' accounts are nicely paid up. You with me so far?'

'Y . . . Yes.'

'Good. After that, one of my men will be in the same place every Saturday for the next thirty weeks. Only on these occasions you will be giving him notes. Three pounds. Still with me?'

Joe spoke without thinking. 'Thirty weeks? That's ninety quid!'

Using his elbow, Jim gave him a hard dig in the ribs. 'Pity you ain't so clever when it comes to cooking the books. You're dead right it's ninety pounds. I'm no bleedin' charitable institution an' don't run away with the idea that you can 'ave it away on yer toes. Because from now on I will 'ave someone keeping their eye on you all day and every day. You got that?'

Joe gasped loudly.

'So you're going to behave yourself, ain't you?'

'Yes.'

'Right then, undo yer belt an' open the door.'

Joe did as he was told.

''Ave a nice walk 'ome.'

Jim pulled back his arm and pushed Joe violently out

on to the gravel. He shut the door, got out his side and was whistling a little tune as he walked towards the pub, leaving Joe lying on the ground.

He was going to have a drink. He felt he had earned one.

Chapter Nineteen

EVIE WAS PUZZLED BY the crowd waiting to greet her. Then she saw her mum, hurrying towards her.

'Aren't you proud of our Jenny, mum?' Evie said.

'Course I am, she's as pretty as a picture,' Flossie agreed, 'an' don't she look 'appy. But I didn't know that Bernie had such a large family, did you?'

'No, I didn't. I think a lot of them are only aunts, uncles and cousins, though. Bernie's only got two brothers, no sisters. They've all got stalls 'ere though. Talk about keep it in the family. I only 'ope they won't expect our Jenny t' get into this business if she does marry Bernie.'

'Jenny could do worse,' Flossie reasoned. 'Ain't a bad life on a day like t' day.'

'No, I suppose not, mum, but what about when the wind's blowing an' it's raining cats an' dogs?'

The South Downs at Brighton were packed on this sunny, August bank holiday. The open market was huge. Bernie had pressed Evie and her mum to come along and meet his family. The intention was for him and Jenny to get engaged at Christmas.

'Trade should be good today,' Dolly Bryant, Bernie's mother, told them as she tied a short navy blue apron, which had two very large pockets, around her thick waist.

Evie felt she already liked this short dumpy woman, with her rosy red cheeks, fair hair and what seemed like a permanent smile set on her lips. There was no hidden side to her. She came straight out with what she had to say.

Flossie stood to one side, her gaze taking in the row of stalls. She knew nothing about market selling but she too liked what she'd seen of Dolly Bryant and she decided to be diplomatic.

'It all looks good stuff, an' you've all laid it out on display so well.'

'Comes natural, luv, all the years we've been at it.' Waving her hand along the line of stalls, Dolly continued, 'all six of these belong to me an' mine. Used to be a helluva lot more when my Bill was alive. Forty-two he was when he 'ad an 'eart attack and died. Still, life goes on. I've got three good boys. Bernie's the only one not married an' he ain't lived at 'ome since he was twenty-two. Got 'is own flat.' Evie was taking her jacket off as Dolly turned to face her. 'Bernie's a good lad ye know. Expect he'll buy a 'ouse when 'im an' your Jenny tie the knot.'

Evie looked rather embarrassed. Where was the money coming from to buy a house? Fortunately at that moment the nearby crowd roared with laughter.

'That'll be Bernie,' Dolly smiled. 'He's started, got the crowd going. I'd best be off. See ye later.'

This was the kind of day Evie enjoyed most. The hustle and the bustle, being part of the crowd, Rosie running back and forth, chatting away to everyone she met, Jenny getting looks of admiration, being teased by Bernie's brothers, her Mum dressed in all her glory, pale blue suit, wide-brimmed straw hat and low-heeled shoes for a change – only because Jim had warned she'd break her bloody neck up on the Downs if she wore those daft stiletto heels. Best of all, Alan Richardson was with them. And he looked so different today. In police uniform he looked very smart but not so tall somehow. Today he wore beige trousers and a cream-coloured short-sleeved shirt. His bare arms were deeply tanned and the backs of his hands showed dark hairs. Open-toed sandals on his feet were an added enjoyment, he admitted, since more often than not he was forced to wear heavy black leather boots or shoes. His blazer-like jacket had lain unwanted on the back seat of the car.

Alan and her father were a long time coming back from the car park. Evie grinned to herself. She'd bet a dollar the pair of them had sneaked off to the beer tent. It was over a week ago that Alan had phoned and asked what she intended doing over the bank holiday.

'Will you be on your own?' he'd asked.

That had touched her on the raw. Why did he suppose she would be? She had been alone for too long, and the prospect of staying alone, especially when the girls had all left home, was frightening.

'Evie? Are you still there?' he'd called down the line when she hadn't answered his question.

'Yes, Alan,' she'd told him, wishing he were there with her so that she might reach out to hold his hand. 'Me and the girls are going with Mum and Jim to Brighton. Gonna meet the Bryant family. Have to sometime, won't I, if Jenny is serious about marrying Bernie? Bit quick for my liking really, but Jenny's turning out no different to what Catherine was. She won't listen to me. Whatever I say, in the end she'll go her own way. Rosie will be just the same, I expect, when she's a bit older. All that aside, I think she's got a good 'un. D'you think so Alan?'

Alan had agreed wholeheartedly, which had put Evie's mind at rest.

Jenny and Rosie had travelled in their granddad's car. Evie had ridden with Alan. The journey had been a bit strained really, and that did worry Evie – not much in the way of conversation. *Oh well,* she thought, *let's hope he comes back from having had a pint in a more jovial frame of mind.*

'Snap out of it.' Flossie was tugging at Evie's arm. 'Whatever it is that's making you frown, for Christ's sake put it out of ye mind for today an' come an' listen to this lot.' With that, Flossie threw back her head and roared with laughter. 'It's better than many a music 'all turn I've seen at Chelsea Palace. Come on, luv, come an' listen.'

The selling ability of the Bryant family amazed Evie. Maud Anderson, sister of Bernie's mum, was selling curtain material and nets. Her husband, Percy, was surrounded by towels and bed linen. Evie stood back, alongside her mother, and listened. My God, you'd have to be right poe-faced not to laugh at his line of patter.

'Put one of our bedspreads over yer bed an' if that don't make yer ole man randy I'll come round an' see t' ye meself.' Percy Anderson spread wide a pink two-tone folk-weave counterpane that had a deep fringed border. 'Now me ole darling, who could resist a beautiful woman like you if they saw ye spread out in ye flimsy nightie lying on top of this?'

He'd singled out a nice plump homely woman for his teasing. He knew what he was about. All heads turned in the direction of the woman, their smiles broadening.

'Go on, I'll 'ave one,' she called, flicking two pound notes from her purse, her cheeks shiny and red by now.

Flossie and Evie moved further along. Bernie had drawn the biggest crowd. Younger women were attracted to this tall, slim fellow. Dressed only in shorts and sleeveless tops, sundresses or mini skirts, the ladies loved Bernie's saucy remarks and many a one in the crowd was giving him the eye.

'If ye can't afford t' buy them,' Bernie yelled, holding up a whole set of coloured casserole dishes, 'you can borrow them. Bring 'em back tonight.'

'Does that go f' you too, luv?' A young mother bellowed saucily, looking cool in a short white dress, with two toddlers in a pushchair at her side.

'Looks t' me like your ole man ain't keeping you short,' Bernie yelled back, grinning while nodding towards her youngsters. 'You wanna buy a set of these fireproof dishes, give him a 'ot dinner for a change. You can't live on love all the time.'

'No.' She laughed as the crowd roared. 'But I'll 'ave one of those large saucepans. I can always leave a stew on to simmer while I give 'im his deserts first, can't I?'

The crowd loved it. Trade for Bernie was very brisk.

'You gonna marry our Bernie?' Harriet Anderson sidestepped a group of men to stand beside Jenny. At thirteen years old, Harriet still had a baby face and lovely dark hair that framed her face with ringlets. She was very shy and tended to be pushed aside by all her boy cousins.

'I hope so,' Jenny told her, then made a friend for life by saying, 'Would you like to be one of my bridesmaids? My sister Rosie is almost the same age as you. You'd make a pretty pair.'

Harriet's eyes widened. 'D' you mean it? Really? I love Bernie better than all my other cousins. Cos . . . I mean . . . oh you know, I love them all, but Bernie is special.'

'I do know what you mean,' Jenny assured her, 'and I wouldn't ask you if I didn't mean it. I'll even let you and Rosie help me choose what colour dresses the bridesmaids will have.'

'I'm gonna find Rosie an' tell her what you've just said.' Harriet was flushed with excitement as she sped away through the crowds.

The noisy chaos continued as Jenny waved to Bernie and mouthed, 'See you later.'

She went across the grass, the light breeze blowing her green cotton dress and her long dark hair, which today was not plaited and coiled around her head but held back by pretty side combs.

Jim Tyler lay back on the dry grass, resting on his elbows, and watched his family pack up the remains of their picnic. His acquired family, he reminded himself. Flossie, bless her – no man had a better wife; Evie, his step-daughter; and her two daughters, now his grandchildren. Only Catherine was missing, and she had done so very well for herself, living in her and Stan's own hotel in Weymouth. He grinned. Cathy and Stan had made him a great-granddad. Mustn't forget Jamie! Then there was Alan, Sergeant Alan Richardson to give him his full title. Alan was all right, he was sure of that, but by God he was as deep as the ocean!

Evie, his darling Evie. From the day she had been born to Flossie he had kept an eye on her. Her own father, Jack Smith, had done right by Flossie. He'd married her in time to give the baby a name, but he hadn't stayed around for long after that. As it turned out, Jack Smith had done Jim a favour. Now they were all his family and he loved each and every one of them. His only wish was that he should live to see Evie happy and settled. He wished he could read Alan's mind. Did he intend to marry Evie? Jim decided he wouldn't lay odds on it. Flossie was for ever going on about how you had to make allowances for the man. He'd lost his wife and only child in such a tragic way. That was all very well, but it had happened a long time ago, and no one could grieve forever. Besides, if he didn't want Evie, why the hell did he hang around? Whatever they seemed to do as a family these days, Alan was included. Fine, he was a good bloke, good company. They often enjoyed a pint together. But that didn't do much for Evie. Alan was only queering her pitch. Should he have a word with Alan? What would he say? 'For Christ's sake make up your mind whether you want to marry our Evie, or sling your bloody hook.'? That's what it boiled down to. Flossie would kill him! He had better give the matter a bit more thought.

It was almost six o'clock in the evening. It had been a smashing day, now he was ready to go home. They had been here since ten o'clock. He was looking forward to a bath, a decent cup of tea and settling down in front of the telly.

Flossie was doing up the straps of the picnic basket at last.

Jim called wistfully, 'D' ye think we could go 'ome now?'

'Oh, my luv.' Flossie scrambled across the grass on her knees. ''Ad enough 'ave ye? I'll round 'em all up. Jenny's coming back in our car cos Bernie will be a while yet loading up his van an' he's driving 'is mum 'ome. We'll 'ave to wait till Jenny's been and said goodbye to 'im.'

They looked towards Jenny and Rosie. Rosie was holding up a hand mirror while Jenny attempted to tidy up her face and hair. The sun had caught Rosie: her face was bright red. It was a good job Evie had made her keep her shoulders and back covered. Jenny, being dark, had tanned even more today and it suited her.

'I'm going with Jenny to say goodbye to Harriet,' Rosie called.

'Jim,' Alan shouted.

'Yes, what is it?'

'We're going now. What do you want to do?'

'We've got to wait a bit, till the girls get back.'

'All right. Evie has packed some of the baskets in my car. There's only those few over there to go into yours. We'll see you later.'

'Bye Mum,' Evie called.

'Bye luv.'

The journey home wasn't much better than the one coming down that morning. Alan kept his eyes on the road and his thoughts to himself. Evie might have felt differently if she had known what was going through Alan's mind.

I wonder if men ever really understand women, Alan was asking himself. *I certainly don't know where I stand with Evie. Do I really know her?* he wondered. Some of the tales his colleagues had told him had hurt. Not that one of them had said anything bad about Evie. Quite the opposite. Still, she had got three girls and if the stories were true she had never been married. Didn't seem possible, did it? The fellow that had died in the fire, just before they were to be wed, he hadn't been the father. Strange. It must have been a very sad time for Evie. Nobody knew of sorrow at first hand better than he did. His entire life had been swept away the day that bus driver had had that heart attack. It still hurt him to remember his wife, and seeing young Rosie at times, the sweet pretty face of his only child, Angie, would be there as clear as day in his mind's eye. It was wicked, he knew, but there were times when he felt resentful that Evie had three daughters and now a grandson when his only daughter had been taken away from him so cruelly.

He was quite sure that he was in love with Evie. Not a soul on this earth had moved him since his wife's death, not until he had met Evie. She was a good, kind person.

A damn good mother. But none of that was important when he was near her. Those big blue eyes would focus on him, and he was lost. If only he could bring himself to let go, take a chance and say the words, 'Oh Evie, I love you, how I love you.' But how would she react?

Do I really know her? he wondered. Would she be agreeable to marriage? Because he couldn't stand the thought of anything less. Hopping in and out of bed, as youngsters seemed to do these days, wasn't for him. The thought of being married again, happily married, with Evie there waiting when he got home from a late shift. Evie in his bed. Evie there to hold, to make love to.

He had long ago sold his house, paid off the mortgage and moved back into police accommodation. He could soon alter that. They were building some really nice houses up by Wandsworth Common.

Would Evie even consider being married to a policeman? *How would I know? I've never screwed up the courage to tell her that I love her, never mind anything else.*

He turned the car into Chetwode Road and was lucky to find an empty parking place outside Evie's house. As the car drew to a halt, Evie yawned and Alan laughed.

'You're sleepy.'

'Too much fresh air,' Evie answered, tipping her head back to look up into his big brown eyes.

Suddenly they were very close. Alan took her shoulders between his hands. She felt his fingers tighten. He wasn't laughing any more. Those deep-set eyes held an expression she had never seen before.

Evie began to say, 'It's been a lovely day,' but that was as far as she got, because his lips came down gently on hers. He was kissing her and he went on doing so for some time.

When at last he drew away Evie's feelings were in such

a turmoil that all she could do was lean limply against him, wanting to cry with happiness, wanting him to start kissing her all over again, feeling a fool because she had been cross with him for not talking to her on the journey home. Her cheek was against his chest, and his arms held her so close that she could feel the throb of his heart, like the beating of a drum. It was ages before either of them moved.

'Aren't you going to come indoors?' she asked, in a voice that was barely a whisper.

'No, I don't think I'd better. Not tonight. Jim and your mum will be back with the girls soon.'

He got out of the car, came round to the passenger side, held the door open for her and lifted out her bags and baskets, setting them down at her feet.

'I'll phone you tomorrow,' he said, waved his hand, got back in the car and drove off. Evie couldn't believe it! He was gone! For a moment she felt guilty, then angry. *What the hell have I got to feel guilty for? He made the first move and that took him long enough.* She knew then, without any doubt, that she loved Alan Richardson. 'And a lot of good it's going to do me,' she said out loud as she put her key in the lock and started to think about putting the kettle on.

You're a bloody fool, she decided. *You always pick the strangest of men to fall in love with. You'd never believe that we'd been kissing so passionately for the last quarter of an hour.* Christ, she had been on the verge of begging him to go further, and it hadn't seemed to her that he was made of stone either! *Bugger him. I'm not going to even think about him any more tonight. I'll put him right out of my mind. I'm so damn tired the sooner I get to bed and have a good night's sleep, the better.*

But sleep didn't come for Evie as easily as she had supposed it would.

Chapter Twenty

THE LONG DAYS OF SUMMER were over and the year would soon be drawing to an end. Autumn had been lovely with the ever-changing colours of the trees and shrubs. With the coming of the chrysanthemums and the smell of log fires in the air, there was no mistaking that winter was on them and that very soon it would be Christmas once more. And what a busy holiday this year was going to be.

'Mum, don't you think it odd that Bernie's persuaded Jenny to have the wedding at Christmas instead of just getting engaged?' Evie asked.

'Oh, I don't know. Bernie got a chance of that big house in Wimbledon, a yard at the side as well, and Jim told me he's let 'is flat on a long lease. The bloke's supposed to be paying Bernie a good rent an' all.'

Evie was glad to be having this talk with her mother, not that she seemed to be of the same mind as her.

I'd much rather my Jenny hung on for a bit, Evie thought to herself.

Every day they learned a bit more about Bernie. He was going too far too quick. He now had six men working for him – nothing to do with the market stalls: he still managed all that himself. This was the building trade he'd got himself into. He already had things moving. That's what the yard at the side of the house was all about, a main office and site for materials, according to Bernie.

Evie ladled soup from the saucepan into the two bowls she'd set out ready for her and her mother to have lunch. 'I almost forgot,' she cried, 'I've got some bread rolls I put in the oven to warm about twenty minutes ago. I won't be a second – you start.'

Evie came back with the hot rolls and a dish of butter. 'Good job I'd only put the oven on low,' she said, breaking open a roll and watching the steam rise from it.

'Lovely soup,' Flossie commented. 'Can't beat mine-strone when it's home-made like this.'

Mother and daughter sat, heads close together, and sighed over the rushed arrangements. Even Flossie, though she wouldn't say so aloud, couldn't help wondering where all the money was coming from. On the other hand Flossie couldn't keep her mouth shut when she'd gleaned a bit of news.

'Did our Jenny tell you that Bernie was thinking of dabbling in the 'oliday trade?'

Evie almost choked on her spoonful of soup. She swallowed, wiped her mouth with her serviette, and said, 'What?'

Flossie laughed. That had been her own reaction when Jim had related the story to her. 'Tourist industry, that's the word Bernie used. Jim told 'im it was a very tempting idea, very nice business to be in.'

'Are you telling me that Bernie asked Jim to put money into one of his schemes?'

'No, course not. Bernie was saying that he'd got the blokes that work for him taking big old fireplaces out of derelict buildings. Seems some of them are real marble, worth a bomb. I don't think money is any problem for Bernie, that's 'ow it come up.'

'What d'ye mean? "Come up." What came up?'

'All right, Miss Clever Clogs, came up.'

Flossie put a big lump of butter onto one half of her roll, took a bite and smacked her lips, deliberately keeping Evie waiting for an answer. 'Bernie's been away about five days, down in Kent.'

'I know that, Mother. Jenny's been mooning about the 'ouse like some lost sheep.'

'Well he called in at the office and 'im an' yer father 'ad a bit of lunch together, that's 'ow he come to tell Jim about this new idea of 'is. Bernie reckons there's a piece of land near the coast in Kent that he could pick up for a song. Put 'is men on to it, converting cottages for holiday-makers, building log cabins, even a big barn or some suchlike place where he could set up a bar, provide entertainment, even some sports facilities. No flies on Bernie, is there?'

Evie sighed. 'I just 'ope he doesn't bite off more than he can chew.'

'Well, you know what they say, luv: unto him that 'as shall be given. He's obviously a 'ard-working lad with his 'ead screwed on right. He makes a bit of money but he don't just sit back or spend it on 'imself, he makes it work to make more. He could 'ave sold that flat of 'is, but no, lets it instead. No matter what, for as long as that lease runs he's got a nice little sum coming in.'

'I told you Bernie's mum rang me, didn't I?'

'Yeah, something about they were seeing to the reception and all the drinks, wasn't it?'

'Oh, she's been on to me again since then. The reception is all fixed. They've settled on a hall at the back of the Surrey Tavern. Landlord's going to see to the booze, and a catering firm are doing the food. All down to them, so Dolly insists: wouldn't stand for no refusal.'

'Thank Gawd f'that! Be like feeding the ruddy five thousand if all that lot are gonna turn up.'

'Mum! They're not as bad as that. I told 'er that dad 'as made a stand about the dresses, flowers and the cars. As he said, he paid for Cathy's an' he's gonna do exactly the same for Jenny.'

'Be a good job when it's all over. Fancy booking a wedding three days before Christmas.'

Evie grinned. 'Jenny told me they wanted to spend Christmas in Majorca – lovely place for a 'oneymoon.' Suddenly her eyes clouded over. 'Bit different to us, eh Mum? Don't suppose you 'ad a 'oneymoon, did you? And I certainly didn't, seeing as 'ow I ain't never got as far as the altar.'

'Oh, Evie, luv! Things ain't exactly gone your way, 'ave they?'

'Don't start crying over me,' Evie said, but all the same there was a sob to be heard in her own voice.

Flossie decided to change the subject. ''Ave ye thought what you're gonna give them for a wedding present?'

'Mum, I 'aven't got a clue. Afraid it won't be much, what with Christmas presents an' all. The only one I 'ave got is little Jamie's. I'm paying so much a week off a rocking horse for 'im.'

'Makes it worse, Wally and Ada 'aving their do only a fortnight after Christmas.'

'Y'know, Mum, I've been trying to think of a way to get out of that one.'

'You can't do that, luv. Ada would be ever so upset an' Wally would never forgive you.'

'What is forty years? Ruby anniversary, isn't it?'

'That's right. Tell you what, Evie, you won't 'ave to lay out on clothes. Ye can wear what ye wore to Jenny's wedding, an' me an' yer dad will get a nice present for Ada an' Wally. We'll all sign the card, the girls an' all, say it's from our family. How about that?'

'Mum, you an' Dad do so much for us already.'

'Leave it out. Say no more, I'm only glad I've got a bit to splash around. I've known days when I didn't 'ave a shilling in me purse till I made an' sold a load of pies.'

Evie grinned, remembering their front room with the window open and a table display of her mother's cooking. 'It's a wonder you 'ad any women customers. You were only interested in the men.'

'You cheeky bitch! For that you can wash up on your own, cos I'm off.'

Flossie was still smiling to herself as she walked the few yards to her own house. Things had altered a hell of a lot since she'd had Jim to take care of her. Marvellous really. She'd ignored the man for years. Only used him. *Trouble is, we often don't see what good there is right under our very noses. We're all too busy looking further afield for that hidden pot of gold.*

She was still musing to herself as she opened her front door. She wished to God that Evie would do something about Alan Richardson. She laughed out loud as the next thought came into her head. *At Evie's age I'd have had that copper in my bed long before now. And I'd have made damn sure that he came back for more.*

Evie stood at the bottom of the stairs and called, 'Catherine.'

Catherine, who had spent the last two hours sorting out buttonholes and pins, ironing ribbons and her mother's blouse, not to mention brushing out the hair of the two bridesmaids in order to fix their floral head-dresses, straightened up from buckling her shoes, had a final look at herself in the mirror, patted her own elegant hairstyle and went to open the bedroom door.

'I'm ready.'

'Yer nan and grandad's 'ere. Come on down. We're 'aving a drink.'

It was nearly half past eleven, a bright, cold day but their prayers had been answered: the sun was shining. The car would be back for them very soon now. The church was only five minutes away.

Flossie had taken charge of young Jamie. Evie looked at him again. *My God*, she breathed silently, *he looks marvellous*. Dressed in a blue velvet suit, he was the image of his father, the same grey eyes that twinkled, and Evie's mind went back to the first time Catherine had brought Stanley home and she had nicknamed him Laughing Eyes.

'Drink up,' Jim ordered from where he stood in the bay of the window. 'Car's 'ere.'

The neighbours were all out on their doorsteps: children gathered around the gate. Evie waved as she got in the car. She was off to see her second daughter married in church. She clutched the hand of her eldest girl, Catherine and asked, 'It 'as worked out for you, 'asn't it, luv?'

'More than I could ever put into words, Mum.'

'That's good enough for me, pet. I only 'ope it is as good for our Jenny.' She let go of Catherine's hand and brushed a tear away from her eye.

Catherine put a hand on the shoulder of her mother's silk suit. 'Don't you dare cry, it took me ages to do your make-up. Besides, Mum, this is a happy day. You only had to look at Jenny this morning. She looked like an angel. No one looks like that unless they're really in love. Remember that, Mum. Jenny will be fine.'

Evie was surprised to see how crowded the church was and she hesitated for a moment until she felt her stepfather put slight pressure on her arm, and then she was walking up the aisle, between the rows of pews, surrounded by her family. Jim was arm in arm with her mother, Catherine had her arm linked with Stanley's. Evie held on tight to the tiny hand of her grandson and wondered why it was she never had a partner.

The ceremony was over. Evie said a silent prayer as she watched the photographs being taken. Jenny had had her hair cut. She looked beautiful, with fashionable dark curls peeping out from beneath her veil and her brown eyes glinting with happiness.

Evie and Flossie hadn't spent hours and hours sewing this wedding dress. There hadn't been time. Everything had been such a rush.

Bernie looked splendid, too. Extremely smart in his grey morning suit and silk cravat, and with a grey top hat! It was marvellous really, how well everything was turning out.

'Now the parents and the grandparents, please,' the man with the camera called.

Bernie's mother went forward, arm in arm with a smart gentleman whom Evie hadn't yet met. Dolly had a fur stole around her shoulders and beautiful pearls around her neck. At the other end of the line Flossie stood with Jim. Flossie was wearing a three-quarter-length creamy-coloured fur coat, her Christmas present from Jim.

There was no rivalry between the relations. Indeed, on the occasion when Evie, her two girls, and her mother and father had been invited to tea with Dolly, Evie had felt very much at home in the warmth and laughter of the Bryants' big kitchen.

At last enough photographs had been taken, and they could all set off for the reception. Bernie endeared himself to Evie for life. He broke away from his family, all pressing round to kiss the bride. Hand in hand with Jenny, he stood in front of Evie, and said, 'Thank you. I'm the luckiest man alive to 'ave found Jenny. To 'ave her for my wife is more than I dreamed of.' He bent his head and gently placed his lips to Evie's cheek.

It was too much. Evie burst out crying.

'Please don't,' her new son-in-law pleaded.

Jenny laughed. 'She's only crying because she's so happy.'

'Women!' Bernie smiled. 'By the way, is it all right if I call you Evie? You're much too young f'me to call you mother.'

Evie laughed through her tears. 'And you, Bernie Bryant, are full of blarney.'

A few days into 1965, Evie got home from work at about three o'clock in the afternoon. She put her key in the lock, promising herself to put the kettle on first and while it boiled to get the fire going. It was bitterly cold. Her feet felt frozen in spite of the fact that she was wearing fur-lined boots.

'Evie! Evie!' She heard her mother's voice calling her from down the street and turned to see her beckoning. 'Come on down,' she called, and Evie was mildly surprised to hear a frantic note in her voice.

Evie half ran the few yards. The front door stood open and Evie sighed thankfully as she stepped into the warmth of the passageway and closed the door behind her. She opened the door to the living room and blinked with delight at the roaring fire, in front of which Flossie had drawn up a small table with tea things set out for two.

'Oh, you're a real luv, Mum,' she said crossing the floor, hands spread wide to the hot coals. 'I think we're in for some snow, though Dad said it's too cold for that.'

Flossie, with a piece of cake in one hand, picked up the teapot, and said, with something like dread in her voice, 'Evie, you've got to go to the police station again.'

'What?'

Flossie, having already balanced a strainer on the edge of a cup, poured the tea before she repeated, 'You have! Sergeant Walker was round 'ere.'

Thoroughly alarmed, Evie sank down into a chair and gratefully accepted the cup of tea from her mother. She took several sips before she said, 'Mum, what d'you think it is this time? Surely they can't still be harping on about that blessed tin box.'

Flossie sighed deeply. 'I couldn't get much out of the sergeant but he seemed to hint that that was what it was about.'

'Oh, my God!' Evie muttered. 'What more can I tell them?'

Flossie cut a thick wedge of fruit cake, placed it on a plate, and pushed it in front of Evie. 'I phoned the office, but you'd just left. Yer father said to tell ye to let them stew. You're not to go traipsing round there on your own tonight. He's gonna go with you tomorrow. Anyway he said he'll get off early, be home soon, so if you go and meet Rosie from school, I'll nip down and put a match t'ye fire so's it's warm for later on, but you can 'ave yer dinner 'ere with us. I've got a lovely bit of loin of lamb. Rosie loves picking chop bones, don't she?'

Throughout the night Evie tossed sleeplessly, wracked by nerves. Could they charge her with concealing stolen goods? Surely she couldn't be sent to prison for something she'd known nothing about. They were certainly dragging this case out.

In the morning, she built the living room fire up and had a nice hot bath before waking Rosie.

'Come on, luv, I've laid your undies out on the fender in front of the fire and I've lit the gas oven an' opened the door to make the kitchen warm so you can wash out there an' then run to get dressed in front of the fire.'

Evie came back from taking Rosie to school and, as she parked her Mini, Jim came out of his house. Evie had dressed with care. A long straight navy blue skirt, topped with a pale blue jumper and cardigan, over which she wore her big winter coat, beige with a narrow braid trim in brown round the collar and cuffs. A hat was necessary, if only to keep her ears warm. It was a soft woollen trilby, the brim of which she tugged well down over her forehead.

Jim wore a light-coloured belted raincoat and a fawn checked cap. You could see your face in his well-polished shoes.

'We might as well walk,' he said, taking a firm grip on Evie's arm. 'We'll never get parked anywhere near the station an' it's not far.' After that he was silent and very grave-looking.

Going up the steps to the station he murmured to Evie, 'Think before you speak. Just answer their questions truthfully but don't volunteer any other information.'

Evie wanted to protest that she didn't have any other information. But she had protested that fact till she was blue in the face and nobody took the slightest bit of notice.

They were passed from a uniformed constable to a sergeant and then to a plain-clothes policeman, who led the way up a flight of stairs.

Finally they were ushered into a large room and asked to be seated at a long table, where they were left alone.

Evie stared up at the high ceiling, white a long time ago, now brown with one corner discoloured, probably from a leakage or where the rain had come in from the roof.

Superintendent Thompson came to join them and with him was a plain-clothes man who was introduced to them as Detective Sergeant Burrows. Once their names and relationship were established, Jim was asked to move away from the table and sit on a chair by the wall, out of Evie's line of vision.

A young woman now entered the room, pulled another chair forward and sat down. She was smartly dressed in a grey costume. She laid out in front of her a lined note pad, some buff-coloured folders and three well-sharpened pencils. She arranged a shorthand notebook on her knee, looked up at the superintendent and said, 'Ready when you are.'

Obviously she was going to take notes of everything that was said. This made Evie feel even more alarmed.

'State your full name, age, place of birth and your full address.' The man named Burrows was in charge.

Evie did as he asked, her voice holding a note of defiance.

'How long had you known George Higgins before he died?'

'I don't remember, not exactly.'

'Were you aware that he associated with known criminals?'

Evie shook her head.

'You never met anyone who aroused your suspicions?'

'No,' Evie snapped indignantly. 'All George's friends were very nice, kind people.'

'Why did you never ask the council to open up that room for you?'

Evie looked at him dumbly. 'You don't look a gift-horse in the mouth. That was the condition when I was given the tenancy of the house. The main outside wall on that side was unsafe.'

There was a long silence. Sergeant Walker was looking

keenly at her. His grey eyes were cold and hard. Evie felt physically weak. She wished she could see her stepfather's face. Why were they going on about George so much? They seemed to be pretty sure that it was George who had hidden the diamonds, but when all was said and done, what could they do about it? George was dead and buried. *Why are they bothering me like this?* she asked herself in desperation.

The detective was reading notes from the folder. 'How did you first come into contact with George Higgins?'

'I can tell you that.' Jim Tyler rose to his feet. He had assumed a quiet air of authority and the language of the well-off businessman that he was.

The detective swivelled round to face Jim. 'Really?' His tone was heavily sarcastic.

'I knew George Higgins from the time when he was a young lad. And now if you don't mind I'm getting fed up with sitting 'ere listening to you grill my young daughter about something that she knows nothing about.'

Jim had snapped and Sergeant Walker cleared his throat reprovingly. 'She is not young, she's a grown woman,' retorted the detective tartly. 'Sit down Mr Tyler, or I'll have you removed from the room.'

Jim was undeniably upset, but he wasn't going to let them walk all over him. He looked at his watch. 'Thirty minutes. And by then you either allow me to take my daughter home or you charge her, in which case I shall ask to use a telephone and have my solicitor here without any more delay.'

Evie looked at Sergeant Walker in bewilderment. She couldn't believe it! He was actually smiling.

The dark-haired young detective stood up and stretched himself, nodded at the young lady who had been taking notes and said, quite pleasantly, 'See if you can rustle up some tea for all of us.'

Sergeant Walker also got to his feet, came round to Evie's side of the table, rested his large hand on her shoulder and said softly, 'Sorry, lass.'

'Is that the end of it?' Evie asked in a very quiet voice.

'Almost. Won't be long now.'

After a short while, the secretary brought a heavily loaded tea tray which also held a plate of plain biscuits.

'Here you are, Mrs Smith,' she said politely. Having poured out the first cup, she handed it to Evie.

Everyone ate their biscuits and drank the tea in total silence.

It was almost midday when a uniformed constable knocked on the door and the detective took several sheets of typed paper from him.

'Sorry you've had to wait so long,' he said quite friendly as he returned to sit at the other side of the table. He started to read the closely typed pages very carefully.

At last he looked up, beckoned the secretary to his side and said to Evie, 'It all seems to be in order. Just a record of this morning's conversation. Will you read it through, please, Mrs Smith? And then if you agree that it is in order I'll get you to sign at the bottom of each page.'

Jim got to his feet again and came to where Evie sat. He looked very anxious. 'Read it very carefully, Evie. If you don't agree with any paragraph don't sign, or if you don't understand anything pass it to me to read.'

The detective sighed and looked at his watch.

Jim couldn't help himself. 'Suddenly you're in a hurry?' he asked, having his turn at being sarcastic.

Fifteen minutes later, Evie took the pen offered by Sergeant Walker and signed everywhere he indicated.

'Thank you, Miss Haywood.' The secretary was dismissed.

The detective said, 'Good day,' his nod taking in Evie

and Jim, then, turning to Sergeant Walker, 'I'll be in touch, Jack,' and he too left.

The big room suddenly felt cold. Sergeant Walker leaned back in his chair and stretched himself. He rubbed his chin and grinned at Evie. All the rocklike hardness of his manner had vanished completely and it was suddenly as if he was their friend.

'Did you bring your car?' he asked Jim.

'No, it doesn't take us a couple of minutes to walk.'

'It's snowing hard, at least it was when I went downstairs a while ago. If you'd like to wait a few minutes I'll drop you off in my car.'

'No thanks,' Jim replied firmly. 'We'll be indoors in no time.'

The sergeant gazed at Evie. 'Still mad at me?' he asked with a smile.

He got no smile from Evie. 'Suppose you 'ave to go through with things like this. Part of the job, isn't it? But I wish to God you'd show a bit of kindness an' tell me what it's all about.'

He stood up, moved around the table and then perched his backside on the edge of it, facing both Evie and her father. 'Well, I can tell you this much. We know now that we're never going to learn any more from you than what we know already. We're satisfied as far as you are concerned, Mrs Smith.' He paused. 'We had to check and check again. There was a great deal of money involved. We had to be sure that you, young lady, weren't part of the master plan.'

Evie gasped, and he grinned at her.

'It's been known before, an intelligent lady being heavily incriminated.'

Evie said loyally, 'George wouldn't have dreamed of me being mixed up in whatever it was he was doing.'

'Well . . .' He swung himself off the table and abruptly

held out his hand to Jim. 'I'll come downstairs with you, see you off the premises.'

'Bloody waste of time,' Jim grumbled as he steered Evie towards home, heads bent against the wind that had by now turned the falling snow into a blizzard. Jim stopped at the corner of the road. He was seething with anger.

'Come on, luv,' he yelled, nodding towards the Wheatsheaf, 'I'm gonna buy us both a stiff drink.'

Later that evening, when Rosie was fast asleep in bed, the house seemed so silent, Evie knew she wouldn't be able to lie in bed. For the second night running sleep would be impossible. It wasn't often that she allowed herself to dwell on her early life but today had been more than she could bear. It had brought home to her just how very much she was on her own. Her stepfather had been marvellous. No one could have done more. As always, where she was concerned, he was kindness itself. If she told him she wanted the top brick off the chimney he'd do his best to get it for her. That didn't alter the fact that when night fell and doors were closed she had no one.

Now, in her mind, the years slid away and exposed all the heartache that Ted Hopkins had caused her, the promises that she had lived on for so long. Then there had been George. He had been going to turn her life around. He would have been her husband, her lover, companion and friend. More than that even, he would have been a real father to her three daughters.

As she paced the floor, the loneliness, the bitterness and the anger overwhelmed her. She lowered herself down into an armchair. Had today seen the last of the police and their damn enquiries? One thing she was sure of, she couldn't take much more. She closed her eyes. *Oh George! You certainly left me some legacy!*

Chapter Twenty-one

EVIE GOT OFF THE bus at St Leonard's Church and turned to walk along Streatham High Street. She felt a bit daft, really, even thinking about buying a new dress just for Wally's do. Mum was right, she should wear the dress she'd worn for Jenny's wedding, but somehow it seemed too weddingified. The thing was, she couldn't afford to lash out; she'd just ordered another half ton of coal. She'd got the money put by for it and there was no way she could break into that. *To hell with it.* She raised her head, pulled her shoulders back and grinned. Doesn't cost anything to look.

She was outside Pratt's department store.

Once inside she made her way to the dress department. An assistant was attending to an elderly lady, taking dresses off the rail and fanning them expertly.

Evie watched spellbound. They were all such lovely dresses.

'Can I help you?' A tall, older sales lady stared down at Evie. Evie noticed she was immaculately presented in a black silk dress, expensive shoes and a thin string of pearls.

'Yes, please,' she said nervously. 'I'd like to look at some dresses.'

'Has madam any special occasion in mind?'

'Well, not really. I just thought I'd like to browse.'

The woman smiled. 'By all means. I'll leave you to it. Let me know if I can be of any assistance.'

Evie wandered off. Around her were other women, some with children, some with friends, a few with men. She wished she had someone with her.

She pulled a few dresses from the rail, noticing the stitching and the details, but most of all the prices. They were staggering.

'I'd like to try these three on, if I may.'

The sales lady was pleased. Taking the dresses from Evie, she led the way.

Inside the changing room, Evie looked at her flushed face in the mirror. 'You must be mad,' she mouthed. She pulled a black dress on first. The feel of the material was soft and nice. It was a really lovely dress. The low neckline showed the smooth, round mounds of her breasts. The gathered material fell from beneath her bust in gentle folds down to her calves. The three-quarter sleeves flowed.

Evie loved it. *It could have been made just for me,* she declared to herself.

She didn't want to be bothered with the other two dresses, not after seeing what this one did for her. She imagined walking down the stairs, any flight of stairs, to see Alan Richardson's face smiling up at her. Would he think how good her figure still was? Would he yearn to take her in his arms? *Stop it!* she said to herself. *Why do I always have Alan Richardson on the brain?*

She looked at the price tag again. It hadn't altered. Sixty guineas! From her handbag, Evie took out a notebook and a pencil. Quickly she drew an outline of the dress. Several glances in the mirror and then one last slow twirl, and she was sure she had all the details that were necessary.

'I'm so sorry,' Evie said, feeling very uncomfortable as she handed back the dresses.

The sales lady sighed. *Such a dowdy little thing*, she thought, *but such lovely blue eyes and fair hair. A jolly good figure too*, she added, patting her own ample waistline.

Evie felt very much more at home down in the basement. In less than twenty minutes she had bought a length of the most gorgeous black material, and already in her mind's eye she was picturing herself and Flossie cutting a pattern out of brown paper before putting the scissors to the cloth.

Clutching the glossy bag, Evie smiled smugly. *In for a penny, in for a pound*, she thought, as she made her way to the underwear department. Besides, I'll have saved more than fifty-five pounds on the dress.

Evie pored over the wisps of pretty underwear. There were such lovely colours. It was so long since she'd fingered such articles. Her undergarments had always been sensible rather than glamorous. Another time perhaps. What was needed now was black to wear beneath the bewitching dress that she was going to make.

She found a bra and matching French knickers, and an extra-long petticoat, the hem and plunging neckline trimmed with lace.

'Such a lovely set, don't you think, madam?' remarked the young lady as Evie laid her choice out on the glass-topped counter.

'Oh, I do think so. I'm really pleased with them.'

Evie felt she was walking on air as she came out of the store and made her way to the bus stop.

Later, in the quiet of her own home, Evie spread the material out on the table. She ran her hands over the soft fabric. If she had to stay up all night and every night she was going to end up with a dress that she could be proud of.

And it wouldn't have cost her sixty guineas.

After forty years of being married to Ada, Wally Harris had come a long way. He was not as physically strong now as he would have liked, but his mind was still keen and very alert. He listened attentively to everything anyone had to say on horse racing. On or off the course, he had his daily bet, never exceeding his limit.

With one exception. Six months ago, Jim Tyler, his boss and his friend, had given him a tip. This in itself was most unusual.

'Advance odds will be damned good. Don't lay out more than you can afford to lose, and don't spread the word,' had been Jim's advice.

Wally hadn't needed to be told to lay the bet off elsewhere.

'You don't make a mess on your own doorstep,' he had said to Ada when she questioned why it was that she had to go up to Brixton to place the bet.

Jim's advice had been solid! It was that one horse that had paid for this spread tonight.

Ada Harris smiled at Flossie as they raised their gin and tonics in a toast to each other.

'Forty years wed!' Flossie grinned. 'Never thought you'd 'ave made it.'

'To tell ye the truth, luv, neither did I.' They both burst out laughing. 'There's been many a time I've nearly killed Wally. Bloody know-all, he was, when we were first wed. And that old bitch of a mother of 'is. Proper big sendoff Wally gave her; 'alf the East End turned out for the funeral but I 'ave to tell ye, I breathed a sigh of relief.'

'I remember, we 'ad 'am tea in Brixton Co-Op Hall when we came back from the graveside.'

'Long time ago, wasn't it, Floss?'

'Yeah, my mum was still alive then. Things ain't 'alf altered, ain't they?'

'Altered! That's not the word that I would use. All the councils are the same: "We're making huge improvements throughout the East End," that's what they tell us. All they've bloody done is demolish our way of life. Still they go on, knocking down what's left of the old corner shops. All the streets where we were brought up 'ave long since gone. Damn shame!'

'I know what ye mean, Ada. It was a blessing in disguise when Jack moved me to Tooting. About the only favour he ever did f' me. I did 'ave a run up to the Elephant the other week, thought I'd look up some of our old neighbours. Got a shock, didn't I? All the old folk we knew are not there any more. Whole bloody streets 'ave disappeared.'

'I know what ye mean. It's awful living in a block of flats. I still miss our little old 'ouse, even if it didn't 'ave a bathroom. When I complained to our rent collector that our lift never works an' told 'im that me an' Wally 'ated living in that great block of flats, know what he said?'

Flossie drained her drink and set the empty glass down on the table. 'Ain't got a clue, Ada, but if ours is anything to go by then it wouldn't 'ave made much sense.'

'It didn't, luv. He said we were lucky that Wandsworth housed us at all. Bloody cheek, when you come to think about all the blitz our area suffered. Now all they think about is supermarkets and high-rise flats. To my mind it's ten times worse in the summer. We all used to 'ave a bit of back garden, didn't we? The men grew a few bits of vegetables, we could 'ang our washing out in the fresh air. Front doors were never closed, let alone locked, and on nice evenings us women always brought a chair out on to our front path and had a natter with our neighbours. Kids 'ad a bit of respect for their elders, an' all. Many a time I've given my two boys a clip round the ear for cheeking old Grannie Kent that lived next door.' Ada sighed deeply.

Flossie nodded her agreement before saying, 'Ye know what strikes me as funny, every family in them days 'ad a cat or a dog. Everyone who lived in the street knew the animals by name, and as for us kids, we were in an' out of each other's 'ouses all the time. I don't know 'alf the people who live in Chetwode Road these days.'

Ada gave a cynical laugh. 'Floss, would ye believe me if I tell you that there's four flats on our landin' and I couldn't tell ye from Adam who lives in any of them.'

A roll on the drums cut through the noisy chattering. A man dressed in an evening suit tapped a microphone, intensifying the sound.

Ada squinted up towards the stage at the end of the hall, trying to see through the haze of cigarette smoke. 'I thought that was my Wally gonna make a fool of 'imself,' she whispered to Flossie.

'Ladies and gentlemen, boys and girls, dinner is now being served.' The Master of Ceremonies' voice was loud, his face flushed as if he'd drunk a considerable amount of spirits.

The babble of talk broke out again as parents looked for their children and wives signalled for the men to come away from the bar.

The four long tables were set out beautifully: white damask cloths, crystal clear glasses, with red being the theme for the floral arrangements and serviettes. A huge two-tier cake raised on a silver stand and set on a table stood against the wall, a ruby wedding creation for all to see.

The first course was mussels in white wine sauce.

Flossie stage-whispered to Jim, 'I wouldn't 'ave been at all surprised if Wally had given us jellied eels.'

'Behave yerself, woman.' Jim had a hard job to suppress his laughter. 'Our Wally put a lot of time and effort into deciding what we were to eat tonight.'

Four more courses, and now champagne was being served. Time for speeches and toasts to be made.

Wally, bolstered by several glasses of champagne, rose to his feet and insisted on singing. 'We've bin t'gether now for forty years and it don't seem a day too much. . . . Cos there ain't a lady living in the land as I'd swap fer me dear old duch.'

This rendering was greeted by much stomping of feet and calls for more.

Back in the main hall, Evie was seated with her mother and Ada at one of the several small tables set around the walls. Rosie was off having a good time with all the other children and teenagers. The band was playing popular dance tunes.

The cigarette smoke made the room blue, making faces hazy. The lights were dimmed and the MC called, 'Take your partners for an old-fashioned waltz.'

The band struck up 'The Blue Danube'.

'Like to dance with me?' A smiling young man was standing looking down at Evie.

She was about to rise, when Ada spoke up. 'Evie, this is me nephew, Mike. He's me sister's boy, just got divorced he 'as, so watch 'im.'

'Aunt Ada, with your beady eyes on me I promise I won't put a foot wrong, not unless this lovely young lady encourages me.'

Evie was indignant. She opened her mouth to reply, but Mike had already leaned down and put his hand firmly under her elbow to help her up. Before she even had time to look at him properly, she was out on the floor.

What Mike lacked in know-how, he made up for in energy. An old-fashioned waltz takes a lot more vigour than a modern one at the best of times. Not only was Evie breathless by the time the band ceased to play, she was laughing her head off. Not a word had been spoken between them. His ever-changing grimaces and the mad way in which he spun her into turns was enough to make anyone laugh.

With a final spin, he whirled her to the narrow end of the room, furthest away from the band. They flopped on to two chairs, and Mike pulled a handkerchief from his pocket and mopped his perspiring brow. Brown eyes beneath brown, bushy brows laughed at Evie under the damp cotton.

Evie was panting. She couldn't speak. Mike's eyes were so merry, though, that she had to smile back.

'Well, young Evie, how was that?'

'Fun,' she gasped.

'Shall I tell you something? I 'ad you earmarked from the moment I walked into the hall. You're the sexiest lady I've come across in a long while.'

Evie felt herself blush. 'Don't spoil it by stringing me along with a load of lies.'

'I tell her the truth, and she calls me a liar. That's not nice. Not nice at all.'

He slowly tucked the crumpled handkerchief back into his pocket, then leaned back in his chair, hands lying loosely on his thighs. He stared at Evie, with a smile curving under his thin dark moustache.

He could be a professional gigolo, Evie thought, smiling quietly to herself.

'I meant it, you know. That dress is a stunner, looks as if you were poured into it. Shows your every curve up top.' His eyes roamed over her from head to toe.

Though he was subjecting Evie to this intense examination, she didn't feel offended, rather pleased actually.

With the help of her mother, a lot of effort had gone into the making of this dress. Now, she told herself, every stitch had been well worthwhile. She wore her expensive black silk underwear beneath the dress. It felt gorgeous.

She caught a glimpse of herself in a long mirror. She had brushed her hair up into high sweeps around her face, and at the back bouncing curls fell to her shoulders. Perhaps it wasn't only the dress that made her look seductive. Sexy, Mike had said.

Well, I'm here, having just been whirled around a dance floor, sitting alone with a man who is openly admiring me. I almost feel like a teenager again.

'Evie, do you like me?'

She burst out laughing, embarrassed by the question. 'Well . . . I 'ardly know you.' She looked at his smiling face, and then added, 'Of course I do.'

He grinned at her confusion. 'Not knowing me can soon be put to rights. Come on, sexy, let's dance.'

So they took to the floor again, this time to a quickstep. He was an expert. Evie was content to go where he led, twirling, scissoring, rising and falling on the balls of her feet.

The next dance was a slow foxtrot. Evie forgot that she had come with her young daughter, mother and father. Mike was silent as he held her close. She was again content to let herself float in the arms of this most unusual man, a man who was a bit brash, a man who was now nuzzling her neck with his moist lips, a man she knew she wouldn't want to have a relationship with.

Evie turned her head and looked back. She couldn't believe her eyes. But they were right. Alan Richardson was leaning against a pillar, watching them. He looked away quickly. But not quickly enough. Evie caught a resentful glance and noticed his tight-lipped expression. Dear God! What was he doing here?

Across the other side of the hall, Flossie sat watching her daughter She had hardly taken her eyes off her. It made her heart sing with joy to see Evie so happy. Tonight Evie looked years younger. To see her dancing, not with another woman as so many were because their men preferred the bar to the dance floor, but with a man, an attractive man at that.

She had seen Alan arrive, watched as Jim had shaken hands with him and Wally had welcomed him with a pint of beer. Now she noted the changes of expression that were flooding Alan Richardson's face. What did he expect? That Evie should sit behind the door waiting for him to decide if he was man enough to make his feelings known? All right, he had had a rough time in the past, but then who hadn't? Only the very lucky ones. Her Evie deserved some happiness. It was long overdue.

Alan strode across the floor and left the room. If Flossie had been on her own she would have dropped her head in her hands and cried for her daughter.

'Maybe it's for the best,' she whispered as a comfort to herself. In her heart she knew that wasn't true. Any fool could see that her Evie and Alan were in love. Both of them were acting so cagey. If one of them didn't make the first move soon it would be a great pity. Two lives were being ruined all because the past had been hurtful and they were afraid to take a chance.

I think I'll have to open my big mouth and tell the daft pair that life doesn't come with any guarantees. You have to grab what's going and make the best of it.

Chapter Twenty-two

ALAN CAME THE NEXT afternoon. Evie was sweeping the front path. Several times in the past months it had snowed, never settling, just leaving dirty slush to pile up in the gutters and on the paths, creating black ice come nightfall.

Evie leant on her broom and watched him open the gate and cross the space between them, all broad and solid in a tweed overcoat, his hair ruffled by the wind. In that moment she wondered how she would get through the rest of her life if it had to be without him. He was everything good, solid as a rock, and yet so guarded where his feelings were concerned.

He sidestepped the mound of dirty snow and in a single stride was at her side. 'Evie, what on earth are you doing out here in the cold? Go inside, go on, get in the warm. Leave the broom, I'll finish it. Have you got a shovel and some salt?'

In silence she handed him the broom and went inside the house. From the top shelf of the kitchen cabinet she took down a large brown earthenware jar which held cooking salt.

The jar was less than half full. 'Damn,' she muttered, getting down on her knees and opening the door of the bottom cupboard. Reaching into the back of the shelf she gave a sigh of relief. 'Thank God for that,' she said as she pulled a large unopened packet towards her.

Then she opened the back door and felt chilled to the bone as she cautiously made her way down the path to the shed and found the only shovel she possessed. She handed it to Alan with a mixing bowl into which she had poured all the salt.

Evie backed away to stand in the porch, watching as Alan scraped with the shovel, lifting the small piles of slush, carrying them out and tipping them into the gutter. Then he sprinkled big handfuls of salt in an orderly fashion, working backwards from the gate to where Evie stood.

It was still very cold, and suddenly Evie shivered. Without a word Alan put an arm around her and drew her close into the warm circle of his arm. She let her head rest against his broad tweed-clad shoulder and breathed in his manly smell of soap and aftershave.

'Evie . . .' he began.

'Yes,' she prompted.

'I can't bear to be with you and not hold you, and it's even worse when I stay away from you. I know this isn't the time, but I can't help myself, not any longer. I adore you, Evie. Would you listen if I were to tell you that I can't spend the rest of my life longing for you.'

Evie's voice was little more than a whisper. 'I'd listen. I'd give you my full attention.'

His arm tightened, and she felt his lips brush against the top of her head. Her eyes filled with tears.

Alan laughed, a happy laugh.

Evie drew back and looked up into his face.

'We must be mad,' he said, 'standing out here on the

doorstep for all the neighbours to see, and getting frozen stiff into the bargain.'

'I don't care if the whole world is watching,' she told him, her eyes now sparkling bright.

They abandoned the broom and the shovel and went through the front door into the living room where the glow and the warmth from the fire bade them welcome. They settled themselves on the settee, side by side, and somewhat shyly Alan took her hand between both of his.

'Evie, I've been so worried about you. From the moment I was called out to that attempted break-in you had, I felt there was a danger that you would be implicated.'

'But you never said anything.'

'At the time it wasn't my business.'

'But you worried about me?'

'Of course I did.'

'You weren't there the next day when they found the tin box. Did you learn later about the diamonds?'

'Yes. There was no way I could interfere, not officially, but I promised myself that I would keep an eye on you and the situation.'

'Did you know about the police coming 'ere t' see me, and that I 'ad to come t' the station?'

'Yes. I asked to see my chief inspector. I laid my cards out, straight and honest, told him I knew you slightly from our school days, had met up with you again, taken you out a couple of times and . . .' He broke off, dropped his eyes and examined his fingers.

Evie was overwhelmed with love for him at this moment, but at the same time she wanted to shake the life out of him.

'And what, Alan?' Alan closed his eyes. He couldn't look at Evie. 'I told him that I loved you dearly.'

Evie gasped. 'But that was months ago!'

He licked his lips and nodded.

'You're telling me you knew you loved me as far back as that?'

Alan stared at her defiantly. 'From the moment I set eyes on you again.'

'Well, well, and what did your chief inspector have to say about that?'

'He told me to take a few days' leave, that I wasn't breaking any rules, that you were known to him as a decent, law-abiding young woman.'

'All that time wasted.' Evie's voice was tired.

'Faced with the loneliness of spending the rest of my life without you, I had to come and tell you.'

Evie looked at him closely, a slight smile playing around her lips.

'Last night wouldn't have spurred you on in any way, would it?'

Alan had the grace to grin, albeit sheepishly. 'I could have killed that bleeder, d' you know that? He was pawing you and nibbling yer neck.'

Evie pulled herself up straight and burst out laughing. 'And I thought it was only women that were jealous!'

'Well, he was bloody ridiculous. You looked a million dollars and he was treating you like a tramp. I had to get out of that hall. I couldn't stay. I'd have lost me temper.'

'Shall I tell you something? He lives in Birmingham. We're not likely to set eyes on him again. Come 'ere.' Evie pulled him close.

She was in his arms. He was kissing her.

Evie was well aware of Alan's hand on her breast and of the fact that his breathing was heavy. She opened her eyes as Alan picked her up and made for the stairs.

Slowly he undressed her, his fingers clumsy but gentle. Within minutes he was in bed beside her. The years of being on her own had stored up a hunger in Evie that exploded when he took her into his arms and his bare skin came into contact with her own. She turned and buried her face in his chest, thinking for one dreadful moment that she was going to cry, but that was ridiculous: she had never been so happy, never in the whole of her life.

Alan was whispering in her ear, over and over again, 'I love you, Evie.'

His big hands drew her even closer. Their bodies were locked together. Hands, feet, arms and legs were all entwined. She felt weightless. Now she was crying, but it didn't matter. His kisses changed. Now they were desperate and long. He was breathing loudly and so was she. His fingers moved away from her breasts. She closed her eyes and he kissed her eyelids, then she felt his weight as he lifted himself on top of her.

It was a long time before Alan breathed out and rolled over on to his back. They were both drenched with sweat. They lay there, holding on to one another. They were both quiet now.

Presently she raised her head and looked into his good, kind brown eyes and liked what she saw. Now there was a future ahead. A love to be shared, things to be discovered about each other, and Evie knew she was ready. They lay there, the eiderdown wrapped around them, making plans, daft plans, like being married with a police escort and having Alan handcuffed to her side. The very idea had Evie laughing so hard she eventually ended up with hiccups. Trying to hold her breath was impossible as she again burst into a peal of laughter.

'Now what's the matter?' Alan himself could hardly speak for laughing.

'Imagine, me in bed with a policeman. A sergeant at that!'

Evie had a sudden joyful thought. *Now I can live the rest of my life with a man who really loves me.*

Suddenly Evie frowned. Was this all too good to be true? Why had it taken Alan so long to tell her that he loved her enough to want to marry her?

Alan sensed the change in Evie because she had become still and very quiet. 'Is there any particular reason why you've suddenly stopped laughing?' he asked.

Evie did her best to make light of his question, even though doubts had crept in to spoil this wonderful moment. 'I 'aven't gone off you, if that's what you're asking.'

He smiled. 'I thought you might still be comparing me with lover boy from yesterday.'

'Alan, you know that's not true, but a few things are troubling me, and I don't want there to be any secrets between us.'

'Neither do I, so why don't you talk to me about them?'

'Well, until today you seemed as if you ran hot one moment and cold the next where I was concerned. I've never quite known where I stood with you.'

'Evie, oh my darling Evie, how can I convince you that I have loved you almost from the time I saw you standing out in the street in your nightclothes in the early hours of the morning? Even then I knew I wanted to protect you: you seemed so frightened.'

'I was frightened, scared to death, and boy was I pleased to see you.'

'I tried to tell you about my feelings after we'd been out a few times. I started to several times. Somehow the conversation got changed or another subject came up. And . . . you mustn't forget this, Evie, I had had such a happy marriage, blown apart without any warning. I suppose I was scared to take a chance on the same thing happening again, and yet I wanted to so much. You made me so happy and with you I didn't feel so lonely. I wanted to have you for my wife and look after the girls, a whole family, all of us together, but most times it seemed too much to ask.'

Alan paused, confused as to how he could make Evie understand why he had been so indecisive.

'Besides, you had been going to marry George, and by the sound of what I've been told he would have been able to give you everything. You might have rejected me.'

'Oh, Alan . . .' Evie interrupted and Alan realised she was upset. She had meant to be very sensible, just to ask, calmly and quietly, why he had been so loving one moment and then had let days go by before she would see him again.

Alan pulled her close to him, her face pressed into his chest, and he was saying, 'It's all right. It's all right,' just as though she were a young girl.

They lay close together for a very long time. Then Alan began to whisper, 'I was scared of getting hurt for the second time. Scared that you wouldn't want me, that all that was important to you was that your girls were happy and maybe you thought I wouldn't look after them. I was one on my own, but you had so many things to consider. I wish we'd have talked about all this before now.'

Evie raised herself up onto her elbow and stared into Alan's bright eyes. Then, her voice low, she said, 'I've only one thing to say to you. I love you,' and then she burst into tears, but there was laughter mingled in with those tears. Laughter in which Alan joined.

The light was going: the afternoon was almost over.

'I'll 'ave to get up, Alan. Rosie will be 'ome soon.'

He swung his legs over the side of the bed straightaway. 'All right if I use the bathroom first?'

Downstairs, with the fire made up, the tea things laid out in readiness, Alan shrugged himself into his overcoat.

Evie's heart thumped against her ribs and a knot formed in her throat that threatened to choke her. Surely he wasn't going to walk off, just like that! Not now! Not again! Alan saw the look of dismay on her face.

'Evie, don't ever doubt me again. Not for one moment. From now on I'll be like a limpet, stuck hard an' fast to your side. Believe me, Evie. Please. Because that's how it will be.'

'Well, where are you off to now?'

'To meet Rosie from school. My car is only a few yards up the road. I won't be long.'

'Alan?'

'Yes.'

'Rosie is something we 'ave to talk about. Don't say anything to her without me being there, will you?'

'Trust me. We'll be back in a tick.'

For the first time that afternoon a frown came to Evie's forehead. Rosie! What would her reaction be? Rosie liked Alan. She made that very clear. But there was a vast difference in a friend and a stepfather. Would she throw tantrums? Or would she be pleased? You never could tell. Especially not with young girls.

Life doesn't always run true, does it? she reminded herself. No two girls had been more headstrong and self-willed than Cathy and Jenny. And look how well the pair of them had turned out. Cathy had done really well, living in a hotel; lovely son, Jamie, and Stanley who adored her. And as for Jenny. Her and Bernie! Well! *The sky's the limit where those two are concerned.*

Looking back, she told herself, *they ain't turned out so bad, and they're damned good to me. After today, who knows?* She crossed her arms around her chest and hugged herself. Life was suddenly offering her so much. She heard the front door open. Rosie's jolly laugh rang out and, as she got to her feet to greet her youngest daughter and to make the tea, she grinned to herself. *Maybe there's hope for us all. Who knows?*

It was late that night when they stood kissing each other in the darkness of the hallway. Alan's arms were wrapped around her and Evie felt that her body fitted so well against him. All evening he had teased her unmercifully about her previous night's dancing partner, and he had had Rosie rolling on the floor, doubled up with laughter. But now his kisses and embraces were gentler, softer and not so urgent as they had been that afternoon.

'You have to go.' Evie sighed.

'I love you,' he whispered in her ear. 'I shall go to the town hall first thing in the morning.'

'What for?'

'A special licence.'

She broke away and queried, 'You don't want us to get married as quickly as that, do you?'

'Evie, if I could arrange it we'd be married as soon as the registrar's office opened in the morning.'

'Don't you even want to consider a church wedding?'

'No. All that paraphernalia would take too long. I want you for my wife, now. I want to be able to sleep with you every night, not have you turfing me out in the cold.'

'Oh, Alan.' She found herself blushing.

'You've gone quiet,' Alan said, sounding amused. 'You won't mind a quick wedding will you?'

'Not really,' Evie said dreamily, thinking that a church wedding would have been nice. Faced with Alan's determination, she decided there was a bonus to letting him have his way. She would be his wife that much sooner.

Alan held her securely in his arms and she felt so happy she felt she would burst. 'I'll see you in the morning, my luv.' He gave a quiet chuckle. 'One thing before I leave you, Evie. I'm not marrying you just so that we can sleep together. I'm rather a good dancer, if you'll give me the chance to prove it. I'll even consider growing a thin moustache, though I can't guarantee it will be as black as your Mike's was.'

'Oh, I'll kill you!' She clenched her fists and pummelled away at his chest.

He caught hold of her wrists and she collapsed against him. They were both still laughing as they parted.

Evie listened to the sound of his footsteps die away. Alan had not only told her how much he loved her, he had shown her.

We are both so happy tonight. May it always be so from here on, she prayed.

Chapter Twenty-three

EVIE HAD OVERSLEPT. SHE flew down the stairs, shouted to Rosie, telling her to hurry up, filled the kettle and put it on the gas to boil, lit the grill, cut bread for toast and set the table.

Rosie appeared, already dressed for school but moaning that she had wanted to be early. Heidi started to whine. Evie flew to the back door to let her out and tripped over the mat as she turned quickly to grab the grill pan and prevent the toast from burning. The side of her head had hit the lock of the larder door: it hurt like hell.

She buttered two slices of toast and set them on a plate in front of Rosie. Then she went to the sink and ran the cold water over a cloth, which she held to her throbbing forehead.

'You're not even dressed, Mum. Does that mean I don't get a lift to school today?'

'Rosie, I've said I'm sorry. I'll be as quick as I can.'

She took a mouthful of her tea, almost scalding her tongue. There wasn't time: she'd have to wait till later before having a drink. She rushed out of the room and had got to the foot of the stairs when she heard the letter box being pushed open.

'You're late this morning, gal. If Rosie's ready I'll run her to school f' you.'

Evie let out a long sigh of relief as she turned and went to open the front door.

Bert Killick's red face was wreathed in smiles as he looked at Evie. 'Must admit I've seen ye looking better.'

This statement did nothing for Evie's morale.

'Had a rough time last night did ye? Joan told me what the two of ye got up to.'

'Christ, we only had a couple of drinks and a bite to eat. We were too busy talking.'

Bert laughed. 'I'm on early shift, been 'ome f' me breakfast, and it were Joan that told me you weren't about. Yer milk's still out 'ere on the doorstep.'

Rosie came out of the living room, slinging her school satchel over one shoulder and jamming her velour school hat tight down over her ears. 'Oh thank you, Uncle Bert. You are a life-saver,' she said dramatically as she trooped behind him down the front path, with scarcely time to wave to her mother as she got into his car.

Thank God for that. One of the good things about having friends as neighbours was they kept an eye out for her and were always ready to do a good turn.

Evie sat at the kitchen table and slowly drank her tea. After having had a second cup, she got up and let Heidi in. Filling a bowl with the cold tea that Rosie had left, she added more milk and set the bowl down on the floor for Heidi. Heidi responded with several licks to Evie's hand.

'Good girl, you really are a good girl.' Evie petted her.

After a bit, Evie went upstairs to the bathroom. She put in the bath plug, turned the taps on and sprinkled in scented bath salts that Rosie had bought her for Christmas.

Five minutes later she was feeling great, lying in hot water, wallowing, enveloped in the scented steam. Preparing for a wedding in such a short time was proving a bit much. She allowed herself to indulge in a little self-pity. Alan was going too fast for her liking. He wanted her to move. He was talking of buying a new house. She had been wary in case he suggested that they live in his house. She didn't fancy that. Too many memories for him. She had been trying to think of a way to point this out to Alan, but he forestalled her by saying they were building new houses up by Wandsworth Common and that as soon as the wedding was over he would take her and Rosie to view them. Funny really, because when she'd discussed this with her mum, Flossie had laughed and said everyone seemed to be getting bitten by the property bug. Apparently Bernie had been urging Jim to move house for ages now. Paying rent year after year was a dead loss according to Bernie, much better to own your own property.

No matter whether they left Chetwode Road or stayed, Evie was sure of one thing. Soon she would have the one ingredient that had been missing in her otherwise happy family home. Over the years it had been the nights that had always been the worst, when she had longed for love, for affectionate physical contact, for someone to cuddle up to, someone to hold her and tell her that they loved her. Soon she would have Alan as her husband, and Rosie would have a father. She remembered the conversation she had had with Catherine, how affected Catherine had been by the fact that her father had never been around when she was growing up and how Evie had desperately wanted to prevent that kind of pain from touching Rosie. Try as she might, though, there hadn't been a lot she could do about that. When she thought of Ted Hopkins and the fact that he had never once so much as acknowledged Rosie's existence she still felt so angry.

Suddenly she found herself feeling desperate. *I don't think I could bear it if Rosie didn't take to Alan.* Rosie had been cut up enough when George had died. Maybe, like herself, and Alan too, Rosie was afraid to let her feelings show. Everything would turn out well this time. It had to.

She hoisted herself out of the bath. Dried and powdered, she wrapped a towel around herself and went into her bedroom. She hadn't decided what she was going to do with her day yet. She pulled her best grey skirt from the wardrobe, found a white blouse and started to get dressed. She pulled a black lamb's wool jumper over her head, making sure that the collar of the blouse was tucked outside the round neck of her jumper. Her hair was well brushed and pulled back from her face with the aid of a large glossy hair slide. She was in the middle of putting on her make-up when she heard the knock on the door.

'Blast,' she muttered to herself. She finished outlining her eyebrows and was about to apply her lipstick when the knock was repeated, louder this time.

'All right, all right,' Evie yelled as she ran down the stairs.

She flung the door open and stood back. She was flabbergasted. The gentleman who stood before her was dressed in a belted raincoat, pigskin gloves, with a bowler hat on his head, and he carried a very expensive-looking briefcase. This man was an official of some sort, and that fact worried Evie a lot. She looked at him inquiringly and he doffed his hat.

'Good morning. Mrs Smith?'

'Yes?'

He held out his hand. 'Mr James Harwood, from Simpson and Simpson, Insurance Brokers of Hatton Garden. I would like to talk to you. May I come in?'

He handed Evie a small white business card, and as he did so he smiled at her. The smile transformed his lined face. Up until this moment she had considered him an old man. Now grey eyes twinkled at her and he looked somewhat boyish as he waited for her reply.

Evie studied the embossed card, stood back and allowed Mr Harwood to step into the passage. Hatton Garden! That meant diamond dealers. Oh no! Not that business again.

'Please sit down,' Evie said, once they were inside the living room, 'and tell me what it is you want to see me about.'

He took the offered chair and turned to smile at her in some amusement. 'Why are you so apprehensive?'

'Because according to your card this visit has something to do with diamonds and I'm sick to death of being asked questions to which I 'ave no answers. I've 'ad the police on my back for months an' I still couldn't tell them any more at the end than I could at the beginning.'

'Mrs Smith, I haven't come to question you. I've come to say thank you.'

'Thank me!'

'Yes, thank you.'

Despite the fact that he was smiling broadly at her now, Evie felt shivery with cold. She folded her arms across her chest, and gazed at him in astonishment.

'Mrs Smith, if you would be so kind as to sit down and listen, I will endeavour to explain.'

Evie sank down gratefully into a chair that was facing the one in which he sat.

'First off, let me say how sorry I and my company are that you have undergone such rigorous questioning at the hands of the police.'

Evie wanted to tell him to get to the point, explain what all this was to do with him and what the hell a man from

Hatton Garden was doing sitting in her council house. Her eyes were willing him to give her an explanation.

'The diamonds recovered from this house were the property of my company. They were worth one hundred and fifty thousand pounds.'

Evie could feel her heart thumping. She sat silently.

Mr Harwood said, 'You look very shocked.'

It was ages before Evie could bring herself to reply and when she did the words came pouring out. 'I am shocked. The police 'ave convinced me that George, that's the man I was going to be married to, was mixed up in this awful business. They said it was 'im that put the diamonds in the tea chest and then hid the chest in my room that is boarded up. I've almost come to believe them. But one hundred and fifty thousand pounds. No! I don't believe that. George wouldn't 'ave got mixed up with anything as big as that. No. They were hidden in my room for ages. All that money and no one came round to claim them. No.' She was shaking her head vigorously.

Mr Harwood made no comment on her outburst, only asked her, 'Are you all right?'

'I dunno about being all right. I've just realised that I was living all that time with that fortune lying in that room. D' you know there was another attempt to break in 'ere before they ever found your diamonds? Me an' my girls were in a lot of danger when ye come to think about it.' Suddenly Evie's temper came to the boil. She had had enough. 'So, what is it you want, Mr Harwood?'

The expression in his eyes was very merry. 'I told you I am here to thank you. I am so sorry, it was decided at a company meeting that you could not be considered for the insurance reward.'

Evie thrust out a hand and interrupted him. 'I never thought I would be. I don't want your money. Only for you an' everyone else to back off an' leave me alone.'

'I'm sure that's true.' He grinned at her, trying to coax a smile to her intent and frowning face. 'However, it was a unanimous decision that the board could show their concern for the trouble you have been put to and I have with me a small gift which we hope you will accept.'

He bent his knees, picked up his briefcase from the floor and unlocked the clasp. When he turned back towards Evie he was holding a slim blue leather case in his hand.

'Open it, Mrs Smith,' he urged.

She did as he asked.

She couldn't bring herself to believe what she was looking at. 'Oh,' she gasped. She was fascinated by the gold chain, the heavy V-shaped piece of gold that hung from the centre, from which was suspended a gold pendant the size of a sixpence. It was the centre of the pendant that mesmerised her the most. A single diamond. It was exquisite.

As she gently moved the case, the diamond sparkled, sending all the colours of the rainbow shooting out at her.

'Oh, how beautiful,' she breathed.

'Friends, now, Mrs Smith?'

Mr Harwood's question brought her back to earth.

'I couldn't accept this,' she whispered, holding out the case to him.

'Please, don't offend us. We felt it was the least we could do.' Then he suddenly became very fatherly. He came nearer to Evie, patted her shoulder and said, 'There will be occasions in your life when you can wear that special diamond, and if nothing else it will be a nice nest egg perhaps for your daughters one day.'

'Thank you.' They were the only words that she could think of to say.

He made for the door, turned, came back and shook her hand. And with that, he was gone.

Evie stood with the leather case in one hand and her other hand clamped over her mouth. She didn't know whether to laugh or to cry. She bustled about making herself a fresh pot of tea. When all was ready she carried the tray into the living room, sat down and poured out the first cup. When the cup was drained she opened up the case and sat staring at the piece of jewellery that now belonged to her. 'Unbelievable,' was all she could mutter to herself.

She put the knuckle of her finger in her mouth and sucked until it was wet. Then she slipped the ring that George had given her off her finger and placed it beside the diamond on the velvet lining of the box. A ray of weak sunshine came through the window at that moment, caught the stones and sent the bright colours flashing. They really were beautiful.

Did you really think you would have got away with one hundred and fifty thousand pounds' worth of diamonds, George? She chuckled to herself. She couldn't help it. In her head she could hear George saying, *Nothing ventured, nothing gained.*

Mr Harwood had said he was sorry she didn't qualify for any reward. At this thought she laughed out loud. *That's all you know, sunshine!* She'd got her reward and more. She was satisfied and, wherever he was, she was certain that George felt the same way. If he hadn't planted those stolen gems in her house, there would have been no attempts to break in. The police would never have been called and she and Alan might never have met up. In less than two weeks' time she was to become Mrs Alan Richardson. What it all boiled down to was, George had left her well provided for. A police sergeant to take care of her, no less. You'd have to be barmy not to see the funny side of this ironic tale. She was still laughing as she picked up her ring, put it back where it belonged on her finger and snapped the leather case shut.

Would she ever have the courage to wear that gold chain? It would be nice to do so, just once, on her wedding day. She'd have to ask Alan's advice about that. After all he was going to be the law around here from now on.

For the whole of that week, Evie kept the news of Mr Harwood's visit to herself. By the time she came home from her shift at the betting office on Monday morning she had made her decision.

Having made herself a pot of tea, Evie took it into the front room, shut the door and sat down at the table with the telephone in front of her. She dialled the London number.

'Simpson and Simpson, Diamond Merchants. Can I help you?'

'Please may I speak to Mr James Harwood?'

'Who's calling?'

'Mrs Evelyn Smith.'

'I'll see if Mr Harwood is available, please hold the line.'

Evie felt so nervous she almost put the receiver down.

'James Harwood.'

She recognised his voice, remembered his grey eyes and the fact that they had twinkled. 'Mr Harwood, good afternoon. I'm sorry to bother you, but there are a couple of things that are worrying me.'

'Would you like me to call on you again? If there is something that I can do for you, you only have to ask.'

'Oh no.' Evie was quick with her refusal. 'It's just that I know the gift your company has given me must be very valuable, and . . .' Evie hesitated.

'And that is a problem?' He asked the question in such a kindly manner that Evie imagined he was frowning.

'Insurance.'

Another pause.

Oh to hell with it, she had to come right out and say

what she meant or put the bloody phone down. 'Surely an item such as this has to be insured. Well, I know enough to know that I could never afford the premium that any decent company would ask. So, please, don't think me ungrateful, but I'd like you to arrange to have it collected. You have to take it back.'

'Mrs Smith, how very remiss of me. I really must apologise. Do you have the case near you?'

'No.' She could hardly tell him that she had unscrewed the hardboard panel of her bath and, wrapped in sheets and sheets of newspaper, it now lay on the bare floorboards, well out of sight beneath the bath. He would have a fit if she told him that.

'Have you had the item out of the case at all?'

'I've looked at it for ages, but no, I 'aven't actually lifted it out yet.'

'I suggest you do just that, Mrs Smith.' He laughed softly, and then went on casually, 'There are several documents in the bottom of the case, under the velvet lining. Valuation papers, registered ownership, and full insurance, which is to be met and covered by my company for as long as you remain the owner of the said item.'

Evie gasped. She felt such a fool. Before she could form a reply, Mr Harwood was speaking again.

'I can't believe that I was so thoughtless. Do please forgive me. I imagined that the first thing you would have done when I left you was lift out the chain.'

Most women would have, just to admire it, he thought to himself, but then what little he knew of Evelyn Smith had already brought him to the conclusion that she wasn't at all like most women. He felt he had to be very tactful now.

'Mrs Smith, do you have a bank account?'

'I 'ave a post office savings account.'

'Would you give me your telephone number? I really must visit you again. Set you up with a safety deposit box at a local branch of any bank you care to choose. Your necklace should be kept at the bank, but also where you have easy access to it.'

'There's no need.' Evie was feeling a whole lot more confident now. 'Mr Harwood, I'm going to be married next week. To a police sergeant. I haven't told him of your visit yet, but I will now. He'll go to the bank with me.'

'Congratulations! I am so pleased for you.'

Evie felt that he spoke the truth. She could tell by the tone of his voice. 'Anyway, thank you for listening to me. I'm sorry I was such a dope, not to look in the case.'

This time he gave a hearty laugh. 'My pleasure, Mrs Smith. Wear your chain at your wedding and may it always bring you good luck.'

'I will,' she assured him. 'And thank you again. Goodbye.'

Evie made another quick telephone call to the police station, leaving a message for Sergeant Richardson to call when he came off duty.

Waiting for Alan to arrive, Evie was like a cat on hot bricks. She pottered about her bedroom, dusting the dressing table, tidying her clothes in the wardrobe and finally sitting down to do her hair and make up her face. All the while she was trying to decide how she would look on her wedding day if she wore the expensive piece of jewellery. Not only that, what would people say? Any fool would know that she hadn't bought such an item. Where the hell could she tell them she had got it from?

When, a little after three o'clock, she heard the slam of a car door, she set down her hairbrush and went downstairs to let Alan in. Opening the front door, she was faced with not only Alan but her mother as well.

'Oh well, might as well kill two birds with one stone,' she said, stepping back to let them both in.

'What kind of a way is that to greet yer poor old mother.' Flossie grinned.

'You're not old, an' neither are ye poor, but you sure as 'ell are gonna be very surprised when you 'ear what I've got t' tell you.'

'Don't I even get a kiss?' Alan demanded.

Evie held up her face and Alan took her in his arms. 'What's all the mystery?'

Evie smiled. The smile lit up her blue eyes, and it was as though she was now truly happy.

Flossie was watching her intently and she too felt it was as if all the years that Evie had struggled along on her own were now well and truly gone. Her Evie was in love and the man she was about to marry was decidedly in love with her. Thank God!

Suddenly Evie pushed Alan away. She laughed, shaking her head. 'You've got to listen to me. Both of you. I don't know where to begin. It's all so muddled up. It makes no sense to me. God knows 'ow I'm gonna make you understand.'

'Well, first let's all sit down,' Alan drew a chair forward for Flossie and another for Evie. He remained standing. 'Now, you could try starting at the beginning and then maybe we'll be a lot wiser by the time you get to the end.'

'I don't really know the beginning. I never did. It's all to do with George.'

'Oh my Gawd!' Flossie muttered. Evie ignored her.

'All right,' Evie agreed, 'I'll try not to take all day.'

'Take your time,' Alan urged, seating himself on the settee, legs outstretched.

'Well you, Alan, know better than most about the tea chest and its contents that were found in my boarded up room, an' you, Mum, don't need me to tell you any more than you already know about George.'

Neither of them answered so Evie pressed on.

'I had a visitor last week. A Mr James Harwood, a diamond merchant or insurance broker, something like that. Anyway he came from Hatton Garden. He came cos he said 'is firm didn't think it appropriate that I should get the reward.'

'What reward?' Flossie was astounded.

'Oh, don't start, Mum. Don't ask questions or I'll get in a right muddle. Just listen.'

Alan gave her a smile of encouragement.

'He brought me a gift instead. A diamond, set in gold, and it's on a gold chain. I rang him today an' asked 'im to come and take it back because I was afraid of 'aving it in the 'ouse with no insurance an' all.'

Evie had to laugh at this point. The look on each of their faces had to be seen to be believed.

'It's true – honest, every word, Mum.'

'Well what did ye wanna go an' tell 'im ye didn't want to keep it for. God knows ye put up with enough 'assle one way an' another over those blasted diamonds. A little present! It's no more than you deserve.'

Evie was more interested in Alan's reaction. He now sat up straight, his hands clasped together, hanging loosely between his knees. Evie sighed, wriggled back in her chair, and waited for him to tell her what he thought she ought to do. He gazed at her across the small space that separated them. For a few minutes neither of them spoke.

Then he said, 'I see no reason why you shouldn't keep the gift.'

She was taken back. 'You sounded very much like George then.'

Suddenly Alan laughed, shaking his head.

'What are you laughing at.'

'You, my luv. Most women would be over the moon. What do you do? Phone Hatton Garden and ask them to come and take back their gift. You're unbelievable, you know that, don't you?'

To his astonishment, she looked across at her mother and he saw their faces light up with amusement.

Shaking her head, Flossie said, 'Oh lad, you've a lot to learn about my daughter. Anyway I'm gonna go, leave ye to it.'

''Ang on, Mum, you ain't even 'ad a cup of tea. You've got time for one, 'aven't you?'

'No lass, I'm off t' see about yer Dad's dinner. Wait till I tell 'im. He agreed with me only this morning that you'd been quiet all the week. We wondered what was up.'

'Well, now you know. Sorry it's taken me so long to tell you.'

'Don't let it worry you. I'll see meself out.'

'Bye, Mum.'

Evie turned her attention to Alan, who sat smiling up at her, not in the least put out by what she had told him.

'So.' Evie hesitated, and then went on. 'Should I wear the chain the day we get married?'

'You'd like to, wouldn't you?'

'Yes.'

Alan got to his feet. She raised her face, expecting him to kiss her, but instead he put his arm round her shoulders and drew her close.

'Evie, my darling, when are you going to realise that all I want is for you to be happy. You're afraid that you'll upset me if you so much as refer to George, that's about the truth of it, isn't it?'

Evie turned her face away, she couldn't meet his gaze.

'George is dead. I have nothing to fear from him. If you must know, I feel grateful to him. I'm sure your mother had him taped right. A lovable rogue is how she described him to me. He took care of you and the girls at a time when you must have been pretty low. You'll always be grateful for that and I wouldn't want it any other way.'

'How did you know,' Evie asked, 'that George did so much for us?'

'Because your stepfather told me.'

'That figures. Jim was very fond of George. And to be honest with you Alan, for those few months George made my life very happy. While we are on the subject, may I ask you something?'

'Anything, Evie.'

'It's about my ring.' She held out her hand, spreading her fingers wide. 'I'd like to keep on wearing it . . . I thought I might transfer it to my other hand.'

He took her hand, lacing his fingers with hers. 'Whatever pleases you most. You could wear it through your nose and I wouldn't complain, just so long as you go on loving me.'

'Oh Alan. You are such a kind man. How could I not love you?'

She was in his arms. Their lips met and nothing else mattered in the world. He stayed only for a little while, long enough to drink the tea that she had finally made. After that, he tried hard to stifle his yawns, telling Evie that he had been on duty since five o'clock that morning.

She went to see him out. In the open doorway they kissed for several minutes. Then Alan left.

Evie came indoors and closed the door. She was so grateful that their wedding was only days away. She couldn't wait. Alan was never out of her thoughts. At night she dreamt about him, waking up with drowsy contentment, smiling. Although she had three daughters she had never been married. Never had a husband. Now she clung to the fact that Alan was about to change all that. Soon when she woke up of a morning Alan would be there, lying beside her.

Chapter Twenty-four

IT WAS THE VERY last Saturday in February, a real winter day of bitter cold, frost and pale blue sky showing through puffy white clouds. The sun shone, making everything seem bright and cheerful, but there was little warmth in it, and the grass verges were as hard as iron.

Sitting in the back of the hired car, holding hands with her stepfather, Evie decided that it was the most beautiful day. It was her wedding day.

Flossie and Jim had agreed with Alan that it would be an idiotic waste of money to have a big church wedding. She had settled for a simple family service at the town hall with a lunch party afterwards at the British Legion club. The steward of the club had been more than helpful, offering the huge banqueting hall, masses of room for everybody, and he and his staff would see to the catering.

The road curved sharply. Ahead stood a signpost with an arrow pointing the way to the town hall.

'Nearly there,' the driver said over his shoulder.

Jim Tyler squeezed Evie's hand, which still lay between both of his. She smiled. There was never a time when she couldn't provide a smile for this man who had been a father to her in every sense of the word.

He said, 'You're gonna be fine, Evie. Alan's a good bloke, but you're still a bit uneasy, aren't you?'

She looked up and met his eyes. Very quietly she asked him, 'Does it show so much?'

'Only to me, who knows you so well.'

'Dad, I do love Alan, very much y' know. But I can't shake off the feeling that everything is too good to be true.'

'After today you will. You'll be a married woman.'

'Yeah. I keep trying to reassure myself with that. Third time lucky? Perhaps. I was so daft about Edward Hopkins. How could I 'ave gone on believing him for so long? And what about George? He would 'ave been so good to me and the girls. I know he would. Why did he 'ave to die?'

'Stop it, Evie. The time for looking back is long gone. Today will be the beginning of a new life. A good life. You have to believe that.'

'Dad, d' you think Rosie is going to be all right?'

'Yes, luv, I do. Honestly, you'll see.'

'It's just that Cathy and Jenny did at least know their father. When they were both little he did come and stay with us from time to time. Rosie has never had any one that she could call Dad.'

'Look, luv, you've got to give this marriage a chance. If you're not prepared to do that we might just as well turn round an' go 'ome now.'

'I guess it's just last-minute nerves.'

Jim leaned across and kissed her cheek. 'For years I longed to be married to your mother. Never had the gumption in me to ask her. Now look at us. My one wish for you today is that you and Alan will 'ave many long years together and that you'll be as 'appy as me an' yer mum are.'

Evie withdrew her hand and brushed away a tear, before saying, 'Oh Dad, you're a lovely man.'

He shook his head. 'Well at least you are looking a whole lot more cheerful. And as far as Rosie is concerned, remember this. Nothing is ever as bad as we think it is going to be.'

'Here we are,' the driver called as he drew the car up at the foot of the steps which led up to the main entrance of the town hall.

Jim was out first and he came round to open the door for Evie.

She got out, drawing her fawn cape around her against the cold. The cape looked and felt fantastic, the neck outlined with a soft honey-coloured fur, the whole lined with dark brown silk. It was a present from her mother. The small hat, perched on her recently cut hair, was a soft fawn felt trimmed with the same fur as her cape. Beneath the cape she wore a dress of soft cashmere, the dark red colour of an autumn leaf. She hadn't made this dress. It had cost the earth. It felt soft and very new against her skin.

Joan Killick had fastened the gold chain, with its diamond pendant, around Evie's neck and together they had stood staring at her reflection in the long mirror.

'Oh, it's perfect,' breathed Joan. Evie had been thrilled with her own appearance. No dress had ever given her such confidence. And the diamond, all facets sparkling, sending forth rainbow colours, was the most beautiful finishing touch she could have asked for.

Part of Evie's apprehension today sprang from the fact that she was half afraid that Alan wouldn't turn up, that at the last minute he might have changed his mind. But the moment she caught sight of him, all her anxiety faded.

Everything was all right.

Alan looked as broad and solid as ever and, today, marvellously handsome. Tall and straight-backed, no overcoat, a charcoal grey suit, white shirt and silver grey tie, and a white carnation in his buttonhole. He looked so dignified, his dark eyes bright with happiness as he gazed down at her.

And Flossie stood next to him.

Evie felt her mother never aged. Her thick hair, now grey, was swept up in a French pleat and topped with the flimsiest of creations that could hardly be called a hat. Her eyes, too, were bright, but with amusement. Even the fact that her great-grandson, Jamie, was tugging at her arm only added to her enjoyment.

And Catherine . . . Evie saw her tall, slender eldest daughter, looking so like she herself had when she'd been a young lass. Long fair hair, pale blue eyes and that creamy complexion. Next to her was Stanley, so well turned out, and as always his gaze as it rested on Catherine was full of adoration.

Jenny and Bernie, together, came racing down the steps.

'Oh Mum! You look marvellous.'

Jenny herself looked a picture, the only one of her girls to have dark hair and brown eyes. Today she had colour in her cheeks and still a youthful, long-legged spring to her step despite her tiny frame.

'Hi there Evie, grand day for it.' Bernie was smiling broadly, putting everyone at their ease, and Evie loved him for it. It was as if he had ordered the weather himself. And Evie wouldn't have put that past Bernie.

'Hello, Mum.'

Evie started slightly, turned round and saw her youngest daughter. Her blue eyes were fringed with long, thick, very fair eyelashes and their expression was open and smiling, full of merriment.

Evie breathed a sigh of thankfulness. 'Rosie, darling.'

Evie had not seen her since the previous day. She had stayed with her nanna that night. She'd always been Flossie's precious pet.

Evie bent and kissed Rosie's cheek and was so relieved when she heard Rosie laugh. She looked intently to see if the laughter was forced or if Rosie was showing some sign of sadness. She need not have worried.

'Here, Mum, Nanna said you don't give horseshoes until after the ceremony but I know Norma and Shirley have one for you as well so I wanted you to have mine first.'

Evie took the silver horseshoe, with its long entwined ribbons and a sprig of lilies-of-the-valley spread across the centre.

'Oh, sweetheart, it's beautiful. Thank you.'

'It's for good luck.'

Evie felt the tears burn at the back of her eyes. Rosie looked so grown up today in an emerald green coat and a small black velvet hat, older than her thirteen years. She looked so very much like her eldest sister, Catherine, and Evie found herself mouthing a silent prayer that all would turn out as well for Rosie as it had for both of her sisters.

Rosie disentangled herself from her mother's grasp, tucked a wisp of hair back inside her hat and said, 'Nanna's calling me. See you inside.'

'Wait just one moment, Rosie.'

Evie pressed her lips against Rosie's cold cheek again, smelling the familiar smell of her soap and talcum powder. 'Don't ever forget how much I love you, will you, pet?'

'Course not, Mum.'

And with that she flew back up the steps.

*

The room was warm and very beautiful. The light oak of the panelled walls shone as the winter sunshine came in through the tall windows. Floral arrangements stood both on the huge desk and on the polished table that was set to one side. Chairs were arranged in a semicircle in front of the desk.

'. . . and forsaking all others, take this man to be your lawful wedded husband?'

'I will.'

'I now pronounce you man and wife.'

A bell tolled at a church nearby.

Time stood still.

You could have heard a pin drop.

Alan was the first to move. He put his hands on Evie's shoulders and stooped to place his lips on hers. It was a long, lingering, gentle kiss.

When he straightened up, he said, 'You know something, Mrs Richardson? I really love you.'

His statement had been said loud enough for everyone in the room to hear. It was the signal for congratulations to be called, hugs and kisses to be given and a babble of voices to mingle.

Alan bent his head and whispered into Evie's ear. Her answer was a beaming smile.

Hand in hand they made their way through the throng of friends to the door. Alan was shaking hands with his colleagues, who had turned out in force to wish him and Evie luck. They were clapping him on the back, until Alan stepped aside.

He raised his hand and softly called, 'Rosie.'

Rosie abandoned Joan and Bert Killick, to whom she'd been talking, and came running towards Alan and her mother. She stopped, just short of Alan's arms, unsure of what she should do.

He took a step, caught her up and swung her round,

her legs flying, kissed her soundly and set her down on her feet again.

'Well, my youngest daughter, what have you got to say to me and your mother?' he asked her quietly.

Rosie looked at her mother. 'Are you happy, Mum?' Her dear little mouth trembled and Evie put her arms around her as she told her, 'Deliriously so.' Rosie broke free of her mother's arms, turned to Alan, and asked, 'And how about you . . . Dad?'

Unashamed, Alan let the tears roll down his cheeks. As he once again picked Rosie up, bringing her face to the level of his own, he said, 'Me too.'

And Evie, watching the pair of them hugging tightly, knew that her stepfather had been right and that all her fears were unfounded.

Her daughter had a father.

And she had a husband.

'Are we going to this reception then?' Alan asked, one arm around Evie and the other still holding on to Rosie.

''Course we are, I'm starving,' Rosie told them both.

Laughing merrily, they went to where the cars stood waiting.

As they came up the steps of the British Legion, a steward stepped forward to hold the door open for them.

'It's a cold but bright day,' he said to them.

'It's a beautiful day,' Evie answered.

The door closed behind them.

Rosie flew across the entrance hall to join her nanna.

Evie and Alan both stood still. She gave him a smile, the brightness of which dazzled him.

'One more kiss, before I have to share you with all our guests,' Alan begged.

It was a kiss full of promise.

Evie opened her eyes. The sun had gone in. It didn't matter. Nothing mattered now. Whatever the future had in store for her, she was no longer alone. She wouldn't be lonely any more. She had Alan.

As Evie and Alan entered the reception hall, the band struck up with the tune, 'Love is the sweetest thing'.

They smiled at each other.

It was a smile that said it all.

WHEELING AND DEALING

Elizabeth Waite

Ella has lived in the East End of London all her life and
when her husband is determined to move to Epsom to be
near the racecourse he frequents and loves, Ella's refusal to
move with him breaks up their marriage. It's been a
tempestuous marriage – sometimes they had money, often
not and when he was doing well, he liked the ladies…

Once the marriage breaks up, Ella loses the will to keep
smart, trim and fit. Until her mother steps in, determined to
pick up the pieces. And it works – Ella gets a job as a
barmaid in the British Legion club which gives her an
income and a social life. She begins to take pride in her
appearance again and, when Dennis turns up for a drink one
night, he is taken by surprise – and remembers what attracted
him to her in the first place. But can Dennis win back his
wife? Ella has to decide if Dennis has changed – or indeed
can change – his wheeler-dealer ways…

978 0 7515 3611 9

Other Elizabeth Waite titles available by mail